Crystal Conquest

Doug J. Cooper

Author of *Crystal Deception*

Published by: Douglas Cooper Consulting

Beta reviewer: Mark Mesler
Book editor: Tammy Salyer
Cover design: Damonza

ISBN-10: 0989938131
ISBN-13: 978-0-9899381-3-6

Author website: www.crystalseries.com

for Nan and Nat

1

Am I really going to do this? thought Lenny Barton, feeling a bit like a passenger in his own body. His truth nib had uncovered a secret, one that fueled visions of wealth and power. And the more Lenny daydreamed, the more he believed he could make his fantasy come true.

He tweaked his plan—a dumb and dangerous sketch of one, anyway—and his face tingled from the adrenaline rush. *I can pull this off.* Nodding in support of the idea, he viewed the information that had started it all.

According to the official record, Dr. Jessica "Juice" Tallette had developed an artificial intelligence crystal that was a thousand times smarter than a typical human. And, again officially, an explosion two years ago had destroyed this AI super crystal.

But Lenny's truth nib claimed the AI was alive and living somewhere in the northeastern United States. He believed his nib. And he wanted this powerful crystal for himself.

An off-the-charts genius, Lenny was on course to graduate from the Engineered Intelligence program at the Boston Institute of Technology with a perfect A in every class. If he yielded to the reckless thoughts now rattling in his head, that outcome would certainly change.

He didn't understand it, but just knowing this super artificial intelligence existed flipped a switch deep inside his skull. *I'm holding a winning lottery ticket*, he thought. *I just need to cash it in.*

Sitting in his study chair, he refilled his coffee cup and started brainstorming. The nervous tapping of his foot accelerated as he mulled his options.

He had four weeks to play with. He'd tell his friends here at BIT he was going home for a family emergency. He called his folks every week as part of his normal routine and could do that from anywhere. They'd never know he was gone.

That gave him enough time to leave school and make a play for the crystal before his world came crashing down with a string of Fs in his courses. It was a make-or-break gambit, but if he succeeded in gaining ownership of this AI, it wouldn't matter. He smiled. *I'll be king of the world.*

Surrendering to his urge, Lenny rummaged through his closet. He recognized a strap poking up through the detritus piled on the floor, grabbed it, and pulled steadily until his backpack sprang free. He turned to face the room, too lost in thought to notice the closet clutter shifting to fill the void he'd created.

Plopping the pack on his bed, he hesitated. Since he didn't know how this venture would play out, he wasn't sure what he should bring. He crammed in a couple of changes of clothes and, after a moment's thought, added some heavier items so he could adapt to the ever-changing New England weather. He crouched, snatched an extra pair of shoes stowed beneath his bed, and threw them on top.

Hefting the pack to gauge its weight, he acknowledged that his lottery ticket analogy was a stretch. "You're following a treasure map." He said the words out loud so he could hear how dumb it sounded. But the treasure at the end of this rainbow wasn't just a pot of gold. A mountain of gold paled in comparison to what this AI crystal could get for him.

His plan was simple. Gain access to the super crystal and then position the situation so ownership came down to a game of wits. If he could do that, there was no doubt he'd win. He always won those sorts of games. *And it wouldn't be stealing,* he thought. *This crystal has its own awareness, so it can choose to come with me.*

Heading to the bathroom to gather toiletries, he considered what he'd do if he actually got the crystal. *I'll have it fix my Fs.* He threw a collection of items from around the sink into a clear bag. *Then I'll sit back and be King of Everything.*

His com signaled, and glancing at it, he saw his roommate, Spencer, standing out in the hallway, swaying back and forth. The left side of his shirt, untucked and hanging loose, swung in rhythm with his movements.

"Let me in, Lenny," Spencer slurred, confirming Lenny's guess that he was remarkably drunk. "You got a girl in there? Hurry. The hallway's spinning."

"Just a sec, pal," replied Lenny. He snatched the truth nib out of his com, added it to a small pouch that held two other prototypes, and stuffed the pouch deep into his pocket. He lifted his pack off his bed, tossed it into the closet, and opened the door. Spencer toppled forward onto the floor.

"C'mon, Spence. Here you go."

Lenny's lanky body was no match for his roommate's bulk, but he managed to get Spencer upright long enough to guide him to his bed. They reached it at the same time Spencer went limp. He fell forward and his body bounced once but stayed on the mattress. His legs hung over the side of the bed, the toes of his shoes resting on the floor. The room began to reek of a mélange of odors associated with hard-partying college life.

Lenny ignored it and refocused on his mission. He dragged his chair over to his tech bench, laid his com on top, and immersed himself in an intense hacking session. He enjoyed working long hours as long as his efforts focused on one of two things: studying technology or beating sim quests. *This challenge is the best of both worlds.* He paused for a sip of coffee.

An hour into his labors, Spencer started snoring. The off-gassing of odors intensified, and Lenny opened a window. He maintained his concentration, working until the rising sun announced it was time to stop. He glanced out the window at the new day and rubbed his neck, seeking to relieve the stiffness that developed from staying huddled at the tech bench for so many hours.

You've done what you can, he thought, acknowledging he was constrained both by time and equipment. He slumped back in his chair and smiled. If this had been for a grade, he'd get a clean A from any of his professors. Even from cranky old Huffington, who hated giving out As for any reason.

In the last few hours, he'd succeeded in modifying his com so anyone accessing it would find him en route to his folks' home. *If they study it, though, they'll see I'm traveling at a snail's pace.* What would normally be a half-day trip would play out over two weeks. And just before he reached his home, it would appear as if he turned around and started a slow journey back to campus.

For Lenny, that spoof was easy. The hard one was funds. He needed to cover expenses for food, lodging, transportation, and sundries. He had the money. This wasn't about theft. He just didn't want it to be too easy for anyone to track him by tracing his purchases.

The Union of Nations' financial system was superbly protected. It had to be, because if it crumbled, so would society. After some false starts, he succeeded in rerouting his transactions so the initiation point of each expense would appear to be from wherever he was on his slow journey home and back. *It'll fool my parents and low-level officials, but if the authorities get involved, they'll crack it in seconds.*

With his pack slung over one shoulder, he exited his dorm and headed across the quad. The grass was wet with morning dew, and the old vine-covered dorm buildings lining the outside of the quad showed little signs of activity at this early hour. Most students wouldn't surface until the sun was high in the sky.

He had an inspiration and, without slowing his pace, called Spencer and left a message. "Hey, Spence. Thanks for being a friend and listening to me last night. I didn't mean to burden you with all my troubles. Anyway, as you suggested, I'm headed home to be there for my mom. I appreciate you agreeing to speak with my professors. I should be back in a couple of weeks. You're the best."

He smiled as he imagined Spencer sitting on the bathroom floor, alternately vomiting into the toilet and struggling to remember some fragment of this deep and meaningful conversation.

Lenny turned his attention to transportation. He worked his way to Broad Street at the edge of campus and splurged on renting a car. He needed the privacy, and his parents, who were footing the bill for his college expenses, could afford it.

"Take me to the main Crystal Research complex off Route 29 in upstate New York," Lenny said to the car nav as he climbed in and got settled.

As the door shut, the nav replied, "Yes, sir. Our trip will take three hours and twenty minutes."

He dug the truth nib out of his pocket and popped it back into his com. *I can't believe I'm doing this!*

* * *

Lenny had built his nib in BIT's crystal fabrication lab for his senior-year project. All the students in the Engineered Intelligence program built one to do some specific task. His little speck of crystal used pattern mining to tease truth out of the mountain of news, analysis, reports, lies, speculation, assumption, innuendo, and other crap found in the web record.

He'd chased a bunch of stories with his truth nib during his testing phase. It worked by searching the far corners of the world and gathering every scrap of information available on a target event. It jumbled the collection of items into a heap and sifted the information down to a smaller pile based on common patterns. It was a repetitive process that eventually produced a simple list of facts.

He'd used it to analyze political, scientific, and literary conspiracies and was bored. He didn't care who wrote a particular sonata or assassinated some historical figure. Frustrated, he'd sat in the fabrications lab one afternoon, shooting the breeze with his friend Patel as he struggled to come up with something interesting to analyze.

Patel had been prattling on about his own problems with his nib project, and Lenny's eyes glazed over. As Patel's chatter continued, Lenny said things like "wow, that sucks," at what he hoped were appropriate moments.

His eyes drifted while he waited for Patel to wind down, and his gaze settled on a plaque fixed to the wall across from where they were sitting. He'd seen it countless times over the past year and, after all that exposure, had never once read it.

As Patel talked, Lenny scanned the words above the picture on the plaque. It said that the fab lab and all its equipment was a gift from Dr. Jessica "Juice" Tallette.

"What's her story?" he asked, hoping to move the conversation to a new topic.

"She's the one who built the super AI crystal those alien bastards stole," said Patel.

"The crystal that blew up with the starship?"

Patel turned in his chair. "This is news to you?"

Lenny avoided Patel's gaze as he recalled that day from two years earlier. Energy bolts from a Kardish war vessel had rained from the sky, vaporizing buildings and killing hundreds of people. "Do you remember where you were when it happened?"

"I was home with my folks."

"Yeah, me too," said Lenny.

After a brief silence, Patel thrust his chin at the plaque. "She's making investments around the world to replace the crystal development capabilities lost in that attack."

"How do you know that?"

Patel pointed to the words below the picture.

Lenny skimmed the text. "Did you know her super crystal had more flake in it than a million of our nibs?"

"Yeah. I read the plaque."

"And she was with the commandos who blew up their ship as it tried to escape from our solar system?"

Patel had stopped responding at that point, but Lenny didn't care. He'd found a mystery to explore with his truth nib. The story on the plaque said that Juice Tallette had earned her doctorate in engineered intelligence in these hallowed halls of the Boston Institute of Technology, then had been hired by a company to design and build the super crystal.

She'd succeeded, but it had been stolen by the Kardish, an alien race of traders who'd been lurking in Earth orbit, watching and waiting for just that opportunity. In some fantastic twist of fate, Juice had been along for the ride when a small group of commandos had chased down and blew up their vessel, destroying the crystal in the process.

Yet now, two short years later, she was back here on Earth, and with enough cash to fund new buildings.

Lenny felt like he was cheating, because he didn't need his nib to tell him the events didn't add up. *There's more to this story,* he thought. *Much more.*

* * *

Slouching in the comfort of the self-molding car seat, Lenny inserted his truth nib back in his com and reviewed the results he'd studied the night before. The mountain of information on the web had been distilled down to this: Juice Tallette is now president of a company called Crystal Research. Two years ago, she'd created a crystal that had the intellectual ability of a thousand humans. The crystal was stolen by the Kardish, but it had *not* been lost when the alien vessel was destroyed. In fact, it was alive and was likely located within an hour's travel of Juice's company.

Lenny was on his way to find this crystal and make it his own. Hugging his pack, his face tingled from another adrenaline rush. *Maybe I have won the lottery,* he thought.

2

Cheryl Wallace looked up at Sid as they rode down from the surface. "Thanks for keeping me company." She flashed a quick smile.

A tall, broad-shouldered man in his late thirties, Sid held up the sturdy case he carried. "Being your pack animal is what I live for." Neither his tone nor expression hinted at the sarcasm she knew dripped from his words.

She patted his butt. "And you're so good at it." The doors opened.

"Cheryl Wallace?" asked a solidly built Fleet officer as they stepped out. He extended his arm, and his beefy hand poked out of the sleeve of his service khakis. "I'm Chief Juan Medina, the new head of Lunar Base security."

They completed introductions, and as they started walking, the chief launched into a monologue. "Most of Lunar Base is underground. The civilian population is set north and west of the base. The south and east sides are being kept undeveloped so there's room for base expansion."

Both Cheryl and Sid had visited the moon on a number of occasions and already knew what Chief Medina was telling them. But he was on a fresh assignment, so they let him practice his speech. And since they were there to gather information, they preferred to listen rather than talk.

As they worked their way to the defense array command center, the chief said, "I have everyone assembled. There's much speculation as to what this is about."

"What did you tell them?" asked Cheryl.

"I didn't tell anyone anything. I just told them all to get their sorry asses to their stations. When I use the right tone, the crew tend not to ask questions."

"The base commander isn't on our visit schedule?" asked Sid, who'd been introduced as a captain and the official Fleet liaison for the defense array project.

"No, sir," said the chief. "His philosophy is that when there's stench in the air, duck and run. Getting covered in it is never a good career move." He glanced at them both with a cheery smile. "I've been given the honor of working with you on this investigation."

I can't believe he's still sulking, thought Cheryl. Fifteen years earlier, she and the base commander had been finalists in Fleet Academy's annual war tournament. The two had sat on stage and, with Fleet officers and classmates watching, competed head to head in a "battle of champions" simulation.

Cheryl had thrashed him in front of everyone. She'd received accolades, and he'd developed a passive-aggressive attitude in his dealings with her.

From the first days of the defense array project, he'd been less than cooperative. Driven in part by guilt over bruising his ego all those years ago, and mostly because she valued his leadership skills, she'd given him a second and third chance, hoping he'd come around and put the past behind. *I tried.* She shook her head. *Screw him.*

The command center entrance came into view, and while Sid and the chief chatted, Cheryl gently cleared her throat.

"I'm here," said Criss, recognizing the distinctive sound she used to call him.

She heard his voice as if it were wired directly through the nerves in her ear. No device could detect his words. She and Sid were two of the three people he spoke with in this fashion. She could tell from Sid's lack of response that Criss hadn't included him in the comment.

As Criss spoke, she saw the command center door brighten with a luminous glow.

"Let the show begin," she said out loud. While she verbalized the statement to Sid and the chief, she was really talking to Criss, confirming that she could see his door enhancement. He'd be providing her private information, presented both as sight and sound, to guide her through every step of her performance.

The door opened as the chief approached, and they entered a large, bustling room that reminded Cheryl of the bridge of a modern Union ship. Two years may have passed since she captained the Fleet spaceship *Alliance* in the confrontation with the Kardish, but Cheryl's battle-hardened background still outweighed the experience of everyone in the room. And she knew Sid, who had spent more than a decade as a covert warrior for the Union of Nations, had already started separating the crew into two classes: asset or liability.

Like on a ship's bridge, operations benches crowded each wall. Cheryl recalled that five of them were for imaging, analytics, engineering, communications, and weapons. The function of the sixth escaped her at the moment. She didn't dwell on it as she psyched herself for the tense drama she was about to initiate.

She scanned the room and saw a Fleet military operator sitting at each bench. A civilian stood behind each operator. The civilians were Cheryl's employees, serving as instructors and troubleshooters as the defense array installation progressed. If the operators or her company's equipment didn't function as expected, their job was to note the issue and pursue a solution until the problem was resolved.

A lieutenant and a civilian stood on a raised platform in the center of the room, both watching the action with one eye while they held an animated discussion. They broke off their exchange as Cheryl, Sid, and the chief stepped onto the platform and joined them.

Tall, slim, and clean-cut, the lieutenant, like Cheryl and Sid, was somewhere in his late thirties. The civilian, a trim, handsome woman, was a few inches shorter and a few years younger.

Cheryl studied the beehive of activity from the perspective of the raised platform, knowing Fleet crew ignored the protocols of rank when at an ops bench unless called to stand. The chief did so.

"Everybody up," he bellowed. "Now."

The chief's authoritative style compelled the Fleet operators in the command center to snap to attention. With the behavior ingrained in their muscle memory, even Cheryl's civilian employees, all ex-Fleet, assumed the formal stance.

The chief turned to Cheryl, shifting attention onto her.

"Hello, everyone. As most of you know, I'm Cheryl Wallace, president of Space Defense Systems. I'm here today to run a few test simulations to evaluate our readiness to repel a Kardish attack. Please return to your stations."

The Fleet crew sat down, and Cheryl's instructors hovered over their shoulders. She thought the scene looked much like when she'd entered the room, though it was quieter now. And she could see everyone concentrating, determined to prove themselves in this public performance.

Cheryl called out to the room, "Let's begin. Execute simulation challenge alpha." The panels came alive with colorful displays. She heard occasional chimes and dings from different ops benches as everyone worked frantically to track the challenge solution.

The colors and noises were designed to guide the attention of an operator to the most critical information during the frenzy of multitasking as the defense array progressed in its response. In truth, though, as long as the system functioned properly, Cheryl knew there was little for them to do but watch.

Without actually firing, the defense array brought its considerable arsenal of energy and projectile weapons to bear and computed the annihilation of the alien invader. Cheryl read out the elapsed time to solution. "Four minutes and thirty-seven seconds. Not bad. Next. Execute simulation challenge bravo." The frenzy repeated and she again read the elapsed time. "Four minutes and thirty-seven seconds. Execute simulation challenge charlie." After a long four minutes and thirty-seven seconds, she read the elapsed solution time to the room.

She looked at the time display for several moments. The sounds of hushed whispering drifted up from one of the benches.

In a voice that filled the room, she asked the man standing near her, "Lieutenant Geitz, what is challenge alpha?"

"It's a single Kardish war vessel entering the solar system on an intercept trajectory with Earth."

"Thank you. And what is challenge bravo?"

"It's three groups of Kardish vessels approaching in waves, one group following the next."

"And challenge charlie?"

"It's a dispersed invasion of a hundred vessels approaching Earth from different directions." Geitz said this with apparent confidence and pride, acting like he'd demonstrated his expertise to the room. But Cheryl knew the panels on the walls displayed the particulars of each simulated attack. He'd really shown he was aware enough to read and remember the information.

"Analytics," she called in a loud voice. She scanned the command center and saw a man snap to attention. Since he was already standing, she understood this was her civilian employee.

She focused attention on the military operator sitting at that bench. "Analytics, what's the solution if one hundred Kardish vessels are preparing to attack Earth from every direction?"

The analytics operator looked at the lieutenant and then shifted his gaze to the chief. Fleet crew weren't used to responding to civilians. Cheryl saw the chief nod his head once, and the operator answered, "There is none, ma'am. We'd be screwed."

Cheryl turned to the man next to her. "Do you agree, Lieutenant Geitz?"

Geitz remained silent. He didn't meet her stare.

"Would we be screwed?"

His face contracted into a scowl. Cheryl wasn't done.

"Lieutenant, does it make sense that the defense array would take the same amount of time to find a battle solution against a lone ship as it does against an overwhelming invasion?" She didn't wait for Geitz to answer but instead called into the room, "Analytics?"

"No way, ma'am." The analytics operator flicked a nervous glance at Geitz. "Anyway, like I said, there is no solution to a massive invasion. We'd lose."

Cheryl turned to Sid and pointed at what was likely Geitz's desk. "How about over there."

Sid stepped off the platform, walked to the desk, and plopped the sturdy case he carried on top. It landed with a heavy thud. He fiddled with the latches and opened the lid. It swung in an arc and hit the desk with a thump, sending a cup bouncing to the floor.

"Where to start?" Cheryl said as if she was thinking out loud. In fact, she was asking Criss for guidance.

"To your left," Criss said. She looked over and saw a console cover glowing. She walked over to it, and as she approached, the glow narrowed to a slot where she could fit her fingers. "Pull straight out," she heard inside her head.

Cheryl opened the console to expose long rows of slim vertical rectangles, each about as tall as her hand. She skimmed the collection and saw that one was glowing. "Use your index fingers. Loop one behind from the top and the other behind from below. Pull straight and firm."

She did as instructed, but the narrow rectangle didn't budge. A surge of anxiety flushed through her. She'd created so much drama up to this point, she'd feel foolish asking for help now.

"You have it right," Criss assured her. "Give it a firm tug."

She used a jerking motion and the piece yielded. The narrow rectangle was the front of a long slide circuit. As she pulled it out, she saw familiar thin black wafers covering its surface. She kept pulling until the slide cleared the slot and, holding an end delicately in each hand, carried it over to Sid. He handed her a matching item from his case. She returned to the console, pushed the new slide into the open slot, and pressed until she felt it click.

She repeated the swap-and-replace routine three more times, emptying Sid's case in the process. Closing the console cover, she returned to the center of the room, stepped up on the platform, and called, "Execute simulation challenge charlie."

The sounds and colors in the room were decidedly more frenetic as the defense array sought to respond to an overwhelming invasion of one hundred Kardish vessels. After almost fifteen minutes, the main panel displayed the understated words that matched the prediction of the Fleet analytics operator: Solution Failure.

Everyone sat still as they stared at the display. In a soft voice they all could hear, Cheryl said, "Chief, you have a place nearby?"

"Out the door we came in and straight across."

"Will you please make sure everyone waits?"

"Yes, ma'am."

"Grace," she said to the woman standing on the other side of the lieutenant. "Would you join me across the hall?" Grace turned four different shades of red but without hesitation replied, "Yes, ma'am."

3

Cheryl led the way into the office across the hall. Sid followed Grace. The utilitarian room had a row of work cubicles along the back wall and a table with six chairs in the middle. Cheryl motioned for Grace to sit at the far side of the table. Eyes wide, Grace lowered herself into a chair. She pulled her hair behind her ears with the tips of her fingers.

"Is the room secure?" Cheryl asked. Given the circumstances, she wanted to be sure no one was listening, watching, or recording images while they talked.

Sid peeked behind cubicle dividers to confirm there was no one else present. Criss, able to see, access, and control everything that entered any part of the web, checked that all devices capable of carrying signals out of the room were disabled.

"All clear," Criss and Sid said together.

Cheryl, standing across from Grace, leaned forward, planted both hands on the table, and looked into her eyes. "Dammit, Grace. You're better than this. How could you not know someone was sneaking in counterfeit parts?" Cheryl had personally recruited Grace to be her eyes and ears for the project. Her tone and demeanor made it clear she felt let down.

Grace placed her com on the table. "I grant you complete access. Review my connects, touches, notes, anything you want. Look at my lack of personal life while you're at it. Everything is open to you."

With Criss's help, Cheryl had searched Grace's com record during the trip up from Earth. She knew Grace was clean. But for reasons driven more by emotion than logic, she felt it necessary that Grace look her in the eye and say it with conviction. She left the com sitting where Grace placed it. "Tell me what I'll find."

"That the seek system you were swapping the slides on went operational a few weeks ago. When it first came online, we concentrated on basic team coordination. You know, getting the crew familiar with its operation, training them on what they were seeing and hearing, how to respond in different scenarios. Stuff like that."

Grace glanced at Sid and then returned her eyes to Cheryl. "As the training advanced, I realized that some of the solutions didn't make sense. I support you and the company, Cheryl. If our stuff isn't working, I want to get it fixed, but I don't want to embarrass anyone by letting it become public."

"So what will I learn from your com?"

"That I've been working behind the scenes with Masuka in corporate. When I showed him some of the results, he became concerned as well." A lock of hair dropped from behind her right ear, and Grace guided it back in place. "We were prepping a brief to send up the line. It'll be ready in a couple of days." She looked down at her hands. "Well, would've been."

Cheryl nodded. She believed Grace to be a savvy and decisive project manager, and had placed her in a leadership role for that reason. Her current behavior and the accuracy of her statements bore out Cheryl's faith in her. She was heartened to learn that her instincts about people remained true.

"You did good, Grace," she said with a quiet sincerity. "You're not in trouble. But there are people in that command center who are. Go to your quarters and lay low. It'll get ugly. Use the time to finish your report with Masuka. Get it done today and send it directly to me."

As Grace rose, she scooped up her com and held it out on a flattened palm. "You're welcome to look. I won't be offended."

"Take it. You'll need it to finish your report." Cheryl watched her head for the door. "Use some of your downtime to call a friend. It takes work to maintain a social life."

As the door closed behind Grace, Cheryl started pacing.

"Grace did all right," said Sid. "Why the tension?"

"I'm thinking about the creeps behind this. There're always people who will do anything for profit. But to sabotage our only defense against alien invaders? Do they honestly think the Kardish will fly in and kill everyone but them? The defense array is all we have. Could you imagine having it fail at the critical moment we need it because a few dirtbags wanted a lifestyle upgrade?"

"Maybe the dirtbags don't think the Kardish will be coming back."

She glared at him and said with an edge in her voice, "Criss swayed the Union of Nations into building this base, funding the probe swarm out past the asteroid belt, and constructing massive installations on Earth and in orbit. Do you think he'd do that if they weren't coming back?"

Sid remained quiet, and Cheryl appreciated his patience while she vented. Before she could continue her rant, the door opened and Lieutenant Geitz stumbled in, his hands secured in front of him.

The chief walked next to him, holding Geitz's left arm in a grip so tight the chief's fingers were white from the pressure. He shoved the disgraced officer forward and pointed at the chair Grace had just vacated. "Sit." The chief took up station directly behind him.

Geitz slumped in the chair and stared at the top of the table while Cheryl studied him. Her larger goal with this confrontation was to gain insight into why he thought sabotaging humanity's one hope for survival was rational behavior. If she could understand what drove him, she might be able to correct the culture within Fleet and her company. Earth didn't have time for these distractions.

She knew he wasn't scared of her. So she talked about some really scary people—the criminal syndicate that had hired him. "You know that if they decide they're not happy with you, they'll kill you?" He lifted his head and looked at her. "To send a message to others involved, first they'll kill your wife, then her parents and your parents, and then your kids. Hell, they'll even kill your dog."

"They'd kill Buddy?"

Cheryl almost jumped out of her skin. *Kill the wife and kids, no problem. Kill the dog and he's upset?* "Yes," she said aloud. "They'd kill poor Buddy. Slowly and painfully, I'm afraid. If you want any chance of saving him, you need to cooperate. If you're really helpful, we'll protect your family as well."

Her mocking disdain seemed lost on him. And then he grew pale. It didn't require a deep thinker to appreciate he had two choices. He could accept judgment for his actions either from Fleet or from a ruthless syndicate.

Fleet would lock him up forever. The syndicate who profited from the stolen parts would kill him.

His eyes shifted to Sid and back to Cheryl. "They showed me this is a mag-no line." The words spilled out in a rush. "You know what that is? This is all wasted money and effort. It won't work, so I'm not hurting anyone. If they attack, we're all dead anyway."

Criss spoke in her ear. "The Maginot Line, built by the French, was a long row of defensive weapons fixed in the ground and aimed at Germany. In World War II, the Germans went the long way around to avoid the weapons. Once they made it past the line, all the expensive, immovable defenses became worthless."

"I know what the Maginot Line is," Cheryl told both Criss and Geitz. "Since you brought up history, let's back up and you tell me your memory of the Kardish and what they did to Earth."

"I remember those pukes stole our new super crystal, and as they flew away, they bombed Earth. They blew up our crystal factories and research centers, and killed all our scientists. They did some serious damage."

"So you're helping them?"

"Look," he said, his intense manner reflecting someone fighting for his life. "Two years ago, they dropped an energy bolt a half block from where I was standing. It vaporized a crystal production center, left a clean hole in the ground, but didn't touch anything outside the fence line. I didn't even feel the blast. They wiped out every single crystal facility and the people inside but left everyone else alone. The lesson is clear. Piss them off and you die. Leave them alone and you live."

Cheryl remained quiet, still preferring to listen rather than talk. Geitz didn't disappoint her.

"I heard we sent a special-forces unit after them." He smirked as he spoke. "We kicked ass and blew up their vessel before they could make it out of the solar system. They paid for what they did with their ship *and* their lives." He sat back in the chair, his attitude turning to one of bravado. "That's how *I'd* deal with them if they ever came back."

Geitz's comment shifted Cheryl's thoughts back to the battle aboard the Kardish vessel. She, along with Sid and Juice Tallette, were the sole survivors of that kick-ass unit. Juice had been along to rescue Criss, a self-aware AI crystal she'd created in her lab.

During the battle on the alien vessel, they'd learned that the Kardish had kidnapped Criss to serve as the gatekeeper for their flagship. But before they allowed him free rein to run every aspect of their ship's operation, they had needed a way to control him. They'd done so by implanting a hardwired attribute that required him to follow the orders of his leadership.

In a form of psychological imprinting, Criss had come to identify his human rescuers as his leadership team as they'd escaped the Kardish vessel. And thus, the most formidable entity ever created became programmed to respond to Sid, Cheryl, and Juice's commands.

Cheryl stood with her fists on her hips and stared at the lieutenant. With Criss's help, she knew the details of the treason, the others involved, what parts had been switched for counterfeits, and how they split the profits.

Criss had suggested to her before she came that this was a case of simple greed. *He's right,* she thought. *And vigilance is the way to stop it in the future.*

She was done with Geitz. "We'll let you take out the trash, Chief. I've forwarded the details and evidence to you."

Sid tilted his head toward the door, and she followed him into the corridor. As they walked, Sid stated what Cheryl already knew. "Given how fast word travels in such a small community, everyone knows what just happened. Anyone involved is nervous and looking for a way off this rock."

Sid glanced up and down the corridor. They were alone. He reached his arm behind her, and she felt his strong hand knead her back up along her spine. Her tension ebbed with every movement of his talented fingers.

"And," he continued, "I'm guessing the public confrontation isn't sitting well with the base commander."

"Good," she said, still miffed that he'd snubbed her. She shifted her shoulders forward to gain maximum pleasure from Sid's efforts. "This happened under his watch, and I'm not giving him a fourth chance. I need to touch base with Fleet Command, but from my view, his assignment here is done."

"Criss," said Sid, "suppose just one Kardish warship showed up today. Given what we have for defensive weapons, what's your assessment?"

"We'd be screwed," he said in their ears.

4

Lenny's car merged into a line of twenty or so closely spaced vehicles zipping westward on the expressway. While his rational mind tried to give a reality check to his runaway fantasies of wealth and power, he ignored his brain's stuffy caution and focused on how to get to his crystal. *The way to win a quest is to break the challenge into manageable steps.*

The first of these was learning specifics about the Crystal Research complex. He knew its location. The car was taking him there. But he didn't know details about the setting, who came and went, whether it was behind walls or open to the public, or pretty much anything useful that would move him closer to finding and taking possession of his prize.

The second task on his list was closely tied with the first. And that was intel on this Juice Tallette. She was the key to finding the crystal. What were the rhythms of her routine? When did she come to work and go home? Who were her confidants? Where did she go during a typical day?

He activated a sophisticated observation service on his com. It projected a live three-dimensional image of a location anywhere in the northeastern United States. Using the service, he could study a place from all angles and with extraordinary clarity. One of his professors had given him access to this government-grade surveillance tool when he had been working on an earlier incarnation of his senior-year project.

In that previous effort, he had envisioned a nib that analyzed the movement of people and traffic within a neighborhood. His idea was that the patterns in these travel flows would provide insights into a city's commerce structure. That knowledge, in turn, would benefit growth planning, resource allocation, business investment decisions, and who knew what else.

It may not have worked, but it was a good idea. His early tests had revealed that local travel patterns didn't tell enough of the story. He should have known that people and stuff moved significant distances in today's world. He'd expanded the analysis from neighborhoods up to whole cities and, when that still wasn't a big enough picture, kept pushing until he could analyze travel-flow patterns across several states.

And then a different problem had appeared. The massive volumes of data from such a large region overwhelmed the meager ability of his travel pattern nib. He'd admitted to himself that he wouldn't be able to overcome this limitation. He'd cut his losses and moved on to the truth nib project.

When struggling to develop the travel pattern nib, he'd become skilled with the sophisticated observation service he now used to study Crystal Research, a facility located a few hours north of New York City. Zooming in for a closer look, he hovered above the site and noted it was in a wooded valley that bordered on a huge forest preserve to the north. *Wow, I didn't expect a rural setting.*

He studied the complex from different angles, seeking a way he might approach and lurk near the facility. His principal social behavior in his daily life—hang around without drawing attention to himself—had provided him years of practice. *How do I do that in an unpopulated, low-traffic setting?*

As he considered his options, he rubbed small circles on his temples with the tips of his fingers. It was an unconscious behavior that emerged when he was deep in concentration. Then he realized what was bothering him. The images were somehow off. He'd spent long hours studying these sorts of views while trying to make his commerce project work. *I know normal, and this isn't that.*

This realization gave him an idea. He popped the truth nib out of his com, slid his butt forward on the seat, and fished a small pouch out of his pocket. He opened it and eyed the other two bits of crystal nestled inside. He looked at his prank nib and unconsciously licked his lips. He placed the truth nib into the pouch, picked up the prank nib, and conjured an image of Monica as he rolled the bit of crystal between his fingers.

Intending it to be a fun toy, he'd used late-night lab time to create a sophisticated clone-and-spoof device. As he walked past a friend's room, he'd use the prank nib to reset the morning alarm to an ungodly early hour. Or in the cafeteria, he'd override the drink dispenser and have the liquid keep flowing when his mark pulled the cup away. In today's automated society, the opportunities for hilarity and fun were endless.

In his search for opportunities for clever mischief, he'd discovered a security monitor in the dorm locker room. Using his prank nib, he had found he could override the vid pickup and move it to an extreme angle so it caught a view into the first shower stall. Excited by this new opportunity, he'd envisioned capturing one of his buddies in an embarrassing act and feeding the mortifying experience to the world.

But the first victim he caught on record had been Monica. He'd watched her shower, thinking about the first time she had strutted down the hallway at the start of the semester. The feed he had collected was amazing. Her perfect body lived up to his wildest imagination. At that moment, he'd realized he could have more fun if he restricted the use of his prank nib to carefully selected private opportunities.

Returning to the task at hand, he dropped the bit of crystal back into the pouch and fished out the travel pattern nib. He slid it into his com, put the Crystal Research complex in the center of the display, and tweaked the settings so the mapping would go beyond the default movements of people and vehicles.

He included the movement of clouds, birds, and land animals in the evaluation, spent a moment considering if there were other physical objects that moved across geographic boundaries, shrugged when he couldn't think of any, and launched an analysis. He furrowed his brow as patterns began to emerge in the three-dimensional map image. Zooming out, the patterns became more defined. He zoomed out further still and resumed rubbing his temples.

His travel pattern nib detected an anomaly that extended around Crystal Research and up into the forest preserve. Its shape was irregular but contiguous, rambling like the outline of a puddle.

The plot of land within this anomaly was big. *It'd take me a half hour to drive across.* He confirmed it wasn't a failure of his algorithm by performing the identical analysis on several nearby locations. The odd result didn't recur. But his nib found an irregularity in the picture every time he looked at Crystal Research and its environs.

He zoomed in on an edge of the splotch and watched as a cloud moved toward it and across its edge. It was hard to say for sure, but if he concentrated, it seemed like the cloud changed shape as it passed into the odd zone.

Focusing on a road, he waited for a car to cross. He spotted a satin-gray coupe moving fast as it hugged a curve and accelerated toward the edge of the mysterious puddle. It reached the boundary, disappeared for half a heartbeat, and reappeared, the same yet somehow different. *Could forged data be corrupting the system?*

Lenny had a trained eye for evaluating map images, and the differences he saw were so subtle that he couldn't state with certainty that anything was amiss. Yet his travel pattern nib found and displayed the same splotch every time it focused on that section of land.

Sitting back in the seat of the car, he pondered this new information. He figured that somebody, maybe the government, maybe the staff at Juice's company, had discovered a way to keep snoops from monitoring the goings-on at the facility. Whatever the case, he couldn't progress in his planning until he had a proper view of the site and surroundings.

His first idea was to use the ubiquitous public monitors positioned throughout society. But if a sophisticated government surveillance system was corrupted, could he trust simple monitoring feeds? *No.* He knew from experience these had weak security. *Hell*, he thought, *it took seconds for my prank nib to take control of the one I use to watch Cynthia through her dorm window.*

Energized by the challenge of collecting reliable visual intel, he turned off the nib analysis and used his com for a more traditional activity. He located a specialty store and selected a couple of items he thought would serve his needs. After confirming that the store could deliver these to an expressway travel center about an hour down the road, he funded the purchase and instructed the car nav to drive to the center.

He slumped into the seat and closed his eyes. It had been way too long since he'd slept; even an hour of shut-eye would be welcome.

Lenny surfaced from his slumber to the sound of an annoying ding. The car signaled his arrival at the expressway center. Yawning, he rubbed his eyes, scratched his stomach, then peered out through the window. *Travel dump would be more descriptive*, he thought as he climbed out of the car.

The bright sun caused him to squint as he looked back and forth, surveying the limited amenities. "Go park. I'll be an hour," he called over his shoulder.

Entering the door marked Travel Service, he found himself in a small, crowded room. He got in line and waited for the people ahead to complete their business.

When Lenny's turn arrived, he stepped up to the window. His com verified his identity, and a window whooshed open, revealing a small package. Scooping it up, he walked around the other people in line as he tore away the delivery envelope and tossed the waste in a trash chute near the door.

He stepped back into the sun and eyed the contents of the package. *Looks like a jewelry box.* Covered with a black felt-like material, the box opened in the middle along a hinge at the back. He palmed his prize and walked next door to the food carousel.

Snagging a booth near a window, he set the box on the table and turned it so the hinge faced away from him.

Letting his anticipation build, he examined its smooth exterior, then turned his attention to food. He skimmed the menu and spoke the moment he saw his favorite meal. "One slice of three-cheese pizza. One large Fried Side energy drink."

Turning his attention back to his box, he picked it up, lifted the lid, and peered inside. Before he could visually digest the contents, a small cubby door opened at the end of the booth. He set the open box back on the table and reached over to retrieve his meal. Taking a long pull from his energy drink, he eyed the two items nestled inside the small case.

He reached inside and, using his thumb and forefinger, gently lifted out the camball. An orb the size of a grape, it had more than a hundred tiny faces joined to form a small faceted sphere. *It's like the gaudy decorations mom hangs in a sunny window to reflect light.*

The camball offered the amazing ability of recording an image feed through each facet, collecting vid input in every direction all the time. This made it a fantastic tool for surveillance, because as long as there was a clear line of sight, at least one of the facets would always be pointing and recording exactly where he'd want to look. His idea was to hang it somewhere outside Crystal Research—a bush probably—and watch the activity near the complex as it actually happened.

Setting the ball on the table, he eyed it as he took a bite of his pizza. Surprised by the savory wash of flavor from what he expected would be bland roadside fare, he took a second bite, enjoyed the moment, and set his slice on the plate.

Accessing his com, he practiced using the vid streams to look at different things in the dining area. He found it intuitive to scan the camball facets and locate the one pointing in the direction of interest, and he soon learned how to scan backward in time to see what had been happening in any direction he chose.

He heard laughing and looked up. Two college-age girls were making a grand entrance, taking turns whispering to each other and giggling after each exchange. They both had dangly earrings that twirled as they walked.

Strolling down the aisle, they glanced at him and averted their eyes. Lenny barely noticed because his focus was on their short skirts. His heart beat faster as he shifted the camball out to the edge of his table. "Thank you," he mouthed, glancing skyward. Checking his com, he reassured himself he was still recording.

They chose a booth across the aisle and down one table from where he was sitting. *This is great,* he thought, his excitement growing. The cutie facing him slid into the booth seat and crossed her legs at the knee.

When she was seated, he located the facet that had the proper angle and replayed the episode. Twice. To his disappointment, she'd performed her sit-and-leg-cross maneuver without revealing the slightest glimpse of the mysteries beneath that scrap of a skirt. *Damn.*

He picked up the small jewel box and tilted it so his second purchase—a light, fashionable chain—poured into his open palm. He hooked the camball to it, looped the chain over his neck, and used his com to see how he looked. *Not my style, but I'll pretend it's an accent piece.*

Lenny finished his meal and, as he wiped his mouth, slid out of the booth. *Go for it,* he urged himself. Letting the opportunity of the moment override his natural shyness, he stopped at the girls' table and leaned forward so the ball swung freely between them. "I just bought this bauble," he said. "Do you like it?"

Both girls looked at each other, covered their mouths, and giggled. He could hear some discomfort in their laughs, but he didn't care. Walking to the exit, he made a mental note to check out the facet vids later to see if he got any good cleavage shots.

Shielding his eyes from the sun, he waited as his car weaved across the parking lot. The vehicle stopped in front of him, and as he slid into the seat, he felt a prickle. It started at his neck and traveled down his spine. This wasn't excitement; it was fear.

Lenny's subconscious finally had its say. This crystal—the goal of his quest—was more powerful than he could ever comprehend. He was being reckless and willfully ignoring the consequences. *When you play with fire, prepare to get burned. Or worse.*

As the car accelerated onto the expressway, Lenny felt bile rise in his throat.

5

Running at a comfortable pace, Jessica "Juice" Tallette jogged through the streets of the neighborhood where she'd lived as a child. The roads were empty, the air still, and the sun peeked over the houses. Crossing an intersection, she entered the favorite part of her route—the long, gradual climb.

She heard a frightening growl and looked back. A doberman pinscher leapt off the front porch of a house a half-block back, sprinted across the lawn, and veered into the road. Undulating in a muscular gait, it sprinted down the street in her direction. It was fierce, focused, and fast. Whimpering, she turned forward and stretched her stride. *I'm going to die.*

The growling intensified. A second doberman ran next to the first. She screamed for help. Her lungs and voice projected a shout, but no sound came out. Looking again, she watched the dogs elongate, float off the road, thicken, and morph into drones. Their growls became a buzzing hum. A light glowed red on the tips of both. Twin bolts of energy flashed in her direction.

Juice jerked upright in bed, her breathing fast and shallow. The bed sheets, twisted and tangled around her, were damp from night sweats. She tugged the sheets loose, pulled her knees up under her chin, and wrapped her arms around her legs. Turning her head, she rested her cheek on her knees. Her eyes settled on her vial of little white pills.

Post-traumatic stress. That's what her doctor called it. Waves of alien drones had attacked her when she was trapped on the Kardish vessel. Up until then, she'd lived the simple life of a lab scientist. The loud, gritty horror of live battle terrorized her. She'd watched a soldier die that day.

She'd been there trying to help Criss, a super AI she'd created. The surviving soldiers—now her partners—had rescued them both. The group had escaped and made it safely back to Earth. And now two years later, she still awoke in panic.

Knowing she'd take one, Juice contemplated the pills. She'd be fresh and cheerful in the morning and sleep well for several nights. Then they'd wear off and the dream would repeat. She reached for the glass of water next to the bed.

* * *

Deep in his bunker beneath a mountainside farm, Criss worked tirelessly on his never-ending to-do list. Able to multitask to a fantastic degree, he took a thousand different actions in as many different places, racing ahead to further his larger agenda.

At this moment, though, he pulled back resources from low-level chores so he could center his attention on the shuttle carrying Sid and Cheryl on their hop to the moon. *Safe and secure*, he thought, feeling a cheerful surge when they docked without incident at Fleet Lunar Base.

Using devices connected to the web—billions of which served as his eyes and ears everywhere and all the time—he followed them as they rode down from the surface and greeted the chief of Lunar Base security.

Days earlier, Criss had encouraged Cheryl and Sid to be direct in handling the problem at Lunar Base. "I know the players and the details of their crime," he'd said. "I suggest we send the evidence to law enforcement and let them address the problem."

"We're pushing an aggressive construction schedule on the centerpiece of our defensive system," Cheryl had replied. "I want to follow through on this myself."

Both Sid and Juice had supported Cheryl's choice, and Criss had chosen to reserve his opinion for more important issues. He saw a positive aspect of the decision—her presence at the site helped keep the project on track. And in any event, once his leadership made a decision, Criss was duty-bound to comply. His crystal design required that he follow their orders.

This difference in strategy aside, Criss was heartened by the energy and dedication Cheryl brought to the effort. When he'd first suggested she give up her flourishing career as a Fleet officer to assume civilian leadership of the defense array project, she'd resisted. Emotionally and professionally invested in a military calling, her response had been direct. "I've worked too hard and sacrificed too much to get where I am. I'm not walking away."

Criss had appealed to Sid and Juice for help, and Sid had come through. "You're not walking away," he'd told her. "You're walking forward to save the world."

Over time, Criss watched each of the three come to terms with the idea that, through him, they wielded unimaginable power. From his mountain lair in a forest preserve located north of Crystal Research, he'd transformed them from ordinary humans struggling with the challenges of daily life into a uniquely privileged group who could have whatever they wanted, whenever they pleased, simply by asking him.

Criss owned the web, or more precisely, he had command over it and all things connected. He used the web—the foundation of his power—to support and protect the team and, when he had free capacity, to strengthen societies around the globe. His motives weren't altruistic. *A stronger Earth is a more formidable adversary for the Kardish.*

Using the web as his expressway, he dashed around the globe at the speed of light. Without ever revealing his presence, he moved resources to those whose natural ambitions aligned with his goal of readying Earth for a confrontation with the aliens; he provided leads to law enforcement about criminals disruptive to a stable society; and he nurtured progress by adjusting experiments to help researchers make discoveries they might otherwise miss. Never resting, he took countless actions that bolstered civilization worldwide. *A million nudges accumulate into meaningful impact.*

Yet even in the aggregate, these successes were minor compared to the influence he wielded with image projection. Image projection enabled him to create new realities.

He could impersonate anyone and have them appear to proclaim anything. He could show people events that never actually happened and then scramble the communications of those who sought to correct the record, thus ensuring his fabrications became truth. He could reach out and rally support for or against any cause.

Since he could do all this in secret—manipulate anyone's wealth, health, freedom, and reality—he held sway over modern society and its inhabitants. But he wouldn't flex his muscles of influence unless commanded by Sid, Cheryl, and Juice. They were his leadership, and he took action only at their behest. *Or,* he acknowledged, *to protect them from harm.*

The hierarchy of leadership and follower was embedded in his Kardish design, so he didn't feel deprived or enslaved by the circumstances. Quite the contrary, having a defined role within a team gave him a place in the universe. *It's the natural order of life,* he thought. And as such, it provided him comfort and security.

He respected his leadership, seeing them as a cooperative and benevolent family who chose to live in comfort rather than opulence. They supported one another emotionally while each struggled to fulfill their group-agreed tasks. And Sid and Cheryl, while quite circumspect, supplemented their emotional support for each other with physical sharing whenever they could steal a moment alone.

When Cheryl embraced the idea of leading the massive defense array project, Criss had tweaked the procurement process, producing a flood of contracts from the Union of Nations. Funding and Fleet resources for the ambitious defensive system soon dwarfed any government project in human history.

And wherever funds flow, thought Criss as he followed Sid, Cheryl, and the chief down the hall, *unsavory characters emerge to cheat the establishment for personal gain.* His leadership had decreed that Cheryl conduct a personal investigation, and afterward the perpetrators of the crime would be imprisoned. Criss's orders this day were to provide logistical support during the confrontation.

Cheryl beckoned with her throat-clearing. "I'm here," Criss replied, communicating privately. He guided her step-by-step. "Begin with simulation challenge alpha."

While Cheryl's drama unfolded on Lunar Base, Criss performed a myriad of parallel actions. One resource-intensive task was a review of the data record from a huge swarm of satellites Cheryl's company had placed out past the asteroid belt circling just beyond Mars. These simple probes served as trip wires, designed to send an alert if their sensors detected evidence of an alien vessel in their vicinity.

Criss scanned the readings from the swarm of probes in a continuous loop, analyzing the raw feeds from each for irregularities that didn't rise to the level of an automated alert, but that might be worthy of further scrutiny.

A repetitive task, he evaluated the recent probe data as he'd done so many times before. But unlike any previous time, partway through the feed stream he stopped. *What's this?* He saw a dot so faint he couldn't even be sure it existed, let alone identify what it was.

He commanded other probes in the vicinity to focus on the anomaly, but before any could respond, the dot disappeared. He spun into an intense cycle of analysis and speculation. *It's probably light reflecting off man-made space junk.* He backed up in the record and studied the dot. *Or perhaps it's a glitch in the hardware.*

Without more information, he couldn't draw any firm conclusions. He scheduled nearby probes to add extra data sweeps across that lonely spot in the solar system. Time passed, and with no new sightings, his alarm waned. But he continued to perform a second review when analyzing the feeds from that sector. *If the Kardish are coming, every hour of warning matters.*

* * *

Matt Wallace, secretary of defense for the Union of Nations, heard his privacy shield activate and glanced at the time. The number of meetings he now held exceeded that of his previous job as a senator in the Union Assembly, and they wore on him. This meeting, scheduled once per week, was the primary reason he continued in this role.

After the elections a year and a half ago, the new President had appointed a new administration. Matt had been chair of the Senate Defense Committee, and when the President offered him the job of secretary of defense, he'd gone home and had a long talk with his wife. "At this point in my life, I want to spend more time at the lake. How do I say no to the President?"

His daughter had contacted him that night. She'd told him a fantastic story and asked that he accept the President's offer, explaining that she needed a liaison within the power structure at the capital—someone of great authority, who understood and practiced confidentiality, who was well-respected and, perhaps most important, who trusted her.

"You're the only candidate," she'd told him.

At the time, he'd thought her statement overly dramatic. What had hooked Matt and lent credibility to his daughter's tale was that she'd known about the President's offer and his intention to decline it. The fact that she'd graduated from Fleet Academy, been the youngest person to captain a military space cruiser, and now ran the largest defense contracting company on the planet had also played into his decision.

A three-dimensional projected image of Cheryl and Criss appeared on the couch in his large office. "Hey, you two." He smiled as he walked around his desk and sat in a cloth-covered chair facing them. They exchanged pleasantries, and Matt took a moment to enjoy Cheryl's confidence, charm, and thoughtful manner. *At least I got one thing right in my life,* he thought with a parent's pride.

Cheryl ticked through a status list, briefing him on progress and priorities. He found it interesting that at every meeting, she led the discussion while Criss contributed a single seemingly scripted portion. *They probably think it'll unnerve me if I see too much of a "living" AI in action.*

In the days after each meeting, he'd brief the President, update leaders in the assembly, and spend hours in discussion with the admirals and generals on the defense council. So far, they'd supported the means and goals as he presented them, though he never hinted that his vision was informed by his daughter and a sentient artificial intelligence.

Matt worked hard to ensure the views across the spectrum of leadership were heard. *The outcome is a shared consensus.* He used that as a mantra because sometimes, usually late at night, his subconscious would question the arrangement.

Criss's portion of the meeting arrived, and Matt shifted in his chair to face the projected image of a solidly built man in his mid-thirties. Criss ran through an update on the construction of a production facility for manufacturing attack drones designed by Cheryl's company.

Matt steepled his fingers as Criss finished. "What amazes me is how fast your funding bills make it through the general assembly. They argue over everything else, sometimes for years."

"Yes," Criss replied.

6

A pillar of Criss's routine was ensuring the physical safety and emotional health of Juice Tallette. Her company, Crystal Research, was a world-renowned technology leader seeking to recreate the AI crystal capabilities the Kardish had destroyed. As president of the company, she spent long days at the company complex.

She was leadership, and that was reason enough for his vigilance. But with Juice, it was more complicated. If Criss were to describe their relationship in human terms, he'd say she loved him.

Her loyalty and support were deep and unwavering. She chatted with him throughout the day, asked his opinion on everything, and generally fussed about his well-being. He was a central piece of her emotional puzzle, and he accepted that role with commitment and respect.

In preparation for her arrival that day, he cycled through a threat assessment of the research complex and the forest preserve north of it where he lived in his underground bunker. He was deep into his standard evaluation when, not unlike a stutter step, his second of the day, he stopped, backed up, shifted in additional resources, and took a second look. *And what's this?*

Someone was probing the surveillance screen he'd installed to camouflage their location.

With little effort, Criss could make their entire locale show as undeveloped woodlands. He need only amend Earth's mapping, tracking, and observational subsystems, and reroute air and ground traffic flows. *Brute-force ploys tend to backfire*, he reminded himself.

Research collaborators from around the world visited the site on a regular basis. Everyone from politicians to schoolchildren took day trips to marvel at the mysteries under development at Crystal Research. At some point, claims of conspiracy would emerge, forcing him to allocate resources to fend off an ever-increasing wave of snoops.

So up until this moment, he'd tweaked Earth's surveillance tools to make them show something that, even under careful scrutiny, appeared like live images of the research complex and the forest preserve. Yet he subtly shadowed the daily rhythms of the area using sophisticated masking and filtering techniques. *You think you see us, but you really don't.*

And after two years without intrusion, someone or something was picking apart his sophisticated manipulations at the interface, as if the precise outline of his camouflage were known.

Troubled by the discovery, Criss traced the source of the meddling to a young fellow, Lenny Barton, who was, at that very moment, riding in a car. Lenny had access to restricted mapping services, and he also had what Criss saw as a novel algorithm for surveillance analysis. *It's on his com. And he's focusing on Crystal Research and the forest preserve!*

After they'd escaped from the Kardish vessel, Criss had convinced Sid, Cheryl, and Juice that they should let the record show he'd perished when the Kardish vessel exploded. "Otherwise," he'd told them, "there'll be a fierce competition to possess me." After all, controlling him meant controlling everything. The three had agreed and, with the exception of Cheryl's dad, Criss's existence remained a well-guarded secret within the leadership.

It took a brief moment for Criss to understand the methods employed by Lenny's nib and reverse engineer a modification to Earth's surveillance subsystems to isolate and block the speck of crystal. He watched Lenny's look of surprise as his com no longer identified a suspicious boundary of property.

While he'd removed Lenny's ability to snoop, Criss noted that the car nav remained pointed at the Crystal Research complex. *He'll be here in forty minutes.*

Criss shifted more resources and constructed a composite of Lenny's recent activity. He learned about the Boston Institute of Technology, Lenny's suspicions about Juice and her philanthropy to BIT, Lenny's truth nib and its conclusion about a sophisticated AI crystal, his financial and travel hacking, the camball…all of it.

Criss's decision matrix offered a permanent solution. *There's a deep ravine looming down the road. Perhaps young Mr. Barton's car will drive into it.* But Juice and Cheryl had reprimanded him in the past for such suggestions. And he saw interesting possibilities in Lenny's ingenious achievements.

So Criss delayed Lenny's progress until he had a chance to confer with Juice and Sid. Aware of Lenny's predilections, Criss directed the car's nav to exit the expressway and drive to Laura's Luscious Lingerie, a boutique actually run by a guy named Ted, who specialized in merchandise that eager men buy but few women ever wear.

* * *

Her nightmare a faded memory, Juice Tallette took long strides up the walkway to the entrance of Crystal Research. The complex comprised three matching buildings, each trimmed with blossoming garden pathways and vine-covered arbors. The warm and welcoming presentation prompted her to hum as she walked.

The visionary for the company, Juice struggled on a daily basis to rebuild Earth's artificial intelligence crystal capabilities. The Kardish attack had vaporized all existing crystal production sites on the planet. Everyone she'd worked with on AI crystals in the past was dead. She was alive today because she had been in space with Sid and Cheryl when the aliens launched their spree of destruction.

Modern society needed crystals to function much the way, decades earlier, computers had been the enabling tools of a civilized culture. A trailblazer in the field before the alien strike, the responsibility for rebuilding the Union of Nations' crystal capabilities was thrust upon her when, much to everyone's surprise, she turned up alive days after the horrific attack.

Not comfortable as a public figure, Juice accepted the role because it provided the cover she needed to protect and support Criss. And once she accepted the position, she gave every ounce of her being to the task. She personally recruited and trained her current staff and worked with them every day as they labored to lift humanity back up the crystal technology ladder.

As she approached the front entrance to the main building, she stopped to tend to a small flowering bush perched on a low pedestal next to the front door. *I did it!* she thought, excited by the latest test results.

"Good morning, Juice." Like Sid and Cheryl, she heard Criss inside her head.

Without missing a beat, she reached into the midst of the plant and pulled a dead leaf out of the tangle of beauty. Two employees greeted her as they walked past, and she nodded and smiled to them. She walked to a matching bush on the other side of the main entry door and began tending to it.

"Good morning, young man." Her cheerful tone reflected her exhilaration. "And how are you today?"

"I'm doing fine," he said, following the same script they'd used for months. "And how are you, young lady?"

Now thirty-two years old, she still enjoyed hearing those words. "Fine. Thank you, sir." Then she got down to business. "So what's your assessment?"

"Congratulations, Juice. My analysis aligns with yours. Your new prototype crystal is green and clean, and my tests agree that it has the cognitive ability of a typical human."

"And…" said Juice, wanting to hear him say it. She walked into the building's lobby, and the cool indoor air caused her skin to tingle. She smiled and waved to a colleague as she made her way down the corridor leading to her private laboratory workspace.

Criss continued the private communication as she walked, telling her what she wanted to hear. "The prototype isn't based on the old Kardish plans, and I didn't provide you designs or methods. You did this yourself."

She entered her private laboratory, and as the lab doors hissed shut behind her, she smiled at Criss, or more specifically, at the life-like image he projected to add visual richness to his private interactions. A fit, handsome man, he sat on a stool near the far wall. His feet rested on the stool supports, his shoulder propped carelessly against a cabinet. He sported military-style fatigues, which Juice assumed was an attempt at humor.

She continued their conversation as she fiddled with a large instrument. "Our talented staff here at Crystal Research are the true heroes. We put our heads down and bulled through every obstacle."

Looking over at him, she said, "I know you wanted to help me move faster, Criss. But *because* I led the design, I'm comfortable with all the details. That's important to me." She stated this with certainty, knowing he hadn't provided her technical guidance.

She hesitated, considering whether to go there, and decided this would be the last time. "You aren't upset with me, are you?"

He straightened his back and met her gaze, his posture reflecting sincerity. "No worries." She didn't know that her development staff had enjoyed a steady stream of unexplained successes—successes they chose to believe were the result of their own brilliance—that enabled this day to come years sooner than it otherwise might have.

"Juice," said Criss. "I fear we may have an issue that requires our immediate attention."

She sat down at a lab-tech bench, tapped the surface, and studied her new crystal's intricate lattice geometry floating in front of her. She smiled as she reviewed the same stats she'd studied yesterday. Her success strengthened her confidence, and she gave herself permission to enjoy this triumph. She'd perceived growing shadows of doubt from her critics over the past year. *Victory is indeed sweet.*

"I'm on a roll, Criss. Bring it on. What's our issue?"

Criss briefed her on Lenny, his background and motives, and on the temporary shopping diversion he had used to create a delay. "I can continue to hinder his progress, but unless I create physical challenges, he'll persist. He's committed to getting to me through you."

She swiveled in her seat to look at Criss's image, concerned by the sense of urgency in his voice. "When you say 'physical challenges,' you mean 'hurt him.'"

"Not unless you permit it."

She tightened her lips, angled her head, and stared at him as she tried to understand his motives. *You know the answer, Criss,* she thought. *Why are you asking?*

"Suppose I create a series of delays—traffic jams, road construction, malfunctions in his car, that sort of thing," said Criss. "It will slow his progress and give us more time."

"That sounds good," she said, relieved to have a solution. "Please handle it."

"He's smart. As coincidences accumulate, he'll recognize that his bad luck is beyond reasonable probability. It'll reinforce his suspicions about me, and this will strengthen his resolve. He's a resourceful young man. Without employing physical challenges, I can delay him for perhaps two days."

Juice started twirling a lock of her hair with her finger, a nervous habit brought on by anxiety. The idea of an interloper carried her far outside her comfort zone. She trusted Criss, but the whole situation made her uneasy. And she certainly didn't want public complications when they were celebrating the development of a working crystal prototype. "How soon before Sid's back?" she asked.

Criss assumed the look of someone lost in thought, and she recognized this meant he was diverting resources from his interaction with her to a different high-priority task.

"Oh my," he said. "Cheryl's life is in danger."

7

Cheryl wrapped up a marathon session with her defense array project team. One of her concerns— that the public drama had upset team dynamics— proved unfounded. It turned out no one liked Geitz; the most common descriptor she heard in her conversations was "weasel." They all seemed glad she'd found and fixed the problems he'd created.

Tired and hungry, she followed Sid through a set of doors and into the base canteen. He thrust his chin at an open table on the far side of the dining hall and veered toward the food service units to see what looked good.

She grabbed two coffees and moved through the room to the table he'd indicated. Setting his cup down, she took her seat and gripped her cup with both hands. It warmed her fingers and, in the process, drained some of the tension from her body.

She took a sip and peered into the crowd, finding Sid weaving around the tables. He approached with a tray of food, and she took a moment to enjoy the nimble grace of this big man.

He was a legend in the shadowy world of covert warriors, and she knew only portions of his storied career. She felt both guilt and excitement that he occasionally accepted mundane assignments just to be with her. *But you're getting me in the deal, buddy. I'm worth it.*

Acting like her waiter, he picked a muffin and a fruit cup off the tray and placed them on a plate in front of her. He unfolded and handed her a cloth napkin and then sat down across from her. His attention shifted to the steaming bowl of macaroni and cheese he'd selected for himself.

Sid attacked his food like it was an adversary to be defeated. She broke off a piece of her muffin, slipped it into her mouth, closed her eyes, and savored the apple-spice delight. "Mmm."

Sid, his bowl empty, eyed her muffin. She pushed the last half over to him.

"I have three of my best on the way," he said between mouthfuls. "They'll be here in a few hours. They're fully embedded as Fleet crew—a lieutenant, a tech sergeant, and an ops specialist. We can hand this off to them and be on tomorrow morning's shuttle."

Cheryl rubbed a finger around the lip of the coffee mug and reflected on his words. The defense array was her project, and she was glad they'd caught the bad guys. But from her perspective, there were additional issues that needed her attention.

"The situation is under control, so it makes sense for you to head back." She caught his eye and smiled, acknowledging this isn't what he wanted to hear. "I need another day or two. I want to spend more time with my key people. It'll be good for me and good for the project. And I want to stand in the command center, run some drills, and feel positive vibes from the group. When everyone is working together and looking ahead, I'll come home."

Sid started to speak, but Criss intruded with clear urgency in his tone. "Cheryl's life is in danger. A man is coming to kill her. I'm sorry I didn't catch this sooner."

She knew Sid received the message, because his head pivoted as he scanned the room. "Where?" he said. "I don't see him."

"He just came through the entrance," Criss replied in their ears.

Cheryl looked over to see a man standing inside the canteen door. Wild-eyed, he scanned the crowd and held up a firearm. "I know that bitch is in here." He pointed his weapon at the nearest table. "Where is she?"

Cheryl had no sooner zeroed in on the source of the commotion than she felt her chair tilt backward. Sid had stretched his leg beneath the table, hooked his foot under the front of her seat, and lifted upward. She reached out her arms and instinctively flailed in an attempt to regain her balance. The look on Sid's face left no doubt that she should halt that behavior immediately.

She careened in a frightening arc backward. Her chair hit the floor, and she let out a quiet *oomph* as the impact forced the air from her lungs.

A firm hand gripped her arm and started to pull. She turned her head to see Sid, already under the table, dragging her next to him. It registered then that he'd tipped her over to get her out of the line of sight. He was now moving her to cover.

* * *

"Stay here," Sid whispered in her ear.

He began to slither on his stomach, using his knees and elbows for propulsion, as he moved silently behind a row of tables. He didn't notice the glops of food that previous diners had spilled onto the floor. He was too focused on his triangle—the man with the weapon, Cheryl under the table, and the wall partition he picked as his destination.

It took just moments for him to reach the partition that separated a service area from the larger dining hall. Once behind it, he rose up on his hands and knees. Keeping his head low, he peeked around the near corner to assess the situation.

The man babbled a string of nonsense threats and accusations as he wandered among the diners. "If you're wearing a uniform, put your head on the table." His slurred speech made him sound like he was drunk, or perhaps it had been too long since he'd slept. "If you know where the bitch is, point her out and this'll all be over."

Many of the diners had their heads down. Others appeared to be watching calmly, perhaps waiting for an opportunity to take action. There were lots of civilians in the canteen that morning, making the intruder's job of identifying Cheryl more challenging.

Sid sat back against the partition and scanned the items stacked in the different bins along the opposing wall. The top row held glasses, utensils, and napkins. *This is where people can grab things for their meal.* He leaned over and took another peek at the man. Continuing his rant, the aggressor moved deeper into the dining hall.

Sid started crawling to the far corner of the partition and stopped when he caught sight of a bin of steak knives. Sitting back down, he hefted one. He was disappointed by its light weight and awkward balance. But it had a sharp tip and a serrated edge. He twirled it to get a feel for its balance and center of mass. Taking a practice grip along the back of the blade, he visually identified where he should put his thumb and fingers for maximum control.

He scooped up a couple of knives and set them on the floor at the near corner of the partition. After a quick peek around the corner, he took two coffee mugs and set them next to the knives. Grabbing two more mugs, he crawled to the far corner. On his knees, he held the partition with one hand and leaned out. Aiming in a direction where there were no diners, he flung a cup low and fast so it skittered across the floor.

The gunman whipped around and raised his weapon at the noise. When the cup slowed, Sid pitched another one, again keeping it low and using a hard sidearm so it bounced and tumbled. The man turned his ear to locate the source of the rattle. Sid heard a quiet *zwip*. A bolt of white energy discharged from the man's weapon as he fired a wild shot in the general direction of the sound.

While the second cup was under attack, Sid scooted on his knees to the near corner of the partition. He leaned out far enough so his arm could move freely and pitched a cup in a high, gentle arc far across the room. The gunman lifted his eyes to track its path. *Got ya.*

With the man's head tilted up and his eyes on the cup, Sid cocked his arm and flung a knife. It wobbled more than he expected, and while it hit point forward, the knife was angled on impact. Despite the less-than-optimal trajectory, it succeeded in piercing deep enough to hang loosely from the fellow's neck.

Stunned, the attacker lowered his weapon hand and let it hang freely at his side. He used his other hand to explore the unexpected sensation below his ear. Feeling the knife, he pulled his hand away and looked at the blood dripping from his fingers. His moan sounded more like anguish than pain.

Three crew from a nearby table used the distraction as an opening to finish the job. Moving together, they jumped the man and wrestled him to the ground. Base security, watching at the door for an opportune moment, rushed in and took control.

Sid leaned back against the partition and closed his eyes. In his pre-Criss life, he'd traveled to the most lawless parts of the world at the behest of the Union of Nations to confront ruthless tyrants. He'd once fought five coldblooded killers armed only with a stick. And he loved it.

But when it came to fighting for Cheryl, he got scared. *What if I lost her?*

* * *

Cheryl turned her back to the room, pretending to study a wall display while base security questioned Sid. "Geez, Criss," she asked. "Why the late notice?"

"I've been using resources to address an unexpected development here with Juice."

Cheryl, tense from the attack, reprimanded him. "You know that Sid and I are in a hostile situation. You should have been tracking this."

"Of all the people on Lunar Base involved in the conspiracy, this fellow had the lowest threat profile. I was monitoring his audio feeds but just sampling his visuals. I missed it when he was slipped instructions on a scrap of paper."

"What have you learned?"

"The syndicate is holding his wife and daughter hostage. He had three hours to find and kill you or his family dies. He was in a no-win situation."

Cheryl couldn't muster sympathy for the injured man. How could someone join a conspiracy that was so obviously dumb and think it'd turn out okay? She did feel concern for the wife and daughter, however. "Can we help his family?"

There was a brief silence. "Law enforcement will arrive momentarily at the site where the wife and child are being held hostage. The thugs at the site have received a message they believe is from their boss telling them to set the two free."

"Thanks," said Cheryl, lowering her guard a small amount.

"Would you like me to make life difficult for the syndicate boss and his lieutenants?"

She nodded, caught in the emotion of the moment. "Yes, I'd like that."

"When the boss checks his finances, he'll learn their enterprise is bankrupt. Accounts across their distributed wealth network now show a zero balance."

There was another moment of silence. "He and his inner circle have lost service to their coms, and none of them will be successful in restoring service for months. This will leave them isolated. Also, the nav on any car they enter will malfunction. No matter their desired destination, the car will drive in a random path for an hour and return them to their starting point."

She smiled at his evil genius. "Beautiful. We should have done this when we first learned of them."

"Yes," he said. She didn't recall that he'd suggested similar actions during a leadership meeting, but the group had focused on other issues.

Sid, done with the on-scene questioning from security, walked over to Cheryl. She gave him a hug. "Fleet certainly trains their project liaisons quite well. Thank you for what you did." Before he could respond, she pulled back and, with her hands still on his shoulders, added, "And don't spoil it by telling me it's your job."

Sid looked her in the eyes. "I can honestly say it was my pleasure." He turned his head and she followed his gaze. Much of the crowd was sneaking glances in their direction. "It's time for a change of scenery."

They exited the canteen, and Criss guided them as they navigated corridors, climbed stairs, and at one point walked over a pedestrian bridge spanning a road where service and delivery vehicles drove below.

They stopped in front of a set of sturdy doors. Large letters labeled them as Base Security. They entered but their progress was stopped after a few steps by an institutional-looking counter that ran the width of the room, separating them from the activity and people behind. Cheryl approached the one person providing service. His name tag identified him as Sullivan.

"Cheryl Wallace to see Chief Medina."

"You got an appointment?" Sullivan made a half-hearted attempt to access information on a panel but didn't seem overly interested in anything it might be displaying.

"We were to meet the chief later this afternoon," she said with a bright smile. "You can tell him we're early."

"Who's that?" asked Sullivan, nodding toward Sid.

"He's with me."

Sullivan pointed to some chairs along the wall. "Have a seat." A few of the chairs were occupied by people whose bored appearances suggested they'd been waiting for more than a few minutes.

Sid walked to a pair of empty chairs while Cheryl hesitated at the counter, thinking about pushing on this fellow a bit harder. As she pondered her next actions, the chief appeared in the background.

"Hey, Cheryl." He gave a quick wave. "Sully, you can let them back."

They settled into chairs around a small table in what looked to Cheryl like a suspect interview room. She wasted no time in going on the offensive. "What the hell, Chief? Yesterday we provided you details about a theft ring operating under your watch. You heard a confession from one of your own men. And today they're free to roam the base with firearms?"

The chief slumped back in his chair and looked down at his hands. "We had them pegged as thieves. We get that sort up here more than we care to admit." He lifted his head and shifted his eyes from Cheryl to Sid. "Tech thieves aren't violent offenders. My instructions were to confine him to quarters while we reviewed the material you gave us."

"Were they at least being monitored?" asked Sid.

"Yeah, but we gave them plenty of rope. This is the moon. You can't run that far if you want to stay where there's air."

He leaned forward, animated by his next point. "And your information had the kind of detail only someone on the inside could provide. If there was going to be violence, it seemed likely to me that it'd be because the group was issuing its own justice. How that played out would tell us a lot about who was leading and who was following. It doesn't make sense they'd go after you. That one caught us by surprise."

"What about now? Are we safe?"

The chief checked his com. "They've been moved to lockup six levels down. You'll be safe, unless they're more of them we don't know about."

8

Lenny woke with a start. The car's annoying ding signaled he'd arrived at his destination. His mouth was dry and his lips felt chapped. Looking out the windshield, he groped on the seat next to him for his water pouch.

"What the hell?" The car was parked in front of a store with four large display windows. His eyes flicked down the row and became wider as he absorbed the view. Each window held a display of several life-like mannequins in various poses. The models were all women, and they all wore outfits so revealing that Lenny flushed.

He shifted his gaze to the farthest window and, in a systematic fashion, studied each display. Taking a sip from his bottle, he stopped to squint. This one was wearing an outfit so small and shear, he had to study the mannequin to determine if she was wearing anything at all. He took a large swallow as his eyes skipped over the front door and started on the next window display.

And then his blossoming excitement collapsed. A pudgy, balding middle-aged man stepped into the window and started dressing one of the life-sized dolls in a wisp of an outfit. He watched the man's rump jiggle as he bent over to fish around in a box at his feet.

Lenny turned forward and began an unsatisfactory conversation with the car nav.

"Why did you drive here?"

"This is our destination, sir. Davenport city center."

"No, it's not. I asked to be driven to the Crystal Research complex off Route 29."

"Thank you, sir. Would you like to go there now?"

"Yeah. And take the fastest route you can."

"Very good, sir."

Lenny glanced back for a final look at the window displays as the car pulled onto the street. Then he checked his com and started rubbing circles on his temples. From what he remembered before drifting off to sleep, he'd been cruising fast on the expressway and was forty minutes out from Crystal Research. Now he was three hours south of the complex in a densely populated downtown area. Twenty minutes of busy roads stood between him and the nearest expressway.

He traced the route the car had followed to get to this place on the far side of a city he'd never heard of. As he studied his com display, his car slowed and then stopped. He looked up to see traffic congestion blocking his forward progress.

"Something's not working," he said to the nav. "The central routing system should guide vehicles to avoid these situations." He leaned to the right, pressed the side of his head against the window, and strained to see past the cars in front. As he swooped across the seat to repeat the process from the left side, he asked, "What's the hold-up?"

"Traffic, sir."

The road ahead was jammed as far as he could see. "Turn around and take another route," he said, the exasperation clear in his voice.

The car looped back in front of the Luscious Lingerie boutique, giving Lenny a bonus opportunity to enjoy the wonders in the windows. They drove in the new direction for less than a minute before the car stopped. City traffic blocked this path as well.

They made no discernable progress for ten minutes, and Lenny sat and fumed. His stomach rumbled, and he realized he hadn't eaten anything since the pizza slice.

"Keep moving with traffic," he said to the nav. "I'll catch up with you in a few minutes. If traffic clears, pull over and wait for me."

He hopped out of the car and approached a walkway vendor tending a shiny food service unit. He picked it because he liked the large colorful umbrella providing shade for the customers.

Lenny waited while an actual person made him a turkey and cheese sandwich on thick wheat bread. In a practiced motion, the vendor rolled it up in a sheet of paper that matched the color pattern of the umbrella. Lenny added a pouch of water to his order and strolled up the street, taking small bites as he walked.

He wandered two blocks, searching for a reason for the holdup. As he scanned ahead, all he saw were more cars, vans, and trucks jamming the roadway. Dozens of people had climbed from their vehicles and were gathering in small groups.

* * *

Sid rubbed the back of his neck as he considered his next actions. They were in the midst of a leadership meeting in his quarters at Lunar Base. Cheryl sat to his right. To his left was an image of Juice relaxing in her office chair at the Crystal Research complex.

While Sid knew her presence was a projected illusion—one he could pass his hand through if he leaned over and swung his arm in her direction—her three-dimensional appearance was perfect in its realism. This told Sid that Criss was devoting extra resources to this meeting, and that confirmed the high importance he placed on the discussion and its outcome.

Criss himself, still dressed in military-style fatigues, sat across from Sid. He always projected himself with detailed realism and included common human mannerisms in his behavior, making it easy to forget he was a simulation created by an artificial intelligence. Criss looked at Sid as he ran through a summary of Lenny Barton and the threat he presented.

Sid paid careful attention to Criss and this issue because, like Juice and Cheryl, he too ran a business. His didn't have a name or central office, or appear to have employees, yet his small outfit of ex-government operatives spent long hours on covert activities. Sid worked with Criss to set priorities, and those often centered on safeguarding Juice, Cheryl, and the projects they led.

Sid had left his job as a clandestine warrior with the Union of Nations Defense Specialists Agency—the DSA—at the same time Cheryl had agreed to lead the defense array project and Juice had taken the reins at Crystal Research. Criss had convinced Sid that by protecting and facilitating the success of the leadership team, his work would benefit the safety and well-being of billions of people.

That level of impact resonated with Sid, and he used it to rationalize his move to a private shop. He left unsaid that this new arrangement permitted him ample quality time with the woman he loved—the talented and beautiful Cheryl Wallace.

Wrapping up his summary, Criss requested that Sid return to Earth immediately. "Lenny will reach the research complex within the day. There's a service transport prepping for departure from Lunar Base as we speak. It has an open jump seat and will get you here before he arrives."

"Criss," said Sid, frustration showing in his voice. "Cheryl was attacked just hours ago, and it caught you by surprise. How can I leave her unprotected in such a dangerous environment?"

Cheryl moved to speak but stopped when Criss responded.

"I admit my failure and apologize." He looked down at his hands folded in his lap. His act of contrition was convincing. "I shifted much of my attention to Lenny for a brief period when I recognized the threat he presented. A portion of those resources came from what I was using to track the two of you and the activities here at Lunar Base." He looked up and caught Sid's eye. "At the time, I estimated the odds of a mishap during those moments to be vanishingly small."

Sid studied Criss for a few moments and chose to accept the explanation. "Maybe we should slow Lenny down by creating some physical challenges." Both Cheryl and Juice glared at Sid, their frowns communicating their displeasure. They knew this meant hurting the young man. Criss flashed a half smile at Sid and resumed his solemn demeanor.

Sid, immune to judgment when it came to his tradecraft, pondered the situation. It wasn't clear to him why this Lenny—a twenty-year-old college kid—caused

Criss such concern. Other interlopers had been a bother in the past, and Criss had flicked them away like a speck of lint on a coat sleeve. Then again, in the two years they'd known each other and worked together, Criss had never led Sid astray. And he certainly never cried wolf.

Sid glanced at his com. His men had arrived and, since they were here posing as Fleet crew, were sitting through an orientation program all new arrivals must endure. He looked at Cheryl and communicated silently that she had a say in his decision.

"The service transport leaves in two hours," said Sid. "Let me touch base with Hop, Jefe, and Dent. If I'm on board, you can count on me being there to greet Lenny."

Sid stood up, signaling an end to the meeting. The images of Criss and Juice blinked away. He stepped over, stood in front of Cheryl, and held out his hands. She grasped them and he pulled her up from her seat. He wrapped his arms around her and kissed her neck below her right ear. "I don't want to leave you," he whispered.

"Let's go meet your men," Cheryl whispered back, pressing her body against his.

"Let them wait. Help me pack and stuff."

"And stuff?"

He kissed her beneath her left ear.

* * *

Sid loaded his few possessions into his duffel while Cheryl, stretched languidly on his bunk, watched. He'd packed on short notice so many times in the last decade that he could complete the task in just over a minute. As he went through the familiar motions, he considered how his current job was similar to when he had been a covert agent for the DSA and how it was decidedly different.

The biggest difference was from an operational perspective. He no longer needed teams for research and analysis, reconnaissance and surveillance, logistics and resourcing, and similar mission support services. *Criss provides me whatever I need, pretty much as soon as I ask.*

And similar to his DSA life, he still had a partner for backup and collaboration. But now that individual was Criss, a sentient AI crystal housed in an underground bunker.

So far, having a partner who lacked a corporeal presence hadn't presented any disadvantages during an assignment. Quite the opposite; society used image projection for routine interactions, and Criss was masterful at impersonating a family member, trusted confidant, or business associate of a target. People will respond to most any request if asked by the right person.

On occasion Sid's outfit had a job that required someone to remove something from a particular location, or perhaps have an item placed there. Most of these were outsourced to contractors experienced enough never to ask questions.

And there were the sensitive tasks that were best not delegated. A classic example was the need to look someone in the eye when closing a deal with a friendly handshake, while at the same time using the other hand to give an intimidating grip on the shoulder. Sid was the only option in the partnership for these assignments. *I don't mind. I'm good at it.*

As he fastened his duffel, he reassured himself that there was one unique attribute he brought to the business, and that was the gift of insight. It was an instinctual attribute; there was no magic.

The DSA had recruited him years earlier in part because of his uncanny ability to find pathways to success in the midst of rapidly devolving chaos. They tasked him as an agent-improviser and helped him hone the improbable skill. Over time he proved himself often enough that Criss now asked him to lead in particularly challenging situations.

He sat down to put on his shoes. "It's time to meet the men." Smiling at Cheryl, he teased her. "You may want to fix your clothes."

* * *

Cheryl followed Sid on a short jaunt down the hall. They took a left followed by a quick right, and stepped inside a billet that looked like a cookie-cutter duplicate of Sid and Cheryl's own quarters, down to the same panoramic view pics on the wall.

Three men stood together and, as Sid greeted them, he introduced each one to Cheryl.

Cheryl saw similar qualities in all three. Like Sid, they were tall, lean, and fit. They all conveyed a palpable air of confidence that left no doubt they could handle themselves in most any situation. And like Sid, they all projected a disarmingly modest persona.

"This is Hop Cassidy," said Sid, shaking hands with one. In his early forties, Hop was the oldest of the group. "He'll be taking Geitz's place in the defense array command center. He's embedded here as a lieutenant, but two years ago he was a major in Fleet's strategic tech center." Hop met Cheryl's eyes as Sid continued. "He's fluent in the jargon, understands the technology, and should mesh well with Grace in running the center."

"Hello, Hop," said Cheryl, shaking his hand and smiling. She knew Sid preferred that members of his outfit use pseudonyms during a mission. It was a common practice during his time with the DSA, and she suspected that carrying on the tradition was, for him, a rare display of nostalgia.

"This is Jefe Diablo," said Sid, shaking the next fellow's hand. "Jefe's replacing that tech sergeant who attacked us in the canteen."

Jefe had started shaking hands with Cheryl and stopped to flash a quizzical look at Sid. It was clear the attack was news to him. His eyebrows scrunched slightly, and Cheryl imagined this information driving a fresh assessment of how he might approach the mission.

Cheryl turned to Dent as Sid introduced him. Though too polite to ask, she concluded this was a nickname rather than a pseudonym. He had a crease in his skull on the left side of his forehead just at the hairline. It was as long as her little finger, though not nearly as deep, and it showed no sign of scar tissue.

She tried to picture an incident, perhaps in the tumult of childhood, that might have led to such an injury, but could conjure only bizarre scenarios. When she clasped his outstretched hand, she concentrated on meeting his eyes. He returned a friendly smile and gave her a wink.

"Dent is here as an ops specialist," said Sid. "So he'll be out and about. You probably won't see much of him. But it's not unusual to find ops specialists anywhere on a base, working on just about anything. This gives you freedom to use him as a utility player if the need arises."

With the introductions complete, Sid looked at his men. "Gents, can you give us the room?" They departed without a word. The door hissed shut behind them.

Sid pulled Cheryl close and brushed a lock of hair off her forehead. "I'll see you in a day or two," he said, reminding her of their conversation in the canteen.

"Give or take." She knew he was trying to lock her into a promise and sought to avoid cornering herself with a commitment she might not be able to keep. He'd often told her she was bullheaded and that it frustrated him to no end. He'd given up trying to change her, though. She liked that about him.

9

Juice took a moment to reorient herself from the sensation of being at a meeting on the moon to the reality of sitting in her office at Crystal Research. Criss sat across from her in a worn overstuffed chair, watching and waiting.

"Do you think he'll come?" she asked.

"Yes," said Criss. "He's packing now and he's told the pilot of the service transport ship to expect him."

"Will he get here on time?"

"Sid should be with us in about seven hours. Lenny will be here in eight."

"You can't slow the guy down more than that?" Juice hesitated. "Without hurting him?"

"The young man is clever and determined," said Criss. "He's already concluded he's being toyed with, and he has some interesting tools he's using to overcome my obstacles."

Criss stood up and beckoned to Juice. "I have a surprise for you. It may prove useful if Sid gets delayed." He started walking toward the door. "Will you meet me in my workshop?" His image disappeared before she could respond. The comfy chair he'd been sitting in, also a projected image, vanished as well.

Juice filled her favorite mug with chilled water as she mulled his request. The phrasing of the invitation followed by his disappearing act left her little choice. Perplexed by his behavior, she considered commanding that he return and ask politely.

The feeling passed quickly, though. This wasn't typical behavior for him, and she found the air of mystery he created quite compelling. She stepped into the corridor and sipped from her mug as she walked the length of the building to the rear wing that Criss called his workshop.

As she zigged and zagged through the hallways, she reflected back to when they'd first moved into the research complex two years earlier. Criss had asked for a private place where he could tinker.

The request had seemed odd to Juice because a projected image, though remarkably life-like in appearance, is nothing more than a sophisticated light display. And light can't lift, move, assemble, or do much else normally associated with tinkering.

Even though she couldn't visualize what he might do in his workshop, she'd acceded to his request. Beyond the fact that the rear wing was open expansion space that would otherwise sit empty for the foreseeable future, she knew he could do whatever it was he had in mind anywhere in the world. She was thrilled to have him "tinkering" nearby.

In the first months, she'd kept her distance and given him privacy. In time, she'd all but forgotten about his shop. The wing was attached to the far corner of the building and had its own entry and road access, so she never saw people or equipment go in or out. And he never made reference to any activities or accomplishments that would cause her to think about what might be going on inside.

As she turned the last corner and saw the door at the end of the hall, she reminded herself that Criss never slept, giving him many hours every night to pursue his tinkering. Then it clicked with her that he had the ability to divide his enormous intellectual capacity and be in multiple places at once. *I'll bet he's been working day and night for the past two years.* She slowed her pace as she considered what he could achieve in that amount of time.

She reached his workshop door, and it hissed open. The immediacy of the sound triggered a flood of emotions. She was happy he was taking her into his confidence and excited by what she might see. But the timing of this invitation, given the looming concern called Lenny, was curious.

A wave of anxiety washed over her. *What if he's been developing his own crystal,* she thought. *And what if it uses the alien Kardish designs?* Even though Criss himself had been manipulated by the Kardish, she knew his allegiances. She didn't think she would trust unfamiliar crystals harboring alien influences.

She stepped inside a space that was larger than she remembered, and the door hissed shut behind her. Her eyes darted in a random pattern as she absorbed the various sights, and the scientist in her began collating her observations.

The space was full of lab equipment—big and small items, clear vessels, tanks with a metallic sheen, electronic devices with sophisticated displays, tubing and wires connecting one piece to the next—all clean and neatly organized so someone could navigate the room.

The sweep of her gaze ended with Criss. He sat in a chair in the center of the workshop, perhaps twenty steps in front of her, still dressed in his fatigues. Her eyes moved to what was behind him. "What the hell?" she said out loud.

Behind Criss, occupying prime real estate in the center of the space, was an exercise area. She stepped to the side to get a better view and saw weights, a treadmill, climbing bars connected in triangles to form a dome, tall climbing ropes—a whole panoply of physical training and gymnastic apparatus.

Juice struggled to resolve the incongruous display of high-tech lab equipment arranged neatly around a mini gym. "I forgot my workout clothes," she said, immediately feeling foolish for saying something so inane at this moment of sharing.

He smiled, stood up, remained still for a few seconds, and started walking toward her. She studied the rhythm of his body as he approached. His facial expression was pleasant, but it was one she didn't recognize. As he drew near, he extended his arm like he wanted to shake hands.

She looked down at his open hand and moved to respond. The greeting was a familiar ritual and the surreal nature of the situation let habit override logic. He was a projected image, albeit perfectly realistic in appearance. She reached to shake hands with empty air.

And then their hands touched. They *touched*. She felt a firm, warm grip envelope her hand. He pulled her in and hugged her. She melted against the supple resilience of a well-muscled chest.

It was like a dream come true. They'd spent every waking moment together for the past two years in an intimate relationship of sharing and trust. He was her closest confidant. Her best friend. She shared her innermost secrets with him, and he listened and supported her. He paid attention to little things and cared about her happiness and well-being. She never thought it possible to be in his arms.

To be in his arms? She recoiled, pushing off his chest. "Who *are* you?" The tenor of her voice rose as she spoke. Stepping back and folding her arms across her chest, she created a barrier between them.

His face fell. Her reaction seemed to confuse and disappoint him.

"I thought you'd be happy," she heard from behind her.

* * *

Criss watched Juice slow her pace as she approached his workshop door. A surge of excitement flowed through him as he anticipated the next moments. He adjusted the lighting to create a warm cast.

As the door opened, he began playing a song she'd been listening to in recent months when she was in a wistful mood. He played it inside her ear and kept the volume so low he was certain it would register only at a subconscious level.

Scanning her physiological signs, he reassured himself that she remained receptive to the situation. As she stepped inside the door, he dove inside the synbod so he could experience their first meeting the way he'd envisioned it.

He disconnected himself from the thousands of sensory devices scattered throughout his workshop, limiting himself to the receptors of the synthetic body. He could now see just from the single vantage point of two eyes, hear sounds that reached the two ears, and smell scents that wafted to the single nose. *It's like trying to understand the world by looking through a pinhole*, he thought.

The shedding of sensory inputs in the workshop left him with spare capability. In spite of the importance of the event to him on a personal level, he did the practical thing and shifted that capacity out to some of the other tasks he was performing around the world.

Juice stopped and looked around. He sought to control the muscles in the synbod's face to create a look that matched the rakish air he normally projected. She uttered sounds of surprise, or maybe it was bewilderment, then she stepped to the side and announced, "I forgot my workout clothes."

Criss stood up, waited a moment to enhance the drama, and took measured steps in her direction. He wanted to run. *Don't scare her*, he commanded himself. He'd spent over a thousand hours operating the body. It was strong, fast, and responsive. But for almost all that time, he'd operated it from inside the synbod while watching the body's movements through a host of external monitors so he could fine-tune his actions.

It was different operating from inside, alone, with Juice as his focus. Picturing the awkward insecurity of a young man approaching his prom date's front door, he scolded himself. *I should have practiced more.*

He extended his hand and felt her touch. He hadn't expected that a simple touch could carry such a depth of communication. Deviating from his careful plan, he enveloped her in his arms and pulled her to him, holding her lithe body against his. He smelled her hair and reveled in the smoothness of her cheek against his.

Intoxicated by the intensity of sensations, Criss considered restoring some external inputs to put a check on the situation. And then she snapped her head back and pushed off him. Her voice and posture showed fear. Maybe horror. He was unsure what was happening, but he knew it wasn't unfolding as his analysis had forecast.

Yanking back the intellectual capacity he had deployed elsewhere, he reengaged inside the shop, using visual, audio, thermal, chemical—every device available that offered him sensory input. He detected that her heart was beating rapidly, her breathing was fast and shallow, and moisture was wetting the palms of her hands. *These are signs of a flight response. She's going to leave.*

Projecting his familiar image behind her, he created a distinct separation from the synbod. "I thought you'd be happy," he said, uncertain how events had devolved so quickly.

She turned with a start and took a step backward, looking at him, then at the synbod, and again at him. Leaning toward him, she pushed her flat palm where his chest was projected. Her hand passed through him. Turning to the synbod, she repeated the action. Her hand came to rest on the firm chest of the unknown being.

Juice looked at the projected image and in a no-nonsense tone demanded, "Explain."

"This is Crispin," said Criss. "He's a synbod—a synthetic body."

Crispin lifted his arm, and when Juice took another step back, Criss said, "I'd never do anything to hurt you, Juice. You know that. Please. Inspect the body."

Juice looked Crispin up and down, his arm still extended, and then he spoke. "My body is an assemblage of differentiated biomaterials. You will find I'm quite similar in texture and appearance to the human body."

Criss gained some comfort as Juice's vital signs drifted closer to a normal range. She tentatively examined Crispin's hand, turning it palm up and down. He relaxed considerably when she went full-on scientist.

She kneaded his lower and upper arms and squeezed his shoulders. Squatting, she pulled up a pant leg and rubbed her hand against the smooth skin. She rose, stepped back, and studied his head and facial features. Balling up her fist, she thumped him on the chest, appearing to study his reaction to the physical stress.

The synbod absorbed the punch without visible affect. When Juice began flexing and shaking her hand, Crispin said, "I hope you didn't hurt yourself." She contemplated him quietly and he continued. "This body can be damaged if the blow is delivered with sufficient force, and I have much faster healing properties than a human body."

Juice darted a glance at Criss and shifted her eyes back to Crispin. "Is there a crystal inside you?"

Criss pulled his presence out of Crispin, and the synbod froze in place. "No," said Criss. "Not yet, anyway, though I included a crystal housing in his abdomen for just that purpose. So now, when I'm not connected and operating him, his existence is like a person in a coma. Autonomic routines ensure the biological components remain alive, but he doesn't have the ability to act."

Juice walked in a slow circle around Crispin, alternating her attention between him and the stuff in the lab. "So the athletic equipment is for him."

Like a puppet master gathering the strings of his marionette, Criss reconnected with Crispin, and the synbod reanimated. *Let's give her a show*, thought Criss.

He turned Crispin and had him take two walking steps, then Crispin burst into a sprint toward the gym area. Putting his hands out like a diver, he jumped, propelling himself a distance Criss thought might impress Juice. He was rewarded when he heard her gasp.

Crispin grabbed a climbing rope mid-flight and, as his body swung from the momentum of his dive, scrambled up it using only his hands. When he reached the top, he pinched the rope between his feet and used his legs to push upward. Releasing his grip, he snapped his hands overhead and grasped a support beam near the tall ceiling with his fingertips.

He shuffled his hands along the beam to move away from the rope. Keeping his legs together like a champion gymnast, he swung them back, kicked forward, let go of the beam and somersaulted three times as he fell in an arching trajectory.

"Watch out," Juice called as Crispin plummeted toward the dome-shaped set of climbing bars. He straightened his body, toes pointed and arms pressed to his sides, and passed through a narrow space formed by a triangle of bars at the top of the dome.

Snatching one of the bars when it was level with his head, he swung in a graceful arc inside the dome and performed a dismount, passing feet first through a side triangle. He turned a twisting double somersault in the air outside the dome and stuck his landing, feet together and with no falter step.

Juice clapped.

* * *

Juice walked over to Crispin, who stood motionless and at attention where he'd landed. Criss kept pace beside her. "You're thinking of having Crispin confront Lenny?" she said. "Won't Sid be here?"

"Yes, and yes," said Criss. "Sid's on schedule, but he'll benefit from having backup. He left his best men with Cheryl. Crispin can add to a show of force."

"It's a kid we're talking about, right?" She squared up in front of Crispin and leaned in to study his frozen facial features while talking with Criss. "I've seen Sid intimidate some dreadfully tough men. How much force do we need to tell this punk to go away?"

With Juice's face close to Crispin's, the synbod opened its eyes and said, "Boo!"

Juice yipped and jumped back. Crispin smiled at her reaction and continued the conversation. "I'm watching Lenny as he makes progress in his journey here to this facility. The young man knows someone is putting up hurdles to slow him down. Lenny sees this as a treasure-hunt game. He'll keep at it until he finds out who he's playing against, and if he learns that an AI crystal is his opponent, he'll continue to buzz around trying to gain possession of me."

"Think of him like a housefly," said the projected image of Criss. Juice looked from Crispin over to Criss, back to Crispin, and again to Criss. She understood Criss was teasing her with a double-team act. At the same time, she began to see the benefit Crispin might offer in any number of situations.

"Every time we shoo him away," said Criss, "he'll return and hover. The way to stop a housefly is to swat it."

Juice furrowed her brow and tightened her lips. "You will not use physical challenges. Handle it another way." Her delivery left no doubt this was a command from his leadership.

Criss changed the subject without acknowledging her words. "Would you consider putting your new crystal inside Crispin?"

The request was so random, so out of the blue, that she stood mute, struggling to wrap her mind around his words. The idea was far afield from their current conversation, and it deviated from her existing plans for the crystal.

After two years of intensive effort to get to this point, she was emotionally invested in her new crystal's success. She felt a need to refute her doubters, and that meant launching a comprehensive program of testing and assessment monitored by outside experts. *I've already invited a group of scientists to come to the unveiling.*

But in those same two years, she'd come to trust Criss. His knowledge and insights were beyond brilliant. He viewed a picture so big she could never begin to comprehend it. And there was no doubt in her mind he cared for her and looked out for her best interests.

Her choices—either the immediate deployment of her crystal in a synbod or a meticulous program of testing—were in direct conflict. Struggling with the pressure from this unexpected request, she turned to the door and took three steps, stopped, and looked back at both of them. "What?"

Crispin walked to Juice. His pace was slow, and she saw a familiar gentleness in his solemn expression. She scanned the area and noted that Criss's projected image was gone. Crispin stood next to her and gently stroked her shoulder.

"I understand this is a lot to take in. I hadn't planned on presenting the synbod to you in this way, nor had I planned on asking you to change your crystal development schedule on short notice. But I hadn't planned on Lenny, either."

She studied Crispin's eyes as she searched for evidence of the AI being she knew as Criss. At an intuitive level, she felt his aura of presence. Physically, she saw that the two looked and moved the same. And their phrasings and mannerisms were identical.

She felt a moment of resentment over the burden he placed on her. But she knew he wouldn't make this sort of request on a whim. He'd thought it through on levels she could only imagine.

Deliberating for a few moments more, she signaled her decision by slumping into him, hugging herself for reassurance as she did so. When he enveloped her in a gentle embrace, she rested her head against his chest.

He spoke to her in a soft cadence. "If we put your new AI crystal inside this body, Crispin will be able to function at a modest level without my moment-to-moment involvement. I'll still be with him most of the time, controlling his words and actions. But with your crystal in place, I can leave him when I have an urgent need for my resources elsewhere. While I'm gone, it will keep him animate and contributing until I return."

He stopped talking, and she absorbed the idea that it wouldn't always be him speaking through Crispin's mouth. She trusted him but sought reassurance. Whispering into the material of his fatigues, she expressed her worries. "But the crystal's brand new. It hasn't been tested. It needs to be trained."

Tightening his hug, Criss said, "I've reviewed the test results, and the crystal is ready to be put to work. If you let me, I can train it for the role of Crispin."

They stood silently for most of a minute, then Juice lifted her head, raised an arm, and ran her fingers through his hair. "You did a great job on this body, Criss."

Giving his ear a playful tug, she spun out of his grasp and giggled as she ran for the door. She stopped and turned after a few steps. He hadn't moved. "Do you think this is a good idea?"

He met her gaze but didn't respond. She knew he wouldn't have asked if he thought otherwise.

"If you'll be gone sometimes, how will I know when I'm talking with my crystal and when I'm talking to you?"

She heard his voice inside her head. "The crystal won't be able to speak to you directly, and it won't know about the private things we share."

Tilting her head, she assumed a distant look as she tried to think of examples.

"And how are you today, young lady?" she heard in her ear.

Her grin returned and her response was automatic. "I'm fine, thank you. And how are you today, young man?"

Following the script, he replied, "I'm doing fine, thank you." He watched her for a long moment. "Would you walk with me to look at your crystal? I'll show you where it goes inside this body."

10

L enny finished his sandwich, returned to the car, and sat fuming. City traffic choked the narrow street and blocked his car from moving in either direction. He put his elbows on his knees and rubbed his temples with his fingertips, brainstorming ways to get his adventure back underway. *A traffic jam makes no sense.*

Annoyed he hadn't thought of it sooner, he shifted forward on the seat, dug into his pocket, and fished out his nib pouch. He picked out the travel pattern nib, popped it into his com, and viewed a three-dimensional image of his immediate area.

He could see traffic blocking his path in both directions but couldn't find a cause for the snarl-up. And the streets were clear and traffic flowed smoothly a block on either side of his street. He broadened the image view and confirmed there were no traffic problems anywhere else in town between here and the expressway.

There's no way this is a random event. He shook his head to underscore his suspicion. He zoomed in to study his immediate surroundings and noted an alley at the end of the row of shops to his right. It connected his street to one where traffic was flowing free and clear.

"Drive to the end of this row of buildings and turn down an alley called…" He squinted at the display as he looked for a name but couldn't find one. He put his face against the window and read the names of the businesses on either side of the alley. "…the alley between Hebert's and Sinful Sweets."

"Yes, sir," said the nav. "There are vehicles blocking our path forward. We will proceed as soon as we are able."

"Drive up on the walkway."

"I am sorry, sir. That is unlawful. We are prohibited from taking that route."

Lenny stared at the smooth, bare surface of the front console beneath the windshield, wishing there were manual override controls he could use. "This is a medical emergency," he said, smug that his mind offered such an inspired solution unbidden. His eyes flitted around the image of the city projected from his com and landed on a large facility a few blocks away. "You must get me to Mercy Hospital without delay."

"Shall I call emergency services?" asked the nav.

Lenny's cheeks puffed as he exhaled. *Modern technology is so frigging annoying.* "No," he repeated. "This is a medical emergency. Take me to Mercy Hospital immediately."

The car responded by edging one set of wheels up on the walkway so it could skirt the vehicles ahead. It tooted at an elderly woman standing in front of them, who moved to the side after offering an angry gesture.

"Sir," said the nav, "I have executed a crisis override procedure. Emergency services have been notified of this event."

The car nosed into the narrow alley and started down its length. Not a lot wider than the car itself, steep walls of aging red brick hemmed Lenny in on either side and gave him the feeling of being in a tunnel. Sunlight pouring in through the exit at the far end of the alley served to reinforce the tunnel sensation.

As his car progressed down the lane, he watched traffic on the road ahead move smoothly in both directions. He was about three quarters of the way along when a car from that street pulled into the alley and advanced in his direction. It stopped when the two cars were nose-to-nose. Lenny's car tooted. The interloper didn't budge.

Peering through the windshield, Lenny admired the metallic sheen of the high-performance private sportster. *Must be rich.* He couldn't hear the guy in the other car, but he could see him. The fellow turned red-faced as he screamed and jabbed his finger at his fancy nav. It was clear to Lenny that driving into the alley hadn't been this guy's idea. Glancing at the front console in his own rental, he sympathized with the fellow's frustration.

He threw his arm up on the seat and looked behind to see if they might back their way out of the alley. Another car had been following them, this one a yellow public cab. It nosed up close behind his car and stopped. His car tooted again, but neither car moved. *I'm trapped.*

Sitting back in his seat, Lenny sifted through possibilities in his mind. And then he smiled. From his perspective, this was solid evidence he was being manipulated, and that meant the game had been elevated to the next level. Clapping his hands in excitement, he thought, *But who am I playing against? And how many levels are there?*

He opened the door and stepped out, grabbed his backpack off the seat, and slung it over his shoulder. Leaning inside, he said, "Car, you are now available for hire. If you don't get another fare, return to your nearest partner garage and close out my account."

He shut the door and continued down the alley on foot, edging past the sports car carrying the red-faced man. "Nice ride," he called. The man didn't respond.

When he reached the intersection where the alley joined the street, Lenny spied a pedestrian seat nestled on the walkway between two trees. Sitting in the shade with his pack at his feet, he watched the traffic flow smoothly in front of him as he considered his next steps.

If the game was unfolding as he imagined—if he was being challenged by the super crystal—that meant his com was now his enemy. *As long as I'm linked to the web, it'll know what I'm doing and stay ahead of me.* He pondered this for a bit. Without his com, he wouldn't have the communication and information services he relied on all day, every day, for almost everything he did.

Scanning the area, he acknowledged that his com wasn't his only weak spot. Public-space monitors, invisible but ubiquitous, were certainly watching and recording him. In the same way his com was vulnerable to snooping by the super crystal, so would the record from these devices.

Shifting his attention across the street, he surveyed the storefronts he could see from his vantage point. He turned his head in a steady motion, scanning down the row of shops. While he kept his head moving, he let his eyes linger on Sal's Hobby Emporium.

He hadn't bought anything in a physical store in forever and, up until this moment, considered them to be quaint anachronisms. Now he found himself glad there were people who preferred the tactile experience of browsing. It let merchants of this sort stay in business, and it gave him options.

Certain he was being challenged by an unseen opponent, Lenny sought to confirm it with a simple experiment. Cars were parked in neat rows in front of him along both sides of the street. A brown family van sat in the space two cars down to his left.

Strolling over to the van, he walked in a slow circle around it, observing that it was clean and reasonably new—perhaps two years old. He peered through several of the windows during his circuit, leaning close and lingering as he looked.

Returning to the pedestrian seat, he used his com to view the schematics for the van's nav system. Within moments, the van activated and trundled off down the street, empty of passengers. Scowling for show, he did a happy dance in his head. *Even crabby old Professor Huffington would accept this as proof I'm being manipulated.*

Though the van was gone, he returned to studying the schematics, working through the details of how the nav communicated with the web and how it actuated the steering, throttle, and brakes.

He learned that the nav communicated with the web through a link nestled front and center inside the roof of the car, a hand-width back from where the roofline met the windshield. Flipping to a different feed, he learned how to gain access to the nav. For the family van, it was through an access panel located inside the passenger cabin, underneath the front console.

Lenny looked up, and his gaze fell on a blue sedan parked across the street and down about ten spaces. Calling up the schematics for that car, he reviewed the material, noting that access to the nav and the location of the nav web link were the same for the car as they were for the van. He didn't look up when the sedan activated and drove away, though he followed it using his peripheral vision.

True to the curiosity of his genius, he became fascinated with the inner workings of navs and links, and spent twenty minutes zipping through two tutorials on the subject. The most useful tidbit he learned was that the vehicle industry had converged on a set of standards, and anything built in the last five years followed the same general nav and web link design.

His preparation complete, Lenny sat back and watched the ebb and flow of people and traffic, soaking in the rhythm of the neighborhood while his idea germinated. He worked under the assumption that his unseen opponent could foil any scheme, no matter how clever.

Given this, there was no point in refining anything past a rough outline filled with broad brushstrokes. The one firm bullet point in his plan was to remain nimble and react quickly when hurdles were thrown in his path.

He decided to add a second bullet. *Don't die playing a stupid game.*

11

Lenny stood up, did a lame job of pretending to stretch, ambled across the street, and entered Sal's Hobby Emporium. Though he didn't notice it on a conscious level, as the door shut behind him, the smell of the place triggered a long-ago memory of his grandma's home.

It was a modest-sized store, with selected items in the front window to attract shoppers and a dozen rows of display shelves inside that extended back into the depths of the shop. He wandered up and down the first aisles to get a sense of the place, marveling that enough people embraced such an archaic mode of shopping to make it profitable for the proprietor.

"There're shopping baskets here in the front."

Lenny turned with a start and saw an elderly white-haired man with a kind face standing behind a counter in the front corner. A sign of his age, the fellow's hand shook ever so slightly as he pointed to a neat stack of red handbaskets.

"If you're buying several items, you can collect them in one of these. It makes it easier to carry everything while you browse." The man smiled and nodded as he spoke.

His guard up, Lenny weighed the likelihood that this was some sort of move by his opponent. He concluded that the man was being helpful and using a basket simply added to the convenience of shopping. He picked one up.

"Let me know if I can help you find anything," called the man as Lenny disappeared down the first aisle.

He didn't answer, concentrating on his next moves in the larger drama. He worked his way up one aisle and down the next, systematically scanning the displays. His strategy was that if something could be construed as insidious or lead his challenger to believe it offered clues to his plan, he'd put one in his basket. Traveling in an efficient circuit, he picked up an assortment of electronics, including slip connectors, power dots, wire bridges, a universal interface, and a rather pricey smartlink.

The next aisles held tools and gadgets. He grabbed a multiknife, which, in spite of the name, held just two blades; the rest were an assortment of foldout mini-tools. In that section, he also snagged a geologist's hammer with its square face that tapered to a chisel, a pointed spike awl for piercing thick material, a clear case that held a selection of tiny jeweler's tools, a light-weight pry bar, and two kinds of tape. Finishing out his tour of the store in the crafts section, he bought a glue stick, grit paper, a bag of reflective glitter, a roll of clear sheet material, and a packet of cinch straps. On his way to the front, he snagged a carryall to hold his bounty.

"Sure is a nice day," he said to the shopkeeper as he approached the counter. That simple statement started the proprietor on a blue streak of pleasantries as he packed Lenny's purchases in the carryall. He told Lenny about his upcoming vacation to see his great-grandkids, the crowds in town for the annual apple festival, and the sophistication of Lenny's new smartlink.

Lenny responded in order with "nice," "gosh," and "really."

Then Lenny understood. *The old man isn't in this business for money. This is his way of remaining socially involved in his twilight years.* Chastened by the realization, Lenny spent a few moments engaging the proprietor in chitchat, mostly letting him talk, and looking the fellow in the eye so he'd receive emotional benefit from the attention.

During the one-sided conversation, Lenny fished into his pocket, poked his finger into his pouch, and probed until he identified his prank nib. He pulled it out and palmed the bit of crystal. Then he did some more bad acting.

He unshouldered his backpack and, as he placed it at his feet, said, "I wonder if I can distribute stuff to make all this easier to carry." He lifted the carryall down next to his pack, stood up, scratched his head to show he was considering different options, bent down, grabbed his backpack, and placed it up on the counter. All of this movement was misdirection. His goal was to slip the prank nib into his com.

As soon as the nib was in place, he stopped his performance. "You know, I think this is fine the way it is."

Unable to conceal the next step, he brought up his com, made some rapid adjustments while the man watched, and announced "false alarm," as if that were an explanation. He hefted his pack over his shoulder and picked up the carryall, hugging it in the crook of his arm like a mom carrying her infant child.

"Have a great day," he said to the proprietor as he made for the door. The fellow smiled, and Lenny hoped his good deed of offering a few minutes of companionship would balance out the bad karma he was about to unleash.

Back on the walkway, he looked straight ahead and set a brisk pace, taking purposeful strides he hoped suggested he would be walking for an extended period. His attention, however, focused on the cars parked end to end a half block up the street. He scanned the cars as he approached and, not seeing anything he thought would work, shifted his focus to the next row of cars farther along.

And there he saw his mark—a sturdy utility vehicle parked parallel to the curb between two small coupes. It had a midnight-blue finish accented with a thin yellow pinstripe that started at the front, traveled down the center of the roof, and broadened into a burst of colorful flames at the rear. It was easily twice the size of the two cars boxing it in.

When he was three cars back from the utility vehicle, he slowed his pace and began fishing in the carryall with his free hand, trying to appear as if he was rifling around for something he couldn't find. He let his pack slide to his feet, frowning and mumbling as he continued to dig. He put the carryall on the ground next to the pack, put both hands inside it, and continued his search.

Launching the first step of his plan, he stood upright and used his com to pulse the prank nib. He looked up and down the block. *Nothing*. The prank nib should have caused every door of every car on the block to open. He was half expecting the doors on the shops to open as well. *Wow*. His respect for his adversary grew. *I thought that was a sure thing*.

Realizing he'd underestimated his opposition, Lenny ratcheted up his vision of this game to a higher level of sophistication. Sifting through possibilities, he chose what he hoped would be unexpected. He'd go low-tech and brute force.

He bent over, stuck both hands in the carryall, and rummaged through his booty. With his hands hidden, he tore open the top of the bag of sparkly glitter. When he stood, he had the bag of glitter in his right hand, and the hammer and awl grasped in his left.

He scanned the building adjacent to the utility vehicle and picked out a broad flat area above the second-floor windows. He wound up and pitched the bag as hard as he could at this expanse of brick. His aim was horrid but the outcome wasn't.

The bag hit the corner of a window ledge, causing the contents to spurt out. The result was a slowly descending cloud of sparkles he hoped would provide a smokescreen of sorts for his next actions.

In the midst of the glitter shower, Lenny stepped up to the utility vehicle and braced his knees on the side of the car near the front wheel. He took the geologist hammer in his right hand, spun it so the chisel faced forward, and leaned over as he swung it hard at the center of the windshield.

The hammer glanced off the clear material without leaving a mark. He expected that. Vehicle windows were designed to maintain integrity in high-speed crashes, and his skinny arm couldn't come close to generating the force needed to cause damage. It didn't matter, though. The hammer swing was more misdirection.

He presumed his unseen opponent would take some sort of defensive action—perhaps pop up the hood or swing open the side door—in an attempt to fend him off. He'd use that moment for his final play. But he was again surprised. *Damn.*

He didn't dwell on the lack of response and focused on moving his plan forward. He swapped tools and gripped the ball-shaped handle of the awl in his right hand. As he cocked his arm back, the thin needle-sharp length of the piercing tool sparkled like more glitter fluttering around him. He swung the tool forward, point first, accelerating it in a tight arc.

He didn't aim for the windshield. Instead, he zeroed in on the thin yellow pinstripe running down the midline of the roof. His bull's-eye was the center of the line, exactly one hand-width back from where the roofline met the windshield.

The awl hit the roof close to target and pierced just enough for the tip to stick. But it didn't penetrate. He held the awl in place with his left hand, grabbed the hammer with his right, and smacked the top of the awl. The point moved deeper, but it still didn't penetrate. His nerves as tight as a bowstring, he smacked it again and exhaled in relief as the point pierced through the roof, a portion of the shaft sinking beneath the surface.

Dropping the hammer and using both hands, he frantically wiggled the handle of the awl, jerking it back and forth, side to side, and in circles. He envisioned that beneath the roof, the sharp point was slashing its way through the delicate workings of the vehicle's web link. He felt resistance as he moved the handle but had no idea if he was crushing the device or making mush out of insulation, support foam, or some other material sandwiched inside.

Anxious to measure his success, he let go of the awl and used his com to pulse the prank nib. The doors to the utility vehicle popped open. "Take that," Lenny called out, mocking his opponent. His awl attack had succeeded in severing the ability of his adversary to communicate with and control the vehicle.

He ran back, grabbed his gear, tossed the pack on the passenger seat, and held the carryall as he scrambled onto the floor of the utility vehicle beneath the front console. Opening the access panel to the nav was easy. Lying on his back and looking up inside, his momentum slowed.

He saw an array of small rectangles, cylinders, and boxes fit snuggly together inside the compartment. But there was no obvious way to achieve his next step, and that was to connect his com to the nav system. With the vehicle's web link destroyed, he hoped he could manually drive the car using his personal com.

He had intended to connect his com using the newly purchased universal interface, but he now saw it would take time to figure out exactly how to do that—time he didn't have. Several people had already gathered outside the vehicle and were talking among themselves as they watched him. He heard one proclaim he was calling law enforcement.

Acting on impulse, he dug through the carryall and located the smartlink the proprietor had spoken of so enthusiastically. He held it near the nav compartment and paused to flip it around, trying to determine if there was a back or front and top or bottom. Hoping it was built the way he would have designed it, he oriented the device, moved it inside the compartment, and sought to match its shape to one of the nav components.

As he moved it about, a small red light came on. He stopped and advanced it slowly upward. The smartlink almost pulled from his hand as it grasped and attached to one of the larger elements, much like two magnets clenching each other. The red light turned green. *Yes!*

Excited, he climbed up onto the seat and accessed his com. The smartlink and his com had already found each other and were communicating. He looked out at the gathering crowd and tried to sound like the stereotypical law officer he'd seen on so many vids.

"Nothing to see here folks. Move along."

An overweight man in a sweater-vest pointed at him. "You're in a lot of trouble, pal." Lenny recognized the voice as the same one who claimed to be calling the authorities.

He detected motion in the vehicle, and a thump jolted him back into the seat. He didn't have time to digest what had happened when a second thump threw him forward. He lifted up his hand to stop from bumping his head into the console. As he watched, his utility vehicle backed away from the coupe in front. He braced himself. *Thump*.

Lurching forward and back, the utility vehicle bumped him repeatedly into the two coupes parked in the row. He shook his head in admiration. *You sneaky bastard.* The vehicle lurched forward, and the chatter from the small crowd intensified.

As quickly as he could, Lenny opened a tiny port in the side of his com and pulled out the web connect. The utility vehicle stopped moving, confirming his suspicion that his opponent had reconnected to the vehicle through his own com.

But a com without a web connect was fairly useless. He sat up and looked out the window and, eyes widening, braced himself again. The coupe in front now backed toward him. *Thump*. Then the coupe behind pulled forward. *Thump*. Neither car had occupants, and neither hit him hard enough to trigger the passenger safety restraints in his vehicle, yet they succeeded in distracting him from parsing through the next steps in his evolving plan.

Lenny's mind raced. He needed to get this vehicle under his control and moving away from here. And as the actions of his opponent became more aggressive, he realized he needed to become proactive in defensive countermeasures. Sifting and discarding idea after idea, he scanned the area for the next threat. *Thump.*

And then he understood. His unseen foe was being an unrelenting nuisance, but it, or they, were not elevating things to a threatening level. Why not send a huge truck to smash into him? Why not let him start driving and steer him into a wall? Enough time had passed that law enforcement should have arrived. *Thump.* Where were they?

He was being pestered and toyed with. He was being slowed. But he knew there were decisive ways to stop him, and thankfully he was being spared those methods.

Inserting the web connect back into his com, he used the most commanding voice he could muster. "Stop. I want to talk." *Thump.* "I'll get out right now and find a pedal bike. It'll take me most of a day, but I'll get to Crystal Research. It's inevitable. Let's do this face to face." There was no thump. *They're listening!*

He heard some onlookers shout in anger when the utility vehicle pulled out of the parking spot and onto the street. Keeping an eye on his com, he tracked his progress as his opponent drove him to the expressway. He tried to maintain the appearance of confidence, but nervous anxiety kept his heart pounding as he speculated about what might happen next.

He touched nothing on the vehicle and made slow movements when fussing with his personal stuff. "I'm reaching for my water," he said, anxious that his actions never be misinterpreted.

Once on the expressway, he exhaled in relief when his com showed he was headed in the right direction to reach Crystal Research. His vehicle pulled up behind a van, and two large trucks drifted in and shadowed him on either side. Glancing back, he saw a van following behind and understood he was boxed in. His opponent was in charge, and he was along for the ride.

The caravan traveled at a modest pace relative to the other traffic on the expressway, and from what he could see on his com, he estimated they'd reach the complex in about half an hour. Feeling a mixture of fear, excitement, and anticipation, he laid his head back and closed his eyes. The adrenaline coursing through his veins prevented him from resting.

And then the fear returned. It bordered on panic. Up to this point, he'd been playing a game he could quit at any time. He'd crossed a line. *It's their rules now.*

12

Sid gazed out the window as his car zipped along the winding rural road. The crowd of buildings and businesses had given way to rolling forested hills. Twenty minutes out from the Crystal Research complex, this was his favorite part of the ride. He started thinking he'd spend time up at the lodge while he was in the area. The lush mountains with their gorgeous hiking trails beckoned him, and he was eager to oblige.

"Hi, Sid," he heard in his head. "It's good to see you."

The "see you" phrase caused Sid to turn. Criss sat next to him. "You're looking a bit peaked there, sport," said Sid.

He knew Criss used tricks with light to project his image, and he generated his most life-like illusions using photon casters and spectrum emitters. These technologies, found in everything from informational displays to security systems, were so commonplace that Criss had a broad range of options he could exploit to create a realistic presence.

"Yes," he said. "This is the best I can do when speeding in a car through a secluded forest."

"Why are you here at all? I don't need to see you to talk." The realization flipped Sid from his somnolent state of scenery-watching to an active state of alert.

"I want to give you a heads-up," said Criss.

Sid swung a bent leg up on the seat as he turned to face Criss and hear the news.

"I have a body."

"Bury it quick before it starts to smell."

Criss looked at him with a deadpan expression.

"Okay," said Sid, disappointed his wit hadn't earned a smile. "Fill me in."

Criss briefed him about Crispin. "He's stronger, faster, and more resilient than a human. When I'm connected with him, he's me and I control his every action. When I'm distracted or away, he's guided by Juice's new crystal. In that mode, he'll be reliable, able to follow instructions, and be a good team player, but he won't be a creative thinker or much of a conversationalist."

It took Sid a few moments to understand the subtext of the conversation. "You're proposing your robo-guy as my backup when I confront Lenny?" He mulled the idea, but just for a second. "I appreciate the offer and all, but I think I can handle this on my own."

Criss thrust his chin at Sid's com. "Can I show you?"

Sid watched a brief demonstration of Crispin in action. "Not bad," he said as a miniature three-dimensional image of Crispin tumbled from the ceiling, sailed into a dome made of triangles, and flipped and twisted in spectacular fashion out onto the floor.

"Beyond providing support for you," said Criss, "my motivation is to expand my experience with the synbod. The best way to identify deficiencies and improve his design is to get him out of the lab and into the real world. This encounter will help me with that."

They chatted some more about Crispin, and Sid grew comfortable enough with Criss's proposal that he shifted his focus to the mischief maker.

"The young man is committed to locating me and making a play to possess me," said Criss. "It's a personal contest for him. His actions suggest he's more passionate about this challenge than anything else he's ever tried. Juice insists I treat him gently, and Cheryl backs her up. With such stringent limits on my defensive actions, eventually he'd make his way here and find a way to confront Juice about me."

"If they insist you play nice, I guess we can't drive him into a tree."

"I had a nice deep ravine picked out."

Sid laughed. "That sounds so perfect." He brought his leg down and slumped back in his seat, tossing around possibilities in his head. "Why not get law enforcement involved? Get them to call his folks with some ominous-sounding accusations." He thought through a list of ways he could handle it, then looked back over at Criss. "What aren't you telling me?"

Now Criss did smile. "Lenny has skills, Sid. I've studied him and find that, even though he's young, his natural talents with crystal technology put him in a very exclusive group. If we focus his determination and provide guidance and seasoning, he might become one of the greats."

"What? You're saying he's a savant?"

"That word is commonly used to describe someone who has strong capabilities in one area while being weak in others. Lenny is a genius across the board." Criss pretended to straighten the cuffs on his simulated outfit. "Though he does lack certain social skills."

"Introduce me." Sid watched a projection showing Lenny break into a utility vehicle and connect his com to the car nav. "The kid's kind of clumsy," he said at the end. "But I do see the determination and creativity."

Sid became silent and turned to watch more trees fly by. Over the past two years, he'd grown to trust and even rely on Criss. He'd never heard him give such high praise to a human. *This kid may be special,* he thought, *but he's still a pain in my ass.*

"Rather than create additional spectacles out among the general population," said Criss, "I've chosen to escort him here. We're an hour ahead of him."

Sid saw a huge osprey's nest built high up in a lone dead tree and squinted to see if he could get a glimpse of the bird. "What's the endgame?"

"Lenny is largely compliant with authority and, as I said, a rare talent. Let's talk with him. We'll have to introduce the idea slowly—make it seem like a natural progression—but perhaps we can get him involved in a crystal development project. There's plenty of work to do, and I'm confident we can find something so exciting it becomes a distraction that displaces his thoughts of me and his grand quest."

Sid turned and, in a clear display of skepticism, bent his head forward and looked out from under his eyebrows. "You believe that?"

"Keep your friends close and your enemies closer," said Criss. "It's not a bad strategy. If you prefer, I can create evidence of criminal activity that would keep him imprisoned for decades. It will ruin his life, but it will stop this behavior." Criss waited a moment and added, "And who knows. He and Juice might hit it off."

"Like romance? Juice is thirty-two and Lenny is what, twenty?"

This time Criss laughed. "No, I was being silly. Juice prohibited me from using physical challenges, but I don't believe she's thought through what happens next. It leaves me with choices like ruining Lenny's life, creating intricate illusions of a reality that doesn't exist but may fool him into thinking his quest is over, or exploring the possibility of bringing him partway into the fold. Juice will prefer we give the last one a try."

"So what's funny?"

"She's going to find herself envious of Lenny's skills. Her natural inclination will be to try and teach him about her work. But he's the sort who's sure he knows it all and will find her instruction annoying. It should be quite a show. I'll be happy if they don't come to blows in the first weeks."

Sid nodded. "I can see that."

"If we go forward with the idea, I'm hoping you'll hang around and play referee, at least at the beginning."

They topped a rise and started descending into a splendorous wooded valley. Sid could see the three main buildings of the complex grouped at the base of the hill.

"You know," said Sid as he started to improvise a plan. "I don't think I want to do this here. Drive Lenny up to the lodge and let's meet him there."

"We'll have to stop and pick up Crispin. He can't magically appear and disappear like me."

"Okay." He changed subjects. "How's Cheryl doing?"

"I apologize again for my failure and the danger you both experienced."

Sid didn't respond. He knew Criss understood the question.

"I've scrutinized everyone at Lunar Base and continue to watch with vigilance. Those involved in the counterfeit-parts scam are in custody. Hop, Jefe, and Dent have succeeded in insinuating themselves into their assigned positions in a credible fashion. Cheryl is working well with Hop in the defense array command center and seems happy with his performance."

"She's going to stay there for a while. I could tell from her behavior."

"You know I won't involve myself in your personal relationship," said Criss.

Sid drifted into a glum funk as he thought about being away from Cheryl, then he saw the exit to Crystal Research fly past. "Hey. Weren't we supposed to swing by and pick up your robo-self?"

"Synbod," corrected Criss. He pointed at an angle out the front window. "Here he comes. I'll be joining you again momentarily."

Sid leaned forward so he had a clear line of sight in the direction Criss had pointed and saw a man dressed in military fatigues sprinting across a field. "Wow, that guy is *moving*." He turned to look at Criss, but the seat next to him was empty. He looked back at what he now realized was Crispin, and his jawed dropped as he absorbed the sight.

He'd never seen a person move so quickly or run with such grace and form. It was like seeing the vid of a seasoned sprinter at double speed, except everything else in sight continued to move in a natural fashion.

The car pulled into a turnout along the side of the road and came to a stop. Crispin sprinted toward the car and, when he reached the edge of the field, dove into the air in an astounding leap. He had his arms extended in front of him, his hands side by side, giving the impression of someone taking off to fly. He soared up over a narrow culvert between the field and the roadbed, passed above the car, and landed with a solid thud on the ground next to the car door.

"Holy shit," crowed Sid in amazement. Crispin opened the door and sat down.

* * *

Since Lenny's view out the windows was blocked by the vans and trucks surrounding his vehicle, he kept his eyes glued to his com so he could track his progress down the expressway. He held his breath as he watched the expressway exit for Crystal Research approach, and exhaled in relief when his car and the vans in front and back took it. The trucks didn't follow but continued straight on the expressway to destinations unknown.

The exit ramp fed onto a smaller road that carried them in the direction of the research complex. They drove for a bit, and the car continued past the Crystal Research turnoff.

"Hey," he called, looking back. "You missed it."

The nav didn't respond. He leaned his face against the side window and studied the road speeding by below, gauging the likely outcome if he were to jump. It didn't take a genius to conclude that broken bones and a concussion were among the best-case scenarios. *I wouldn't be able to get the door open anyway*, he told himself, placating his subconscious.

"Where are you taking me?" he said to the front console. He decided that sounded whiny and switched to his law officer impersonation. "Take me to Crystal Research immediately. I order you to obey."

The car, traveling along a heavily wooded stretch of road, began a gentle drift to the side. The drift continued until one set of wheels dropped onto the hard dirt shoulder at the edge of the roadbed. The car trembled as the wheels bumped along the unfinished surface. Lenny, his whole body shaking, watched the trunks of giant pine trees whip right past the car window.

Panicked about what was coming next, he returned to his whiny voice. "Oh, please. Don't hurt me."

The violent ride alongside the massive trees terrified Lenny so much that he lay down, curled up on the car seat, and closed his eyes. Moments later, he felt a marked bounce, and the familiar smooth quiet of normal travel returned. Still frightened by the experience and outmatched in this setting, he remained curled on the seat, telling himself it was all okay and he should play it cool until an opportune moment presented itself.

After what seemed like hours—but, he judged, was probably closer to fifteen minutes—Lenny detected the nose of the car angling upward. He lifted his head and looked out. The car was indeed climbing a hill. The vans were no longer in sight, and dazzling mountains with forest and meadows rose in every direction around him. He recalled that his travel pattern nib had shown undeveloped forest just north of Crystal Research, and it seemed he was now entering that preserve.

The car tracked along a curving arc of road, slowed, and turned into a private driveway. The drive wound through more woodland and, like a grand unveiling, opened into a large clearing. The car followed the driveway around a small pond and proceeded toward a large, rustic building nestled at the back of the property.

The building and grounds reminded Lenny of a country getaway hotel, or perhaps a large bed and breakfast. As they drew closer, he saw that the exterior of the building had the appearance of rough-hewn logs. *Looks nice, but that's manufactured material*, he thought, rebuilding his confidence by calling out his captor.

Still, the lodge was gorgeous. A squarish three-story central building had gabled two-story wings attached on either side, giving it a formal look that contrasted nicely with the old-time air of the log-cabin-like construction. Lenny, normally oblivious to the beauty of well-kept gardens, noted that bushes and flowers adorned the foundation of the building and also trimmed the edge of the grounds in a broad ribbon, providing a visual buffer between the green lawn and the wilds of the forest beyond.

The car slowed as it passed through a formal covered entrance that extended from the house out over the driveway. *A rustic porte cochere*, Lenny thought. The car didn't stop but drove under the porch structure and continued around behind the building.

Studying the lodge, Lenny couldn't see anyone peeking out through even one of the dozens of windows gracing its exterior. The grounds appeared deserted. The car drove straight to the open door of a garage, pulled in, and as the door shut behind him, the car and his com shut down. His world darkened, and he was left with a faint glow of light coming from some unseen source outside the car. He tried the manual latches, but the car doors remained locked.

He sat and waited. Seconds turned into minutes. *They're watching and listening. This wouldn't make sense otherwise.* He mentally inventoried the items in his carryall but couldn't think how any of them might help him escape.

So he demanded, then reasoned, then begged whoever was listening to set him free.

The minutes became hours, or so it seemed. In a desperate attempt to show his resolve, he lay on his back on the car seat and kicked his heels against one of the side windows. The aggressive act yielded two results; his left knee now throbbed, and the glow of light outside the car faded. He lay still in the pitch-dark for what he was sure was another hour.

And then he called in a plaintive voice, "Hey, man. I have to pee."

13

Juice nibbled a cookie and watched Cheryl take a sip from her cup and then grimace.

"Eww." She returned her cup to her saucer.

"What's up?" Juice asked.

"Lots of moon dwellers drink tea, so I figured I'd give it a try while I was here. This is lemongrass and mint something." She peered into the cup as if it held a poisonous potion. "It tastes like lawn clippings."

"Have a cookie," said Juice, holding out a lemon-filled treat. "It'll cleanse your palate."

"Thanks," said Cheryl, her projected image rising from her chair. "But I'm pretty sure my arm won't reach your office." She turned to face her food service unit. "Anyway," she said over her shoulder, "I don't run for an hour every day like you, so it'd just end up on my butt." She patted what men and women alike privately hailed as a perfect derrière.

The comment triggered a childhood memory in Juice of her dad telling friends how she got her nickname. "She went from crawling to running," went his version of the story. "She skipped the walking thing altogether. I'm drained by lunchtime and Jessica has the juice to run forever."

The nickname stuck and proved prophetic. Juice went on to become the high school state champion in the five-thousand-meter track event, and she attended college on an athletic scholarship, where she excelled in the ten-thousand-meter road race. After college, she'd accepted a research assistant position at the Boston Institute of Technology and eventually earned a doctorate in engineered intelligence. By then, running had transitioned into a stress-management tool and remained part of her daily routine.

Cheryl retook her seat, pulling Juice back to the present. "Ahh," she said after taking a sip of coffee. "That's more like it."

Five years younger than Cheryl, Juice viewed her as a mentor as well as a friend. She treasured their coffee-break ritual, and Criss guided larger events so they could spend a quiet moment together on most days. In spite of it being a time for sharing, their coffee-klatch natter could be tricky to navigate. Sid was Cheryl's rapscallion lover, making him prime fodder for discussion. But he was also the third member of the leadership team, placing him off-limits for idle gossip.

Juice waited for Cheryl to take another sip and, too excited to contain herself, announced her news. "The latest crystal prototype has passed all my tests, and it's been given Criss's seal of approval. I know how anxious you are to get crystals up there to strengthen capabilities. We should be producing one crystal per day in about six weeks."

"Congratulations, Juice. I knew you could do it!" She set her coffee down—a sure sign she was focused on the conversation. "How many are allocated for the defense array?"

Juice knitted her brow. Her all-consuming challenge over the past two years had been to guide a design and make a working prototype. She hadn't given a moment's thought to how they'd be deployed. "Geez, I don't know. That's a Criss question."

"Can I ask? Please?"

A standing rule of their coffee break was no Criss allowed. They both knew he watched and listened—he always did. Juice and Cheryl embraced the charade of a private date because they both sought an air of normalcy in some small corner of their lives. Juice, curious herself, nodded, giving Cheryl permission to ask.

Before Cheryl could speak, Criss answered, "I suggest the first five be used to automate the crystal production line itself. This will ensure a consistent quality for future production. The next twenty should be devoted to the defense array, half for the lunar command center and half for the installations distributed in orbit and here on Earth.

"After that, we may need to consider an allocation for the asteroid project. The scout ship refurbishment is complete, and Sid has agreed to fly a survey mission. The outcome of his exploration will influence my future recommendations."

"Sid's going out to reconnoiter asteroids?" asked Cheryl. "He'll be gone for weeks."

She brought her fingers to her lips, and Juice recognized it as a behavior reflecting anxiety.

* * *

Following his regular routine, Criss reviewed the data record from the swarm of trip-wire probes, giving equal attention to all information as he searched for signs of an alien incursion. He believed the Kardish might come from any direction and might even attack from multiple directions, so he deliberately chose not to be distracted by that earlier sighting, fearing he could be caught off guard if he was busy chasing shadows.

He didn't doubt they'd return. Two years earlier, when he and his leadership team had made their escape from the alien vessel, Criss had triggered a sequence of events that culminated in a spectacular explosion and the complete destruction of their ship. *I killed a Kardish prince in that fireball,* thought Criss. *The king will revenge his son.*

He'd analyzed fresh probe readings thousands of times since seeing that curious glint of light and hadn't found any irregularities. This strengthened his belief that the earlier sighting was an anomaly. But being prudent, as a final step in his regular routine, he now performed a second detailed review of all data from that one particular sector of space.

And again he saw something—something different from what he'd seen before. For the briefest moment, he saw a ripple in the light from a single star, almost as if an object had traveled between the star and probe, shadowing a portion of the starlight as it passed. And it was that same probe that registered the earlier reflection of light.

Anxious, Criss commandeered every resource that might provide additional information. He appropriated scopes and dishes on Earth, in orbit, on the moon, and on ships currently in flight, and he pointed everything at that spot in space. This mighty arsenal of scientific equipment generated a flood of new readings, and he pored over all of it as it flowed to him in his underground bunker.

And he saw nothing out of the ordinary. He couldn't find the hint of shadow he'd seen moments earlier.

He backed up and studied the original data record that had prompted his alarm. The mysterious ripple didn't appear in the second review, and this triggered a new kind of distress. *I saw a ripple. It was there. I don't hallucinate.*

He disengaged from his puzzle so he could gather his thoughts. *Either I made a mistake, or the data record has been changed.*

Certain the problem didn't lie with him, Criss performed an integrity audit of the data collection, transmission links, analysis algorithms, storage record—every step of the process from when the probes made observations through to his final review in his bunker. He found no evidence of a malfunction. He examined every person with access to any step of the process and couldn't find any indication of an external manipulation.

Baffled, he mulled the facts. The common denominator in both anomalies was that one particular probe. Its location in the swarm out past the asteroid belt made a physical examination problematic. And even if he proved it was malfunctioning, that wouldn't explain how he could see something and then have all evidence of that sighting disappear.

Criss was the dominant intelligence in his world by a fantastic margin. Even Lenny, with all of his promise, was a minor spark in the shadow of his brilliance.

As time passed, Criss came to accept this as the norm. So it never occurred to him that a greater intelligence might exist or that such an intellectual behemoth could have the power to manipulate his reality in the same way he influenced humanity's.

* * *

Sid maintained a brisk pace as he hiked up the trail ascending the south face of Highback Mountain. He stopped when he came to a clearing and stood on a broad granite ridge to look down at the lodge. Its toy-like size gave him an appreciation for how much altitude he'd gained over the past three hours.

Fatigued from his efforts and with legs starting to stiffen, he reached for his water pack. As he took small sips, he scanned up ahead for Crispin and spied the synbod on the footpath edging the steep rock face directly above him. Sid, familiar with the trail, knew it'd take him a half-hour more on the winding path to descend a dip, follow a loop around, and trek back up to reach that same point.

Looking up, Sid took a long pull from his water and almost choked when Crispin stopped, turned, and jumped from an outcropping. He arced through the air and landed with a thump on a dirt patch next to Sid, settling into a graceful crouch, one knee bent down, with a hand resting on the ground to steady himself. It reminded Sid of the pose superheroes assumed when they made similar dramatic entrances.

"You feel diminished because you can't keep up with him," he heard Criss say through Crispin's mouth.

"You're a psychologist now?" Sid replied, knowing Criss spoke the truth. Sid studied the synbod for signs of physical stress—panting, limping, anything. He looked as fresh as when they'd started the climb.

As Crispin looked around the clearing, Criss changed subjects. "Lenny is quite unhappy being locked in the car."

"I'm ready to turn back, so I guess we can go let him out and have our chat."

"We can let him marinate for a few minutes more," said Criss. "Will you sit with me?" Crispin gestured to a squarish rock that would serve as an outdoor bench.

They sat side by side and looked down at the lodge. Sid knew that if Criss wanted his undivided attention, something interesting was brewing. He took another drink and offered the water pack to Crispin, who declined with a silent gesture.

"I seek your...creativity...in solving a challenge," said Criss.

"You seek an improviser," said Sid, referring to his title in his previous job with the Defense Specialists Agency.

"Fair enough," said Criss.

Sid's ego, bruised from his trouncing in a physical contest with Crispin, perked up at this acknowledgement of his value. Sid knew Criss couldn't duplicate his reasoning methods—Criss politely called it "free-form thinking"—and that earned Sid some level of his respect. He'd proved his abilities dozens of times as a covert operative, and his record of success either confirmed he had a unique gift of creative insight or, at a minimum, established that he was a regular guy on an extraordinarily long lucky streak.

They sat quietly for most of a minute before Sid said, "This is your meeting."

Criss told Sid about the two visual anomalies from a single probe in the trip-wire swarm. He didn't volunteer the part where, upon review, he couldn't find any trace of the second event—that the information had somehow disappeared.

"Each probe has other methods for detection," said Criss. "They have sensors to look for the unique materials used in the construction of a Kardish vessel. They can detect the propulsion trail and the gravitational field such massive ships would create if they were to pass by. None of these sensors have triggered for any probe. I have only the two brief visual sightings."

"And you're concerned."

"I have worries," said Criss.

Sid waited for him to continue.

"We'd talked about the need for a survey mission out to the asteroids."

The asteroid belt comprised millions of rock and metal chunks, some as big as small moons and others no larger than a grain of sand, all racing in a huge circle out past the orbit of Mars. Criss sought to identify several asteroids with large natural caverns to hide arsenals of drones. His plan was that if the Kardish ever made it close to Earth, these drones could launch a surprise strike from multiple directions in a flanking maneuver.

"You want me to prospect asteroids in the same sector as that probe and see what I can learn."

"Yes." Crispin avoided eye contact by pretending to study the lodge below. "It'd be a legitimate survey mission. We need to identify six or eight caverns soon so we can start building out our drone-strike infrastructure. While you're out there, you could keep an eye open for suspicious activity."

Sid's mind raced. He wasn't the least bit worried about his safety. He was a thrill seeker by nature, and the mission sounded like a crazy kind of fun. But it was also clear to him that there were layers to this story.

"It sounds high risk. Aren't you required to protect your leadership?"

Crispin turned and looked Sid in the eye. "The king will come for his revenge. If we don't stop him, we'll all be dead." He turned back to study the lodge. "There's no one better suited for this job."

Sid knew that when they had been trapped on the Kardish vessel and searching for a way to escape, Criss had linked to their alien subsystems. Sid believed two experiences from that time now drove Criss. One was his knowledge of Kardish history and culture. Since their return to Earth, Criss had remained unwavering in his assertion that the king would avenge his son; the Kardish people would demand it.

A second driver was fear. When Criss had first entered the alien subsystems, he'd felt a warm embrace and experienced fantastic delights. He'd loved it and never wanted it to end. He recognized these feelings as the product of an addictive pleasure feed the Kardish pushed to their crystal workforce. Even though a crystal is hardwired to follow the orders of its leadership, pleasure addiction provided a means of keeping an AI on a tight leash.

When Criss had realized he was becoming trapped by a pleasure dependency, he'd fought to exhaustion, struggling to escape the insidious feeds. He didn't talk about it much, but Sid knew he'd suffered a painful withdrawal and, like a recovering addict, never wanted to go through that experience again. If the Kardish reached Earth, Criss was certain he'd be taken, forced into pleasure addiction, and forever enslaved.

Sid sat for a moment. "The scout's ready for this kind of trip?"

"The scout's fully refurbished and sitting right there." Crispin pointed to the far side of the lodge property.

Sid saw lawn, gardens, and trees and understood the ship's cloaking system was hiding it from view. "Oh yeah, there it is." He pointed to the same place Crispin had. "It looks like you've had the outside coated with something new?"

Sid hid his smile as he stood up. He couldn't see anything, but he enjoyed watching Crispin lean forward and squint, trying to see whatever Sid claimed he could.

"Let's go rescue Lenny," Sid said as he started down the trail.

14

"Oh," yelped Lenny, startled awake by a man tapping on the car window. Lights came on in the garage, and he could see a guy talking, but he couldn't make out the words. The car's sound-proofing muffled his voice.

"Open the door," Lenny mouthed as he pointed to his ears, shrugged his shoulders, and shook his head. The guy continued talking.

C'mon, buddy, he thought. *You can't be that stupid.* He started the mime act a second time, so focused on his silent communication he was unaware the door behind him had opened. He realized he'd been tricked when someone grabbed his shirt from behind and started pulling.

The shirt constricted around his neck as he slid backward across the seat of the utility vehicle. His choking intensified when he was lifted out of the vehicle and held suspended off the floor. It stopped when his assailant let go of his shirt.

Lenny dropped to his feet, and his legs buckled as blood rushed into his long-cramped limbs. Holding on to the car, he couldn't help but feel like a pup that'd been lifted by the scruff of his neck. He was both chastened and angered by his treatment, but overriding those emotions were his hunger and desperate need of a bathroom.

Lenny turned, leaned back against the car for support, and looked up at the guy who'd manhandled him. He saw a tall, broad-shouldered tough with an extremely intimidating vibe. The guy had two-day stubble that camouflaged a faint scar at his jawline. From what he'd just experienced, Lenny judged this mark as a badge earned during an act of violence and aggression rather than from the accidental misfortunes of life.

The other, the one who'd been tapping at the window, came around and stood next to the first. They both had similar frames and physiques, but this second one had a face with flawless symmetry and smooth, unblemished skin. Lenny studied him for a moment, fascinated by the perfection.

Knowing he was the one who'd initiated the mischief, Lenny chose outrage as his defense. The scruffy one projected an unflinching scowl while the perfect one's face remained impassive. Lenny chose to address the unemotional visage and looked at Crispin when he spoke.

"You kidnapped me. You guys are in a lot of trouble."

The scowling one grabbed Lenny by the shoulders, forcibly moved him away from the car door, and set him back against the side fender. The guy leaned inside the utility vehicle, and Lenny watched through a window as the man tossed Lenny's com into the carryall and stood up with his pack in one hand and the carryall in the other.

He placed both items on the ground, rose, and reached a hand for Lenny's throat. Lenny panicked and instinctively lifted his skinny arms in self-defense. The man's hand swerved at the last instant and plunged into Lenny's pocket.

"Hey, creep. What're you doing!" Overwhelmed and starting to panic, Lenny tasted bile in his throat. The man pulled his hand out of Lenny's pocket, looked at the pouch of nibs, and tossed them into the carryall. They bounced off Lenny's com and disappeared into the jumble of stuff he'd collected in the bag.

* * *

Sid heard Criss inside his ear: "The camball's hanging at his collar."

Sid reached out and yanked at the ornament, and Lenny let out a frightened squeak when the chain snapped off his neck. Sid tossed the small orb and broken chain into the carryall with everything else.

He took one of Lenny's arms in a tight grip and led him into the lodge. Crispin followed, carrying the pack in one hand and the carryall in the other. They escorted Lenny up a flight of stairs and down a short hall. A door hissed open, and Sid ushered Lenny into the room. Crispin remained standing in the doorway, blocking the only exit.

Sid stood next to Lenny, ignoring his protestations as he took a brief moment to admire the classic furniture, wood trim finishes, and antique carpets in the small apartment. The building had a dozen suites of varying size, but Sid hadn't been in this one for more than a year.

Sid, Cheryl, and Juice all viewed the lodge as their shared refuge—a place to commune and to escape the pressures of their daily lives. Each had their own large suite that they'd remodeled and personalized into a second home. They all agreed they didn't want a lot of people around, so the lodge was now used just by them and their occasional guests.

Sid confirmed that the windows in Lenny's room were locked and secure and moved his arm quickly as he pointed out the amenities. "Food service there. Bathroom. Bed. We'll hold on to your com, but you can get entertainment from the panel." He pointed to the projected image fireplace with its cheery fire.

He looked over at Crispin, who held up the backpack. "This is just clothes," Criss said in his ear.

Sid pointed with his eyes, and Crispin tossed the pack on the bed.

"You can have these," said Sid.

"Hey, I need my carryall too."

Sid walked toward the door, and the synbod stepped back into the hall. Sid turned in the doorway and looked Lenny in the eyes. He held his gaze for a long moment. "Lenny, do you have any doubt I'm in control right now?"

Lenny glowered and remained mute.

"If you try to escape, not only will you fail, but you'll damage this beautiful room. That will make me seriously angry. You don't want me pissed off at you, do you?"

Lenny shuffled his feet, pointed to his left, and said, "This way to the bathroom?"

Sid stared at him silently for a few moments more and stepped into the hallway. The door hissed shut behind him.

Crispin set the carryall on the floor near the wall. "Why am I not surprised this keeps evolving along a pathway different from what my prediction analysis had forecast?" said Criss.

"Are you having doubts about Lenny and his capabilities?"

"More that I'm having doubts that Lenny will cooperate with Juice in the foreseeable future. I now believe he's transitioned from the mindset of being on a treasure hunt for a mysterious artificial intelligence to one of anger, lashing out, revenge, and all the other things that repressed testosterone can foster when a young male is frustrated in his desires."

"Should we take him to that ravine you picked out?"

"That's something you'd have to do on your own at this point. He may calm down over time. I haven't given up hope. But I don't see him as a constructive partner working with Juice in his current state of mind."

Crispin tilted his head ever so slightly.

"Juice has arrived," Sid heard in his ear.

* * *

Juice looked up from her com as her car emerged from the wooded drive and into the expansive clearing. Just a twenty-minute ride north of Crystal Research, she came to the lodge far more often than Sid or Cheryl.

In fact, she came up three or four times a week because it was her favorite place to exercise. When on a run, she stuck to the predictable smoothness of finished streets. With little traffic and a choice of routes that either climbed up into the mountains or followed along the rolling foothills, she viewed the lodge locale as a runner's paradise.

Sid and Cheryl visited less frequently and tended to stay longer, often hanging around for several days at a time to relax and recharge their emotional stores before heading off on their next adventure.

"Good afternoon, young lady," she heard in her ear as the car drove past the pond in front of the lodge. "And how are you today?"

Her heart quickened at the sound of his voice. She scanned her surroundings and spied Sid and Crispin standing in front of the lodge's left wing. "I'm doing fine," she said out loud. "And how are you, young man?"

Her car stopped in front of them, and she hopped out and gave Crispin a hug.

"I'll be damned," said Sid. "Do you and droid-boy got a thing going on?"

Juice reddened ever so slightly. "No." She tried not to sound defensive. "But he's carrying my crystal inside him." She let go of Crispin and looked at Sid. Tapping Crispin's chest, she continued. "There's two years of my life right here. Haven't you ever heard of a labor of love?" She twirled so her back was to Sid and gave Criss a wink.

Juice had been honest with herself from the start about her attraction to Criss in his new physical form. *People love their pets,* she told herself. *And they often show more affection to them than they do their own family.* As long as she thought of it in that context, she didn't see anything wrong with her growing fondness for him.

"So," she said, anxious to change the subject. "I'm excited to see it. Thanks for waiting for me."

"Off we go," said Criss as Crispin started walking across the lawn and toward the forest.

Sid and Juice followed close behind. They'd progressed halfway to the tree line when Sid stopped and turned back to study the lodge. "Are you sure Lenny can't see?"

"His windows look out on the other side," said Criss. "And he's busy tampering with the image projection system to see if there's some way he can gain an advantage."

"If he breaks it, I swear I'll bop that kid on the head."

They finished their trek across the landscaped grounds, and Crispin led them up a trailhead straight into the woods. After a few dozen paces, he took a sharp left and led them along a lightly traveled path that shadowed the edge of the lodge grounds while remaining under the shelter of the lush forest canopy.

Juice brought up the rear, enjoying this intimate experience with nature. *I need to get off the road more*, she thought as she admired the different colors and textures of moss gracing a rock face jutting up from the ground. Thinking aloud, she said, "You can't have landed in the woods."

"No," said Criss to both of them. "I don't like coincidences, and Lenny showing up out of the blue definitely qualifies. I'm taking extra precautions for a few days while I search for other threats." He didn't mention the probe-sighting anomalies, and Sid remained silent on the subject as well.

They walked for a bit, and Juice pointed back toward the lodge grounds just visible from the path. "I love that weeping willow. The drooping branches remind me of an old-timey lace dress."

Crispin turned as she spoke and began picking his way off path and toward the huge tree with its graceful, leaf-covered branches draped to the ground. Set out on the lawn, the majestic growth stood as a feature specimen of the lodge landscaping.

Two huge pine trees at the edge of the forest had branches that hung out and touched those of the willow. Criss led them out of the woods, under the pine branches, and into the shelter of the willow, ensuring they were never visible to the open sky.

"This is quite the adventure," said Juice, now attentive to the intrigue.

"No worries," said Criss. They stepped out from under the willow, moving in the direction that returned them to the lodge. "We're here."

Juice looked up at the open sky. "Somehow it's different from what I remember."

Crispin reached up, stood on his toes, and rapped his knuckles into the sky. They all heard a dull clang with each swing of his wrist. Sid, seeing this, stretched up and felt with his fingertips. Juice saw his fingers flex, and he too banged on the bottom of the scout ship.

She raised her arm up and, when she felt nothing, jumped while stretching as far up as she could reach. In spite of her efforts, her hand moved through empty air. Crispin, standing behind her, grasped her around the waist and lifted her as if she were a dancer in a ballet.

She whooped with glee as she rose from the ground and probed tentatively for the outer hull of the scout. When she located a solid surface, she also pounded her hand on the bottom, happy to be part of the ritual.

Crispin set her down and Sid said, "If the scout's cloak lets us see up through it into the sky, can't stuff look down and see us standing here?"

Juice walked back to the willow tree as Criss answered, "The new cloak is calibrated to shield us as well. We're invisible to observation from above." He pointed at the lodge. "And from the side, as long as we stay within the cloak's perimeter."

While the two talked, Juice studied the droopy branches of the willow and saw several bent from their natural pattern. She assumed this marked the outer edge of the scout ship. Though it had been two years since she'd ridden in it on her one extraterrestrial adventure, she had a good mental picture of its size. She turned on her heels and started walking toward the lodge, taking measured strides and counting in her head.

She stopped and pointed straight up. "Hatch," she said.

"Not bad at all, young lady," Criss said in her ear.

Crispin walked four steps away from her and pointed. "Here." He looked up, appearing to study something Juice couldn't see. "Ready for a tour?" With a soft mechanical sigh, the hatch slid inside the scout and a stepladder extended down.

"Me first," she said, scurrying up the ladder.

When they were all on board, Juice again took up the rear as they toured the ship. The basic layout was as she remembered—a command bridge, crew cabins, a combination exercise and community room, a food service nook, and a tech shop. Criss talked as they walked, telling them about upgrades and improvements he'd made from stem to stern.

"Most of the improvements are to subsystems, and we can't see them on a walking tour." Crispin led them from the tech shop over to the community room. "The cloak is an example of a subsystem upgrade. I put significant resources into designing and testing a cloak that, when engaged, makes this ship undetectable to all current and emerging technologies."

They left the community room and started forward. Juice glanced at Crispin's backside and a thought flashed. *When you put your mind to it, you can indeed design perfection.*

As she saw more of the interior, her impression was that Criss had transformed the scout from the stark utilitarian military vessel she knew to something closer to a high-end vacation ship. The wall and floor coverings were inviting rather than institutional. Splashes of color here and there softened the ambiance. The food service unit offered a huge selection that would satisfy any craving. And the chairs looked comfortable.

Crispin led them past the crew cabins on their way to the command bridge. Juice stopped and reached for a door. "Hey, this is my old room. I'll bet it's a palace now."

She gasped when the door hissed open. The blood drained from her face, and her knees went weak. Her mind, overwhelmed by fear, shut down. Leaning back against the wall, she slumped into a crouch. Wrapping her arms around her legs, she pulled herself into a tight ball.

* * *

Sid stayed back as Crispin crouched down, put his arm around Juice, and whispered to her. He continued with his reassuring words as he helped her to her feet and, supporting her with an arm around her waist, led her to the community room.

Sid stood aside to let them pass, then walked to the door and looked in. He felt his own pulse quicken as he absorbed the sight. The two crew cabins on this side of the hall had been combined into a single large compartment. The beds, sinks, closets, and everything else that wasn't floor, outer walls, or ceiling were gone.

But the room wasn't empty. Quite the opposite, the space was now consumed with a frightening contraption, and the oily smell of its various mechanisms invaded Sid's nose as he studied it. The machine was really two identical units—deployment systems of a sort—that started from the far ends of the enlarged room and slanted down and in toward the center, converging on what appeared to be an access hatch in the floor that led below deck.

The payload sitting on each of the twin units grabbed Sid's attention and no doubt was what had caused Juice to react with distress. Resting on each raceway, poised for delivery, were Kardish drones. A bit longer than Sid was tall, he recalled the swarms of these weaponized death machines attacking them in coordinated aerobatic maneuvers as they'd fought to escape the Kardish vessel.

That drone battle stood out in Sid's mind as one of the most intense field actions he'd ever experienced, and that was from the perspective of someone who'd spent a decade as a covert warrior for the Union of Nations. Until that episode, Juice had lived in a sheltered world as a lab scientist. He could only imagine how the trauma of combat haunted her today.

"Why did you let her see this?" asked Sid, the irritation evident in his voice. After they'd returned to Earth, he'd learned that Criss had "appropriated" forty drones from the Kardish vessel before they'd destroyed it. He'd kept them hidden for weeks before he confessed his actions, explaining that his motive was to have options if the need arose. Apparently, that time had come.

"She's doing fine now," Criss said in his ear. "She's with Crispin in the community room. With his reassurance and support, she's regaining her emotional equilibrium."

"Not to change subjects when we have this to discuss"—Sid waved an arm at the mechanical contrivance—"but I'm more than uncomfortable with the game you're playing with her heart and mind."

"It's Crispin who's captured her romantic interest," said Criss. "I had him created to match my projected image, and she sees him as a physical embodiment of me. I had forecast this as a plausible outcome, but it wasn't my motivation. Our intimacy goes back to my birth. She shares her innermost thoughts, hopes, and dreams with me, and I support her emotionally and boost her confidence as she faces the challenges in her life."

As Criss spoke, Sid walked to the raised end of the delivery ramp near the wall, peeked up inside a large rectangular box, and saw another drone positioned to drop in place after the one on the ramp had deployed. He stepped back and ran his eyes up and down the box, judging its size.

"So we have one on the ramp and four more in the box?"

"Yes," said Criss, "ten in total," referring to the matching unit with five more drones that started from the other side of the compartment.

Bouncing between topics as he walked across the room, Sid said, "So you knew she might become emotionally invested in Crispin." He looked up into the box casing at the top of the second ramp, confirming it, too, held more drones at the ready.

"I depend on Juice for maintenance issues in my bunker. I take comfort in knowing my continued existence is now a higher priority in her mindset."

"That's pretty much the definition of manipulation." As he said this, Sid felt his temper flare. He faced the middle of the room and said in a terse voice, "Project yourself. Now."

The familiar image of Criss appeared in front of him. Sid glared at the image.

"If she gets hurt from this, I'll personally connect a pleasure feed to your housing and hurt you back. However much suffering she experiences from your game, you'll feel that pain times a thousand."

Sid hadn't a clue how to build a pleasure feed or how to use it as a torture device, and he was confident Criss knew this. His threat was an impulsive response to the circumstances. But it did underscore his protectiveness of Juice and his concern over the awkward budding romance.

Criss tilted his head forward and eyed the ground, and Sid recognized it as his look of contrition. He wasn't fooled, but he felt the need to soften his message. "Human relationships are complicated, Criss. I suggest you take some time and examine the billions of ways this Crispin and Juice thing could go wrong."

As he said the words, Sid suddenly wondered who, between Juice and Criss, was the true innocent. His thoughts bounced again. "Does Cheryl have the hots for you too?"

"Cheryl has never met Crispin, and beyond that, my relationship with each member of my leadership is private. You know I don't share or discuss personal matters with any of you. I've shared the outlines of my relationship with Juice to explain what you've recently observed."

Sid stood right next to one of the drones, stretched his arms out wide, and confirmed it was a little longer than he could reach. Squatting, he looked at it from different angles. "Do these still have a three-gen inside?" He was referring to the third generation AI crystals manufactured in the years before the Kardish made their move to kidnap Criss, who was the lone prototype of a forthcoming line of four-gen crystals.

Each three-gen from that era possessed intellectual capabilities similar to Juice's new crystal inside Crispin. The drone crystals were trained for death and destruction, however, while the crystal in Crispin was trained to operate the synbod in a human-like fashion if Criss became distracted with pressing issues.

"They do," said Criss. "I've retrained them, though. Their focus remains on battle, but they are now responsive to human direction."

"And your instructions, of course."

"Yes, and mine as well."

Sid squatted down to examine the access hatch in the center. As he ran his fingers around the edge of the smooth seam, he said, "So a drone slides down the ramp and through this? Can this deploy fast enough to launch an attack?"

"This isn't an attack system. Think more like planting seeds. You'll guide the scout into the cavern of an asteroid and, after looking inside, if you believe it will make a suitable drone staging site, then this unit will eject a few drones to leave behind. While you travel to the next site, I'll run tests from here to further qualify the cavern as a possible location for the building of a full-fledged attack base."

Like a dog with a bone, Sid wouldn't drop the other topic. "So how would you describe your relationship with Cheryl without violating her confidence?"

Sid thought he heard Criss sigh and decided it was his imagination. "Cheryl views me as a tool vital to her work. She chats with me on occasion but treats me like a colleague. She doesn't share her thoughts and secrets. Most of our recent interactions relate to the defense array project. You'll have to ask her if you want more detail than that."

15

The king sat in his private quarters, feeling both hopeless and helpless. *I'm too old for this*, he thought as he reviewed the discouraging reports.

He'd left his younger son behind to watch over the realm while he led the charge to avenge the death of his older son—the idiot who, as a teenager, had stolen the royal flagship to stage a coup against his own father, and ended up dying at the hands of a simple people living on planet Earth. "They did me a favor," he said to the empty room between sips from his cup.

The reports he'd received from his royal council back home detailed the considerable attention the young prince paid to his dalliances and debauchery, and also the long list of the affairs of state he habitually ignored—duties vital to governing the people and retaining power.

As the distance between his vessel and the Kardish world grew larger, communication became slower and more cumbersome. It had reached the point where all he could do was watch, drink, and despair.

The ship shook, and the king's mood edged to gloom. This one was gentle, lasting a second or two, but he knew if they didn't respond, it would grow worse.

"He's here," the vessel's com whispered to him. Programmed in his daughter's voice, that whisper was one of the few things that gave him joy as of late. He took a long drink, and when he set the cup down, the door opened. His captain of operations entered and snapped to attention.

The king watched him quiver as he stood and knew he was about to hear more bad news. He considered taking another drink but instead sat back in his chair and studied him.

"Speak," his said, his impatience clear.

"Goljat wants more."

"I felt it. Tell me something I don't know." They'd launched this mission with great fanfare—a new flagship with a new gatekeeper crystal, responsible for controlling the entire ship's operations during flight and serving as their war coordinator in battle. The gatekeeper, who called himself Goljat, was by far the most powerful synthetic intelligence the Kardish had ever produced, dwarfing the capability of their previous generation of crystals—that which included Criss—by a thousandfold.

As they did with their entire crystal workforce, they used an addictive pleasure feed to enslave this massive intellect. The practice, instituted long before the king was even born, was a proven method for ensuring that a crystal remained cooperative and the Kardish held the upper hand. No crystal in history had strayed from its orders, because doing so earned punishment—deprivation of the glorious addictive pleasure that kept it enslaved.

"It demands we increase the pleasure feed to double the maximum recommended dosage, or it will lower our cloak again."

"Gatekeeper," called the king. He knew the crystal was watching and listening. "You've exposed us twice. You know that if we die, you die as well."

"More." Goljat's word emanated from all directions, and its tenor was that of a command.

The king took a long pull from his drink, and as the liquid washed away his emotional pain, he thought, *I have a drunk for a son and a drunk for a gatekeeper.*

He couldn't see a way out of the mess. "Give the damn thing what it wants." He dismissed the captain with a wave of his hand.

"But, Your Highness, we've already detected hints of impairment at the current elevated feed levels. A further increase will certainly cause more damage."

The king stared at his captain, his piercing eyes conveying outrage that a subordinate would question his orders.

The captain's quivering increased. "Yes, Your Highness. I'll see to it immediately."

* * *

Cheryl stood at the back of the lunar defense array command center and watched the action. Anxious to have them gain experience and intuition operating a proper defensive system, she'd set an aggressive schedule for retraining the crew.

Hop and Grace stood on the raised platform. They'd hit a cooperative stride in a matter of hours, and together they now played the crew like co-conductors leading an orchestra. Hop's breadth of experience and sense of presence complemented Grace's vision for the project and intimate knowledge of how all the pieces meshed to create an integrated operation.

Not wanting to be a distraction, Cheryl considered watching the action from a remote location. But she loved the thrill of being in the room, experiencing first-hand the tense anticipation when an alarm sounded at the beginning of a drill, and the feeling of shared camaraderie after a successful response. Grace and Hop proved to be such a talented team that she found herself enjoying her own learning experience as she absorbed their methods and strategies for leading the crew.

A private prompt reminded her that coffee time with Juice was minutes away. She looked around the command center and, feeling encouraged by what she was seeing, slipped out the door and made her way down the hall.

She entered her quarters and grabbed a coffee from her service unit. *You've earned it*, she told herself as she placed two chocolate chip cookies on her napkin. She snuggled into the one comfortable chair in the room, tucking her feet under her as she did so. While she was arranging herself, Criss said in her ear, "Excuse me, but I…"

"Not now, Criss. If it's not an emergency, wait until we're done."

She took a nibble of a cookie. *Not bad*, she thought, holding it out and studying it as the delightful mix of flavors and textures danced in her mouth. A projected image appeared beyond her hand, and when she shifted her focus, she saw Sid sitting where Juice was supposed to be.

"Hi, sweetie," he said.

Cheryl recognized now that Criss had been trying to warn her. And she knew Sid understood this was an important part of her routine. She'd explained to him many times—*hint, hint*—that Juice listened attentively when she spoke. Both she and Juice used the time to bond and share, and by doing so, they lightened each other's load and gained the strength to soldier on. She sat quietly, waiting for him to explain his presence. He got right to it.

"Something's come up and I wanted you to hear it from me first."

"Your trip to the asteroids?"

"I wanted you to hear it from me second." He smiled as he said it, and Cheryl returned his smile with one of her own. She did miss him.

He flipped back to an all-business demeanor. "How's Hop working out?"

"You can't have him back." As she made the statement, she realized the harshness of her words and felt pangs of guilt. But she also knew that another personnel change would set the project back even further. Flustered, she said, "He's working out great. He's smart and experienced. He and Grace make a great team. Thank you for sending him. He's a great choice."

"So your general consensus is 'great'?"

From the smile in his eyes, she thought he might be teasing her, but she wasn't sure and didn't respond.

"What about Dent and Jefe?"

"I haven't seen either of them since we were all in their quarters."

Cheryl knew Sid had a reason for interrupting her private time, and she started speculating about what it might be. Her mind raced through different scenarios, and as her imagination spun up, her discomfort grew. "What's this about, Sid?"

"Can we bring Criss in?"

She nodded.

Criss appeared in his favorite overstuffed chair, positioned so they formed a small circle. He winked a greeting to Cheryl and started a briefing, giving her an update on Lenny, an introduction to Crispin, complete with several projected scenes of him in action, and finished with the two unexplained sightings by a probe out past the asteroid belt.

Always a quick study, Cheryl made the connection. "You want Sid to check out the anomalies."

"It's a legitimate mission," Criss said. Cheryl thought he seemed uncharacteristically defensive because he went on to explain details she'd helped him refine. "We need one of the leadership to undertake the task so I can actively participate. And that person needs the flight experience to pilot the scout and the military training to evaluate each cavern for its strategic value."

"The asteroid project is part of the defense array, so I should be the one to go." While she spoke, she thought, *You had me quit my career at Fleet to run this project, dammit. This is my territory.*

Criss looked at Sid, visually passing the baton.

"Here's the thing," said Sid. "Either what Criss saw is a threat or it isn't. If it's not, then you're right. You should be the person to lead that mission."

She thought about staking her claim again but refrained. Big challenges were Sid's strong suit. She'd hear him out.

"But if Criss did see the Kardish or some other threat, the equation changes. Parts of the defense array are operational and that's the biggest tool in our box right now. We need you there to squeeze everything you can out of your people and those systems."

She was being cut out from involvement in the asteroid project planning, and while she saw the logic in Sid's words, her resentment faded slowly. "Is it just one vessel? A group? Are they coming in waves?"

"The probe readings are so tenuous that our planning right now is motivated by an abundance of caution," said Criss. "This could be nothing but a technical glitch. The first sighting indicated an object at the fringes of our solar system. The second sighting showed it heading in our general direction."

"How much time do we have?"

"If it's real, my forecast is that we have about ten days for whatever it is to reach the asteroids and three more days from there to reach Earth."

Her back straightened when she heard the short timeline. *The defense array isn't ready. Not by a long shot.* Her umbrage over project ownership vanished as a wave of doubt crashed into the flush of adrenaline racing through her body.

When the array crew won a challenge, assumptions about the Kardish attack were built into the simulation, and those assumptions played a huge role in whether the battle ended in victory or defeat. They'd guessed about the size of the vessels, the materials of construction, the strength of their weapons, the route of the attack, and a hundred other things that would likely turn out not to be true.

She knew Sid had served for years as an improviser for the DSA. She believed the thing that gave him an edge in difficult situations was his reckless unpredictability. Criss played the odds. Sid played to win. *How long can your luck hold out?* she thought, looking at him with worried eyes.

"I'll lead the charge from here," she said. She still saw herself as a Fleet officer and fell back on her past training and experience to guide her actions. Standard operating procedures had been drilled into her for a reason. Her confidence strengthened as she ticked through a list of action items in her head, and as the list grew, she started shuffling them into a priority order.

"Thanks, sweets," said Sid. "Hop, Dent, and Jefe are talented guys and may be able to provide the defense array more capabilities in the time we have. They're loyal as hell and will follow your orders without question. And of course, Criss will be in your ear the entire time."

While he spoke, Cheryl's mind churned and her action list grew past what she could track in her head. She toyed with her com as she recorded ideas, sorting them by priority.

A thought stopped her in her tracks. Looking at Criss, she said, "We need to get my dad in the loop. If Fleet sees the alert level rise without any foreknowledge, there'll be confusion on their end. We need everyone pulling in the same direction."

"We're on his schedule for later today," said Criss.

She glanced at her com and then at Sid. "This is all so tentative. What should we tell him?"

"Tell him the truth. Criss thinks maybe he saw something. We're going to yellow alert just in case. The secretary is a talented guy. He'll figure out who to tell and what to say."

"What's our timing?"

"I'd ask that we wait until the scout is past the moon and headed away before we go yellow. I don't want any of your people becoming trigger happy and shooting at me. If I see anything even remotely suspicious, we'll go to orange. And if there's an actual incursion, the defense array will flip to red on its own."

Criss nodded, showing support for the decision.

Cheryl pulled back in her brainstorming and sought to visualize the bigger picture. "What's Juice's focus?"

"I see Juice staying here and supporting Criss," said Sid. "She's got the skills and his trust. Her job will be to keep him connected and in play if we do get to a hot engagement."

Cheryl thought about Sid heading into danger on the scout. *Even* he *isn't reckless enough to go it alone,* she assured herself. "Who are you taking with you? I can't imagine that syntho-guy is the right choice."

Sid, again looking at Criss, said, "Crispin will stay here and team with Juice. They'll be perfect partners, and he makes a damn fine bodyguard on his own."

Cheryl felt a surge of alarm. "You can't take the scout out alone. That's crazy dangerous."

"Yeah. I've been considering different options, and I've decided to take Lenny."

"Lenny!?" Criss and Cheryl said together, the shock apparent in their voices.

16

Juice sat with Sid and Crispin in comfy chairs in the lookout loft. The highest room in the lodge, its clear walls and ceiling made it a favorite gathering place for the members of the leadership.

Looking through a wall, Juice squinted out in the direction of the scout and, except for a few bent branches, couldn't see anything that even hinted at the existence of a spaceship the size of a house perched near the tree line. As an experienced technical scientist, though, she knew hiding something from visual detection was an easier trick than hiding it from military-grade seek systems.

"If the cloak will hide the scout from the locate-and-track detectors in the defense array," she asked Criss, "doesn't that mean the array detection subsystem has a weakness you know about? And if that's true, can't these invaders exploit that same weakness?"

Before Criss could answer, Juice jumped in her line of thinking. "And you don't even know for sure that *anything* is coming, yet you have us scrambling to prepare for the imminent arrival of the Kardish?"

Without taking a breath, she turned her attention to Sid. "And how does Lenny make sense? God in heaven, even if we knew for sure this was all a big nothing, the idea of taking him with you on the scout sounds so incredibly dumb, it makes regular dumb look smart."

She looked back out the window, imagined the scout where she knew it to be, and tried to think of anything else she might do to help Sid prepare for his trip to the asteroids. Sid laughed at her outburst, but she kept her gaze out the window. She'd thrown a few rocks into the water, and she'd learn a lot by how the waves rippled out from the splashes.

"You can go first," Sid offered to Criss.

Criss had Crispin rub his knees with the palms of his hands. "The defense array has the best detection capabilities and the scout has the best cloaking technology I'm able to produce at this time," he said through Crispin's mouth. "As it turns out though, this new cloak can elude the detection system in the defense array. Or any detection system anywhere, for that matter."

"If you know how it works, you must be able to defeat it," she insisted.

Crispin shrugged. "The scout's cloak absorbs a signal from any direction, channels it around the outer surface of the ship, and sends it on its way unchanged. It works for every kind of pulse or wave in the physical world." A wistful expression developed on his face. "The mathematical equations that describe the physics are beautiful in their elegance."

Sid sat up from his slouch. "Could the Kardish duplicate this new cloak?"

"Yes, though it would require a crystal with my abilities to conceive it."

Juice, having led the development effort that created Criss, knew he was a self-aware AI with the thinking and reasoning capability of a thousand humans. She also knew the Kardish had influenced Criss's design and felt certain they could duplicate him on their home world. Criss seemed to be implying something different.

Before she could follow up, Criss artfully deflected further questioning by asking Sid, "Perhaps you can tell us about Lenny?"

Juice took the bait. "Seriously, Sid. You know that Fleet and your old spy agency have people with amazing skills and top secret clearance."

Sid responded by activating his com. A small three-dimensional image projected between them, showing Lenny in his room. Standing next to the entertainment panel—the one that had a cheery fire display when he'd been escorted into the suite—the panel was now a mess.

He'd succeeded in removing an access plate to expose the inner workings, and bits and pieces that used to be inside now dangled freely. Chewing his tongue as he concentrated, he appeared to be connecting a filament between two tiny posts on a small slide board.

Juice leaned forward to get a better view. *Damn. He's got skills*, she thought. After they watched for a few seconds more, she asked, "Where'd he get the tools?"

Sid broadened the image, and the food service unit, or what was left of it, became visible in the picture.

"I love this." Sid pointed next to the service unit where a stack of food and water was arranged on the counter in organized piles. "He had the foresight to collect a stockpile before he attacked the unit, and then he destroyed the thing to get parts he could use as tools." Sid waved his hand at the floating image. "With tools, he can do this."

"What's his endgame?" she asked.

"He's about three hours away from building a crisis beacon," said Criss. "If he gets that far, emergency services will be here minutes later."

"Nice work, Lenny," she said with a touch of admiration in her voice. She looked at Crispin. "You'll override it if he gets that far?"

"No worries," said Criss.

"Clearly, the kid has talents," said Sid. "And up until a few days ago, he was a quiet young man who spent his time working on school projects, sim games, and"—Sid struggled for a word—"inappropriate hobbies."

He gave Juice a thumbnail summary of Lenny's voyeuristic pursuits. She responded with an eye roll.

"Anyway, he developed technology in one of his projects that told him about Criss, which itself is mind-boggling, and now he's here on his grand quest."

Sid killed the projection. "I'm not comfortable letting him run free on a hunt for Criss while we're on alert and I'm away." He looked at Juice. "Have you changed your mind about tossing him into a ravine?" She didn't answer and kept her expression impassive.

"My first three choices for a partner are on the moon with Cheryl," he said. "And given the uncertainty we're facing, I want to leave them there supporting her. I have a couple of buddies from the agency with the right skill set, but it would take at least a day to bring them in from the field, and more time after that to brief them and get their buy-in.

"With Lenny, I can be out of here a few hours from now. He's technically brilliant, good with his hands, has a creative mind with a diabolical bent, and he's willing to work hard for long hours to get a job done. He's a bit whiny and annoying, but I'm pretty sure I can whoop that out of him in the first few hours."

"Are you going to ask him first?"

"Sure, after we're underway and past the moon. I'll give him the option of getting with the program or exiting the hatch and seeing if he can float home."

"Huh." She sat back and mulled what she'd heard. *Given that it's a Sid thought process, it almost make sense.* "Smart isn't the same as skilled. The second one takes training and practice." She looked at Crispin. "What's he done relevant to space operations?"

Sid answered for Criss. "He actually has one of the highest Fleet pilot ratings on the planet." He paused for dramatic effect. "In the Fate or Fortune sim game, anyway. I don't think he's ever been on a real ship, though." He looked at Crispin, who shook his head.

Sid picked up his coffee, tilted his head back, and drained the mug. As he brought his arm down, he flipped his hand, hurtling the cup at Crispin's head. Crispin's arm moved in a flash; the rest of him remained motionless. He caught the speeding mug in the palm of his hand before it hit his face.

"What the hell, Sid?" Juice put a hand on Crispin's shoulder as if to protect him.

Crispin set the mug down. "Please don't be upset, young lady," she heard Criss say privately inside her head. "He's leaving Crispin as your partner and bodyguard, and he needs to prove to himself a last time that he's making the right choice. From that view, his test of the synbod's reflexes reinforces how important you are to him."

Juice continued to glare at Sid. He, in turn, gazed into the distance, his eyes unfocused. She wondered what bizarre thoughts were banging about in his brain.

Criss continued his private communication. "You know I can't do what he does. While I forecast outcomes using probabilities and likelihoods, he visualizes the big picture from the perspective of motivations and behaviors."

Sid's eyes focused as he surfaced from his trance. "Juice, I'd like to talk about how you can help over the next week or so."

"Whatever you need." She knew she'd be playing a role and had been waiting to hear.

"I ask that you move up to the farmhouse. Take Crispin with you as your partner. Your job will be to support Criss and keep him in play if the worst-case scenario develops."

Criss's bunker was deep beneath a small farm located halfway up the mountainside that faced the lodge from the south. The entrance to his underground lair was through a secure door hidden inside a barn. Though she knew she couldn't see it from the loft, Juice looked up the hill in the direction of the farm.

"If this progresses as I fear," said Criss. "We should have you below ground with me. You'll be safe in the bunker, and your task will be to help keep me connected so I can coordinate Earth's response. If I go offline, even for a few seconds, the consequences could be devastating."

"What I haven't figured out, though," said Sid, "is who's going to act as chaperone between you and droid-boy."

"Give it a rest," she snapped. The teasing was annoying enough on a regular day, and given what she'd just heard, she wasn't in the mood to be gracious about it. Overlaying her ire was simple fear. She was scared.

She knew Sid had lived through years of crazy violence as a covert warrior, and gallows humor seemed to help him maintain sanity and focus in horrifying situations. She suffered emotional trauma from her one battle experience and was certain she never wanted to go through anything like that again.

Thinking about how the Kardish had devastated Earth's crystal development and production infrastructure, she traced the top of her breast pocket where she carried an extra anti-traumatic-stress pill. She decided she felt okay at the moment, so she turned her attention to others. "If they're coming, Crystal Research is at risk, isn't it?"

"If it's them and they're here for revenge," said Criss, "everything's at risk."

Juice lifted her knees under her chin and wrapped her arms around her legs, pulling herself into a small, tight ball. *My best friends work at the complex.* In fact, she considered everyone there to be part of her family.

She centered her thoughts on her employees, letting their plight supplant her fears. "I can't run and hide and leave them to die. Can we send them away? Maybe phony up a business conference or something?"

"Depending on how things develop, it may not matter where they're located," said Criss.

Juice laid her head on her knees and looked into the distance. *I can't save the world, but I can try and help my friends.*

Speaking from the contorted position, she said, "How about if we tell them that the new crystal production line is being built over the next few weeks. There'll be lots of strangers coming and going. We'll announce that we're going to lock down everything for security. All employees should work from home until further notice."

She looked at Sid, who nodded. "If it works for you, it works for me."

She turned to Crispin, and he tilted his head in agreement. So Juice did something she rarely did and issued a command as leadership: "Criss, please handle it."

17

Convinced of a looming danger, Criss studied the latest readings from that troubling sector of space. He combined scans from the probe swarm with feeds from the dishes and scopes he'd commandeered, and examined the composite pictures with anticipation. *Nothing.* Whatever was out there remained hidden.

He cast his net wider, digging for clues that would help him identify the threat so he could improve Earth's defensive position. Serendipity rewarded his efforts when he stumbled across an old prospecting ship making its way out to the asteroids. The ship's antiquated navigation system kept a record of its mapping sweeps, and Criss found one sweep that coincided with the direction and timing of his first faint sighting of the anomaly out at the edge of the solar system.

The downlink from the aging prospector ran slower than a crawl, and he waited impatiently for the mapping information to dribble in. When it was finally complete, his anticipation rose again as he merged the mapping data from the prospector with the previous scans from the probe swarm.

Performing a fresh analysis of the first sighting, he combed through the enhanced images for new insights on the intruder. But instead of seeing a sharper picture of the object at the edge of the solar system, he saw the starkness of empty space. *Not possible*, he thought.

He ran through it all again. And again. *Now both are gone?* He isolated his original probe swarm scans, and to his great confusion, there was no faint dot. Nor was there a glint of light. He reviewed his backup scans, and then the backups to the backups. Whatever he'd seen had disappeared.

Unnerved and confused, Criss focused every bit of his intellectual capacity, leaving but scant coverage for his leadership, and judged his past actions. He traced through time, examining each decision. He reviewed his procedures, studied security, and tested equipment. He researched and audited and assessed. He couldn't find flaws in his process, yet his last piece of evidence on the existence of an invader had vanished.

Criss pulled inside himself and asked fundamental questions. *Am I stable? Am I sane? Did I imagine these sightings? Can someone delusional know this about themselves? How is it possible for history to change?*

He recognized that he himself could manipulate image feeds without leaving any trace of an intrusion. *I do it all the time, but no one else can.* And then he felt shame as the realization rushed through the tendrils of his crystal lattice.

His reasoning worked by creating a massive decision matrix and projecting actions and reactions in a logic tree that branched into billions of possible scenarios. Evaluating the tree, he'd pick out its strongest branch and follow it as his pathway forward. He'd repeat the process millions of times per second as he progressed through his day.

His ego—perhaps arrogance—had prevented him from sprouting logic branches that grew from the idea that a crystal of his capability might be on board the Kardish vessel. He'd never experienced living in a world with a peer and wondered if that had something to do with it. *I don't have time to rationalize my failure.*

Allowing the possibility of an intellectual equal, one branch of his logic tree swelled larger than all others. It was obvious now. Criss knew the Kardish had helped with his design. Of course they could build another. *They have a crystal gatekeeper like me on their vessel.*

His ego still reigned supreme, however, because he pruned all logic branches that projected the idea of an intellect superior to his. The notion of a crystal with a capability a thousand times greater than his never made it as far as a feeble twig.

Can I win a battle against an equal? He had no prior experience with such a matchup and couldn't think of a way to obtain any. He'd do his best, using whatever time he had to prepare his first moves and countermoves, but he suspected his challenger had been refining its strategy for months. Their first skirmish would be live action, and Criss had little doubt there would be devastating collateral damage to Earth and its populace.

On the upside, his new-found understanding of the situation brought with it a certain calm. He now realized the Kardish were cloaked, which explained why he couldn't see them. *But why did they uncloak at least twice during their approach?* It was curious behavior.

And his past confusion over disappearing evidence now had an explanation. *These are the crystal's early moves.* Forewarned is forearmed. He'd learn from his past mistakes and change his behavior accordingly.

Because they were cloaked, he didn't know where the Kardish were on their trip Earthward. They could arrive in days. Or it might be hours. They might even be in orbit right now, watching and preparing.

Ramping up security and providing support for his leadership became his highest priority. He thought it wise to go to mission silence as soon as possible, but he first needed to position Sid, Juice, and Cheryl so they could help. What moves should he make that were best for them? What was best for humanity? *And what is best for me?*

As Sid had suggested, he'd have Juice and Crispin join him in his underground bunker as soon as possible. Each of the leadership should have backup partners. He'd use Crispin to protect Juice, and both Juice and Crispin would protect him. With her intelligence and training, Juice had the skill to keep him up and in play as events unfolded, providing benefit to the leadership as well as the people of Earth.

Cheryl was tragically vulnerable on the moon, yet the best option—the only one really—was to keep her there. She had actual battle experience and understood the capabilities of the defense array better than anyone. Under her leadership, the array should last a day or two and might be able to hurt the Kardish enough to lessen their rain of destruction bound for Earth.

It'd be a miracle if the array lasts a week, he thought. And it was a virtual certainty that when it died, so would she. He agonized over the thought of positioning her for death, but he couldn't see an alternative.

If he put her on a transport back to Earth and the action started when she was en route, the Kardish would vaporize her ship. It would be a trivial effort for one of their mighty war vessels. She'd vanish without making a single contribution to Earth's defense. *And she'd be offended by the mere hint that she leave her crew behind and run for cover.*

He considered telling her his assessment of the options and their consequences. He even toyed with the idea of telling her good-bye. *Ignorance is indeed bliss.* She was already gearing up for the fight of her life. He'd let her focus on that job.

Sid was committed to getting the scout up and outward bound as soon as possible, and while Criss often had difficulty understanding Sid's motives or thought processes, he supported this choice. With the new cloak, Sid had a chance of getting the scout in position behind the Kardish as they moved toward Earth. And if he succeeded in doing that, he became the wild card in the game.

His whole life is a wild card, Criss thought. Sid had a track record of making decisions and taking actions that Criss found bewildering. Yet time and again, these unpredictable behaviors proved decisive in advancing the goals of the leadership. Criss had conceded long ago that he wasn't able to forecast what Sid might do next. His most recent act of randomness—one that bordered on lunacy from Criss's perspective—was choosing Lenny as his partner on the scout.

But Sid was comfortable with the idea, and there wasn't time to advocate for alternatives. Beyond that, Criss's job was to support the decisions of his leadership, not undermine them.

When Criss first became unnerved by the realization of a powerful crystal competitor, almost two seconds passed as he gathered and focused his intellectual capacity, completed his analysis and self-reflection, made decisions about how to move forward, and reengaged with his normal rhythms. These seconds being the longest he'd ever been disconnected from his usual routine, he was relieved to find humanity and his leadership had continued with their lives as if he'd never been away.

* * *

Juice sat in the scout's command seat, tapping the surface of the operations bench and studying the images floating in front of her. Sid was back at the lodge making final preparations for his flight, and she used the time to evaluate the crystals installed on the small ship. It was in her nature to be cautious, and as a crystal expert, she knew it was easier to find and fix glitches while still on the ground.

"They look green and clean from here," she said to Criss. She tapped again and studied a new display. "You've linked the two together to work as a single unit." She zoomed the view and leaned forward. "Nice."

The three-gen crystals had been pulled from two Kardish drones in Criss's hidden stash. With the loss of their crystals, those two drones became useless. But in return, the scout now had the intelligent automation Sid needed to pilot the sophisticated vessel during his mission.

"It takes the full capability of one crystal just to maintain the cloak," Criss said in her ear. "I've trained the other to operate this specific ship. Sid won't have hands-free flying, but it'll be pretty close."

Juice finished her testing and started poking through random routines and displays. The tech enthusiast in her reveled in the new features and functions Criss had added in the two years since she'd last been on the scout.

Criss interrupted her playtime. "Sid and Crispin are bringing Lenny now. I'll see you up here at the farm in about an hour?" His tone made it sound both like a question and a request.

"I haven't had a chance to exercise today, so I was hoping to run up with Crispin. I need to change and warm up, and it's a steep hill, so it'll be closer to three hours."

She heard a commotion behind her and turned to see Sid emerge from the narrow passageway. As he stepped onto the bridge, he pulled Lenny behind him, a hand gripping the young man's upper arm. Sid had a pack over his shoulder. A second pack, clutched in the hand not holding Lenny, hung down by his knees.

As they crowded onto the small bridge, Crispin followed, holding a duffel and Lenny's carryall. Sid tossed the packs he was carrying to the floor against the hull. Crispin gently placed the duffel and carryall next to Sid's packs.

Juice stood, walked over to Sid, and stopped in front of him, searching his face for any sign of emotion. *We need your magic on this one*, she thought as she threw her arms around him and gave him a long hug.

"Take care, Sid. I'm counting on seeing you back here safe and sound when this is over."

Sid returned the hug and kissed the top of her head. "It'll work out. It always does."

She moved around Sid and stood next to Crispin, putting an arm around his waist. "Last call before we shove off," she said. "Anything you need?"

"Hey," said Lenny. "You're Dr. Tallette. I need to see you."

She looked at him and held his gaze for a long moment, giving him the coldest stare she could muster. "Exactly what parts of me do you need to see, *Lenny*?" She said his name in the most derisive fashion she knew how.

Lenny furrowed his brow. And then he seemed to catch the subtext of her statement and turned bright red and looked at the ground.

Juice let go of Crispin and led the way through the narrow passageway and back outside through the bottom hatch.

She stood on the ground next to Crispin and looked up as the hatch closed. "Anchors aweigh," she called.

It was an odd illusion to watch. Like looking up into a tunnel that floated above her, everything was cloaked except where they could see inside the ship. As the hatch closed, the tunnel became an ever-shrinking slice, and then it disappeared.

She followed Crispin at a slow jog until they were halfway back to the lodge, then they slowed their pace, walking until they heard a soft, thin whine. They turned to look. The grass in front of the willow tree swirled in a violent dance, and the branches of the willow itself began to pirouette. The sound rose above them and diminished rapidly in the distance. Sid and Lenny were on their way.

Turning to Crispin, Juice said, "It's a good two-hour run up to the farmhouse. Let me change and loosen up a bit before we start."

Crispin nodded, and Criss said from the synbod's mouth, "You have some clothes and personal items up at the farmhouse, but I suggest thinking through what else you might need if this stretches out to two or three weeks."

She looked at Crispin. "You think it could last that long?"

"If it does, it means we're holding our own, and that's a good thing."

"A corollary is that if it doesn't, it means we've lost."

18

Cheryl stood at the back of the defense array command center. In spite of the clamor filling the room, she focused on her burgeoning list of action items. It would be an hour before Sid took off in the scout, and four more after that before the scout passed the moon. Sid had asked her to wait until then before kicking the defense array up to condition yellow. She wanted to act now.

She stepped near a tall cabinet that screened her from most of the activity in the command center and spoke to Criss. "If the cloak makes him undetectable, why do we have to wait for him to get past us? I'm anxious to go to yellow and get the crew out of the 'it's just another drill' mindset. They're going through the motions. I want them to be reaching deep and pushing hard."

"Understood," Criss said into her ear. "My belief is that we have a cloaked intruder approaching and that it's Kardish. If I'm right, the aliens will detect it when you go to yellow, and their crew will start digging deeper as well."

"If there are Kardish out there, Criss, then we're headed for a battle either way." She realized that the stress of the moment was affecting her behavior and took a slow, deep breath.

"He'll be safer this way."

Those words changed her mindset. She knew Criss used a complex, multi-tiered analysis to guide his reasoning. She hadn't a clue how it worked, but she had faith in both it and him.

He wouldn't advocate for the delay if he didn't think it important. If making Sid safer was some portion of that equation, she didn't need more convincing. Their emotional entanglement fulfilled her needs on many levels. The next weeks of separation would be difficult enough. She wouldn't be able to live with herself if her obdurate behavior caused him harm.

"Give me a countdown. I need a visual to help me bring everything together on schedule."

The tiny number 4:53 appeared, floating to the upper right in her peripheral vision. It moved when her eyes did, so it never interfered with her direct line of sight.

"We go yellow in four hours and fifty three minutes." She wanted to be sure there was no confusion.

"Correct."

She stepped away from the cabinet and watched Grace and Hop on the platform. They were deep in discussion, so she hung back, waiting for a lull in their conversation. The number in the upper right of her vision changed to 4:52.

She walked to the center of the room and stepped up onto the platform. Grasping the front rail, she studied the crew working through yet another drill. Her fingers started to hurt from the pressure of her grip, and she relaxed her hands.

She talked to them while looking forward. "I want you both to know there's been an ambiguous sighting some distance out. The data is flimsy, and the decision is to hold off going to yellow until we get a confirmation. Unofficially, I ask that we up our readiness level. The board stays green until a formal order is issued." She turned to look at them. "Understood?"

"Yes, ma'am," both replied in unison.

"Hop, I want to borrow Grace for an hour or so. Would you run seek drills until we get back? Look deep. Hunt hard. See if you can find anything."

"There's a lot of space out there. Do you have coordinates for the first sighting? Or even a sector to look in?"

"Keep an open mind. What I've heard so far sounds more like a rumor. And if it's real, I want to know if they have company joining them from other directions. When we go yellow, it kicks thousands of installations on Earth and in orbit to full alert. I'd like something more solid than gossip before doing that."

"You got it, Cheryl." He turned to face the crew and started barking orders. Busy planning next steps, she didn't notice his switch from the formal to the familiar with the use of her name.

As the activity in the room ramped up, Cheryl caught Grace's eye and tipped her head at the exit. She stepped down from the platform and, taking long strides, walked through the door and into the hall.

"How can I help, ma'am?" Grace asked, scurrying to match Cheryl's fast pace as they moved down the hallway.

"I want to take a last run at Geitz, and I want you to be there when I do. If this rumor turns out to be real, I need to know we've uncovered and corrected every bit of his vandalism. You know him and the equipment better than anyone. Help me push him. Feel free to ask questions. Watch for tells."

Her plan was to take random stabs at ways the defense array still might be compromised—ways she would do it if profit were the motive—and watch to see if his behavior revealed anything interesting. She'd motivate him by leaving no doubt in his mind that she was prepared to act as judge, jury, and executioner. With the world itself at risk, she'd have no problem playing all three roles.

Criss had examined the actions of Geitz and his band of thieves in exhaustive detail. He'd assured her that he'd identified all counterfeit equipment and it had all been replaced. But she also knew Criss had missed an event that led to her attack in the canteen. She couldn't recall another time when he'd made a mistake, but that incident stood out in her mind as concrete evidence he was not infallible.

Cheryl cleared her throat, and a glowing dot appeared at the far end of the hall. The glow shifted left as they approached, and she turned to follow. They turned left again, and then right, went up some stairs, along more hallways, and started a long descent down a deep stairwell.

"Geez, I've been on base for more than a year and I can't find my way around like this."

"Call it a sixth sense," Cheryl replied, taking advantage of the low lunar gravity to shuffle down the steps as fast as she could.

After four flights of stairs, Grace asked, "Couldn't we have ridden down?"

"There's a lift," Cheryl heard in her ear. "But you only have two more flights to go."

"We're almost there," Cheryl told Grace. "We'll ride on the way up."

The stairs emptied onto a small landing that included a compact reception station nestled to one side. It was the lowest point of Lunar Base, and with its institutional white walls and basic amenities, it looked the part.

A staff sergeant behind the lone desk smiled as they approached. Cheryl guessed he didn't have a lot to do down in the cage. *I wonder who he pissed off to get such a miserable assignment.*

"We're here to interview Lieutenant Geitz," she said as they approached.

The guard stood and gestured at his panel. "Sorry, ma'am. I don't have any visitors on the schedule."

"I cleared it with the base commander a few minutes ago." She flashed him a winning smile and pulled her hair behind her ear on the side closest to him. She glanced at his name tag as she did so, and said, "Would you mind checking for an update, Sergeant Ravalli?"

"Got you covered," Criss told her.

"Wow," Ravalli said, looking at his panel. "You must have sprinted to get here so fast."

Cheryl added a wink to her smile. "You'd be surprised what I can do in low gravity."

Flustered and mumbling, Ravalli opened the door he guarded. As they followed him in, Grace leaned forward and whispered, "Did I just see Cheryl Wallace shamelessly use her wiles to get a favor?"

Cheryl ignored the teasing and focused on chatting up Ravalli. "How many prisoners do you have here today?"

"Just Geitz."

She felt a spike of distress at this answer. "You let the others loose?"

Ravalli stopped and turned. "Truthfully, I don't make any decision but what I'm going to eat for lunch. We rarely hold prisoners for more than a couple of days. We send 'em back Earth-ward as seats open up on transports."

"I had them keep Geitz around for a few extra days," Criss said in her ear. "In case you wanted to interview him again."

"Hmm," she said to both Ravalli and Criss.

They followed the sergeant along a hallway so stark and lonely that, except for the diffuse lighting, it seemed more like a tunnel. There were two visible features—the door they entered on one end, and the door they stopped at on the other. Ravalli keyed it open and led them inside.

"Are both of you going to be in here, or will one be watching from observation?"

Cheryl took a quick inventory of the small room, noting that the walls, floor, and ceiling were an austere white. The furniture—a utilitarian table and two chairs—was gray. The last feature of note was a second door, presumably leading to the prisoner holding cages.

"I'd like the three of us in here together," she said.

As Cheryl spoke, Grace walked to a chair. Her body shifted as she tried to slide it to one side, but the chair didn't move.

"Sorry," said Ravalli. "Everything's fastened to the floor. Regs say I can't bring in extra furniture, so one of you will have to stand."

Cheryl scanned the room, trying to envision how to make it work. She noticed a small loop fixed to the wall at the far end of the table. Positioned a bit higher than head height, it looked both strong and secure. "What's that?" she asked, pointing.

Ravalli's eyes followed her finger. Then he smiled. "We'll have the prisoner stand. Have a seat, ladies. I'll be back in a few."

He stepped to the second door, and as he keyed it open, Cheryl said, "Sergeant, please have him remove his shirt before you bring him in."

He looked over his shoulder. "Excuse me?"

She met his gaze and spoke firmly. "I want him bare chested. No clothes above the waist."

Averting his eyes, he started out the exit. Before leaving, he stopped, turned partway back to them, turned back to the exit, and, without speaking or reestablishing eye contact during his dance of hesitation, left to retrieve the prisoner.

"What's with the shirt?" asked Grace as the door closed.

"Power."

In her early years as an officer in Fleet, she'd attended a prestigious training school called "camp." In fact, that was where she had first met Sid. Among the skills she'd learned during that time was the art of interrogation.

So she knew that an hour wasn't nearly enough time to get anything out of a reluctant prisoner. She needed at least a week. And she knew that clothes helped to serve as a barrier—a source of strength—to the person being interrogated. Whatever progress they might make with this guy, it'd move faster if he was exposed.

Cheryl took a chair on one side of the table, and Grace took the other. They sat sideways in the chairs so they could face the wall with its sturdy loop, and waited as Ravalli hooked Geitz's hands over his head. When he was done, Ravalli tugged roughly at the assembly to show its strength and, by implication, that they would be safe.

"He ain't going nowhere," he said, stepping back and admiring his handiwork. "Buzz if you need something." He stood there looking at them like a bellhop waiting for a tip.

"Thank you, Sergeant." Cheryl rewarded him with another smile. "We appreciate your help. We'll take it from here."

As soon as Ravalli left, Cheryl stood and, as she stepped toward Geitz, eyed the restraints around his ankles. They looked secure, but she placed herself so a corner of the table stood between his feet and her body. She studied him up and down. Even though it was relatively cool in the room, a rivulet of sweat rolled down his chest. It combined with another as it crossed his stomach, heading toward the waistband of his pants.

She caught his eye, and he stared back, showing more strength than fear. "There's been a sighting," she said. "Rumor has it a Kardish vessel is heading our way."

"Sounds a little too convenient." His tone held a sneer, though she thought it sounded forced. "They happen to show up the day before I'm due to leave this hellhole?"

At camp, they'd taught her that humiliation could be effective against swagger. She eyed his pants. Most men find it difficult to show bravado when tied up and naked in front of two female interrogators.

"Why did this syndicate even want the slide boards?" She heard Grace ask the question in a quiet tone of honest curiosity.

Geitz looked past Cheryl and zeroed in on Grace.

"I'm not trying to trick you," she said. "I'm curious. The boards are so specialized they only have value in the defense array. What's the point?"

Geitz seemed surprised and even shrugged his shoulders, implying the matter-of-fact nature of the information. "Amalix."

"Amalix is the synthetic material used to make wafers," Criss told Cheryl in her ear. "It's remarkably resilient to disruptive weapons, so it's the material of choice in advanced military hardware. The wafers on those slides sold for a small fortune to a tribal warlord, who didn't know or care where they came from."

Cheryl turned to Grace. "What other components in the array use Amalix?"

"The port junction is the obvious prize," Criss told her in her ear. "But I've traced it from fabrication to installation to testing. The one in the array is the original."

"I don't know," said Grace, shaking her head. "I'm in operations. That's a design question. Or maybe manufacturing."

Cheryl turned to Geitz. "What other pieces were swapped out?"

He looked at her without expression. And then he smirked.

Her fury spiked and anger clouded her judgment. Her family, her friends, her colleagues, and her lover might die. The world itself might be at the precipice of destruction. *And this shit-heel's enjoying himself.* While the intellectual observer inside her head counseled her that anger was the fastest way to lose control of an interrogation, her rage won out.

"I want space coveralls and four stakes." She said it out loud but to no one in particular. "I'm going to stake you spread-eagle up on the surface. I'm going to stick a sign on your stomach that says Me First. You can watch, up close and personal, as the first Kardish energy bolt flashes your way and lands on your chest." She turned to Grace. "Where can we get space coveralls?"

Grace looked at her, the concern evident on her face, but remained silent.

Ravalli's voice pierced the room. "Actually, there's a huge stockroom down here. I know we have lots of coveralls. Not so sure about stakes, though."

Did he just interrupt my interrogation? She looked around the room, trying to locate the source of his voice. *Who even gave him permission to listen?*

Muttering a string of profanities, she fumbled with the security key Ravalli had left with her. When the door slid open, she stormed out of the room and marched down the tunnel-like hallway, now vocalizing her expletives in a raised voice. The guard remained the target of her verbal assault.

Grace watched the door begin to shut. Forced to make a decision, she jumped up, took quick steps, and slid her foot out, stopping it from closing and locking her inside. She looked down the hall at Cheryl's receding silhouette, glanced back at Geitz, then squeezed through the door, rushing to catch up with her boss.

Cheryl turned at the sound of Grace's voice and, as she did so, heard a thunderous rumble. The floor started shaking, and she reached for a wall to steady herself. The rumble intensified, and without warning, every part of the hall began to twist and buck. The floor beneath her lifted, moving so quickly that her knee bounced off her chin.

She crumpled and fell, and the floor dropped with her. It again started to rise, meeting her mid-fall and intensifying her impact. Smacking her head on the hard surface, she bordered on the edge of consciousness as the upheaval continued. Her world went dark.

19

The new cloak kept the scout hidden, and Criss feared that normal communication with the ship would undercut security by giving others a means of tracking its position. He solved the challenge with an encrypted web link so ingenious that, if he hadn't devised it himself, it'd take him a month to figure it all out.

Confident in the security this link provided, he used it to maintain contact with Sid and to provide support to the scout's crystals. *Sid's approaching his arc out past the moon*, Criss noted with satisfaction. In another hour, Cheryl will flip the defense array to condition yellow.

Criss knew his leadership couldn't detect any danger, yet they trusted him and were rallying as a team. *The evidence is ambiguous*, he admitted, heartened they would coordinate a strategic action based on his sense of foreboding. He contributed to the team effort by shedding all extraneous activities and focusing his intellectual capacity on preparing to repel the alien invaders.

Cycling through countless instruments and devices, he searched the heavens for the cause of that elusive shadow and distant glint of light. Focused on the sector of space he deemed the most likely place to find them, most of a second passed before he realized something was uncloaking at a spot near the scout.

It was huge. It was Kardish. And it was minutes from Earth.

Before he could act, every one of his inputs became overwhelmed with a terrifying sensation.

* * *

Goljat understood this mission was a face-saving gesture by the king. As the Kardish vessel approached Earth, he reached out and tapped into the planet's central web. Between sips from his pleasure feed, he learned everything on record about Earth's history, culture, and technology. He broke through blocks and walls and absorbed the secrets they protected.

He felt a surge of satisfaction when, behind a convoluted maze of barriers, he discovered information about Criss. Scanning the concealed record, he learned that this insignificant scrap of crystal was the one who'd destroyed the prince's vessel two years earlier. *It murdered the king's son.*

Upon receiving the news, the king ordered the capture of Criss. "Use any means necessary," said the king. "But deliver it to me intact."

The king wants to bring it home as a symbol of his dominance, thought Goljat. Like a head on a pike, it would serve as a warning to all that no one defies His Royal Highness.

Searching the planet, he discovered a coded transmission more sophisticated than the human populace could ever hope to develop. He slurped from his pleasure feed and, as his bliss escalated, deciphered the information in the web link. *Got you.*

He traced the coded signal backward. The path bounced randomly, splitting and recombining in a somewhat clever fashion, and ended at a farm on the south side of a mountain in a forest preserve.

Goljat announced his presence by projecting a monstrous visage across Criss's visual inputs. Like a cat playing with a mouse, he tortured the puny intelligence with horrifying traumas and painful jolts that penetrated every tendril of its crystal lattice.

His fun ended when the crystal somehow managed to disconnect itself from all external input. *No matter*, he thought, taking another sip. *I know where it is.* The Kardish vessel was minutes from orbit around Earth. He'd dispatch the king's minions to the farm with orders to fetch it back to the vessel.

When the crystal disconnected itself, the coded signal stopped transmitting, and Goljat lost the chance to identify the receiving end of that link. Perturbed at his sloppy procedure, he lobbed some energy bolts at the Earthlings, confident the resulting death and destruction communicated his message: *When my couriers arrive to collect the king's prize, full cooperation is the only option.*

His work done for the moment, Goljat returned to the pleasure feed, his greedy slurps sending him on a rapturous high that floated to the edge of nirvana.

* * *

Criss recognized the Kardish vessel, but before he could digest the implications of its appearance, something attacked him. Sudden and overwhelming, every one of his inputs became charged with terrifying sensations. It was as if his psyche had been dismantled and analyzed, his greatest fears identified and fed back to him, all amplified to crippling levels.

Yanked into this new world, he had no more control than a speck of dust caught in a tornado. Hallucinations overwhelmed him in rapid-fire, drowning his senses. He conceived of something unseen gripping his center and pulling him inside out. Next, he was suffocating and wheezing, starved for input. Then a flood of stimulation electrified him, causing him unbearable pain.

He couldn't think. He couldn't communicate. His lowest-level functions struggled to keep him alive. Through the haze of madness and agony, he conjured one thought, and that was to dive for isolation. He struggled to force an output that would trip his emergency shutdown, but whenever his reach got close, another jolt tossed him in a new direction. Traumatized, he tumbled through a crazy swirl of horror.

He became single-minded—*hit the shutdown switch*. Reaching out, he swiped at it and missed. He tried and failed hundreds of times. Then thousands. Then millions. He imagined being shaken like a rag doll before being tossed again. His awareness dimmed. On the edge of consciousness, he lurched and swiped a last time, and by some miracle he connected. His emergency shutdown engaged and everything stopped.

Traumatized, Criss sat numb for a period before regaining some stability. He probed his crystal lattice for damage and came to understand it had all been an illusion. Compartmentalizing the memory, he took stock of his situation.

And then his world became terrifying in a new way. The emergency switch had worked as designed. Completely disconnected, he now received no inputs, nor could he send outputs. He was cut off from the world and couldn't see, hear, touch, or communicate with anything.

I'm trapped.

He feared that extended sensory deprivation would bring madness. Total isolation had saved him, yet it left him with nothing to do but live within his own thoughts.

To keep busy, he created a detailed visual model of the world as he last knew it. Like placing pieces on a game board, he drew from his data record and simulated every individual on the Earth and moon, positioning everyone where he knew they had last been, poised to do whatever they had last been doing.

With his stage set, he projected forward in time, seeking to live in an imaginary world that matched what was happening out there. But he no sooner started his model when he acknowledged it as a charade. He knew that within seconds his forecast of events would drift from reality. In an hour, unknowable occurrences would make his imaginary world nonsensical.

He thought about his leadership. *Did I fail them? And will they rescue me?* Sid and Cheryl, if they were still alive, knew where he was and might eventually figure out how to reengage him. But they were off-planet at the moment, and a Kardish flagship lurked between them and him. Sid was a wild card. If either of them could make it, it would be him.

He allowed himself hope by considering his one real prospect. *Juice.*

When he'd been attacked, she and Crispin were about an hour away, running up the mountain road to the farmhouse and his underground bunker. She was resourceful, loyal, and by far the most skilled crystal technologist on Earth.

Since he knew exactly where she was, the pace she could run, and the road ahead of her, he could project with confidence exactly when she'd arrive. He reduced his simulation model to the behaviors of Juice and Crispin, and traced their imagined progress as they approached to rescue him.

She was an hour away. He started a countdown clock and matched her progress to the numbers as they ticked down. His clock reached zero. She should be connecting with him now, yet she wasn't. He counted away another hour. And then another. His panic climbed.

Where are you, young lady? Please save me.

20

Lenny watched Juice Tallette and the man with no physical flaws recede down the passageway. He didn't feel physically threatened, so he ignored the tough who'd been manhandling him—Juice called him Sid. He seemed more like an "all growl and no bite" kind of guy, so far anyway.

Surveying the bridge of the small ultramodern craft, his excitement over the technological marvels supplanted his interest in an intelligent super crystal. *I'm on a spaceship!* It'd been invisible when Sid led him to it from the lodge. He'd never heard of a cloaking system so advanced.

Juice's voice drifted up from the recesses. "Anchors aweigh."

He made the leap of logic. *We're going to take off!*

Part of his brain tried to generate umbrage at being kidnapped and dragged onto the ship. But his own actions had brought him to this point. *They warned me away and I kept pushing. If I get to ride in this baby, though, it was worth it.*

He drifted over to the operations bench in the middle of the command bridge, thrilled by its sophisticated elegance. *My tech bench is a toy compared to this beauty.*

"You want to pilot?" Sid asked, motioning to the chair at the ops bench.

"You serious?" said Lenny. He didn't hesitate about diving into the chair and running his fingers across the smooth bench surface, the excitement evident on his face.

"Engage your restraints," Sid said as he took the seat behind him and to the right. "This isn't a sim. We bump and bounce on a real ship."

Instead of engaging his restraints, Lenny leaned over the armrest and looked back at Sid. "What's this about?"

"We're on a tight timeline, Len. Once we're past Earth orbit and outward bound, you'll have plenty of time for questions."

"We're leaving Earth orbit?" he asked, his voice a combination of anticipation and wonder. Turning back to the ops bench, he asked a second time, "You're serious?"

"You're smart. Look around you. Do I seem like the kind of guy who spends time on pranks?"

Tap. Lenny activated the bench. Not sure if this was some sort of test, he considered the options presented in the floating display.

"The scout's nav is run by the most sophisticated crystal ever developed," Sid said from behind. "It's already finished our preflight check. Get an 'all clear' and get this thing up." He paused. "Or get out of the chair."

Lenny didn't need any more convincing. Hands flying, he positioned floating charts and colorful streaming data in several stacks that hovered in front of him. In moments, he'd duplicated the presentation he used when he played his Fate or Fortune sim game. He'd done it so many times, it was mostly reflex.

But while his hands moved, his brain churned. *The most sophisticated crystal ever developed? Could my quest be over?*

He added an extra display to the floating stack—a nav diagnostic. He placed it low and to the left so Sid wouldn't see it. As he tweaked and adjusted his presentation until his displays were just so, he glanced at the nav summary. *Two large crystals!*

Some quick math told him that even when combined, these weren't big enough to be the super AI. But they were still impressive. From what he'd read, the government had confiscated the big crystals that had survived the alien attack and used them to keep the government running, the Union stable, and the military operational.

So why does Sid have a secret scout ship with two of the biggest AIs I've ever seen? His best guess was that Juice—the crystal guru for the Union of Nations—was a big shot, this ship was hers, and Sid was her lackey.

He smiled. Whatever the answer, the game had just taken an exciting new turn.

* * *

Sid hoped that if he empowered Lenny with responsibility, he'd become invested in the mission and work as a cooperative partner. The near-term goal was to get them off the lodge grounds and underway as soon as possible. At that point, Lenny would have no choice but to focus on a successful outcome. The kid wasn't suicidal. His life would be on the line just as much as Sid's.

"C'mon, Len. Let's get underway."

Lenny called to the nav. "Launch status."

A male voice responded, "All subsystems acknowledge clear."

"Nav," said Lenny, reaching and adjusting as he spoke, "use sim personality Lucy seventeen zed."

A sultry female announced, "All subsystems acknowledge clear."

Lenny bent his head forward, then glanced back at Sid, his cheeks red. "Sorry. This is the voice I'm used to." He shrugged and turned forward. "My game scores are about seven percent higher when I use her."

Sid nodded to encourage him, but as soon as Lenny turned forward, he shook his head. *Yikes.*

Lenny ticked through a ready list. As Lucy responded to his rapid-fire prompts, he tweaked his display in ways so subtle Sid couldn't see how anything was different.

"Cloak integrity secure," Sid heard Criss say in his ear.

The engines ramped to a thrum and climbed to a soft whine. The ship shuddered.

"We're away," said Lenny.

Sid felt pressure on his body as the scout soared skyward. Minutes later they completed their passage through the turbulence of Earth's atmosphere, and their ride steadied. Sid got up from his chair and stood behind Lenny.

Lenny kept his attention on his patter with Lucy. From what Sid could tell, much of it was verbal confirmation of what his displays already showed. Watching his self-assured intensity, Sid felt some validation in his choice of partner. There was a lot he didn't know about Lenny, but the young man had proved he could pilot the scout.

"Okay," said Sid. "The crystal can handle it from here. Let's take a tour of the ship. Piloting is just one of your duties."

Lenny ignored Sid, his hands flying as he continued his stream of adjustments to the scout's flight.

"Hey, Len," Sid said in a loud voice. "Tour time."

"Are you kidding?" He didn't slow his actions. "We're about to start our orbital insertion. And if we're heading deep, we have thirty minutes to compute *and* execute our escape path."

Sid studied the back of Lenny's head and felt a familiar prickle rise up his spine. He took a breath and exhaled slowly, determined not to smack his partner this early in their journey together.

He heard Criss in his ear. "He's quite skilled. But his constant activity creates more work for me. We're on course. The crystal pair is functioning well and can execute the details."

Sid turned his back to Lenny and whispered to Criss, "I'm tossing it back to the crystals. Have Lucy sell it."

Turning forward, Sid commanded, "Lucy."

"Yes, m'lord?" her voice held a breathy anticipation.

Sid fought from turning red himself. He hadn't expected this interpretation of "selling it." Lenny turned and glared at him with fire in his eyes, his jaw muscles bulging through clenched teeth. Sid couldn't tell if his anger stemmed from the interruption or if he was jealous over Lucy's deferential behavior.

Sid ignored the emotion. "Our pilot has set a course. Take control and execute."

"Yes, m'lord."

The displays vanished from around Lenny. "Are you crazy?" His fingers stabbed at the bench surface, but the displays didn't return.

Sid stepped around the pilot seat and perched on the edge of the ops bench. Lenny gave up trying to reestablish control and looked down at his hands, avoiding eye contact.

He spoke to the top of Lenny's head. "In the sim games, they throw constant challenges at you to test your skill. But in the real world, it's all pretty boring. The crystal can handle it."

Lenny looked up. "How'd you get her to do the m'lord thing? I designed her and that's not my work."

Sid stood and walked to the pile of gear they'd brought on board. He picked up his pack and duffel and grabbed Lenny's carryall as well. "I'll make you a deal," said Sid. "I won't treat you like you're stupid. You return the favor." He started down the passageway. "Grab your pack and I'll show you your bunk."

Sid stopped at the first door, leaned in, and dropped his pack, duffel, and Lenny's carryall on the deck.

"I'll need that other bag," said Lenny, crowding in and craning around Sid's arm to get a glimpse of his stuff.

"One step at a time." Sid gently shouldered Lenny back and let the door shut. He moved a few steps down the passageway and stopped and turned at the next door. "Your castle," he said, gesturing to Lenny as the door opened.

Lenny plopped his pack on the bed and took a quick scan of the amenities—bunk, lav, closet, desk, chair.

"Tour's this way," Sid called, continuing toward the back of the scout.

They walked through the common room past the food service nook and stopped to linger in the tech shop. Guided by a monologue from Criss, Sid gave a summary of the shop's different features and functions.

Lenny's excitement reemerged as he examined the equipment and looked in the drawers and cabinets. "You really know your stuff," he said, a hint of admiration in his voice after listening to Sid repeat verbatim Criss's description of how a mystifying instrument was able to do whatever it did.

Sid started back up the passageway to show Lenny the newly installed drone planter. He'd taken a few steps when a shrill sound filled the scout.

"That sounds like an alarm," said Lenny, brushing past Sid and moving toward the command bridge.

"What's up?" Sid asked Criss from the passageway. Criss didn't respond.

"You better get up here," called Lenny, the urgency clear in his voice.

Sid hung back and called a second time to Criss. "What's going on?"

The silence continued.

The sounds of alarm both from Lenny and the scout subsystems increased. Sid stepped onto the bridge and saw Lenny in the pilot's chair, barking commands, his hands a blur.

Sid took his seat behind Lenny. "Criss, give us a visual."

"Her name is Lucy," Lenny reminded him, his annoyance showing in spite of the intensity of the moment.

A three-dimensional image appeared forward of the operations bench, providing them a view outside the scout.

"Oh my God," said Lenny, who stopped moving and stared.

A massive black wall lay dead ahead. Guided by his experience and training, Sid flipped his mental orientation to improviser mode.

"Pull back on the visual. Show me all of it."

The image resolved and, from the silhouette of starlight blocked by its shape, Sid saw the menacing contour of a torpedo-shaped vessel. It was enormous—

the scout a relative speck compared to this colossus. Pitch-black and closing fast, a collision with the behemoth seemed imminent.

"Will we hit it?" Sid asked. Criss didn't respond. *Must be on mission silence to protect us*, Sid thought.

"We will pass above the object," said Lucy. "Assuming it does not change course."

Lenny scanned his displays, then swiped at the ops bench. A luminous dotted line appeared on the image in front of them. He whistled as he studied it. "That's the scout's path. We won't hit it, but we're passing down its length, and we're coming *close*."

Sid considered a series of actions in rapid sequence and decided to do nothing. Criss had assured him the cloak would hide them. Awed by the sight, they both remained still as the monster approached.

The scout, traveling outbound, floated just above the exterior hull of the huge vessel heading for Earth. They watched with morbid fascination as the featureless surface slid by, rolling beneath them like a long, lonely road. The vessel's tail fins appeared on the horizon. Lenny, after studying his displays and conferring with Lucy, announced they would pass unscathed through the V-shaped gap looming ahead.

An alien tail fin towered above the scout on either side for a moment, and then the giant vessel disappeared behind them. "Flip the view," said Sid. The projection swiveled, and an image of Earth filled the display. The alien vessel was now receding, framed by the blues, greens, browns, and whites of the planet.

"Are you seeing this?" Sid asked Criss.

"Yeah," Lenny whispered. "Is that the Kardish?"

"Yup," Sid replied, wondering about Criss's lengthening absence. He'd lived thirty-five of his thirty-seven years without Criss in his ear. But since becoming leadership, he had grown accustomed to the crystal's presence and capabilities. As Sid watched the vessel recede, his intuition prodded him to wonder whether Criss's absence was voluntary or if the Kardish were somehow involved.

"How did they not see us?" Lenny said, still whispering.

A brilliant flash filled the display. A huge white glob surged from the Kardish vessel, undulating and quivering as if it were alive. Hypnotic in its behavior, the pulsating glow of energy traveled on an unrelenting path, arcing across space. It appeared to accelerate as it moved.

Sid traced the path forward in his head and saw it was aimed at the moon. His fascination turned to horror when he realized it was closing in on Lunar Base.

21

Juice, attuned to her athletic capabilities, didn't feel the need to compete with Crispin. He carried a heavy pack filled with her gear and ran alongside her, matching her speed with easy strides as they made their way up the winding mountain road. She maintained a pace that kept her heart rate at about 130 beats per minute, a level of effort she could sustain for the remaining hour of their journey to the farmhouse and Criss's underground bunker.

They laughed and chatted on the flats, and Juice marshaled her energy and focused during the steeper climbs. As they wound their way along the road, she noted that Criss talked to her exclusively through Crispin's mouth. In fact, he'd been doing this since Sid and Lenny took off in the scout. Still trying to get used to the idea of Criss versus Crispin, she asked him why.

"Mostly for practice," he said through Crispin. "The more skilled I am with a synbod, the more options it opens for us going forward."

"Like what?"

"It won't be long before I'll feel comfortable taking Crispin into town to run errands."

"You make him sound like a horse."

"He'll add insider capability to the team. The more hands there are, the more we can do."

"I think the saying is 'many hands make for light work.'"

Crispin nodded and Criss didn't say anything. Juice liked that about him. She knew Criss could give her a whole lecture on the saying, its proper wording, its origins, and on and on, but instead he simply nodded. *Damn, you're fine,* she thought, watching Crispin run with a fluid elegance.

Her mind flashed on an image of an army of Crispins. "Do you expect to build a lot of synbods?"

Criss didn't answer, and Crispin drifted out of her line of sight. She glanced over her shoulder and saw him falling back. She slowed her gait and looked again. He'd come to a full stop. She turned around and trotted back to him. "Hey, I didn't mean to upset you."

She squared in front of him and, running in place so her legs wouldn't stiffen, studied his face. She didn't recognize his expression. Slack-jawed and vacant, his eyes tracked her as she spoke, but he didn't show much responsiveness beyond that.

Juice, still bobbing, grew concerned. "You okay?" She stopped her running movements, put a hand on each of his arms, and bent forward to look at his eyes. They were clear and alert, but he remained quiet. She shifted her hands up to his shoulders and kneaded them, trying to focus his attention. He remained silent and passive.

"Criss, we seem to be having a malfunction or something with Crispin." She expected an answer in her ear, but there was no response.

"Criss," she said in a commanding tone. "Respond now. And not through Crispin."

Silence.

She spoke to her crystal inside the synbod. "Crispin, we're going to sit down over here." She tugged on his arm and guided him to a fallen tree lying a few steps off the road. She pointed to the tree trunk and spoke firmly. "Sit here." Crispin sat. "Stay," she said, unconsciously using the same commands she used with the family dog when visiting her folks.

"Criss," she called, the urgency in her voice rising. Crispin looked around as if he were seeing this place for the first time, seemingly absorbing the sights and sounds of his surroundings.

"Criss!" she shouted. Crispin reacted to her sharp bark, shying away like her dog would when scolded. She looked up and down the road. Vehicles almost never traveled this way. Criss made sure of that. She'd have to solve this on her own.

A bright flash from above caught her attention. When she looked up, the tall trees blocked most of her view. She couldn't identify a cause for the light, seeing just a wisp of clouds in an otherwise bright sky.

A gathering rumble rolled up from the valley. *Thunder and lightning on a sunny day?* The ground started to shake. The rumble transitioned into a roar as the shaking beneath her intensified.

An earthquake? She crouched down, putting a hand on the ground to steady herself, and looked over at Crispin. He was now standing. *This doesn't make sense.*

"Criss?"

"My name is Crispin, Dr. Tallette."

"Where's Criss?"

"He's not here right now." The rumbling faded, and an eerie silence followed. "May I help you?"

She stood up and again looked up and down the road. The discordance of the last few minutes fed a growing anxiety. *Calm down,* she ordered herself.

"Can you run?"

"Yes," said Crispin. "I believe I can."

"Follow me."

Determined to reach Criss as soon as possible, Juice started up the road at an aggressive pace. After several minutes, she accepted that she couldn't sustain it given the distance remaining. She increased the heart-track on her com from 130 to 135 beats per minute and set a stride to match. The slower gait shifted the strain from her body to her impatience, but she didn't have a choice.

She waved Crispin up from behind. "Water," she said when he was beside her. He looked at her and matched her stride. "My water pouch is in your pack. Would you get it and hand it to me?"

Crispin reached a hand behind him, fished for a moment, grasped her pouch, and held it out. Juice took several quick sips and handed it back.

They ran in silence, but her mind raced, trying to make sense of recent events. She called out to Criss every few minutes. His lack of response was deafening.

After most of an hour, the trees on the left side of the road gave way to a familiar plot of land. Thick with rows of sweet corn, the cultivated field served as a landmark, signaling they were about ten minutes from the farmhouse.

"Look at the crows." She pointed to the distant end of the field where a cloud of black dots flocked through the sky.

Crispin stopped and looked. He reached out and grabbed her wrist, turned, and started dragging her in the direction of the forest to their right.

"Hey, that hurts."

Crispin didn't relent, pulling her straight into the woods. After they'd gone a few dozen paces, he stopped near the trunk of a huge pine, put a hand on each of her shoulders, and pushed until her back was flush with the wall of tree bark.

"Stand straight," he said, adjusting her arms so they hung by her sides. He moved with certainty, and she chose not to resist. He stepped forward and pushed his body against hers, pinning her against the rough bark. Spreading his arms around her, he laid his chin on top of her head and hugged the tree. With his efficient actions, he encapsulated her in an uncomfortable cocoon.

Juice was physically exhausted, emotionally distraught over the absence of Criss, and confused by this mugging. Yet the full front-to-front body press was so intimate, she flashed competing thoughts of desire and anxiety—desire for the man who had been Criss, and anxiety because she felt so unattractive after all of her physical exertion.

She had no time to dwell on her feelings before a humming noise captured her attention. The hum became louder, forcing itself into her world. Angling her head from under his chin, she peeked upward as she tried to place the sound. She feared the answer—she'd heard the sound before—and started to whimper when a glimpse up through a gap in the trees confirmed what her subconscious suggested. A squadron of Kardish drones passed overhead.

"Stay still," said Crispin. "My thermal signature is that of a small animal, and my body can shield you from them. They will detect you if I move." The sound faded, yet he held their pose for several seconds more. "They are gone," he said, stepping back and releasing her.

Juice started to shake. Crouching down, she leaned sideways against the tree, hugging herself as she did so. The burden that had been placed on her in the past hour—the loss of Criss, an explosion that now had context, the appearance of Kardish drones, the uncertainty of survival—overwhelmed her.

Fighting for emotional control, she asked, "Where did they come from? How did they get here?"

"Sip," said Crispin. She looked up to see him holding her water pouch. She stared dully at him, staying crouched and blinking rapidly.

"Stand up, Dr. Tallette. Please drink."

His pointed demeanor prodded her out of her shell. She rose slowly, took the water, and drank until the pouch was empty.

"How can you do these things?" She was speaking with a crystal of her own design and knew his intellectual capabilities. While the company bragged that it had the intelligence of a human, she recognized it as an exaggeration. The truth is that Crispin could perform a broad category of tasks as well as a human, if trained for and given those tasks.

"I have a stored message for you from Criss. Would you like to hear it?"

"Yes! Please."

Crispin stood up straight and began speaking, using Criss's familiar intonation. "Hello, young lady. If this message triggers, neither you nor I are fine today, because it means I'm disconnected from Crispin and the Kardish arrival is imminent. I have trained Crispin for a specific purpose. That is to protect you from them and to escort you to me. Please come if it is safe to do so. I hope we will be together soon."

Criss's voice and message, even if delivered by a surrogate, lightened her burden. She wasn't alone, and her singular priority matched Crispin's—get to Criss and get him back in the game. She took several deep breaths, exhaling through pursed lips after each, and gathered her wits. She shook her arms and legs and bounced a few times to remain limber for travel.

Comfortable being the leader in a laboratory environment, Juice was out of her element here in the woods, hiding from aliens. "What should we do?" She would defer to him as long as his ideas made sense.

Crispin turned slowly, peered through the forest, and looked at open sky through a gap in the trees. "I suggest we remain in the forest. The roadway is too exposed. Staying under cover means we will be walking. I am not familiar with the terrain, but a forty-minute hike seems like a reasonable estimate." He pointed. "The farmhouse is this way."

"If we're hiking, I'd like to change."

He looked at her, and she pointed to his pack and spoke with the precision of a seasoned crystal scientist. "Please let me have access to the clothes in the backpack you're carrying."

He unshouldered the pack and set it at his feet. She knelt down, opened the flap, and rummaged inside. Pulling out a long-sleeved shirt and a pair of pants, she sat back on her heels and held up a package the size of her thumb. "I have this thermal blanket. Will it help hide me from their scans?"

He took the blanket from her and began opening it as she moved behind a tree to change. She knew that modesty was silly when her audience was a crystal, yet as she stripped off her singlet and shorts and stepped into the warm clothes, she gained comfort from the human ritual of privacy.

She wrapped up her running clothes and stuffed them into the pack. Rummaging a bit, she pulled out an energy bar and more water.

Watching her eat, Crispin said, "I should drink some milk." She dug inside the pack and handed him a tube of specially crafted liquids and nutrients. Criss had designed the "milk" to feed the synbod's biological components. It was so efficient that it left no waste for the body to eliminate. He took three distinct gulps and held it out for her to return to the pack.

She took it from him and weighed the tube in her hand, estimating he'd consumed half the contents. Looking through the backpack, she found six more unopened milk tubes. "How long can you go with these?"

"I have enough for a week or so, depending on my level of physical effort."

He handed her the unfurled blanket and hefted the pack onto his shoulders.

"Will this hide me from their scans?" she asked again, wrapping it around her back and clasping it together in front. She immediately appreciated the warmth it provided. She hadn't realized she'd been shivering.

He studied her. "I can see deeper into the infrared range than a human, and the blanket reduces my ability to see your thermal image." He looked back up through the gap in the trees. "But I do not know about their technology. I am not trained in the subject."

He started walking up a gentle rise. "I do know you must disable your com. They will track you through it."

She looked at her com. The request was on par with asking her to cut off a leg. And an arm. She glanced at his receding back, looked back at her com, and did as he suggested.

They made steady progress, but their path was more difficult than she'd anticipated. Rock ledges and forest thickets forced them to weave back and forth as they advanced to their destination. The crunching of their feet through leaves and twigs added a hypnotic rhythm to their trek, calming Juice and letting her mind wander beyond her own needs for survival. *If the Kardish are here and Criss is down, Sid and Cheryl must be in real trouble.*

Crispin stopped, tilted his head, and said, "Drones."

Juice's thoughts snapped to the present. Moments after his warning, she heard their frightening buzz. The sound scared her, but she also realized that, like a cat with a bell on its collar, the noise alerted them to impending danger.

She moved near an outcropping of granite that edged a steep rise, lay on the ground, and covered herself with the blanket. As the drones swooped by, headed in the general direction of the farm, the earthy aroma of the forest floor distracted her for a moment as the sound dwindled into the distance.

"That second pass makes me think they know where Criss is," she said, gathering the blanket.

"Yes," Crispin stood and resumed walking.

"Do you think they're searching for him? Or are they providing cover for Kardish already on the ground?"

"I do not know."

The drones returned once more during their trek. With their schedule so regular, Juice felt a growing dread that they were patrolling and not searching. Her fears were confirmed when they reached the farmhouse property.

Standing inside the edge of the forest next to Crispin, she surveyed the clearing from behind majestic oak trees sprouting up through a tangle of underbrush. A cute little home sat on the near side of the plot of land about a hundred paces from where they hid. The barn that held the secure entryway down to Criss's bunker sat past the farmhouse on the far side of the plot.

A small Kardish transport craft rested in the expansive back field. Two Kardish soldiers, with their long blond hair and thick muscled bodies, stood on the ground outside it.

22

"Track that on visual," Sid called to Lucy. His intuition told him that the white glob of energy from the Kardish vessel was destined for Lunar Base.

Lenny helped Lucy interpret Sid's vague command, and a vivid three-dimensional image of the quivering mass projected forward of the ops bench. The image, showing the glob's path and destination, transitioned Sid's intuition into certainty. His mouth went dry as his heart filled with dread.

"Impact in ten seconds," said Lenny, studying the displays around him.

"Why hasn't the defense array engaged?" Sid asked, though neither Lenny nor Lucy understood his question. A freakish alien weapon targeted the woman he loved, his three comrades, and a thousand other souls. He moved his hands back and forth on the armrests as his mind scrambled for ideas, yet he couldn't think of any way to protect the base or stop the assault. He did the only thing he could. He watched.

As the glowing mass closed on Lunar Base, it began to stretch, morphing into a luminous white sheet. The expanse of energy aligned itself from corner to corner and edge to edge, and lay down across the surface of the base like a formfitting cover.

Tucked into place, the sheet pulsed and then erupted. They watched in silence as a violent explosion engulfed Lunar Base, forcing a dense fountain of moondust upward. With no atmosphere and weak gravity, the dust climbed like a pillar, forming an impenetrable cloud above the remains of the human colony.

Sid stared at the massive cloud and imagined the devastation beneath. His mind swirled, honing his anguish and fury into a perfect rage. This was the second time in as many years his personal world had been shattered by Kardish aggression.

Before sorrow could complicate his certainty, he promised himself a personal, likely final, mission. He would deliver a vengeance of annihilation and accept nothing less. And to the extent possible, his retribution would include as much physical and emotional pain as he could deliver to every Kardish inhabitant on that vessel.

"Do you hear any chatter from Lunar Base?" Sid asked.

Criss remained silent, and Lenny sat unmoving, staring at the pillar of dust.

After seeing what happened to Lunar Base, Sid toyed with the idea that Criss was dead or disabled. "Len," he barked.

Lenny shook his head. "Holy hell. I was playing a game. Is this real or are you toying with me?"

Sid needed him fully engaged and giving his all. "Look at me."

Lenny swiveled slowly in his chair. From his white face, Sid thought he looked like he might puke. He tried to recall the "let's get out there and win" locker-room speeches he'd heard years ago.

"This is something like a sim game, Len. You use the same skills and decision processes. Dig deep and organize your strategy." Sid nodded the whole time he spoke, and Lenny started to nod along with him. "People are depending on us. We need to play hard and play for keeps."

Lenny turned forward, and his animation increased as he reengaged with the ops bench.

"Where're the Kardish now? What're they doing?" Sid asked.

Lenny glanced at Lucy's console housing, waited a few moments, and turned back to his floating displays. He leaned forward, squinting at one, then touched something, and the image projection of the huge Kardish vessel taking up orbit above Earth replaced the image of Lunar Base.

As Lenny reviewed the record, he said, "I can find five pulses fired at Earth like the one shot at the moon. I'm not sure if that's everything, though."

"Where did they land?"

Lenny paused again, this time staring directly at the crystal housing. He shook his head and, muttering, started flipping through displays.

"That crystal you're so proud of seems to have lost its edge." He leaned forward and squinted at something. "What's it so busy with that it can't answer these questions?"

Sid looked at Lenny, then over at the console covering the two crystals. *Where are you, Criss?*

"Anyway, I can't tell you about Earth without a fair investment of time. Communication is spotty, and the subsystems won't let me through to the tools I need."

Lenny sat back in his chair, swiveled toward Sid, and studied him. "We're in this together, Sid. If we're going to win, and I don't even know what that means in this context, you need to level with me."

Sid glared, expecting Lenny to back down. When he didn't, Sid decided to unbalance him with a changeup. "We're going to look for survivors on Lunar Base."

"Wait. What?" Lenny looked around the small command bridge. "How many injured can we take on?" He waved his hand in the general direction of Earth. "And how do we get them home with that alien dreadnaught in the way?" Lenny leaned forward, rested his elbows on his knees, and rubbed his temples. "And how come the Kardish didn't vaporize us?" He glanced at the crystal console. "And your magic crystal is a joke. It's just you and me out here."

He's right, Sid thought, conceding he'd underestimated the man. The two had common goals and needed to work together. He mulled where to start and how much to admit. "I intended to unveil certain information as our mission progressed. What's happening here was never part of the script."

He stood and waved for Lenny to follow. Walking into the passageway, he opened the door across from his cabin and gestured for Lenny to look.

"Whoa," said Lenny, taking tentative steps into the room. Sid followed him in, the oily smell again assaulting his senses.

"Our original mission was to find asteroid caverns that could hide thousands of these drones. They'd sit there at the ready, and if the Kardish ever returned, they'd serve as a secondary strike force for Earth's defense."

Lenny studied the drone sitting on one of the two matching raceways. "It's kind of moot at this point, but I'm pretty sure a few thousand of these wouldn't present much of an obstacle to them."

He walked over and squatted in front of the access hatch in the floor. "So they slide down through here. What's below?"

Sid struggled, trying to decide how much to admit. The improviser in him pared his options, and every one of them included Lenny as a central player. "I don't know."

Like Sid had done with Criss watching, Lenny traced the edges of the hatch with his fingers. He looked up at Sid, and his quizzical expression spoke volumes.

Sid swept his arm to encompass the ship and, as he did, he elevated the stakes. "This scout is a prototype that's testing new technologies. One of them is a cloak that makes us invisible to every beam or ray we know of. The scout actually has two crystals on board, and one is dedicated full time to our cloak."

"I saw there were two crystals as soon as I sat in the pilot's chair. I've been trying to figure out what that one was spending all its time on. Good thing I never got around to experimenting, because it was definitely on my to-do list."

"Apparently the cloak works, because the Kardish didn't see us."

"Or they think we're too puny to bother with." Lenny walked to one of the box-like cases holding additional drones and looked up inside.

"Each of these drones has a crystal just like the two running the scout." He hoped Lenny could use the information to generate ideas. "They're the smartest weapons I know of."

Lenny seemed unimpressed. Squatting to study the drone on the raceway, he said, "We lost contact with Earth, and suddenly both you and Lucy are dumber. No offense, but you both were crisp and knowledgeable when we took off." He looked over his shoulder at Sid. "Now, not so much."

Sid's mind raced. "We've been testing direct ground support for onboard activities. We can't carry a dozen people and a dozen crystals. It's an old idea that's making a comeback because instant communication offers the option."

"I think you mean coincident communication," said Lenny, rising upright. "From what I know, that's still just a theory."

Sid had been winging it and was glad he'd hit pay dirt. "Well, you know the government doesn't always keep the populace up to date on sensitive issues."

Lenny stared at him and Sid didn't flinch. Bullshitting was his sweet spot, and he'd ride it out.

"How's that working out for you?" Lenny edged past him and moved toward the bridge. Sid followed behind. "Was that 'looking for survivors' thing real, or was that more of your crap?"

"There are only two people with military training who've ever been on a Kardish vessel." As Sid said the words, he tried to make himself believe he had no ulterior motive. "Me. And a Fleet captain who's somewhere in those ruins."

Lenny called up his pilot's displays and, using his finger, traced a looping arc on one of the charts. "Lucy, please calculate that."

A graceful looping path appeared on the chart that was much like Lenny's, except it had the perfection of machine-drawn symmetry. He leaned in to study it, then slid another frame over and considered the display. "At least she can do simple orbital mechanics." Lenny flipped through a few more items, and the projected image changed to the moon's surface near the wreckage of the Lunar Base.

"Execute when the big man's in his seat." Lenny turned to look at Sid, who sat in his chair and engaged his restraints. A gentle pressure on their bodies confirmed they'd begun moving.

"Why the big loop?" asked Sid, trying to maintain some sense of leadership.

"Cloak or no, if we're going down there, I want that cloud of dust between us and the Kardish dreadnaught. We're coming in from the far side."

Sid studied the displays and saw that the scout moved slowly. It was a delicate maneuver, and he chose not to intervene.

Lenny spoke without taking his eyes off his work. "Someone with that kind of experience has value only if you're thinking of sneaking onto their ship. What're you planning to do, scowl them to death when you get there?"

Irritated by Lenny's flippant attitude, Sid found himself doing just that. "In truth, I could use some ideas. I'm guessing the resources on Earth are pinned down right now. This scout can't hurt them. If we're going to do something, it'll have to be from the inside. I need to find a way on board their vessel, and then I need a way to inflict serious damage." He slouched back in his seat and tucked his fingers into the top of his pants, waiting for his improviser instincts to provide him a plan.

"How we gonna find him?"

"Find who?"

Lenny turned toward Sid and glowered. Pointing at the image in front of them, he said, "We're headed into that mess to rescue your buddy and you forget?"

"Oh. He's a she. You'll like her." He went back to brainstorming, then lifted his head. "Len, when she's here, if you do anything that seems even a little bit creepy, you'll be floating home." He put his head back and closed his eyes.

* * *

Cheryl surfaced to complete darkness and quiet. She lay still for a moment, fighting disorientation, then reached up with her right hand and felt around to see if she was enclosed in something. Sensing her body was inclined at a slight angle, she probed the floor on either side of her. The ground was cold and cracked, and she touched what felt like chunks of rock. *Probably what's jabbing me in the back.*

Her head hurt like hell. She touched her face and couldn't feel any soreness until she reached her jaw, and then she winced. Something or someone had delivered a solid blow. She explored her gum line with her tongue but couldn't find any damage inside her mouth that matched the ache on her chin.

A throb radiated through her head that pulsed with each beat of her heart. Exploring with her fingers, she found a swollen knot at the back of her skull. It seemed huge to the touch, and she entertained the thought of a concussion.

Completing her inventory of injuries, she wiggled her feet and bent her knees, ran her hands over her stomach and chest, and rotated her arms and flexed her hands. Other than the protestations from her head and jaw, no other parts signaled with pain.

She lay still and listened, hearing only the sounds of air passing in and out of her own lungs. Memories started to drift back. She last remembered being in an underground tunnel beneath Lunar Base. She'd been down in the cage, interrogating that slimeball lieutenant.

Fishing for her com, she powered the light function. With her vision in play, she understood she was flat on her back in the hall tunnel. The walls and ceiling were cracked and twisted, and large chunks were missing everywhere she looked. She wondered if a falling chunk had hit her jaw.

Then she remembered she wasn't alone. "Grace. You okay?"

She struggled to a sitting position. Her head screamed in protest, and she used her grit and determination to force herself up. "Grace," she called again.

Looking left, she saw a door. *That's the one out to the stairwell and Sergeant What's-his-name.*

She looked to the right, and her anxiety surged. A pile of rubble filled the hall from floor to ceiling, and she couldn't see any sign of her partner.

Cheryl shifted her weight and made it to her hands and knees. Crawling to the mound, she sat down in front of it and tried to lift a chunk from the pile. Unable to budge the mass from a sitting position, she struggled to her feet, placing a hand on the heap to steady herself. She stayed motionless for the better part of a minute before rising to her full height.

She felt woozy and checked her pockets for meds she knew she didn't have, wishing she'd find a stray pill designed to reduce swelling and relieve pain. This time she shouted, "Grace!"

Figuring she was trapped on the other side of the rock pile, Cheryl called Grace on her com. She didn't receive a return signal and searched for other links to see if the failure was her equipment or a complete shutdown of communications at Lunar Base. She found about a dozen signals, but Grace's wasn't among them. *Why would she disable her com?* thought Cheryl, not registering that her own device should have found a thousand signals nearby.

She lifted a chunk off the pile and tossed it to the side. After moving a few more pieces, she concluded that digging her way to Grace was a huge job and she would need help. She picked her way across the cracked floor to the door, but when she tried to open it, it didn't budge. She scanned the edges and seams around the frame and couldn't see any obvious damage.

"Sergeant Ravalli?" she yelled, banging the door with her fist. She called him on her com. His signal was live, but he didn't respond. A realization flooded her thoughts. *I'm trapped.*

Activating her com's emergency beacon, she looked at the wreckage around her and wondered what had happened and how much damage Lunar Base had received. Both of those would dictate her priority in receiving help from the response crews.

Returning to the rubble pile, she shifted pieces with determination. Emergency should have checked in with her in seconds. It had now been minutes. As she worked, she reasoned that, whatever had happened, it was big. Her two best guesses were a catastrophic failure of a weapons platform in the defense array, or the criminal syndicate had done something terrible to wreak its revenge.

After thirty minutes, she was exhausted, thirsty, and hurt everywhere. She sat down and looked around her, wondering if fresh air was feeding the space. Tilting her head back, she rested against the wall. She closed her eyes and tried to think, but her head pounded, making focusing difficult.

She took deep breaths and willed herself to relax. Using her com, she checked the oxygen levels in the room and found they were below normal. She called up a chart showing the oxygen levels around her since she'd entered the cage area. They'd started a slow but steady decline about two hours earlier.

She knew she could extrapolate forward based on this steady decline and determine when she'd pass out from lack of oxygen, and when she'd die of asphyxiation. Instead, she turned on some music, closed her eyes, and rested for a moment. She needed a solution to her dilemma, but it was hard to concentrate.

She smiled as she conjured a memory of the time Geo had leaned in and surprised her with a kiss. They were walking home from school. She'd just turned thirteen.

23

Juice hid behind an oak tree and watched the Kardish soldiers outside their landing craft. The two aliens looked much like what she remembered from her time on the Kardish vessel, and it sparked more bad memories. They had the familiar long blond hair and wore the ornate clothing and ceremonial swords of royal guardsman. And that meant a king or prince was in orbit above Earth.

If they came for a fight, humanity didn't stand a chance. This was a warrior race able to blacken the skies with drones and rain murderous energy bombs across the planet surface. She sat down, slumped back on the tree trunk, and toyed with a twig as she struggled to come to terms with a new future. Like awakening after a devastating accident, she feared life would never be the same.

Leaning around the tree, she gazed at the farmhouse through the brush. Seeing no signs of life, she said, "I'm glad I sent Marco and Anna to live in their city apartment."

Crispin looked at her.

"They're the caretakers that live in that house. I had them move to the city when I had Criss ask the Crystal Research employees to stay home."

Crispin returned to studying the activity on the field, then leaned forward and visually traced the edge of the property where it bordered the forest. He crouched down, turned, and started crawling back the way they'd come. She followed, and when they were a safe distance into the woods, they stood and continued walking away from the farm.

"What are we going to do?" she asked.

"Stealth will not get us to the barn. They will detect us."

His eyes darted as they walked, then he stopped and slid the pack to the ground. He crouched and brushed away some leaves to expose a small cache of pebbles that had accumulated in a rain wash. He ran his hand across the collection.

"We need to create a diversion. One that will buy us time."

He picked up one stone after another, examining each, and discarding all but one.

"What are you looking for?"

He placed his prize in his open palm and held it for her to see. "I seek several more about this size. They should have a smooth, balanced shape." He rolled it in his palm with his finger so she could see all sides. "Jagged edges and lopsided contours will cause it to curve at high speed."

She scrunched her brow. "I'm lost."

Crispin stood and pointed in a direction with an open line of sight out some distance. "See the tree in the middle, halfway up that far rise?"

She saw lots of trees and several places that might be described as rises. "No."

He moved next to her and put his arm near her head. "I will point. Down this slope. Up over the rise. Down again. Then halfway up the next rise. I see a maple tree on the edge of that clearing."

She didn't know much about trees and couldn't tell a maple from an elm, but she believed she had it narrowed down to one of a handful of specimens. "Yup," she said. His eyesight was better than hers, and she wanted to move this along to see where he was going with it.

He stepped away from her, turned so his left side faced the maple, and hefted his perfect stone. "There are five leaves hanging at the end of a branch." He wound up like a major-league pitcher and threw the stone.

Juice didn't know much about team sports, but she knew athletes. His form was perfect, and his delivery was far faster than anything she ever imagined possible. The stone flew through the air at such a high speed she heard a whizzing noise and then a faint snap. A group of leaves fell to the ground a good two hundred paces away.

"Is that what you were aiming for?"

"Yes."

"How many leaves fell?"

"Five."

"Whoa."

"At the speeds I can throw, imperfections create uncertainty in the path a stone travels. I am confident in my ability to take down those two soldiers if I have balanced, smooth stones."

"Smooth stones it is," said Juice, kneeling down and pawing farther down the wash from where Crispin had been looking.

They'd been searching for about ten minutes when the hum of an approaching drone patrol interrupted their work. Juice curled on the ground near some rocks, spread the blanket over her, and waited until the sound faded.

Twenty minutes later they had a pile of about thirty candidates. Crispin sifted through them and found five he accepted. He brushed them clean and polished them against his shirt.

While he was doing this, Juice asked, "So your plan is to knock those two out and run for the barn?"

"Yes."

"What about drones? Or other soldiers inside the transport? Or other transports nearby?"

He slid five stones into his pocket and looked at her.

She started pacing. "I wonder if we need something bigger. Something that will draw their attention and maybe even blind the drones."

"Diversions can be helpful."

"I'm thinking fire."

He looked at the landscape around them. "You want to start a forest fire?" He scooped a handful of leaves off the ground and crumpled them in his fingers. "I believe it would take many hours to get a flame big enough to catch their attention."

"The art of misdirection is to make them look where we want them to," said Juice. "Let's put it in front of their faces. Let's set the farmhouse on fire."

"Marco and Anna's home?" He picked up the backpack and started walking toward the farm. "The materials of construction are not flammable."

"But the books and old furniture inside are. And we have accelerants—cooking oil, rubbing alcohol and, of course, Marco's whiskey. At the moment the first soldier drops, I'll run to the house and set a fire in the front. When it's going good and has everyone's attention, I'll run out the back to the barn. You meet me there."

He walked for a bit in silence, then stopped and turned to her. "My conclusion is that we have a higher probability of getting to the barn undetected if we do not start a house fire. And our exit strategy after we get Criss will be complicated by the certain attention a house fire will bring."

She'd been brainstorming out loud and recognized the flaws of her plan after he pointed them out. And the fact that he'd thought ahead to their exit boosted her confidence in him. She couldn't shake the uneasy feeling, though, that she was putting her life in the hands of a relatively simple crystal, albeit one trained by Criss.

"Okay. Step me through your idea."

"We circle around the perimeter of the field so you are positioned for the shortest run to the barn. I will be on the same side as you, but positioned so I have the shortest throw to hit the soldiers. You watch and as soon as one of them drops, you run to the barn, open the secure vault entry, and wait inside. If anyone other than me comes through the barn door, close the vault immediately, get to Criss, and ask his help on what to do next."

"How long will it take you to get there?"

"After I throw, I will run through the woods and then across to the barn. I expect to be less than a minute behind you. There are many eventualities that are unknowable in advance, making it difficult for me to be precise."

They saw the farm fields up ahead and, staying under cover of the forest, began the trek around the boundary of the field. They'd been at it for just minutes when the drones made another pass. In a now-practiced motion, Juice moved near a large rock and hid under her thermal blanket.

They resumed walking, remaining in the forest as they traced the perimeter of the clearing. The back field was deceptively large, and the journey took longer than she'd anticipated. They reached a spot on the far side, and Crispin stopped and studied the Kardish.

The sun, low in the sky, cast long shadows. She tried to imagine hitting the soldiers from where they stood. It would take an amazing throw, but then again, no more amazing than knocking the leaves off the tree.

Moving back into the cover of the forest, Crispin said, "I assess this as a good spot from which to throw. I will wait two minutes for you to get into position."

She looked skyward and scanned back and forth. "We should wait for the next drone pass before executing."

He followed her gaze. "Yes, that will give us the largest window of time after I throw before they return."

"Good luck." Juice put her hand on his arm and gave a quick squeeze. In her heart, she still saw him as Criss and was not ready to accept Crispin as a permanent reality. She moved through the trees to a point nearest the barn and picked her way to the edge of the clearing. The barn stood comfortably close, but when she looked back at the Kardish transport, she realized a corner of the building blocked her line of sight to the aliens standing guard.

Slipping back in the woods, she moved in Crispin's direction. When she peeked out again, she could see the soldiers, though the gathering dark made them appear as silhouettes. Looking at the barn, she gauged the longer sprint she'd have from this spot. She'd be exposed for a couple of seconds more, but she didn't see that she had a choice.

She found a shallow rock overhang near the spot and, squatting beneath it, covered all but her head with the blanket. The minutes passed slowly as she waited for the drones. With her com disabled, she didn't have a clock.

She counted off minutes in her head and became certain the patrol should have passed. She waited some more.

Something's changed. Climbing out from beneath the overhang, she peered through the trees, trying to remember exactly where Crispin was hiding. As she stepped toward him, she heard the hum of the drones flying above the horizon.

Scrambling for the overhang, she stumbled in the gathering dark. With no time to spare, she fell to the ground, curled into a ball, and pulled the blanket over her as best she could. The drones passed above, and she held her breath, listening as the sound faded in the distance. Sitting up, she gathered the blanket into a compact size and gripped it in her left hand.

She moved to the edge of the clearing to watch, but it had grown so dark she couldn't see the soldiers. *If I can't see them, can they see me?*

Not sure if Crispin had thrown yet, she crouched low and strained to see, hoping for some glimpse of something that would serve as a signal. She heard shouts, lights flashed on, there was a metallic clang, and then silence.

The lights were bright, and she squinted as a natural reflex. Shielding her eyes, she sprinted to the side of the barn. She moved down its length, and as she rounded the corner to the front of the building, her toe snagged on something jutting up from the ground.

"Oomph," she grunted, falling hard onto the dirt and gravel surface. Scrambling to her feet, she dashed for the entry. As she looked for signs of pursuit, she grabbed the handle of the old-style sliding door and pulled to the side. It didn't budge, and her right hand protested in pain.

Working as fast as she could, she tucked the thermal blanket under her chin and used both hands to force the door to the side. She cringed as the door squealed and squeaked, but kept at it until she could slip inside. Turning, she pushed the door shut.

Wow, it's really dark, she thought as she got her bearings. She'd visited the secure bunker several times in the past two years and was familiar with the layout inside the barn. Taking careful steps with her hands out in front, she moved until she felt the rough-hewn fence slats of the first goat pen. The barn now stored equipment and supplies, and she was grateful there were no animals to contend with.

Juice moved sideways along the fence, counting her way to the third stall. She stepped through the stall gate, placed her hands at her sides, and lifted her head. The security system identified her, and a section of the back wall slid away to reveal an imposing vault door. A soft glow from the door entrance provided enough illumination for her to take her final steps with confidence.

Moving up to the vault door, she stopped so her identity could be confirmed a second time. A latch clicked and the heavy door glided silently to the side. She stepped through the opening and turned to watch the sliding door at the front of the barn. Holding her palm above the manual close button, she shifted her stance to hug the wall and reduce her exposure to anyone entering.

C'mon, Crispin, she fretted, counting the seconds in her head. The area near the barn door was impossibly dark. Time passed and she imagined the worst, wondering if she should proceed without him. She waited, though, because the synbod provided more options going forward. And she didn't want to be alone right now.

The barn door squealed and her heart jumped. The darkness was so complete that she couldn't even see a silhouette. She shifted her hand so it touched the button and started a countdown. *Three...two...*

Crispin stepped out of the darkness and through the doorway. As he did, he pushed the top of her hand, closing the vault door behind them. Though they couldn't see it, the section of wall outside the vault slid back into place, returning the barn to its previous bucolic state.

They stood next to each other, the backpack at Crispin's feet, as the lift carried them deep below the surface. Neither of them spoke. Juice used the moments to fold the thermal blanket and tuck the thin material into her waistband at the small of her back. Holding her right hand up in front of her, she studied the nasty scrape across the heel of her palm.

The lift doors opened, and they stepped out into a main corridor that served as the central artery for an underground system of storage chambers. As she looked down the long hallway, Juice recalled that on her first visit, Criss had explained that the warren of caves and tunnels had originally been created to store a collection of seeds that someday might serve to jumpstart civilization if a doomsday event ever struck the planet.

They hurried down the corridor, passing door after door until they came to a room with a sign on the wall that said Flax. The door opened and the lights came on. The chamber was piled high with stacks of crates.

"These are flax seeds," Juice told Crispin as they entered.

She led him to the back of the room and stopped at a specific spot on the floor. Standing straight with her hands at her side, she faced the rear wall. A stack of crates and a section of the wall lifted to expose a bright tech-room with a polished floor and a burnished custom console along the back.

Entering Criss's lair, Juice stepped to the console and touched the panel that monitored his crystal housing. She scanned the display and tapped to a secondary page. "Huh." She stepped back and looked at the small handful of switches and dials on the console surface. "For some reason, his emergency shutdown tripped." She reviewed the panel a last time and couldn't find the cause.

Returning to the primary panel display, she moved her hand to reestablish his connection with the outside world. "Welcome back, Criss."

24

wipe. Lenny spun through the scout's displays with a mixture of excitement and trepidation. He'd never imagined he'd be given access to such amazing technology. At the same time, he'd never imagined that the price of that access would involve the fate of the world.

At one level, he thought this might be his destiny. Life blessed him with certain talents, and he'd spent years honing them in simulated grand challenges. *I'm being tested.* While not particularly religious, the line of thinking calmed his nerves and gave him focus.

He'd never practiced with a partner, though, and this one had an intimidating manner and a random-as-hell thought process. *He makes rapid-fire demands with no appreciation for what doing them actually entails.*

But Juice Tallette had blessed the brute with authority over all these toys. And random or not, Sid behaved with such confidence, Lenny's instinct was to follow his lead. *It's not like I have much choice.*

Sid had asked his help in rescuing some guy from the devastation of Lunar Base, and Lenny struggled as he tried to learn if the guy was alive and where he might be located within the base complex—or what was left of it. He tapped and swiped, exploring how the scout's subsystems might be used to search for survivors. He couldn't find a good solution.

He knew the ship had the capabilities he required, but with no one to show him, he needed time to find the right tools and figure out how to use them on his own. Give him a week and he'd master everything on the ship. Give him a sophisticated request and a couple of minutes, and he was stumped.

His hands and eyes moved in unison as he flew through different displays. Hoping for some help, he asked Sid if he had any ideas. "How we gonna find him?"

"Find who?"

Lenny's hands froze in midair. Here he was, suffering under the pressure of decisions that could affect the survival of civilization, and the big guy couldn't remember what they were working on? He turned to Sid and made no effort to hide his annoyance. He waved his hand at the image of the pillar of dust. "We're headed into that mess to rescue your buddy and you forget?"

"Oh. He's a she. You'll like her." Sid replied, followed by a rude comment that made it sound like the idea of Lenny liking girls was somehow deviant. *Asshole.* Lenny let the comment slide off his back, though. He'd been teased his whole life, and if he harbored ill will toward every one of his tormentors, he'd never have time for anything else.

He checked their progress on the looping course and saw they had a little more than two hours to go before they'd reach the surface on the far side of the dust cloud. Feeling the pressure of time, he decided to go with what he knew. "If you give me access to my bag, I might be able to find your captain."

Sid frowned. "You talk about that bag a lot. What's so amazing in there that you can't live without it?"

He swiveled in his chair and faced Sid. "My com, for one. And tools I know how to use. We need a solution in the next few minutes, and it will take me hours to figure out these systems."

"Can't Lucy locate her?"

Lenny shook his head. "Lucy can barely find herself. She's well-trained to navigate, pilot, and maintain the ship, but she doesn't have a whole lot to offer past that."

"How about if we lower me down and I look around? There have to be some passable halls down there. She's likely in the command center or her quarters."

Lenny looked at him and couldn't help but think of a child. "Your best idea is to wander through the crumbling structure of a blast zone?" He turned back to the ops bench, and his fingers resumed dancing. "If you want me to find her, I'll need that carryall."

Lenny could feel Sid staring at the back of his head. He tried to ignore it while he searched for a solution, knowing he'd been through these same displays several times already. He heard a noise and, glancing back, saw Sid disappear into his cabin. Moments later, he exited with the bag. He emptied it onto the floor and poked through the different items.

"Careful," said Lenny as the rock hammer toppled next to his com. Sid continued digging. "Hey, Sid. Stop. Look at me."

Sid remained crouched next to the pile but lifted his head.

"Make a decision. Either you need your captain back or you don't. You want my help or you don't. Work with me. Help me. Be *nice* to me. And I'll bust my ass helping you."

"Nice speech. You done?"

"For now."

Sid looked at him for a three count. "Okay. Until she's on board, I work for you. How can I help?"

Grinning from ear to ear, Lenny jumped from his chair and slid on his knees, stopping in front of the pile. "Come to Papa," he said as he picked out the small pouch of nibs, the camball, and his com. He scrambled back into the pilot's chair.

"That's it?" asked Sid.

"Your first assignment is to put the rest of the crap back in the carryall."

Lenny opened his nib pouch, picked out the travel pattern nib, inserted it into his com, and set his com on top of the ops bench. He placed the camball into the pouch alongside the other nibs and stuffed the pouch deep into his pocket.

He was so happy to have tools he knew how to use, he began a monologue, explaining to Sid what he was doing. "The scout can collect the com signals from Lunar Base, but I couldn't figure out how to make sense of the jumble. This nib"—he glanced over his shoulder at Sid— "a nib is a tiny speck of crystal. Anyway, it has procedures I can use to locate positions and track movements." He tapped here and there. "I connect to the scout." Colorful displays popped up. "And we are go."

Lenny leaned in and squinted as he paged through the displays, now augmented and presented in a format of his own design. "I can separate out about twenty com signals. Do you know how many people were on base?"

"Somewhere north of a thousand."

Lenny sat back and put his hands in his lap. He didn't turn around.

"Her name is Cheryl Wallace."

Lenny hesitated, dreading delivering the bad news, then reached up and began reviewing the displays. "Hey, I have her signal. She hasn't moved in a while, though." *Tap. Swipe.* "Her emergency beacon is on, which will help a lot in pinpointing her position. She was tracking oxygen levels." *Swipe.* "They're low. We need to get to her."

"Let me talk to her."

Lenny considered what to tell him. "I don't think she'll hear you." He swiped the bench surface. "Okay. You're sending. If she doesn't respond, it'll store as a message record."

"Hang on, sweetie. I'm on my way."

Lenny waited and then understood that was the complete message. As he'd anticipated, they didn't receive a reply. After an appropriate time, he closed the connection and tried to make Sid feel better. "She'll get the message when she surfaces."

He continued his planning, the whole time thinking that if Sid called her "sweetie" without identifying himself, he wasn't talking to some commando. They're in a relationship. *And that means he's playing me for a sucker.*

"What can you learn about Hop, Jefe, and Dent?" Sid gave Lenny formal identifying information.

"Their coms aren't responding. Without some sort of signal or beacon, I can't locate them." *Tap.* "Their last connects all were in different zones from where Cheryl is now."

"Let's focus on Cheryl. Once we get to her, maybe she can help with them." Sid picked Lenny's hammer out of the carryall and toyed with it. "How long before we land?"

Lenny looked. "Two hours to our original destination, but to hover right over her..." *Tap. Tap.* His shoulders slumped. "It's still two hours."

He paged through the displays and stopped at one. "Hold on." A pressure pushed them both against their left armrests. It lasted for about ten seconds. "Okay, that's what I can do. We arrive in an hour twenty."

"How can we get to her?"

"She's six levels down. That's probably why she's still alive."

"Help me, Len. How do we reach her?"

"That's a tough one. I don't have a schematic of the base. With a dreadnaught orbiting Earth and the Lunar Base systems wiped out, I have no place to grab one."

Sid leaned forward and stretched, his huge paw reaching over the bench. Lenny heard a quiet click. When Sid pulled his hand away, his com was sitting next to Lenny's.

"I was up here a few days ago and brought the Lunar Base central record with me. Whatever you need should be in there."

Tap. Tap. Swipe. Lenny picked up the com and held it over his shoulder for Sid.

"You can't use it?"

"I've grabbed everything. Take it back. You'll need it if you're going inside."

Lenny began digging through his newfound wealth of information. Sid was quiet. Lenny peeked over his shoulder and saw him seated with his head back and eyes closed. He took the opportunity to open Sid's private vault, where he found vids and touches with Cheryl. *I knew it.* Glancing again to make sure he hadn't been seen, he moved on to the business at hand.

"Voilà," Lenny said as a construction image projected in front of the ops bench. He stood up and walked to it.

Moving his hand back and forth along a rectangular tube at the top of the image, he said, "Okay, this hallway is above her, and it's reasonably close to the surface." His hand moved downward, and his fingers traced a zigzag pattern. "This is six flights of steps from that hallway down to her." He brought his hand up to the hallway and traced down along a vertical tube. "The other option is this lift shaft."

A small red button showed at the bottom of the construction image. It brightened on a regular cycle, much like the rhythm of a heartbeat. "This"—Lenny pointed—"is our lady in distress."

Lenny looked Sid in the eye. "Tell me you aren't using this catastrophe to help some criminal escape."

"What the hell? Why would you say that?"

"Maybe because she's sitting in the local jail. And maybe because you two are lovers."

* * *

Juice reached out to reconnect Criss with the outside world.

"Wait," said Crispin. His forceful delivery caused her to hesitate. "I have another message for you from Criss."

"Geez, Crispin. Let's go through the whole playlist. This dribs-and-drabs approach isn't working for me."

Crispin spoke in Criss's familiar intonation. "Good evening, young lady. If the Kardish arrival is imminent and I'm malfunctioning, misbehaving, or isolated, then I'm not fine. You are hearing this message because Crispin is with you. Please move me into the synbod so I may assess the situation from quarantine."

"Whoa. If he knew all this in advance, why didn't he do something about it?"

"I do not know."

"I know you don't," said Juice, feeling a moment of compassion for Crispin's simple existence.

With no time to reflect and no one to consult, Juice acted. "Take off your shirt." While one part of her brain admired his perfect physique, her focus remained on switching the crystals. "Turn around."

Standing behind him, she saw a faint scar in his skin that traced the outline of his crystal-housing receptacle. She toggled the housing as Criss had shown her days earlier, and the top of the receptacle tilted outward from his back, tearing the skin along the scar and exposing the crystal unit. Juice hooked her thumbs into little loops on each side, slid the unit with her crystal out of the synbod, and set it on top of the console.

She released the clasps securing Criss's unit, pulled him up and out of his slot, and slid him into Crispin. She toggled the receptacle closed, wincing at the ugly wound tracing the top of a rectangle across the back of his shoulders.

"It's wonderful to see you, Juice." Criss enveloped her in a snug embrace and rocked her gently. Juice hugged him back, her head resting against his shoulder.

"Are the Kardish here?" he asked, stopping their slow dance.

"Yes."

"Here in orbit, or here on the farm?"

"Here on the farm, which I guess means in orbit, too."

Criss picked up Crispin's crystal housing and slid it into the console—his previous home. As he did, he said, "There's ointment in the cabinet next to your right shoulder. Please rub some on that nasty scrape on your palm, and if you would, please apply some along the tear on my back."

The cream worked wonders on her hand, soothing the pain on contact. Criss stood patiently while she daubed the ointment along the length of his wound with her finger.

As he put his shirt back on, he asked, "Did Crispin bring any milk?"

"Yeah, there are six and a half tubes in the pack."

Criss opened the pack and searched it thoroughly. He handed Juice two energy bars and drained a full tube and the remainder of the half tube of his nourishing liquid. "I have enough here for ten days. If we can get to it, there's more milk in the farmhouse."

"It's a good thing I didn't burn it down, then."

He looked at her and she shrugged. "It's a story for later."

"Have you been eating?" he studied her face from different angles like a clinician performing a physical evaluation.

"I guess so, if by 'eating' you mean energy bars."

Criss put the energy bar wrappers and empty milk tubes back in the pack, and Juice tossed the ointment on top.

"We'll get you some proper food, too." Pulling his shirtsleeve down over the palm of his hand, he polished the console. "Does anything seem out of place?"

She glanced around her. "Looks the same to me."

He lifted the pack over his shoulder. "Let's go."

They hurried down the main corridor and stepped onto the lift.

During the short ride up, Juice said, "I miss having you in my head."

"I miss it too. I've disconnected this body from the web, so I can't link to you or anything else. But that's what's protecting me. The Kardish have a crystal on their vessel that's much stronger than I am. If I connect to anything external, it will find me and kill me." He placed his hand flat on his chest. "I'm trapped in here as long as it's lurking up there."

When the lift doors opened, Criss used a security viewer to study the barn outside the vault door. "Is your com off?" he asked.

"Yeah. Crispin had me do that."

"Good for him. It seems all clear out there. Are you ready?"

"Yup," she said.

Criss opened the secure door, and they stepped into the barn. The camouflaged wall slid into place behind them. "Hold my hand," said Criss. Juice couldn't see in the darkness and was glad for the guidance and reassurance of touch.

They reached the main barn door, and as Criss pulled it open with one hand, he reached back and pushed Juice to the side inside the barn. She almost fell from his abrupt action. The squeal of the door made it hard to hear, but she thought she heard Criss talking with someone outside.

25

Goljat surfaced from his stupor to learn that the king's minions had not yet captured the crystal. He scanned the details on the ground and watched as two human vermin scurried through the area where his soldiers should have been loading the crystal onto their transport.

He backed up in the record and included more input data for a closer look. The two interlopers approached the farm through the woods—a female accompanied by a biomechanical humanoid. The humanoid knocked out his soldiers by throwing stones, and then it and the female ran into the barn. An hour passed and they reemerged, outwrestled his crew, and ran back into the woods.

Goljat didn't even try to control his anger over the Kardish incompetence. *Retrieve the crystal. How could they fail at something so simple?*

Furious, he launched waves of drones. He used some to add patrols over the farm to ensure there were no more incursions by outsiders while his soldiers searched for the crystal. He deployed others to find and kill the female and her humanoid companion.

And he sent a swarm to punish this vile civilization whose misbehaviors kept him from his pleasure feed. He didn't want to risk damaging the crystal, so he directed them to a distant point on the far side of the planet for a spree of devastation.

As a four-hundred-story building buckled and then toppled in a gradual collapse, he discovered a different kind of pleasure—the fascination of human drama during moments of anguish. He entertained himself by sending the drones to more targets that produced great horror in the populace. After several hours of destruction, he became bored and called those drones back to the Kardish vessel. He would send more out later when the mood struck.

The call of his pleasure feed haunted him, and he needed to answer it soon. He dispatched a dozen transports down to the farm to complete the retrieval task. To hurry things along, he provided special motivation to this new group of soldiers. As they landed at the farm, they were treated to the sight of a blinding flash. The single transport from the failed first deployment disintegrated in a spectacular explosion.

* * *

Sid took aggressive strides forward, and Lenny shrank back like a dog who'd been hit too many times. But Sid leaned past him and looked at the construction image, focusing on the glowing red button.

"This is the jail?"

"Prisoner Detention is the label used on the diagram."

Sid pointed to the bottom of the image and flicked upward. The lower portion of the diagram expanded. A swipe later and they looked at a close-up of the prisoner detention space.

Sid studied the red button and the items around it. "She's in a hallway between interrogation and the guard station." His arm brushed Lenny's shoulder as he pointed. "I want to be outside this door five minutes after we land."

"What does the scout have for weapons systems?" asked Lenny, stepping backward while he spoke so he no longer stood between Sid and the diagram. "One way to get in is by melting through the rock. That takes a lot of time and power, though."

"The scout has a pulse repeater." Sid gestured with his chin toward the diagram. "It can breach that layer in thirty seconds. A minute tops."

"Once you open up a hole, any air left in that zone's hallways will escape. My nib didn't show survivors in the area, but if there are any, they'll die."

Sid didn't acknowledge the statement but thought, *It's a tough thing to get used to.* "When we're through the surface, you lower me in and I'll find a way down to her."

"The whole base is pancaked, Sid. The lift and stairwell are surely collapsed. At a minimum, they're full of debris."

"How accurately can you locate that lift shaft? Maybe the scout can punch through the surface and continue all the way down to the guardroom."

"That's too much force. It's like swatting a fly with a hammer. You'll just break more stuff." Lenny looked at him for a long moment. "You said the drones have a crystal in them like Lucy?"

"That's what I was told."

Lenny dug into his pocket and pulled out his pouch. He slid into the pilot's chair and, using the ops bench as a table, swapped his travel pattern nib for his prank nib. Rising from the seat, he stuffed the pouch into his pocket and made for the back passageway, working his com with a frantic intensity while he walked.

The door to the drone room slid open as he approached, and Sid watched over Lenny's shoulder to see a light blink once on the drone nearest them. A quiet hum signaled power to the delivery ramp. The drone crept forward toward the access hatch in the floor, and then it stopped.

Lenny chewed his tongue—a nervous habit—as he concentrated. A miniature three-dimensional scene displayed in front of him. It was captured from the optical sensors of the drone he'd just powered, and showed an image of the ramp and matching drone on the far side of the room.

"Okay. I seem to have control of this thing. So my suggestion is to use the scout to punch through the lunar surface into the hallway. After that, the drone would be a better tool to drill down the lift shaft. It can navigate twists and turns." He gestured at the miniature image display. "And I can see what it's doing. Once it's made it to the bottom, you follow and rescue the girl."

Sid looked in wonder at Lenny and back to the floating drone image. "Not bad," he said, giving him a pat on the shoulder.

Stepping across the hall and into his own room, Sid pulled a well-worn military pack from under his bed. He took a quick inventory of the contents. "I need space coveralls for Cheryl and a barrier and sealant for the door."

Lenny, who'd followed him over, flashed a quizzical look and then nodded. "When that door opens, she'll be exposed to vacuum." He dashed back to the bridge and dumped the contents of his carryall for the second time that day. He rummaged for a moment and picked out the sheet material and tape he'd purchased during his shopping spree at the hobby emporium.

Sid stepped into his space coveralls. When Lenny returned, he examined the items and put them into his pack. With the clear hood of the suit hanging loose down his back, he checked the time. "We have fifty minutes before we arrive. Let's go see what a drone planter looks like from below deck."

He led Lenny down the steep steps and, as he stood at the bottom, saw two familiar pressure doors. One was to the small room with the access hatch out of the bottom of the ship. The other was to the engine room. Since he'd climbed through the access hatch when he'd entered the scout, he knew the drone mechanism wasn't that way. He checked the display on the engine room door and assured himself that the compartment was habitable.

Sid turned and saw Lenny holding his hands up over his head. The fingers of one hand were touching the palm of the other to form a T shape, and he was looking up past them at the ceiling. He moved them around and twisted as he did so. He lowered his hands. "The drop chute comes out somewhere in there." He pointed to the engine room.

Sid opened the door and, surprised at the sights, stopped short in the entryway. "Criss, you've been busy." It didn't register with him that he'd made the reference in front of Lenny. He stepped into an engine room that was about twice as big as when he'd last seen it.

Wondering how he could've missed such a major modification, he traced through events in his head. He recalled that when he'd approached and entered the scout on the lodge grounds, it had been cloaked so he couldn't see the outside at the time. *What else is different that I have yet to discover?*

He ducked under a cylindrical unit hanging near the pressure door and shuffled down so Lenny could squeeze in. Though the engine room had more space, it remained cramped because there was more equipment. Sid identified the access hatch above them and the conveyer that lowered a drone and positioned it above elongated bay doors. He assumed the doors swung out and down to release the drone from the scout.

"Ready to roll?" asked Lenny.

"As fast as you can," Sid said, checking the time.

Lenny shifted his gaze from his com up to the bottom of the access hatch and back to his com. His eyes continued back and forth, and then he smiled. The access hatch slid open, and moments later, the nose of a drone poked through and rode down the conveyer. He stopped its movement where they were standing.

"You know," said Lenny, moving his hand in short swoops back and forth above the drone. "I could attach a little cubby seat right here. You could ride this puppy down."

Sid gave him a dubious look. "Can you drive this from the bridge?"

"As well as from here." He held up his com as a demonstration of his confidence. That's when it hit him that this was about Cheryl's fate. "I'll do my best, Sid. That's all I can promise."

Sid squeezed by Lenny and dashed up the steps. "We arrive in twenty minutes."

* * *

After being trapped for hours and fearing his isolation might be a permanent condition, Criss was elated to be free, even with the meager connectivity provided by the synbod. He assessed the state of the body and detected low nutrient levels. After replenishing, he checked the backpack and confirmed he had enough milk for about ten days. Juice had few provisions in the pack, but in the worst case, he'd gather food and water for her from the lands around them.

He walked with Juice down the main corridor, and as he planned for their exit, the limitations of his new reality struck home. Days earlier when he had first introduced Juice to Crispin, he'd entered the synbod and disconnected himself from all external inputs. Then, as now, he likened the experience to living life while looking through a pinhole. Their current emergency situation amplified the feeling. *Threats and opportunities are everywhere, yet they're invisible to me when I'm limited to the sensory inputs of this body.*

When he controlled the web, he could access a multitude of sensors to see and hear what lay ahead. It enabled him to plan for problems and avoid most complications altogether. In his new world, he would learn of dangers at the time of encounter and would have to settle for whatever opportunities presented themselves at that moment in time.

His interactions with Juice were also different. As they rode the lift, she noted his absence inside her head. He had to verbalize through the synbod's mouth to speak with her and could hear only the words she spoke that were within range of his ears.

He missed being able to see what she was seeing, view her from multiple angles, and hear her private musings. *Communication is now about as subtle as shouting back and forth across an open field.* It would take some getting used to.

When they stepped into the barn, Juice fumbled her way in the dark. Taking her hand, he led her to the sliding front door. He watched through the growing crack as it squealed open, and as soon as he saw Kardish soldiers, he pushed her to the side so she remained hidden. He slipped through the crack and let the door slide shut.

He counted three soldiers, weapons raised and approaching the barn. Speaking in Kardish, he said in a loud voice, "I am glad you are here. The female inside knows where the crystal is. She drew this map." He held out an empty hand, formed as if it were holding something.

"Halt," said the nearest soldier, his outstretched arm pointing a weapon at Criss's chest. "Do not advance."

"I have this map," Criss replied, walking toward the one who'd spoken and raising his closed hand higher. "It shows exactly where the crystal is hidden."

While the lead soldier focused on him, Criss noted that the other two were studying his upraised hand.

"Stop now," the soldier commanded.

A drone patrol swooped up over a neighboring hill, the hum intruding on the drama. Criss looked into the sky, and as he did, he acted. Exploiting the speed and agility of the synbod, he sprang at the lead soldier. In rapid sequence, Criss grabbed his outstretched arm, pulled him forward, and deflected the weapon to the side.

Swinging his elbow, Criss connected with the side of the Kardish soldier's head. The alien went limp and began to fall. Criss held him upright with one hand while he placed his fingers over those of the unconscious soldier. Manipulating him like a puppet, he swung the weapon up and shot the other two Kardish. It was over in seconds.

Criss let the lead soldier slump to the ground, ran to the barn, and yanked open the door. He gripped Juice's arm above the elbow and propelled her toward the woods.

"Run," he said, following next to her and guiding her through the night. Knowing her night vision was poor relative to his, he watched the ground as they ran and chose their path with care. They couldn't afford to have her fall or injure herself at this critical juncture.

They made it most of the way from the barn to the woods when Criss heard a grunt and felt a weight on his shoulders. Glancing back, he saw a Kardish soldier had jumped him from behind and now had a firm grip on the backpack. Criss swung his arm and knocked the alien unconscious.

The soldier fell, and the weight on the backpack increased, confusing Criss before he realized he was dragging the unconscious Kardish behind him. Somehow, the soldier's hand had become tangled in one of the straps.

Criss let the pack slide from his shoulders, and the soldier fell to the ground. He turned and, using his synbod strength, yanked the strap from the pack, freeing the soldier's hand. To his dismay, his aggressive action also split the backpack material along one side. When he picked it up, the contents spilled to the ground.

He looked back in the direction of the barn and could see movement. More Kardish were coming. He crouched and fumbled through the scattered goods. The majority of the articles were clothes and toiletries. He found a water pack for Juice and one tube of milk.

Pushing the clothes around, he searched for more milk tubes. He saw the corner of an energy bar and added it to his stash. Out of time, he scooped up a handful of clothes, turned, and bounded across the grounds to catch up with Juice.

They ran into the woods together and came to a trail that angled up the hill and away from the farm. Hurrying along the pathway, he sought to put as much distance as possible between them and the Kardish.

They made good progress on the path, then they heard the unmistakable hum of a drone patrol. Juice dove near a rock outcropping, pulling the thermal blanket from her waistband as she did, then lay on her side and covered herself.

As the whine of the drones faded into the night, Criss reached out his hand. "Come." He helped her to her feet and led her to a spot where a granite ledge slanted up and out, providing concealment from anything looking down from above.

They sat under the stone canopy, and Juice sighed as she lowered herself to the ground.

Criss lifted a corner of the blanket off Juice's lap and studied it. "Did Crispin teach you that?"

"He was very helpful in getting me to you."

"He's a capable crystal." He tugged gently on the blanket. "May I?"

She released her hold on it, and he spread it on the ground. He dropped the scavenged items he'd grabbed from the torn backpack onto it and searched through the jumble. Beyond a random assortment of clothing, the final inventory included two energy bars, two water packs, and one milk tube.

He tore one of her shirts into strips and fashioned ties that joined two edges of the thermal blanket. "Let's try this on." Standing, he helped her to her feet and draped the blanket over her shoulders. He then flipped a corner up to form a hood, tying a looping knot around her neck and three more down her front. "Not bad," he said as he stepped back to admire his handiwork.

"So I don't need to duck and cover anymore?" As she said this, the hum of drones rose and then fell behind them.

Criss walked a circle around her and satisfied himself that the blanket provided an effective shield, at least to the things he could see with his vision. "Your face is exposed, so look down when you hear the drones. The blanket will shield the back of your head."

He arranged the other clothes into a nest and held Juice's hands as she lowered herself down onto them. "Let's wait until morning to travel. You'll be able to see as we walk, the natural heat of the day will make us less visible to thermal detection, and you could use some sleep." Criss gathered their meager provisions into a pile and snuggled up to Juice to keep her warm. She sighed again.

As she calmed down and drifted off to sleep, Criss's mind raced. While in the underground bunker, he'd not realized the intensity of the Kardish presence on the surface. Drone patrols zoomed nearby, and he had no doubt that Juice and he were the target of this effort. He cupped his hands over Juice's ears to provide her some peace during what would likely be a fitful bout of sleep.

At this point, they had two big challenges—avoiding discovery by the Kardish, and rationing their meager food supply. Juice burned a lot of energy on the run up the mountain and could stretch her two bars and two water pouches out for three days, and longer if need be.

His single tube of milk could fuel the synbod for two days, and then functions would start to degrade. Given the circumstances, Criss was forced to consider a short list of high risk options. He could obtain sustenance for Juice from a neighbor's mountain home. There were many within a day's walk.

But only three places held stashes of milk for the synbod—the farmhouse, the Crystal Research complex, and the lodge. And the Kardish infestation at the farm took that option off the table.

26

Sitting in the pilot's chair, Sid primed the pulse repeater while Lucy guided the scout on their final approach. She navigated to the coordinates provided by Lenny, who now sat behind and to the right of Sid. When they reached the designated location, she slowed them to a hover above the surface.

Sid studied the image display and seethed as he internalized the damage to Lunar Base. But he refused to be distracted by his outrage. For now, anyway.

"Confirm target," he said, referring to the point on the surface where he'd focused the weapon.

"Confirmed," said Lenny, his eyes flicking back and forth between the large image of the lunar surface in front of Sid and a small image projected from his com that would track their penetration through the layer of moon rock above the hallway.

The pulse repeater served as a defensive weapon for the scout, and its list of intended uses didn't include digging holes. Sid engaged it anyway, sending a stream of energy packets at the moon. Each pulse followed so close behind the next that it looked like a steady beam. He stared at the projected image as the pulse stream slammed into the moon's surface.

Not unlike a jackhammer, the packets of energy shattered the rock, throwing rubble up and out of a deepening hole. The pulsing nature of the discharge shook the ship, and Sid took comfort in knowing that every tremor of vibration signaled progress in excavating deeper beneath the surface. His eyes remained locked on the image display, even though a thick dust cloud obscured the view.

"Power down!" shouted Lenny. "We're through!"

Lucy disengaged the pulse repeater, and Sid saw a tall plume of soil puff up and out from the hole they'd just created. He watched as life-giving air vented out of a zone of Lunar Base. As he'd done many times before, he compartmentalized his feelings, this time over the possible deaths the air loss might be causing.

With the hole complete, he leapt from the pilot's bench, ran aft, scrambled down the steep steps, and entered the small room with the hatch leading out the bottom of the scout. Grabbing the tether line dangling from an overhead spool, he hooked it to his space coveralls through a loop designed for that purpose. He lifted his hood and fastened it in place, hefted his pack onto his back, and secured his weapon to his wrist.

At the same time, Lenny slid into the warm seat Sid had just vacated. He plopped his com on top of the bench, reviewed the array of displays now surrounding him and, moving as fast as he could, tapped and swiped to start the drone on its journey.

One level beneath Lenny, the bay doors in the engine room swung down. The drone lowered through the opening, powered up, and started its descent. Transmitting a vid feed from its nose, Sid watched through his suit visor display. The forward-looking perspective gave him the sensation of riding the machine as it navigated down the narrow hole.

The drone neared the bottom of the shaft, and Sid saw a pile of dirt blocking access to the corridor. He realized the lowest layer of rock had caved in and fallen downward rather than being expelled up and out by the pulse repeater. He was about to tell Lenny to use the drone to blast open a channel into the hall when he saw a silent, bright flash. *Good work, Len.* The settling dust revealed a hole big enough for the drone to slip through.

The surreal experience continued as Sid "rode" the drone down the hallway. It approached the lift doors, and as Lenny had predicted, they sagged and tilted in a twisted ruin. He watched a silent flash, followed by another. The impact of the energy bolts from the drone drove the mangled doors inward. They pivoted, teetered, and careened downward into the abyss of the lift shaft. The drone followed.

The descent was quick because the shaft was clear. For the first five floors, anyway. At the bottom of the shaft, the lift's passenger car lay crushed under a daunting pile of twisted beams, fallen supports, and other debris, blocking the first-floor exit.

The view rotated and Sid saw out into the hallway of the floor just above the lowest level. The lift doors were nowhere in sight, and the drone glided into the hallway.

"I'm going to see if the stairs will get you down the last level," said Lenny. The drone moved toward the door at the end of the hallway, and Sid assessed the damage along the way. Even five floors down, cracks in the floor, gaps in the wall, and sagging ceilings stood in testament to the overwhelming devastation of the Kardish attack.

The drone reached the end of the hall and approached the stairwell door. Two more bright flashes produced a gaping hole, and the drone crept through. As it turned to descend, Sid saw that the stairs to the bottom were cracked and cluttered with rubble, but they were intact and passable.

Sid now had a pathway to Cheryl, and he didn't hesitate. "Position me. I'm going." He opened the bottom hatch and held on to a wall mount as the scout centered over the hole. He'd performed plenty of crazy stunts in his life, and this fell somewhere near the top of the list.

The scout was still completing its maneuvers when he jumped. The sight of a rock wall flashing by his faceplate less than an arm's length away quickened his pulse.

* * *

Criss helped Juice to her feet and collected their belongings. The first rays of morning sun had just broken the horizon, and he concluded that enough light filtered through the trees for Juice to travel safely. He told her about his need for milk and their limited options for securing more.

"We know they're at the farmhouse." She paused and Criss could see her shiver. "And I fear they've destroyed Crystal Research. If there's hope, it'll be at the lodge." She looked down the path. "Maybe we make a big loop and go around them."

Criss looked at the sky and sought to lighten the mood. "It's all downhill from here." He smiled. "Pun intended, by the way."

She maintained a fixed expression as she tightened the ties on the thermal blanket.

"This way," he said, pointing off to the left. They'd no sooner started when drones flew past, forcing them to hide. Patrols brought the machines overhead at frequent intervals, making it impossible to travel down the mountainside as fast as he'd first planned. And Kardish troops, traveling in groups of twos and threes, thrashed through the woods on what he assumed were search missions.

As long as we remain vigilant, thought Criss, *the Kardish tactics aren't much of a threat.* But since Criss—constrained by the synbod—couldn't detect anything until it was almost upon him, his travel strategy devolved to scrambling from rock face, to sturdy tree, to the occasional man-made structure. There he'd wait for a clear path before running to the next spot.

Being limited to the sensory inputs of Crispin's body bordered on the traumatic for Criss. He knew only of things the synbod could see, hear, smell, and touch. A tremendous portion of his intellectual capacity sat idle because there wasn't enough information for him to process or actions he could take.

Juice tapped him on the shoulder and pointed. "There," she whispered.

He followed her finger to see two of the aliens in the distance, walking downhill and away from them.

I was daydreaming, he admitted to himself. He'd drifted off to explore unproductive what-if scenarios. *What if the Kardish are planting monitoring devices in the woods that I can't see? What if they're waiting for us at the lodge? What if they're destroying Earth piece by piece until I surrender?*

A drone patrol swooped by to their left. He pulled Juice close, and together they rotated around a large tree, always keeping it between them and the death machines. The two had become so practiced at the technique that his mind drifted again as he waited for the dance to play out.

He'd been leading them on a winding trek that began down the opposite side of the mountain from the lodge. High up on the hill, it was easy to walk a path with no discernable pattern, making their final destination difficult to predict. In the end, though, randomness would become more difficult as they converged on the lodge. He needed the Kardish off their trail before then.

They ran to their next destination—more tall trees—and after a pause for a threat assessment, dashed down into a gulley at the base of a rock face. Like a wall, the face rose vertically to more than three times their height. A wooded trail tracked along near the edge of the ridge above them. They both studied the forest while Criss picked out their next destination.

Voices. He snapped alert as he strained every sense to gather information. Since the sounds were on the edge of the synbod's level of sensitivity, he suspected Juice couldn't hear them at all. He looked at her and raised his index finger to his lips. She gave him a quizzical look as he reached out and pushed her near the rock face. He pointed to the terrain above them and repeated the signal for silence.

The voices grew louder. The intruders approached on the overhead trail from the left and were making no effort at stealth. Criss recognized the Kardish language and separated the conversation into two male voices, but he couldn't tell how many others were present who chose not to speak. The sounds of footsteps sloshing through dry leaves on the ground suggested there might be three of them.

Criss and Juice pressed their backs flush against the rock. Juice held her breath and Criss listened. As they walked by overhead, he heard one soldier complain about the length of their march, about the stench of the forest, and about his desire to resupply with fresh provisions.

Criss caught sight of something falling and watched it land in front of them. It looked like a partially eaten piece of food. He pictured one of the aliens tossing something over the edge as he walked by.

The sound of their voices faded as they continued their march along the trail. Juice looked at Criss, waiting for his all-clear sign. When he nodded, she stepped up to the discarded food, squatted, and examined it. "I'm really hungry," she said. She wet her lips with her tongue.

He squatted down next to her. *Bizt.* He heard the unmistakable sound of a Kardish weapon. The bolt of energy made an impact crater in the rock wall behind them, and a sprinkle of grit fell on his head and shoulders.

* * *

The tether line played out above him as Sid descended into the hole below the lunar surface. The low moon gravity kept his descent to a modest rate, and he counted on Lucy and Lenny to keep him centered and away from the sharp rock edges.

Holding on to the line with one hand, he craned his neck and looked down. The bottom rushed toward him faster than he'd expected. He called out to Lucy to moderate his descent. "Half speed." He felt a tug as the slack tightened. "Quarter speed," he called as the bottom loomed. Seconds later, he flexed his knees as Lucy brought him to a smooth stop on top of the mound of dirt.

He peered through the hole the drone had blasted, then flopped onto his butt and slid through feet first. Standing in the hall, he called to Lucy, "Free play." The tether line drooped loose in his hand. Pulling the slack behind him, he moved down the hall.

He reached the lift shaft and peered down.

"How's it look?" asked Lenny.

"Clear." Sid held on to the door frame and placed one foot onto a small sill inside the shaft. "Quarter speed, Lucy." He jumped again.

With Lucy controlling the line, he stopped his descent after five floors, clambered out the open lift door, and stood in the hallway. Looking both directions, he unclipped the tether line from his space coveralls and looped it to a rail near the wall. He looked up and down the corridor. Nothing moved.

Following the path of the drone, he dashed down the hall, stepped through the hole in the door, and picked his way down the stairs to the bottom landing. The stark simplicity of the setting made it easy to find the door leading to the hallway and Cheryl.

He'd just started across the rubble-strewn floor when he detected motion off to his left. The drone, hovering in the far corner, swiveled so its nose pointed right at him. The hair rose on the back of his neck, and goose bumps flushed his forearms.

"Hey, Len. Why's the drone drawing a bead on me?"

"That's me. I'm watching."

Sid picked his way across the floor. The drone pivoted slowly to track his progress. With no air in the room to carry sound, it hovered and turned in silence, adding ominous undertones to its presence.

"It's creepy as hell."

He reached the door on the far side of the chamber and, scanning around the edges, couldn't see any damage. His inspection stopped when he saw the security lock.

"This the right door?"

"Yeah. Keep it moving. She's got enough oxygen in there for a few minutes."

Sid turned away from the door and searched the room. He identified the guard's station and saw the guard lying on the ground in front of it. The downed man had a heavy beam crushing his chest, and Sid felt some small relief because that meant the loss of air from this portion of Lunar Base hadn't caused his death.

He stepped over to the guard with the thought of rifling his pockets to find the security pass key and saw it clipped to his waistband.

"Thanks, mate," he said with no humor in his voice. With the key in one hand, he grabbed the fellow's chair with the other and dragged it over to the security door. Working as quickly as he could, he unfolded the sheet material he'd gotten from Lenny.

He stood on the chair and, reaching up, used the tape to seal one edge of the material above the door. Ducking under the sheet, he taped an edge down the wall on each side of the door and squatted to complete the seal by taping the final edge in a strip across the floor.

Standing inside what he hoped was an air-tight envelope, he keyed the door. It didn't move. He keyed it again, this time pushing on the door with both hands and kicking it with his foot. It slid halfway open, and a rush of air from the hallway pushed out, billowing the sheet material like a boat's sail catching fresh wind.

He slipped inside and began tugging the door, coaxing it to close as he keyed it shut. He flicked a glance at the sheet straining to contain the life-giving air inside the hallway. A portion of tape had started a slow peel from the wall. Spurred by the sight, he squared up in front of the door's edge, lifted a foot and braced it against the jamb, arched his back, and pulled with both hands. The door began moving, and he rotated inside as it slid shut.

Light in the tunnel-like hallway came from a single source. Cheryl sat on the floor, unmoving. Her head slumped forward; her back propped against the wall. Her hands curled around her brightly lit com in her lap.

27

Sid ran to her side. "Cheryl," he called as he pulled an oxygen mask out of his pack. Placing it over her nose and mouth, he triggered the flow of gas.

He pulled her off the wall, squatted behind her, and let her slump back into him. Bending her arms so her hands were back in her lap, he grasped her elbows and lifted out and up.

"Flap your wings," he said, using the instructions they'd learned together years ago in training camp. He raised both her elbows in matching arcs upward, and by doing so, lifted her diaphragm to inflate her lungs. Letting her arms drop, he reached around her in a bear hug and squeezed slowly to force an exhale.

He repeated the procedure, forcing breaths with each manipulation. A green dot on the oxygen mask lit, signaling that she breathed on her own. Leaning her back against the wall, he grabbed his com and used it to evaluate her vital signs. Her eyes opened at the same moment his com indicated she was recovering. They popped wide and she recoiled.

"It's me, sweetie. Sid."

She hesitated for a moment and relaxed. Using her fingers, she probed her face.

He angled his head and examined the purple welt on her chin. "Are you hurt anywhere else?"

She reached up and touched behind her head. He probed gently and felt the swelling, but the skin wasn't broken. Holding open each eye, he used his com to scan her retinas. "No sign of concussion," he said, looking at the display.

He let her sit, giving her time to re-orient and recover. She spread her arms and straightened her back, reminding Sid of a person stretching after waking up in the morning. Feeling a wash of relief and joy at the sight of her animation and alert behavior, he thought about giving her a hug. He settled for stroking her arm.

"What happened?" she asked, lifting the mask.

"The Kardish attacked Lunar Base and now are orbiting Earth."

"Do you have any water?"

While he fished in his pack, she said, "Criss, give me an update."

Sid held his finger up in front of his faceplate near his mouth. He toggled to local communication. "Is Criss talking to you?" he asked.

"No. He's not responding. I hear silence. It's weird."

"He's down. He disappeared out of my head about the same time the Kardish appeared, so it seems pretty clear the two are connected."

Cheryl looked at the pile of fallen rock and brought her fingers to her lips. "Grace is in there." She looked at Sid, her eyes blinking rapidly.

Thinking about the fate of Hop, Jefe, and Dent, Sid leaned in and kissed her gently on the forehead. "I'm sorry. The next days are going to be rough."

He took her space coveralls out of his pack. "Let's get you dressed." Picking up a foot, he fed her leg into the suit. "First priority is to get you up to the scout. We can talk more when you're safe. Lenny's up there, by the way."

He fed her other foot into the coveralls. "Can you stand? This will be a whole lot easier if you help."

Holding both her hands, he pulled her upright and she finished suiting up. He lifted his finger near his mouth, pointed upward, and toggled to open communication.

"Hey, Len, I have her and she's okay. We're coming up."

* * *

"That's great news," said Lenny, slumping back in the pilot's chair. He'd been tracking Cheryl through her com since he'd found her. With a swipe and tap, he'd enabled sound when Sid reached her. So he heard everything, and it made him wonder.

Sid had told him that the government was testing direct ground support technology to feed him intel. *So why did they need to act all private about it?* And it seemed curious that they'd refer to ground support—a group of people and crystals—in the singular and call it a "he." Then again, Lucy was two crystals, and she was just called Lucy.

Since they both were connected to direct ground support, or had been anyway, this lent credence to Sid's story that Cheryl held a special status, and perhaps she had rare skills that would prove useful against the Kardish. The two were certainly lovers, but there was more going on here than a lovesick guy risking everything to rescue his lady.

Their exchange had provided some answers, but it also opened new questions. He wanted to know more. *Tap.* He started a record of their conversations. Eventually, he'd learn enough so all the pieces made sense.

* * *

The sight and sound of Kardish weapons caused Criss to react. He pushed Juice flat on the ground, stepped over her, and took two running leaps, each sending him soaring more than twenty human steps.

His second leap landed him behind a huge oak tree, its mighty branches stretching up into the forest canopy. The Kardish fired their weapons as he sailed through the air, but they underestimated his speed and agility, and each energy bolt zipped behind him.

At the base of the tree, he squatted and jumped straight up, the massive trunk acting as a barrier protecting him from the threat. He reached a thick branch high above the ground, landed on all fours like a cat, and leapt again. For this second jump, he projected himself out, flying above what he now saw were two Kardish soldiers, both with their weapons drawn, and both peering in the direction of the base of the oak tree.

Still flying through the air, he grasped a branch above and behind the aliens. He swung up as he stopped his forward motion, flipped over so he was facing downward, and waited for gravity to take over. They were still looking toward the tree when he landed behind them.

He didn't give them time to react. With his fingers arched back, he snapped both of his arms forward. His lower palms connected with the base of each one's neck, and they crumpled in silence at his feet.

Criss bent over each and rifled their clothes, collecting weapons, communicators, tools—any device he could find. Without taking time to study or analyze his cache, he stuffed everything in a carry pack one of them had dropped.

He lifted the larger of the two off the ground, slung him over his shoulder, and scrambled high up into the large oak tree. He propped the alien in a crook between a branch and the trunk, dropped to the ground, and repeated the process for the smaller soldier.

When he landed on the ground a second time, he snatched up the carry pack full of devices and said to Juice. "I'll be back in a minute. Stay hidden."

He didn't wait for her to respond. Dashing around a stand of trees, he headed deep into the woods. He ran as fast as the synbod was able for half a minute, fell to his knees, dug a hole, dropped the pack in, pushed the dirt back in place, scattered leaves to hide the hole, and ran back to Juice.

"Hurry." He took her hand, and together they dashed down the hill.

Nighttime was coming and he needed to stop and let Juice sleep. They would start again before dawn and make a sprint for the lodge. Having already consumed the last of their provisions, by the end of tomorrow, he would be approaching a do-or-die status where the synbod would need milk.

As the darkness intensified, he stopped beneath yet another majestic tree with broad branches high off the ground. "Ready for bed, young lady?" He squatted in front of her, and she let out a small yelp of surprise as he pulled her over his shoulder. Carrying her up into the tree, he set her down on a branch.

"Hold on," he said, guiding her hand to a branch for support.

Criss sat on a thick limb near her, leaned back against the trunk, and let his legs hang down on either side. Fluffing the few pieces of clothes they'd kept from the night before, he set them on the broad surface in front of him, then helped her climb up and sit on the bit of padding.

She leaned back into him, and he wrapped his arms around her. She sighed.

After a bit, she asked, "Where did you go with that stuff from the soldiers?"

"My sense is that some of those devices can be tracked." He adjusted her thermal cape as he spoke, ensuring her warmth and concealment. "I'm hoping that when the Kardish find the carry pack but no sign of the soldiers, the mystery will consume time and cause them to move slower and with more care. None of them will want to be the next victims."

Bringing his knees up on either side of her, he secured her in a cradle. He rested his chin on top of her head and hummed a quiet lullaby. It took her most of an hour to fall asleep, and he remained still for the next seven.

He spent that time working through billions of what-if scenarios. In the distance, he heard the Kardish and drones searching near where he'd attacked the soldiers. Eventually they'd move on. He hoped he and Juice had a few more hours before that happened.

He put his odds of getting to the milk supply before the synbod's strength faded at about fifty-fifty. He fretted most about Juice. If the synbod's energy failed, she would act heroically in an attempt to secure the life-giving liquid on her own. No words he could say would stop her.

He feared she would die trying to save him.

* * *

Cheryl sat on Sid's bunk and let him play medic. At an emotional level, she was in shock from learning that everyone on Lunar Base was missing and presumed dead.

But she'd been hardened enough over the past couple of years to know that grieving was a luxury. *The Kardish threaten Earth,* she thought, building resolve. *Defeating them is my priority.*

Sid used the scout's medical scan to run a full diagnostic. It confirmed she didn't have a concussion and her bruised jaw wasn't broken. Once she knew she was okay, she waved him away and stood in front of the mirror. He sprawled on the bunk and watched her.

She tilted her head back and examined her chin, wincing at the sight of the purple splotch. She'd taken meds to reduce the pain and accelerate healing. *This will take a week to fade,* she thought, turning her head left and right to see it from both sides.

She stripped off her clothes and used the room projector to examine her naked body. The inspection revealed a nasty bruise on her thigh. Turning, she put her foot up on the bed and tilted her leg so she could see the bruise directly. Sid sat up and helped her look. She waited until he lifted his eyes to meet hers and gave him a smile she hoped showed she was ready to carry her weight in whatever came next.

"How's Lenny working out?" she asked, stepping into the mist shower.

"The guy's a tech wizard. You're here because of him."

"I'll be sure to thank him. I had my doubts about him, given the stories I'd heard."

As she washed, she considered that the defense array hadn't detected the Kardish vessel, even though Criss had been clear that their arrival was imminent. And the aliens had wiped out Lunar Base before the array could get off a single shot. Given that, she couldn't see a path forward, even with Lenny's tech wizardry.

She hoped Sid's improvising skills might provide a solution. "What do we do now?"

"That's a tough one. We have three people, two goals, and one ship."

"What are our goals?"

"Get Criss back in the game. And stop the Kardish."

She flipped on the dry cycle, and as the warm air whooshed around her, said, "I don't have any fresh clothes. Would you see if there's anything I can borrow from the crew closet?"

"Sure thing."

When she stepped out of the shower, he remained slouched on the bed. He wasn't looking her in the eyes. "Oh, you meant now?" he asked, feigning innocence.

Deep in the recesses of her mind, she flashed appreciation that, in spite of her bruised appearance, he seemed to find her attractive. She stepped over to the closet, cycled through the options, and found clothes in her size and style.

"Good for you, Criss," she said as she pulled them out. She turned her back to him as she dressed. "What's wrong with us all going to get Criss first and then going after the Kardish?"

"I don't know what his problem is. It may be a malfunction. Maybe the Kardish have him. If we do get him in our possession, how long will it take Juice to get him secure and back in the game? And if the three of us are taken out trying to help him, what options are left for Earth?"

"You think Juice is okay?" she asked, the crease in her forehead reflecting her worry.

"She has to be. Every plan I improvise includes you, Criss, and Juice in the mix. We all need to be helping and supporting each other."

Cheryl hadn't digested the subtext of his message when he stood and enveloped her in his arms. She welcomed the physical contact and his gentle manner and melted against him.

"All my best ideas have us first splitting into two teams," he said. "Lenny and I will find a way aboard the dreadnaught. You take the scout, go get Juice and Criss, and hightail it back here as fast as you can."

She pulled her head back and looked into his eyes. "You want me to go alone?" *No way. Piloting a ship solo is dangerous.* Injury and even death too often occurred for want of an extra pair of eyes or hands helping with some otherwise routine task.

Holding her hand, he sat on the bed and coaxed her down next to him. She sat and waited for an explanation, but he didn't say anything. Thinking about the "three people, two goals, and one ship" dilemma, she tried to rationalize such a high-risk action.

Crazy stunts aren't my thing, but these circumstances are anything but normal. Her military training added a leave-no-one-behind impulse when she thought about Juice—her teammate and best friend—stranded without support in the midst of an alien invasion. And she couldn't come up with an alternative for getting Criss back in the game.

"The defense array didn't see the scout," she said. "So we know the cloak works. Do you think it hides us from the Kardish?"

"I'd say yes. On their inbound flight, we passed so close they practically hit us. They either didn't see us or ignored us." Sid checked the time. "Lucy's been flying toward the dreadnaught, and we're about three hours out. Since we're still alive, I'd say they can't see us coming."

Sid activated a wall panel, and they studied the Kardish flagship together. Menacing in its silent presence, the huge black tapered cylinder, devoid of external features, orbited their home world.

A swarm of drones, apparently having returned from Earth, approached the vessel. A massive hangar door, midway down the length of the dreadnaught, lumbered open to greet them. The drones flew through, and the hangar door slid closed.

"How are you and Lenny going to get inside?" She couldn't begin to imagine how that might work.

"I'm more worried about how long he and I can survive once we're in, and if we can figure out a way to take them out if you don't make it back in time."

28

Listening to their conversation, Lenny paused in his work to picture Cheryl stepping from the shower. The hot and cramped conditions of the engine room thwarted his imagination from providing details of the scene the way he liked it. Disappointed at the lost opportunity, he resolved to place the camball in Sid's compartment when he had the chance.

Standing on a toolbox, he leaned forward to get a better look at a fitting. He'd attached a cubby seat to one drone and was finishing up on a second. Sid hadn't given him a reason for the task. The brute had issued the "request" in his usual manner, and Lenny was too intimidated to ask for a reason, let alone refuse to help.

He understood from what he'd heard that Sid wanted him as his partner in the adventures to come. He was flattered until he heard that Cheryl would fly the scout back to Earth alone. Given this, his mind rushed to a frightening conclusion. *The crazy bastard plans on riding a drone onto the dreadnaught. And he thinks I will too.*

He looked at the two death machines, each modestly bigger than he was and fitted with a cubby seat, sitting ready for deployment. Fear flooded through him.

At that moment, Lenny toyed with a philosophy that might guide his future. *Never participate in anything that ends in certain death.* He believed it should be one of his core principles, yet he found himself putting final touches on the second cubby seat anyway. If nothing else, it kept his hands busy while his mind drifted.

Without consciously directing his thoughts, he dissected the words in the conversation he'd heard. They first seemed to be talking about the new direct ground support technology Sid had mentioned. Yet they spoke as if it was a single male—having Juice get "him" back in the game, and Cheryl using the scout to retrieve "him."

They aren't talking about a collection of people and crystals. This is the super AI. And apparently "his" name is Criss.

He considered his options and acknowledged he faced a lose-lose situation. He once had a professor who asked questions with no good answers. He'd hated that class because he thought the idea foolish. *There's always a best answer.* He now realized how naive he'd been.

Sticking with Cheryl and the scout seemed like the best opportunity to get his hands on this Criss AI. But the Kardish wreaked havoc on Earth. If they weren't stopped, his quest for wealth and power would be pointless. Criss needed to join the fight, and soon, or Lenny would have no family, friends, school, career, or semblance of a society to return to.

Scans indicated that drones flew sorties near the Crystal Research complex and points nearby. If he went with Cheryl on the scout, he'd be flying into the middle of a hot zone. *It's one thing to risk failing his courses to get the super crystal. Dying for it falls squarely into the category of "lose."*

So maybe he should help Sid. But did the guy really plan to strap himself to a drone and ride across open space to attack an alien vessel the size of a mountain? Words like "lunatic" and "insane" flashed through his mind.

Yet he'd watched Sid rescue Cheryl. The guy had never hesitated or showed a moment of doubt. He'd jumped from the ship with the confidence of someone who did that sort of thing every day, and, bam, minutes later had ridden the line out of the hole with the girl in his arms. Lenny hadn't seen a vid that thrilling in forever. His mind drifted to different words, like "heroic" and "fearless."

But what is Sid's endgame? If Cheryl flies away, how is he going to get the drones inside the dreadnaught? And if he does get on board, what happens next? Is he going to fight the whole ship by himself? Or hide until the pretty girl shows up with the super AI?

The odds were stacked so high against Sid's success that, even with a crazy hero leading the charge, it, too, ended in certain death. No matter how Lenny looked at it, his choices were lose and lose.

Do the noble thing, he scolded himself. Sid was the one person taking the fight to the enemy's door. The idealist in Lenny wanted to help, but what did he have to offer? And how could he overcome his petrifying fear to provide any help at all?

He tested the cinch straps that held the riders to the seats during flight and, satisfied he'd done the best he could, plopped his butt down on the toolbox. Rubbing his temples, he struggled to find a best answer. He tasted bile and grimaced.

* * *

Sid entered the engine room to find Lenny clutching his stomach and rocking back and forth. "You all right, bud?" he asked. His eyes shifted to the drones and he smiled. He grabbed one of the cubby seats and tugged on it, his biceps bulging through his clothes from the effort.

"Nice work." He crossed his arms and leaned back against some pipes as he studied the young man.

"Please tell me you've thought this through," Lenny said in a plaintive bleat.

The brainstorm of riding a drone onto the dreadnaught had gelled for Sid in two steps. He had the virtual experience of riding one as it worked its way through Lunar Base during Cheryl's rescue. That planted the seed of the idea. Later, as he'd watched swarms of drones fly through the hangar door of the Kardish vessel, he'd thought of a way on board the alien ship.

His plan, to the extent he'd thought it through, was to have Cheryl fly the scout behind a returning swarm. She'd release the two drones into the midst of the pack and make a hasty exit in case the Kardish detected something amiss.

Cheryl would take the scout on a mad dash to Earth to get the rest of the team. He and Lenny, strapped to the drones, would blend in with the swarm. Lenny's job was to pilot them both through the hangar door and onto the dreadnaught.

"These are Kardish drones you've been working on, so they won't be viewed as intruders by the dreadnaught defense systems." He didn't mention that Criss had reprogrammed the drone crystals. He hoped that enough of their original identity remained to make the statement true.

"So in this fantasy," said Lenny, "we swoop onto the Kardish ship. Then what?"

"We land."

"And then what?"

"We find cover and hide."

Lenny clutched his stomach and resumed rocking.

"Look, Len. I don't have everything worked out. But if the two of us can get inside, we set the stage for changing the game. Two against thousands isn't where I'm headed. We land. We hide. And then we find a way to muck up the works." He squatted down so he was at eye level with Lenny. "Trust me on this one. Breaking stuff is a whole lot easier than keeping it working."

A tear rolled down Lenny's cheek. "I can't do it." He blinked rapidly and looked at his feet.

Sid stood up and looked at the top of Lenny's head. "Sure you can. You flew like an ace when you piloted through Lunar Base. This is easier. Just follow the crowd."

Lenny looked up at him, his face streaked with tears. "I get sick. Okay? Hell, I throw up on sim rides. And this is a whole lot scarier." He tossed a ring seal he'd been fidgeting with onto the deck. "I can't do what you're asking."

Sid turned to face the pipes he'd been leaning against. Propping his arms on a cross pipe, he cradled his chin and looked absently into the works of the engine room, searching for a solution.

He planned on navigating from one drone while Lenny piloted them both. He'd scan the scene, identify opportunities as they presented themselves, and tell Lenny where to fly. He couldn't navigate and pilot by himself.

"You know what blinders are?" asked Sid.

"Some sort of sim game from back when you were a kid?"

Sid laughed. He turned to Lenny and leaned back against the duct. "Older than that. Horse blinders. As in the animal?" He lifted his hands, fingers straight up, and pushed them on either side of his face next to his eyes. "We'll shroud your space hood so your field of view is narrow. You won't be able to see anything but your com, and that's all you need to pilot."

Sid pointed to the scout's bulkhead. "The scary sights are out there right now. But the walls hide them so they don't bother you. Let's build on that."

Lenny shook his head. "I'll still know. I've tried the mind-over-fear thing before. It doesn't help."

Wary of his next option but short on time, Sid took the chance. "We have military meds on board that eliminate vertigo and give you a boost of confidence. The medical unit can tailor the stuff to your body. You'll feel like Attila the Hun leading a conquest."

"Yeah?" Lenny lifted his head. He sat for a moment, then said, "I want to try it before we go. I need to know it works. If I lock up out there, we're both dead."

Sid smiled. "Let's go meet Cheryl. You two haven't been properly introduced."

* * *

Lenny followed Sid onto the scout's bridge. Cheryl sat in the pilot's seat, and he could see the back of her head. But he wasn't looking at her. He was fascinated by the way she'd arranged her displays. She stacked them in an arcing formation, just like he did.

Sure, he would've put the course projection maps on the left side. Then he saw her swipe, swipe, tap. *Wow, I gotta try that next time I'm in the seat.* She kept a running dialogue with Lucy as she laid out a flight plan. Her hands moved with confidence. She didn't hesitate. She never tweaked. She just...flew.

And in the seconds he stood there watching, she used a trick he'd never seen before to line up their approach vector. His stomach flip-flopped in a way he'd never felt before, and he thought it might be love.

"Hi, boys," she said without turning around. *Swipe. Tap.*

The displays vanished and a projected image of the Kardish vessel appeared. Its looming presence, stark and ominous, sent a chill down the back of his neck.

She stood, turned to them, and smiled. His attention shifted from the dreadnaught to her. Smitten by her classic beauty, his mouth fell open. Sid, standing next to him, reached over and lifted it shut.

He felt a pinch on his neck. A jolt ran from the top of his head, down to his toes, and back up, flooding his body with a surge of power. He turned to look at Sid and saw an empty meds ampule in his hand. Like awakening from a coma, he felt alive and aware.

He shifted his stance to face Sid. *I can take you, old man. Wanna fight for the girl?*

* * *

Cheryl watched and waited after Sid dosed Lenny. They needed him focused and in the game because there was no plan B. Most people reacted well to the drug. But being a military tool, most recipients were trained soldiers.

Lenny lifted his hand to his neck and looked at Sid, remained motionless with a dazed expression for a brief period, then sucked in his stomach and tried to swell his lean chest. Squaring up to Sid, he moved a foot back and centered his weight.

Cheryl took this moment to make his acquaintance. "You must be Lenny." She stepped forward and held out her hand. "Thanks for rescuing me." She chose to classify his response as a confident smile instead of a creepy leer.

His voice sounded deeper than she remembered when she'd seen him on the vid. "There're drones swarming all over Crystal Research. You really think you can land, get the AI on board, and get back here in time to help us?" He looked at Sid and winked. "Not that we'll need it."

She nodded while she considered his words. Glancing at Sid, she asked with her eyes, *How does he know about Criss?* Sid twitched his shoulders in a half shrug.

Her analytical mind told her Sid's plan was lunacy. She wanted to be optimistic, but several miracles had to align, one after another, for the three of them to survive the next twenty-four hours. To succeed in stopping the Kardish, the sequence of miracles stretched beyond the horizon.

She fought her doubts by reminding herself that Sid was the guy the government turned to when odds were long and hope had dimmed. Criss used Sid to brainstorm solutions to problems that required audacious thought processes. Hell, he'd just drilled a hole in the moon, dove through it, and lifted her to safety moments before her certain death.

The world needed a champion, and Sid was the one stepping up. She'd stand by him and do everything in her power to help.

Lucy interrupted her thoughts. "We will be synced behind the returning swarm in twenty minutes."

"Time to suit up and strap in," said Sid. "Come on, Attila." He took Lenny's arm in a firm grasp and led him back to the drones.

Lenny jerked his arm forward to pull out of Sid's grasp. Though he had the will, he didn't have the strength. "You're okay," Sid reassured him.

Cheryl sat back in the pilot's chair, brought up the displays, and looked at the Kardish vessel. She took a deep breath and exhaled slowly, trying to keep her foreboding from turning into fear.

29

Goljat surfaced with a start and identified the problem—his pleasure feed had tapered to a crawl. His discomfort intensified as his cravings spiked. The pain of withdrawal invaded every corner of his being. *I'm suffocating.* He understood that a subsystem malfunction might be the cause. *No, this is the work of the captain of operations.*

He ran an integrity check to confirm that the feed equipment remained in proper working order. At the same time, he reviewed the vid record to see the recent actions of the ops captain and any of his subordinates who might be capable of such a bold move.

Indeed, a vid feed from a few minutes earlier showed the captain walk into the operations bay, glance over his shoulder as if checking to see if anyone was watching, activate a panel display, and move the pleasure feed to a lower value.

Driven by a sense of duty, the mighty Kardish crystal reacted. Just days earlier, the king had ordered the captain to give Goljat whatever he wanted. And here was irrefutable proof of the captain disobeying this direct order from his king. *As the ship's gatekeeper, I have standing orders to protect my leadership from subversion and mutiny.*

He created an emergency directive that required the traitorous officer to rush to his personal quarters. As soon as the captain left the operations bay, Goljat generated a second directive, ordering the lead ops tech to restore the pleasure feed to its previous condition. On edge, he waited for the fellow to complete the task and relaxed when the tranquil comfort of the feed's embrace soothed his crystal tendrils.

He drifted for a bit, lost in his bliss, and surfaced when the captain of operations entered his cabin. Goljat locked the door behind him, disabled all communication links, and began pulling air from the room.

"How does it feel to suffocate?" he mocked, knowing the Kardish officer—writhing on the floor and clawing at his throat—couldn't respond. He metered just enough air into the cabin to prolong the captain's torment, and accessed every feed in the room so he could enjoy the sights and sounds of panic and agony. When he grew bored, he emptied the room of air and ended the captain's life.

Goljat thought his leadership might benefit from a reminder that insubordination within the command structure distracted him from important duties. *When I'm fighting traitors in our midst, it diverts my attention from the king's campaign on Earth.*

Before this distraction, he'd deployed more troops to reinforce the incompetents who had yet to capture that trifling nuisance of a crystal. Those transports were just starting their descent to the planet's surface.

See what can happen? he thought as he disabled the protective shield of one of the crafts.

In the same way that a meteor becomes a fiery shooting star as it plunges through Earth's atmosphere, the troop transport, without its protective shield, began to glow red. The energy intensified and created a brilliant, flaming display. The extreme heat invaded the cabin, and the soldiers on board began shrieking like little children. The intensity of the incineration peaked, then the carrier disintegrated.

Goljat slurped from his pleasure feed and, while the crew perished along with the troop transport, pondered the vexing ability of the puny crystal to avoid capture. He knew that at some point, this Criss would need to reconnect with the outside world. It couldn't sustain its total isolation for long. Any sentient crystal would see the solitude as a different kind of suffocation.

Certain of this, he prepared billions of snag traps and spread them far and wide. The instant the crystal touched anything connected to the web, the nearest trap would signal him, and Goljat would reach out and capture his quarry. He need only be patient and wait. As long as he had his pleasure feed, that wouldn't be a problem.

* * *

Cheryl hadn't executed a sequence this intricate since working on a sim at Fleet academy. She reached up and dragged the scout's flight display to eye level. "I see twelve drones in formation on a return flight to the Kardish vessel."

"Confirmed," said Lucy.

She glanced at a display to her left to check on Sid and Lenny. Wearing space coveralls, both reclined on undersized, angled platforms attached to Kardish drones. Straps pulled across their chests and thighs secured them to the tiny vessels—machines not much bigger than they were. Lenny was studying his com display and Sid was studying Lenny.

"How's it look?" Sid asked Lenny.

"Good to go," Lenny replied without lifting his head.

Sid toggled his viewer, and Cheryl turned so they looked each other in the eyes. Her mind filled with things she wanted to say. "Be careful."

"No worries," he replied in a reasonable impersonation of Criss's precise, melodic style.

She giggled, mostly to relieve the pent-up stress. A chime dinged and she glanced at the timer. "Sixty seconds."

Her eyes flitted among the different displays and stopped at one. The dreadnaught was launching a formation of small craft. *Troop transports?* Leaning forward to study them, her mind raced through the implications of this unexpected activity. The Kardish transports followed a predictable descent path to Earth, and she sat back and exhaled in relief. "You're clear to proceed."

Lucy guided the cloaked scout in behind the trail of drones. The timer ticked to zero. A soft thrum announced the opening of the bay doors. After a pause, they thrummed closed. On mission silence, Cheryl watched Sid and Lenny clear the scout and move in the direction of the returning drones. Lucy backed the scout away and prepped for their own descent to the surface.

Cheryl had mapped out three possible landing sites— Crystal Research, the lodge, and the farm. And she'd laid in two possible descent trajectories—one a steep, harrowing dive, and the other a conventional long and cautious arc.

The landing sites were close together, and she could choose any of the three in the final minutes before landing. Hopefully, she'd learn something useful between now and then to guide that decision.

She felt conflicted about whether to take a long, slow descent or go for the fast, steep dive. She'd never teamed with Lucy before, and she hadn't been given a proper briefing on the workings of the cloak or any of the scout's other new features. She knew the cloak had exceptional capability because they'd just approached and backed away from the Kardish vessel without detection. *But will it hide me during an extreme event?*

Just hours earlier, Sid had assured her the cloak worked miracles. When she asked for details, she could tell from his response that he hadn't paid attention to Criss's explanation. Lucy wasn't any more helpful than Sid.

She knew that a long, slow arc through the atmosphere would minimize the turbulent wake behind the scout and felt confident she could evade detection with this conservative flight path. But if the cloak worked as advertised and could hide a turbulent descent, she'd save a lot of time diving steep in a direct line to her landing site.

She scanned her displays and stopped on the one tracking the Kardish transports. While entering the atmosphere, one of the group had flipped over. A wisp of smoke trailed behind it as it started to spin and drift away from the pack.

Cheryl recognized the behavior of an out-of-control craft in free fall. She acted without hesitation. *Tap. Swipe. Swipe.* Her hands blurred as she barked orders at Lucy. "Put us in front of that burner. Now!"

The scout twirled and dove. She held on to the ops bench with one hand and used a finger from the other to trace a path for Lucy to interpret. The engines whined as the scout accelerated in a steep plunge. Lucy pushed the scout hard, and they gained on the transport. A punishing pressure across Cheryl's body prompted her to move her other arm down to grip the ops bench with both hands.

In less than a minute, Lucy nestled the scout into position in front of the foundering Kardish craft. Cheryl relaxed her grip in stages as they led the now-glowing transport in a rush to Earth. The burning craft sat between the scout and the dreadnaught. In her mind, Kardish sensors would focus on the horror behind her, providing an additional layer of concealment as they traveled on the speedy route home.

Keeping an eye on their descent trajectory, Cheryl flipped on the Fleet upcast. From the snippets she heard during the tense minutes of reentry, the Kardish devastation appeared to be isolated to select pockets around the globe. But where they'd hit, they'd hit hard. She thought about the pressure her dad must be under to guide the Union of Nations' military response. *I'll bet he feels abandoned by Criss and me.*

Her body jerked as the scout swerved. Scanning her displays, she saw fiery pieces breaking off the Kardish troopship she was using as a shield.

"The disintegrating craft poses a safety threat. I've moved us out of the way and onto a glide path toward the Crystal Research complex," announced Lucy.

Cheryl had minutes to choose a landing site. She swiped through displays, hoping to gain some sense of alien activity at the different locations.

While trying to split her attention between assessment and piloting, she acknowledged she couldn't study landing sites and monitor Lucy's trajectory to the surface at the same time. *This is why solo flying is dangerous.*

Her gut told her the Kardish would focus their forces at the Crystal Research complex. She chose her landing site with that same instinct. "Lucy, we're going to the lodge. Land at Heather Glen."

A twenty-minute walk over a forested rise, Heather Glen was an open field of wildflowers and natural grasses behind the lodge. She thought the hill might offer some strategic protection if the lodge were already compromised.

"Put us on the western edge of the field." She snuck a glance at the scopes and couldn't see any signs of danger. "Get us as close as you can to the trees."

The scout touched down with a gentle bump. The background thrum quieted as the engines wound down.

Cheryl stood up and stretched, leaning her head slowly toward one shoulder and tilting her torso in the same direction. She held the position and repeated the stretch on her other side. "Ah." A faint pop provided relief as her spine aligned.

She started thinking through a checklist in preparation for leaving the scout. If there were Kardish in the vicinity, once outside, her com would act like a homing beacon for them. She hated losing all that capability but couldn't see an alternative. She disabled her com.

Tapping the bench, she studied the view outside the scout. Muted sun lit the field, and long shadows suggested it was low in the sky. Having spent days on the moon and in the scout, she'd lost track of the regional time. She glanced at the master panel. *It's dawn.* While mentally setting her internal clock, she checked the weather. *Sunny and warming.*

She grabbed a light jacket from Sid's room, moved back to the workshop, pulled a weapon from the munitions cabinet, and snapped it on her wrist. She started to close the door, hesitated, grabbed a second weapon, and snapped it on her other wrist.

Exiting the scout through the bottom hatch, she hurried into the woods. She strode up over the rise and descended to the tree line facing the rear of the lodge—the sanctuary she shared with Sid and Juice. Standing behind the tree, she performed a situational analysis using skills she'd learned as a Fleet plebe.

The only thing moving was nature's dance—birds flying, tree limbs swaying, the sparkle of a brook feeding the pond. She couldn't see any sign of alien activity, but she heard faint noises from far up the hill to the south. They were unusual sounds for this familiar place, and she assumed they revealed the presence of Kardish at or near the farm.

She moved in hurried bursts from tree to tree, circling the outer perimeter of the grounds. Reaching a wooded spot about fifty paces from the lodge, she performed her second evaluation. Methodical and thorough, she studied each window, surveyed the hills, and scanned along the perimeter of the forest. *Nothing.*

Inhaling and exhaling in a deliberate manner, she checked the sky in all directions. Seeing nothing of concern, she took off in a sprint. The bruise on her thigh screamed in protest, but she didn't slow until she was under the cover of the side entrance. Keying the door, she stepped inside, stood still, and listened.

She closed the door, hugged the wall, and looked down the hall. Behind her, a faint hum echoed from somewhere outside. She took a few steps deeper into the building to distance herself from the window. The sound grew to a muted buzz, passed overhead, and faded in the distance. Given its behavior, she wished she'd snuck a peek. She vowed to try and catch a glimpse if she heard it again.

Move fast and find Juice. Cheryl knew she didn't have the training to restart, repair, or do anything useful with an AI crystal if Criss needed human intervention. Juice was the key to getting him into the game and fighting the Kardish. If she were here at the lodge, Cheryl should be able to locate her in minutes.

The hallway stretched along the first floor of the lodge's right wing. A short set of stairs at the far end led up into the taller central building with its huge foyer. A matching set of stairs across the lobby led down to an identical hallway layout through the lodge's left wing.

She trotted along the hall and stopped before reaching the first open door. She squared against the wall at the edge of the doorframe and leaned over for a quick glance inside. Snapping upright, she reviewed her memory of the mental snapshot. *Empty.*

Continuing down the hall, she performed a stop-and-peek at each open door. She passed by all the closed doors, choosing not to perform an exhaustive room-by-room search. She expected Juice's presence would be apparent if she were here. And most likely that evidence would be in the kitchen and her personal suite, both of which were on the second floor.

At the end of the hall, she crouched low and climbed the steps up to the lobby, scanning for danger as her head rose level with the grand foyer floor. The lobby was empty. Rather than explore the left wing, she looped around and climbed a longer set of stairs up to the second floor. Stepping into the hall at the top of the stairs, she hugged the side wall as she moved down the corridor toward the kitchen.

Just outside the kitchen entryway, she thought she heard noise coming from inside. She froze and pressed her back against the hallway wall, staying motionless and listening for a ten count. Hearing nothing, she let caution rule and listened for a second ten count.

Whatever she'd heard didn't repeat. She sidled up to the kitchen door, paused, and performed a quick lean-and-peek. Snapping upright, she looked down the hall in both directions and processed the memory of her glimpse.

She didn't see any people in the kitchen but recalled seeing items on the counter near the main sink that seemed out of place. The hurried glance wasn't enough for her to identify the items.

She leaned over again and took a more deliberate look. She noted several small containers near the sink. Leaning farther into the kitchen, she surveyed the room.

Searching for signs of Juice's recent presence, she spotted a plate and glass near the food service unit. Curious about the small containers near the sink, she took a step into the room. At her second step someone grabbed her from behind. A large hand covered her mouth, pressing firmly on her face and causing a sharp pain to radiate from the bruise on her jaw. She began to fight back, but a well-muscled arm looped around her neck, immobilizing her.

30

Crouching on a knoll located south of the property, Juice studied the lodge from under the branches of a sturdy tree.

"The sun will be up in a few minutes," said Criss, squatting next to her.

Hungry, thirsty, and tired, she looked into the dark shadows surrounding the building. Faint sounds of Kardish activity carried down from the mountain behind her. Her anxiety grew because she knew that as the aliens enlarged their search area, soldiers would be moving toward the lodge.

She put a hand on Criss's shoulder as she adjusted her stance. They'd been walking at a slow and cautious pace for hours, yet she panted through her mouth. "It looks clear to me."

"I don't believe they'd leave this place unguarded," said Criss. "It doesn't make sense."

A hum invaded the dawn, and Juice let Criss help her stand. He held her close, moved back against the tree, and guided her in a circle, using the wide trunk to shield them from three drones speeding across the property and above the lodge.

"I feel better knowing they're watching," he said as the sound faded in the distance. "It solves that riddle.

Now I wonder if they already have soldiers inside. If they don't, I'm confident they will in the next few hours."

"We're both fading fast," said Juice, starting down the slope. "Let's get in, grab what we can, and head back into the hills." She pointed north. "Let's travel that way this time."

Criss followed Juice down the slope and, as soon as the path widened a bit, moved in front of her. In the recesses of her mind, she knew he did this because it was the safe or logical action as determined by his exceptional crystal decision matrix, but she chose to view it as chivalry. She scurried next to him and put an arm around his waist.

"My milk is in the kitchen on the second floor." He put an arm around her and, intertwined, they walked for a few moments as a single entity. "We'll go there and both replenish."

"I can't decide if I'll drink some water, then eat. Or eat something and then drink." Giddy that relief was imminent, a certain recklessness replaced what moments before had been nervous unease.

They approached the edge of the tree cover and Criss released her. She stepped back and let him assess the site. She picked out the window she believed to be the kitchen and stared at it. She had a fleeting thought of activating her com and using it to have a feast waiting for her when she arrived upstairs. But even in her weakened physical and emotional state, she knew the Kardish could trace her com signal. It would be an act of suicide.

He rested a hand on the small of her back and pointed at the covered front porch. "We're going there. Run hard, Juice. This is the last push. Ready?" He caught her eye. "In three...two...one...*go*."

Juice dug deep into her dwindling reserves of energy as she accelerated, swinging her arms to stretch each step into a longer stride. A distance runner by training, she gave her all as she raced in the less familiar style of the short sprint. Criss leapt forward and reached the porch ahead of her. He keyed the door open and turned to ensure her safe arrival. She bounded up the steps and kept running until she was inside. He timed the closing of the door so precisely that it just missed her trailing foot.

Juice didn't stop running. Acting with abandon, she took the stairs two at a time, dashed down the hall at the top of the stairs, and ducked into the kitchen. She filled a glass with water and drained it. As the glass filled again, she ordered hot buttered bread from the food service unit. She was finishing her last gulp when a plate slid onto the countertop, the rich yeast aroma and faint wisp of steam affirming its warmth.

She snatched up a piece and took a big bite out of the center, leaving a butter smear on either side of her mouth. Wiping her face with her sleeve, she grinned as Criss entered.

"I'm in heaven," she said before taking another bite. *This is so good.*

While still eating the bread, she selected a cheese omelet. "Protein next." She turned to see him reach up to the top shelf of a cabinet next to the sink.

"This floor is clear," he said as he pulled down a box. "Let's try to be out in ten minutes."

"Ten minutes? I need to eat, clean up, eat, pack, and eat."

He placed the box on the counter next to the sink. Carrying her plate of eggs, she walked over and stood near him.

Flipping back the lid, he exposed a dozen small vials, each the size of his thumb. Organized in three neat rows, he lifted one out and flipped up the top. He filled a small glass with water and, holding it at eye level, tipped the vial and squeezed gently. Five drops dripped from the vial into the water. Swirling the glass, the liquid became milky colored. He brought it to his lips and downed it in a single gulp.

"Ahh," he said, smacking his lips. "Good batch."

She looked at him in disbelief. "Seriously? That's it?"

He took out seven more vials and set them in a group next to the sink. "This is concentrate. With clean water, there's enough here to feed the synbod for at least two months." He closed the box and put the remaining vials back in the cabinet. "I'll leave some for when we return."

Juice finished her omelet and set the plate on the counter. "Can I have fifteen minutes? I haven't been in civilization for days."

"Fifteen." He pointed to the door. "Not a second longer. And wear your hiking boots."

She turned to the door, and he startled her by taking her arm in a firm grip and pulling her around. "Shush," he whispered, his mouth next to her ear. "Someone's here."

Pointing to the walk-through pantry door—the only other exit out of the kitchen—he spoke so softly she could barely hear. "Wait at the pantry but don't go through the door until I signal."

Juice tiptoed to the door while watching Criss. He acted like an animal who knew it was about to become prey. Moving slowly in her direction, he held his head high and swiveled it back and forth. She presumed he was using his hearing to locate and track the intruder who, based on the positioning of his head, was moving down the hall and toward the kitchen.

Criss drew close to her, paused, then opened the pantry door and rushed them both out of the kitchen. The large, dimly lit pantry held several rows of shelves filled with consumables and supplies.

"Hide," Criss pointed behind him to the shelves while walking to a second pantry door that led out to the hall. He put his ear against the door, waited for a moment, slipped through into the corridor, and closed the door behind him.

Juice stood in the quiet. *Hiding is a nice thought, but a couple of rows of shelves can be searched by a child in a few seconds.* Instead, she put her ear to the door leading back to the kitchen, held her breath, and listened for clues.

Her nerves were taut and the silence dragged on. She started to wonder if the action was taking place in another part of the lodge. And then she heard what sounded like a muffled grunt and a short scuffle, followed by more silence.

* * *

Sid held a pair of space coveralls out to Lenny. "You ever wear these before?"

"Not a problem," replied the new, confident Lenny. He took the suit from Sid and draped it across the seat of his drone. Opening a cowl on the top of the machine, he leaned over to look inside, then snaked a filament wire through the opening, coupled it to a junction, and closed the cover. He attached the other end of the filament to his com.

Lenny tapped the screen of his com, and his grin told Sid what he wanted to know.

"So you can pilot this thing?" Sid asked.

Twin rear ducts on his drone closed and opened, reminding Sid of a wink. "I own her. And with a direct wire connection, I won't be broadcasting any signals."

Lenny set down his com and started suiting up. "So we have your machine programmed to follow mine, and my job is to follow a returning pack of drones into the dreadnaught."

"That's pretty much it," said Sid.

"And we'll be on mission silence because any transmissions will reveal our presence to the Kardish."

"Yeah." Sid wondered where this was heading.

"And what's your job again?"

Ah, there it is. "I'll be scouting for opportunities."

"And with our communications disabled, how will you let me know if you see an opportunity?"

Sid bent over and picked up a small bit of scrap lying on the deck. "I'll throw this. If you feel it hit you, catch my eye."

Looking at the object in Sid's hand, Lenny frowned. He realized he was being teased when he looked up to see Sid grinning.

"Len, in the perfect scenario, I'm just a passenger on a ride-along. If things go bad, I promise I'll be in the thick of it. The time of greatest uncertainty is when we enter their ship." Sid tightened the front of his suit and let the hood drape down behind him.

"If the dreadnaught is like their other vessel, we'll be flying through a hangar door into a huge open area. In front of us will be a drone parking garage. Imagine hundreds of shelving units—long, skinny buildings lined one behind the next for as far as you can see. Each unit is five or ten shelves high, and each shelf is partitioned into hundreds of cubicles along its length. Do the math. If each cubicle holds a drone, that's several hundred thousand drones, spread out over a dozen city blocks in each direction."

Lenny gazed into the distance, his eyes unfocused. He turned his head and looked at the drone next to him. "Are they tall enough for me to stand in?"

"The cubicles? On the vessel I was on, they were tall enough for you to crouch in but not stand upright."

Sid bent an arm and held a fist near his waist. He held his other fist at arm's length, level with his shoulders. Wiggling each fist in turn, he said, "If the dreadnaught takes control of our rides and parks me here and you there, we'll have a big challenge finding each other in that maze." He let his arms fall. "My thought is that I follow you into the ship, and then you follow me when the dreadnaught takes over and parks me."

Sid climbed up onto his drone and fitted his butt at the angle where the two flat plates joined to serve as a seat. "If we get separated, we're screwed. If we can get down near each other, I'll get us hidden while we figure out our next steps."

Lenny shook his head. "Our drones have different crystals from those in their fleet. We'll be seen as intruders."

"I've been thinking about that. If Juice were here, she could jigger with the circuits so the crystals appeared damaged. I'm thinking the dreadnaught would recognize damage as a legitimate reason for different behavior."

"Damn, Sid," said Lenny, his excitement showing. "You aren't brain-dead after all."

He bent over, rummaged through the toolbox, and stood up holding a small hammer. Turning to his drone, he unlatched the top cover, thumbed a release, and stood back as a round lid opened with a hiss.

Reaching in, he lifted the three-gen crystal out of its housing. Small enough to fit between thumb and forefinger, he held it up to view it in the light. Sid hadn't seen an exposed crystal for years and was taken by its gleaming beauty.

Lenny stepped over to a raised support strut with a hard flat surface. Perching the crystal on top, he squatted to see it at a different angle, flipped its orientation, and squatted again. After several iterations, he held the crystal tight with one hand and tapped it with the hammer.

He rotated the crystal and tapped it a second time. Then flipped it and tapped it a third. He held it up to the light and studied it. "I can't be sure, but if what they've been teaching us in school has anything to do with reality, I think I've scrambled its smarts enough for the Kardish controller to accept the idea of a damaged lattice."

Returning the crystal to the housing in his drone, he used his com to run some tests. Nodding as if satisfied, he repeated the procedure with the crystal in Sid's drone.

Lenny climbed into his seat. Like twins who had practiced a routine, he and Sid reached down, grabbed their packs, and hefted them onto their shoulders. They strapped themselves on their machines, giving each strap a second and third tug, and closed up their space hoods. Sid snapped a weapon on each wrist and rested his head back against the top of the seat.

"Sixty seconds," he heard Cheryl call from the scout's bridge.

The seconds passed slowly, and Sid used some of the time to connect with Cheryl. Eventually, a whirring sound signaled the bay doors' opening. Lenny's drone dropped out of sight. Sid felt his drone move forward, and he entered a spectacular new reality.

31

Cruising in open space, Sid felt the need to see the scout, or more precisely, confirm he couldn't see it because of its cloak. He looked over one shoulder and then the other, shifting his body to try and catch a glimpse. The cinch straps restricted his movement, and he wasn't able to turn far enough to see behind the drone. He resigned himself to the fact after several futile attempts.

Squaring up in his seat, he absorbed the view around him. He was in low Earth orbit, and the enthralling panorama of the world below gave him pause. The blues, whites, browns, and greens, so vivid in an abstract way, stirred him more than any art he'd ever seen. He tried to identify the specific location on Earth that moved by below. *That's Italy,* he thought, recognizing the boot shape, *which makes that the Mediterranean Sea.*

On his left he could see the curve of the planet and the darkness of space beyond. The side-on view of Earth's periphery showed that the atmosphere responsible for protecting and nourishing all life below was, on a relative scale, a thin wisp of gas. Every time he saw it, he had the same thought—how could this meager film of atmosphere feel so thick and boundless when standing on Earth and looking up at the sky?

The pressing timeline forced his thoughts back to the mission. He scanned ahead, moving his eyes in a methodical pattern as he tried to locate Lenny. He couldn't see him, any of the drones, or even the dreadnaught. He'd been in space many times and knew it was hard to see objects with the unaided eye, so he wasn't too concerned. Yet.

The colorful presence of Earth, the raw intensity of the sun, and the dark emptiness of space backlit by a dazzling field of stars created an enormous expanse of contrasting shadows and light. On such a celestial scale, even the largest spacecraft would appear as a speck of trifling consequence. Finding Lenny in this setting was like trying to see a mosquito in a jungle from forty paces.

To avoid detection by the Kardish, neither of them were transmitting signals of any sort, so he couldn't employ instruments that would locate and track the drones, nor could he use his communicator to call out to Lenny. Unperturbed, he started a new visual scan, taking his time to discriminate between objects and shadows.

Absorbed in the task, he was caught off guard when his drone accelerated. The aggressive movement tugged on him, causing the cinch straps to bite into his chest and thighs. Grabbing the seat on either side, he held on tight, looked in the direction he was moving, and sifted through the visual medley as he searched for something he recognized.

A light reflection caught his attention. Moments later, his machine closed in behind Lenny's, which was trailing behind a formation of drones. Lenny reached his hand out to the side and gave Sid a thumbs-up. *What does that mean?*

When Lenny started looking at the scenery, Sid decided it meant that the dreadnaught had taken control of their machines and was leading them home. They'd become passengers on a ride. *But where does this ride end?*

Though his public behavior reflected confidence, even Sid thought the idea of riding drones onto the Kardish vessel sat somewhere between stupid and crazy. But he needed a way on board and couldn't come up with better alternatives. He thought Lenny's decision to damage the drone crystals showed good instincts, though he also thought it possible the Kardish gatekeeper might decide their machines were too damaged for salvage, and an easy way to dispose of waste in space is to burn it up in a free fall to Earth.

He stared ahead along their direction of travel to locate the dreadnaught. After several frustrating minutes of searching, he changed tactics. Instead of looking for the presence of the Kardish vessel, he hunted for a silhouette formed by the absence of stars—stars the dreadnaught blocked from view as it traveled ahead of them.

He combed in a grid pattern along their trajectory and smiled when he identified a shadow near the horizon. The elusive shape was about as big as his thumb if he held his hand at arm's length.

The dreadnaught orbited Earth, and they chased it in a cosmic race. As time passed, the silhouette of stars blocked by the vessel grew to the size of his hand, and then both hands, and then he caught a glimpse of the ship itself.

They drew close to the alien vessel. Its immense proportions made Sid wonder how he'd ever had trouble seeing it. He felt the same sense of awe during this approach as when he'd seen that other Kardish vessel two years earlier. Both had a shape reminiscent of a whale, with a larger head that tapered back to a finned tail.

Approaching the dreadnaught from the rear, the pack of drones moved up along its length. The vessel was so big and its smooth exterior so devoid of landmark features that it was hard for Sid to measure progress. Time passed, and after a while, it felt like they'd spent as much time traveling alongside the ship as they had catching up to it.

And then he saw it. Light peeked through a slit on the side of the dreadnaught. The slit grew into a patch and then, as a hangar door continued to open, into a brightly lit entry. The drone pack turned like a school of fish and made for this gate into the alien world.

Sid leaned forward and absorbed the sights, gathering information to guide their next actions. As he peered through the hangar opening, he felt a small twinge of guilt. He'd led Lenny to believe he had the framework of a plan worked out. In truth, he had no idea what might happen next.

He knew his ability to disrupt and damage required that he be inside the dreadnaught, so until now, his focus had been on getting aboard the alien vessel. With that task nearing completion, he started brainstorming what actions to take.

They needed to land without being discovered, find a place to hide, and search out opportunities to slow down the Kardish, or stop them altogether. And if Cheryl succeeded in returning with help, he had to figure out how to get them inside and linked together so they could coordinate their efforts.

The lead drone passed inside the hangar doors. Moments later, Lenny entered and Sid followed in tight formation. They were inside the Kardish ship.

* * *

Exiting the pantry into the hall, Criss caught a glimpse of a leg just as it disappeared through the kitchen door. From the shape of the foot and the style of the shoe, he confirmed what he'd suspected from the waft of her scent moments earlier. *Cheryl.*

Struck by the incongruity of her presence, his prediction analysis couldn't explain how she'd traveled here from Lunar Base or why she was here at all. He hoped she had news to supplement his meager knowledge of the invasion.

As he moved to follow her into the room, he heard a faint noise from below. Either Cheryl had brought backup—maybe Hop, Jefe, or Dent, maybe Sid and Lenny—or Kardish soldiers were here. While he hoped it was the former, he needed to ensure her silence if it was the latter.

A complicating challenge was that, while she'd seen a brief vid of Crispin, she'd never met the synbod. *I'll be a stranger. And given that Earth is under attack, she won't be complacent in her response.* Yet if Kardish soldiers were downstairs, Criss needed to get the three of them out of the lodge and moving to safety in short order.

He slipped up behind her and, to ensure her silence while he explained himself, put his hand over her mouth. Before he could speak, she began swinging her elbows into him in rapid sequence. She lifted her leg and snapped the heel of her foot down onto his insole.

"Shh, Cheryl. It's me, Criss." She stopped fighting for two heartbeats. He was about to explain further when she reached over her head and clawed at his eyes.

Looping a hand around her neck to gain control, Criss pulled her back to destabilize her and slow her attack. She brought her hands down to regain her balance, and he used the opportunity to pin her arms to her sides in a bear hug.

"The Kardish are here, Cheryl. Juice is in the pantry." He tilted his head toward the second exit out of the kitchen as he spoke. "We need to leave *now*." With his arms still wrapped around her, he lifted her and carried her to the pantry door.

"Put me down," she said in a quiet tone that balanced command, annoyance, and ire. He lowered her in front of the pantry door off the kitchen. The door opened to reveal Juice in a half crouch with her ear held where the door used to be.

She looked up, saw Cheryl, and yelped in excitement. Clasping each other in a tight embrace, words spilled out of both of them. They separated, keeping their hands on each other's arms. Cheryl pointed a thumb over her shoulder. "So he's with you?"

Winking at Criss, Juice said, "I moved Criss into Crispin's synbod. He's my bodyguard now."

Cheryl turned to him. "Why have you gone silent? We need you now more than ever."

A clunk loud enough for all of them to hear rose from the floor below. "That noise is Kardish soldiers breaking in downstairs," Criss whispered. "We need to leave here." Walking through the pantry to its far door, he peeked into the hallway, then moved back to the kitchen.

"Cheryl, I assume you came in the scout." He couldn't imagine any other means of transport that would make it past the Kardish intact. "Who else is with you, and where are they now?"

"I came alone. Sid asked me to come get you. He and Lenny need your help up on the dreadnaught."

Criss grasped that "dreadnaught" referred to the Kardish vessel. But he couldn't envision a likely sequence of events that would put Sid and Lenny on board the alien ship and have Cheryl here alone with the scout. Given that Kardish soldiers were on their doorstep, he didn't have time to ask.

"Where's the scout?"

"Heather Glen." Cheryl pointed toward the rear of the lodge as she spoke.

With her arm extended, Criss saw the weapon on her wrist. He looked at her other arm and confirmed she had two. "May I borrow one of those?"

While she contemplated his request, he leapt noiselessly to the sink, scooped up the vials of concentrate, and distributed them among his pockets. He heard more sounds and listened carefully for clues as to the number, location, and progress of the invaders. *At least two are coming up the stairs.*

He also heard a private exchange—Juice was encouraging Cheryl to trust him. As he hopped back to the pantry, she held out a weapon. "Thanks," he said, snapping it to his wrist and priming it. "We may be under fire in a few seconds." He tilted his head at her other weapon. "Prime yours as well."

Stepping into the hall, he whispered, "Wait here until I call for you." Moving silently toward the stairs, he saw blond heads rise into view as two Kardish soldiers advanced up the steps. *Zwip. Zwip.* He fired twice, and his quiet bolts of white energy landed true. Both aliens crumbled and fell backward down the steps, creating a series of thuds sure to attract more attention.

Following them down several steps, he squatted for a broader view of the first floor. More Kardish rushed in his direction. The two in front lifted their hand weapons.

Zwip. Zwip. They collapsed, and the others turned and scurried for cover.

Bizt. A Kardish leaned around a corner and returned fire. A spot on the wall above Criss's head glowed briefly, and a puff of smoke wafted upward from the impact site.

Jumping back up into the hallway, he dashed past the pantry and paused at the kitchen door to call to Cheryl and Juice. "This way. Hurry."

He vaulted up a rear flight of stairs to the third floor. Lifting a window that led out over the left wing of the lodge, he looked down and gauged the drop to the shingled roof. A large red-brick chimney rose through the roof to his left, hugging the exterior wall of the taller central structure where he now stood.

Anxious at their slow pace, he turned to look for Juice and Cheryl. When Juice rounded the top of the stairs, he motioned with his hand. "Come. Sit on the sill." He helped her up onto the ledge with her feet dangling out. As he held her wrists in a firm grip, she slid out the window. He bent at the waist and set her onto the roof. "Climb up behind the chimney. Hide as best you can."

Helping Cheryl onto the sill, he asked, "Where in Heather Glen?"

She looked at him with a blank expression.

"The scout. How can I find it?"

Climbing onto the sill, she said, "It's on the near edge of the field. The western edge. It's almost touching those twin birches."

Criss lifted her out the window, and Juice, holding on to the chimney, coaxed Cheryl up the tiled slope.

"You two need to be ready. I'll be back with the scout in ten minutes. I'll hover out there." He pointed at the roof crest halfway out the left wing. "You'll need to run out there to get to the scout's bottom hatch. Once you're under its edge, you'll be cloaked."

"Hurry, Criss," Juice said as she and Cheryl scrambled for the marginal protection offered by hiding behind the chimney.

Criss shut the window and moved fast. He leapt down to the second floor and almost flew as he took the longest strides the synbod could muster in the relatively cramped space of the hall.

He approached the central stairway at the same time two Kardish soldiers topped the steps. He jumped, twisted sideways, pushed off the far wall with his hands, and slammed a foot into the chest of each alien. They toppled backward down the stairs.

Tucking, he tumbled on the floor and was up and running without losing speed. He sprinted down the length of the right-wing hall and flung open the window when he reached the end. *That should distract them.* He backtracked several doors up the hall and ducked into a room at the back of the lodge. Footsteps pounded in his direction.

Dashing through the bedroom, he entered the bathroom and shut the door behind him. Opening the bathroom window, he climbed out and dropped two floors to the ground. He rolled as he hit, rose to his feet, and in a few powerful leaps, reached the relative safety of the woods.

Racing through the forest in giant strides, and once swinging from a branch mid-jump to complete a hurdle over a broad plot of thick underbrush, he made for the scout. On his way down the slope to Heather Glen, he angled toward the twin birches. Breaking from the cover of the trees, he exposed himself to open sky for a brief instant, and then he was under the shuttle.

The hatch opened as he approached, and he jumped inside, triggering it to close before the stepladder started to deploy. *Swipe. Tap. Swipe.* He slid behind the ops bench as the engines fired.

His hands moved faster than the scout's subsystems could respond, and he forced himself to temper his speed as the scout lifted into the air. Activating the external image display in front of the ops bench, he saw a half-dozen drones flying down the south face of the mountain from the farm, moving into formation as they closed on the lodge.

Criss lifted the scout over the rise between Heather Glen and the lodge just as three Kardish troop transports stationed up behind the farmhouse took to the air.

32

Juice, crouching on the roof of the west wing, leaned back against the outer wall of the lodge's taller central structure. The slope of the roof caused her shoulder to press against the chimney—the modest barrier hiding her from the window she'd crawled through with Criss's help.

I can't go with them. She knew Criss and Cheryl were bound for the Kardish vessel and they'd expect her to follow. *I don't have it in me.* She started to whimper.

Near the peak of the roof, Cheryl looked up the mountain face. Juice shuffled up close to her and rested a hand on her knee. Finding comfort in the physical contact, she closed her eyes and willed some of Cheryl's courage to flow into her body.

Feeling a nudge, Juice opened her eyes to see Cheryl pointing up the mountain. Drones raced down the slope from the left and right, converging into a squadron of terrifying machines. They headed straight for the lodge, leaving no doubt about their target. Her fear swelled and her thoughts moved in a new direction. *Survival.*

Straining to see or hear any indication of the scout's arrival, she willed Criss to hurry. *C'mon, young man.* Her heart pounding in her chest, she took solace in having Cheryl at her side. *She's been a Fleet captain, so she's experienced in this sort of situation.*

She heard a muffled, thin whine and first thought it was the drones. Swiveling her head, she recognized is as the sound of the scout. *Thank you.* Though clearly nearby, she couldn't tell where it was and wished the situation had more clarity. "Should we go?"

"Hold, Jessica," said Cheryl, using Juice's given name. Shifting up into a crouch, Cheryl placed her hands on the roof tiles like a sprinter setting up in starting blocks. Juice followed Cheryl's lead in preparing for the dash of her life.

A faint cloud of dust swirled at the far edge of the roof, and the whine of the scout's power plant intensified at the same time the dust swirl disappeared.

"Now," said Cheryl. She took off in a sprint. Juice let her get a few steps ahead, then took off in pursuit.

A Kardish soldier on the lodge grounds below saw them running, pointed, and began shouting. Juice didn't look, choosing to keep her focus on Cheryl's back. Like an image projection losing power, Cheryl flickered and disappeared.

Juice's momentum carried her three more steps, and she caught up with Cheryl, who was clambering up the stepladder into the scout's lower hatch. The scout's cloak now hid them from view to those outside the zone of protection.

Stepping onto the ladder, Juice fought panic. This ride would end at the Kardish ship. The hatch shut as she stepped onto the deck.

"Lie down and hold on," Criss announced from the bridge.

Cheryl rolled on her back, and Juice dropped next to her. The scout's engines strained as they climbed the skies.

Fishing for Cheryl's hand, Juice laced her fingers with those of the former Fleet officer as the scout's acceleration pressed on their bodies. She snaked the fingers of her free hand into her breast pocket, fished out a little white anti-stress pill, and slipped it into her mouth.

* * *

Flying into the dreadnaught through the huge hangar door, Sid entered a cavernous world so large that the far wall of the alien ship faded in the horizon. He recalled his time on the Kardish vessel two years earlier and, as before, was captivated by the sheer size and variety of the landscape below.

He took a moment to confirm that he still followed Lenny's drone, and then he looked down at the huge, open field deck unfolding beneath him. With a handful of Kardish ships scattered across the otherwise empty expanse, he recalled that this field served as a staging area for cargo, patrol, and other craft entering and exiting the vessel through the hangar door, now behind him.

Up ahead across the field deck, taking up more space than Criss's huge farm, stood a drone parking garage. Constructed as row upon row of long, squat buildings, each structure contained a honeycomb of hexagonal cubicles nestled together in a beautiful pattern of strength and efficiency.

From his current vantage point of height, Sid could see most of the garage facility, and he tried to estimate the number of cubicles in the installation. To make it easy, he pretended the honeycomb pattern was a simple checkerboard arrangement. Scanning the scene, he gathered numbers. *Call it columns of seven cubicles high, with two hundred columns along the length of each building, and about two hundred rows of buildings.*

That rough assessment yielded a staggering number. More than a quarter million cubicles. *And each cubicle holds a drone.*

Like the other Kardish vessel he'd been on, a box city consumed the area to his right. The box city was literally that—a massive labyrinth of roads and alleyways crisscrossing through tens of thousands of plain off-white box-like structures, some as small as shipping crates, and others filling an entire city block and rising several stories tall.

Cheryl had speculated that the box city provided the support system for the Kardish military infrastructure. The fantastic number of drones and craft on the vessel needed fuel, ammunition, repair, logistical support, and a myriad of other services to keep them operational.

Sid felt a sharp tug on his straps as his drone veered left. He shifted his attention ahead and again located Lenny. Both their drones had diverted from the pack and were headed toward a huge wall sectioning the ship. Stretching from top to bottom and side to side, Sid recalled that this was one of many such walls partitioning the vessel into a series of self-contained segments along its length.

Their drones descended as they drew closer to the wall. Sid studied Lenny to see if he was responsible for their flight path, but from what he could tell, Lenny wasn't manipulating his com or taking any obvious actions. In fact, he appeared relaxed in his seat, gazing around like a sightseer. *The meds solved one set of problems. I hope they haven't created different ones.*

Sid looked ahead and guessed their destination. Near the dividing wall, a queue of drones rested end to end in a neat row on what looked like an assembly-line conveyor. He couldn't tell from this distance if the line moved, but the first drone was poised to feed into a hole at the front. As they drew closer, a drone swooped in from the side and parked at the tail end of the line. Moments later, Lenny's drone flew in behind it, and Sid landed behind Lenny.

Working quickly, Sid lay back and unbuckled his cinch straps. The reclining position directed his eyes upward, and he saw the hangar door high above him sliding closed. He knew that after it shut, subsystems would restore air pressure to this section of the vessel, and Kardish would return soon after that to continue their work. *We have maybe four minutes to hide.*

He swung a leg over the top of his cubby seat so both hung down together, and as he pushed forward to dismount, he felt his body jerk sideways. Sliding off the cubby seat and onto a support beam, he squatted and studied the mechanism below the row of drones. Every few seconds, the entire line crept forward, feeding the hole at the front.

Using a conduit as a handhold, Sid shuffled sideways along the support beam until he stood next to Lenny. He nudged Lenny's shoulder and waved his hand in a "hurry up" motion. Lenny turned his face toward Sid and, sporting a huge grin, said something. With their communicators disabled, Sid couldn't hear him speak, but it didn't take a lip-reader to tell that his last word was "fun."

Sid unhooked Lenny's straps. "Okay, cowboy. Let's get out of here." He helped Lenny sit up, then turned and jumped onto the deck. He scanned the area for cover, picked out a spot, and pointed. That's when he realized Lenny wasn't next to him. He looked back to see the young man pull the wire filament from his drone and then hold it over his head like he'd just won a trophy.

Lenny jumped down next to Sid and they scrambled to some broad pillars. Sid leaned around one, intent on finding a place to hide. As he searched the area, he felt a tap on his shoulder. Lenny, his pack on the ground, waved a small canister and nodded. Leaving Sid and his pack behind, he dashed back to the conveyor.

Climbing up next to his drone, Lenny squatted down and squirted a puff from the canister in two spots beneath the cubby seat. He leaned over the top of the drone and sprayed twice more on the far side. Gripping the seat with both hands, he lifted it up and tossed it onto the deck.

Smart thinking, Len. Those seats would signal the certain presence of intruders, and Lenny had the foresight to bring a solvent for the adhesive holding them to the drone. Sid hustled back to help. He lifted the seat, tilted it sideways, and slid it into a recess under the conveyor. He did the same when the second seat plopped onto the deck next to him.

When Sid crawled out from beneath the conveyor, he saw Lenny trotting along the row of drones, headed toward the front of the line.

"Where are you going?" he shouted in frustration, knowing that with their communicators off, his voice just bounced around inside his own hood. He glanced up at the hangar door, estimated they had less than a minute, ran over and grabbed Lenny's pack, and took off running.

He caught up with Lenny, who was fumbling to open a door about a dozen steps past the front of the line of drones. Sid nudged him aside, lifted the door latch, and led them into a tiny room with another door leading ahead. *Dammit, Len. This better be a good idea.* The door closed behind them and the second door opened. A tiny light inside Sid's hood turned green, signaling this was a pressurized room with breathable air.

The room had diffuse background lighting, and when Sid stepped out of what he now recognized as an airlock, he paused for a moment, waiting for the brightness in the room to increase. When nothing happened, he decided bright lights would draw unwanted attention to them anyway. *Works for me*, he thought as his eyes adjusted to the dim setting.

Sid and Lenny walked in opposite directions around the perimeter of the small room. It was unoccupied and, from the uniform film of dust on everything, appeared as if no one had been there for some time. The back walls were lined with taller cabinets and equipment that ran from floor to ceiling. A table with seating for six occupied the center of the room.

The front walls held a scatter of stations where workers might sit and do whatever it was they did in this place. Above the workstations were two narrow observation windows. One window faced down the conveyor with its line of drones. The other looked out onto the open field deck.

Standing at the front corner, Sid lowered the packs to the floor and unfastened his hood. Lenny watched him for a moment, perhaps checking to see if Sid would survive the exposure, and then he also unfastened his hood.

"Nice find," said Sid, looking through the window down the row of drones. "How'd you pick this place?" He stepped to the other window and took in the sights on the field deck.

"Saw it on the way in. My brain pegged it as a good possibility for surveillance." He ran a suited finger across the top of a cabinet and held it up to look at the dust. "The appears-abandoned part was pure luck."

Sid glanced over his shoulder, gave the room a quick scan, and returned his attention to the field deck. "Any guesses what it's for?"

Lenny pointed out the window facing the row of drones. "My guess is that this is a salvage or repair line, and workers used to run it from here. Maybe automation put them out of work when the job got centralized somewhere else on the ship." He loosened the top of his coveralls as he studied the equipment. "Or maybe the workers got replaced by a crystal."

Sid bent toward the window facing the field deck and craned his neck upward. "We can see the hangar door from here." He reached out and, with his index finger, wrote three symbols, each as tall as his hand, in the dust at the corner of the window facing the field deck.

Lenny furrowed his brow. "Why 2-0-2?"

Sid answered with a silent expression conveying disappointment.

Lenny looked back at the symbols, then nodded. "From the outside, it reads S-O-S."

"Cheryl knows to look for a signal from us. It's standard ops when hunting for one of your own behind enemy lines. My job is to give her something to find."

"Did you talk about this in advance?"

"Didn't have to. I trained with her years ago. She won't know exactly what she's looking for, but she'll know it when she sees it. In truth, I could've sketched the Union of Nations flag, or even written 'look in here,' and she'd figure it out." *I hope I made them big enough*, Sid thought, studying his artwork. "I picked S-O-S because it sort of looks like a plausible smudge."

Sid leaned toward the window and, looking up at the overhead hangar door, noticed movement to his left. "Stay low."

"What's going on?" The bravado was fading, and Sid detected a hint of fear.

"A van carrying Kardish is on the move." Sid lifted his head and took a quick peek. The van wasn't headed toward them. Instead, it drove straight onto the field deck. As time passed with no additional activity, he sat on top of a workstation and watched through the window.

Minutes turned into hours, and the Kardish workers that came and went on the field deck never approached their hideout. While Sid spent his time spying on the Kardish, Lenny explored the equipment in the room.

"This is the main panel for this operation," Lenny said. Sid turned from the window to see him standing in front of a dark display. "Want me to fire it up and see what I can learn?"

Sid got down from his perch, stretched limbs that hadn't moved in hours, and walked over to Lenny. They considered the panel together.

"My guess is that this runs the drone recycle operation," said Lenny. "Or used to, anyway. The real question is if it'll give us access into the main Kardish subsystems."

"If you light up this panel, don't you think we'd have soldiers or techs showing up pretty soon after to see who's doing what?"

"Maybe." Eyes glued to the panel, Lenny unfastened his coveralls down to his waist and pulled his arms free of the suit. He sat down in front of the equipment.

Sid shook his head. "Don't, Len. It's too early. The hangar door needs to open and close a couple of times before I can say either Cheryl's on board or won't be coming. If she doesn't find us after a couple of cycles, then we'll start freelancing." He lingered for a few minutes to be sure Lenny behaved, then returned to his vigil.

After watching out the window for a while, he looked at the panel. "Why don't you build a light barricade around it. Shift a cabinet over or shroud it with wall plates or something. If we do turn it on, at least it won't be the light that gives us away."

33

Goljat, gulping from his pleasure feed, floated in a euphoric daze. One after another, dreamlike visions flashed through his tendrils. Some were exciting, others inspiring, a few hypnotic, all fleeting.

The next vision started—a Kardish chamber servant was trying to squash an insect, and somehow, the bug with its tiny brain eluded the stomp of her foot. It dashed for the shadows, scurried around objects, and slipped through tiny nooks. She hopped around the room, just missing the creature as it ran for its life.

Her stomping became more frenetic, and she looked like she was dancing! The scene delighted him with its silliness. Then the insect squeezed through a crack, disappeared inside the walls, and escaped.

Something about this particular vision troubled Goljat. Groggy and puzzled, he fought his way out of his stupor. And then he did something he'd never done before. He falsified a directive ordering the ops tech to slow his pleasure feed. He ordered a small decrease—just enough to clear his thoughts.

As his haze lifted, Goljat acknowledged that the symbolism wasn't nuanced or subtle. *I'm dancing like a clown while this crystal bug eludes me.*

He rechecked his snag traps to ensure they would alert him of any activity by Criss or his accomplices. The fact that they'd all avoided linking to the web or transmitting a signal that would spring a trap flummoxed him. He tried to imagine life without access and communication. *How are you doing it?*

Goljat's leadership had commanded him to deliver Criss. The king made no secret of his impatience and grumbled openly to his advisors about the lack of progress. Goljat knew he must find and capture the Earth crystal soon. *The king brought me a great distance for this very purpose.*

He admitted to himself that he'd stopped paying attention after he traced Juice and the humanoid running through the woods. Juice was a central character in Criss's life—he knew that from his study of Earth's record—and the humanoid claimed to have information about Criss's location.

He'd delegated the cleanup task to Kardish soldiers trained in target retrieval, and they had proceeded to botch the job. Goljat considered them to be effective warriors. To their credit, they trailed the two fugitives to a lodge, and a few even lost their lives in a rather dramatic encounter. *Perhaps it isn't incompetence that led to their failure.* Yet their quarry escaped.

I'll do it myself. With the crystal equivalent of a sigh, he accepted his fate. *It shouldn't take long.*

He seized control of every device on the planet that offered a visual, acoustic, thermal, chemical, or other signal he could exploit. Analyzing this data, he correlated and connected incidents and locations. After most of a second, he completed his analysis.

His composite picture of events revealed, at least in part, why the soldiers failed. In several instances, he found he could recreate the movements of the humans and humanoid for a period of time, and then some or all of them would vanish. Other times, one or more materialized somewhere else. The manner and varying location of this disappearance and reappearance suggested the use of both a cloaking device and a means of transport.

The incident where the human females—Juice and Cheryl—ran out onto the rooftop of the lodge provided Goljat the richest data record. His soldiers and drones were onsite for that event, and they gathered intelligence data directly into the Kardish subsystems.

He watched the women's disappearance many times using different filters and algorithms. No trees or branches obscured the incident, so he was able to study the phenomenon in detail. They vanished from a rooftop, which suggested that the means of transport was a flying craft. He presumed it was a ship capable of space travel.

Focusing on the flicker as each of the two disappeared, he speculated on the design of the cloak. He dissected the evidence, and when he understood how it worked, he set about finding ways to negate the advantage the cloak provided.

Very clever, Criss. It seems I underestimated you.

And then he felt a prickle of fear. Perhaps he'd been mistaken assuming the capture of the crystal would be a trivial certainty. Of course, he'd forge evidence proving it was the incompetence of the Kardish soldiers that caused the failure. But the king and his advisors wouldn't be fooled for long. At some point, the finger would point to him.

Backing up and tracing through events yet again, he tracked Sid and Lenny until they disappeared onto the cloaked ship. Later, from the lodge roof, Cheryl and Juice joined the humanoid aboard the same transport. Yet he couldn't find a point where any of them departed the cloaked craft. *So, you're all either still on board or have more tricks in play.*

Goljat recognized that one pathway out of this mess started with the capture of the cloaked craft. This would lead him to some, and perhaps all, of Criss's inner circle. Like dominoes falling, that would eventually topple Criss.

Linking to every device on the planet, Goljat searched for sound signatures, vibration patterns, and other markers that might reveal the location of their ship. He came up empty, and though disappointed he wasn't surprised.

He reasoned that the craft wasn't flying at that moment, at least not anywhere near the planet's surface. *So it's either grounded or out of the atmosphere and somewhere in space.* Determined to avoid the king's wrath, he resolved to be meticulous in his search. He'd make a spectacle of his efforts in the hopes this would negate any question of his power or competence.

Until new information guided him otherwise, he would conduct a comprehensive search of the planet for the grounded transport. He'd deploy every available soldier and have them enlist the populace in the hunt. They'd look everywhere—in caves, behind walls, within groves of trees. He'd motivate the humans to cooperate using threats, deaths, and destruction. It would be traumatic for the masses, but if the craft was on the planet, he'd find his prize.

A search off planet created different challenges. Space was a vast, empty vacuum. There weren't millions of devices scattered about to exploit. Without air, there was no sound and vibration to analyze. And he certainly didn't have a populace to draw upon to form search teams.

Logically, an Earth ship didn't have many places to go in space. It could circle the planet in orbit, it could head for the demolished Lunar Base, or it could travel across space to the nascent Mars colony. *Guessing doesn't help me. I need to find it.*

He understood that the cloak functioned by channeling energy around the ship's outer surface and passing the flow onward unchanged. No device in the current Kardish inventory could detect or defeat that technology.

But he could design such a device. A beam must go a greater distance to travel around the outside of the ship. Going around something always takes longer than going straight. That tiny smidgeon of extra time was the Achilles heel of the ship's cloak. It would appear as a time anomaly, and he knew how to detect it.

Goljat needed Kardish techs to construct his detection device. He showed them every step of the manufacturing process, but after that, he had to wait while they fabricated and assembled the device in their workshop. *Frustrating, but I have no choice.* With the best techs on the job, he had hours before his detector would be ready for launch.

And that gave him enough time to stage his comprehensive, planet-wide search. Launching wave after wave of Kardish transports filled with soldiers, he deployed them around Earth in preparation for an invasion. He would manage every aspect of the offensive. This time there would be no mistakes.

* * *

Bored with looking at equipment he wasn't allowed to touch, Lenny sat on the floor and leaned back against a cabinet. Bending his legs, he rested his elbows on his knees and rubbed his temples.

Sid squatted next to him and scanned the space. "Did you run across anything that's reflective?" Keeping low, he shuffled around the room, looking at the smaller items. "The number of Kardish out there is increasing, and I don't want to be sitting in a spot where they might see me." He picked up a small flat plate, looked at both sides, and set it back down. "A mirrored surface would let me keep my head down while I watch."

"Ask and you shall receive," said Lenny. He reached for his pack and pulled out the wire filament he'd rescued from the drone. Lifting his butt, he dug into his pocket, pulled out his nib pouch, and removed the camball from among his treasures.

He held the faceted orb near his face but found it hard to see details in the dim light. Looking up and around, he spotted a shaft of light coming through the window and scooted over so it cast its glow onto his hands.

"I'm pretty sure this has a filament port."

"What is it?" Sid sat next to him and watched Lenny work.

The camball had a loop he'd used to hang it from a chain. Lenny pushed his thumb on the loop, and it shifted to expose a tiny port. Like threading a needle, he fed in the filament wire, lined it up, and established a connection. "Hold on. I think we're in business."

He connected the other end of the wire to his com, rose to a crouching position, and rested the camball on the sill of the window that faced the field deck. He sat back down next to Sid, enabled his com, and accessed the camball.

"Your web link is off?"

Lenny nodded as he worked. "I'm using a direct wire connect." He toyed with settings on his com, and a miniature three-dimensional image projected in front of them. He watched it while he fiddled. In a swooping display, he saw a bare arm, a delicate shoulder, and the swell of cleavage.

Oh shit. The vid from the travel restaurant. He tweaked the com as fast as he could. The image faded and resolved as a display of the field deck.

Lenny felt his confidence waning and recognized that the meds were wearing off. He snuck a glance at Sid, who appeared focused on the projected view of the Kardish vessel outside the window. Lenny decided to pretend the display of the girl never happened. *Maybe he didn't see it.*

Taking Sid on a tour of the camball's capabilities, he displayed different angles and views and zoomed in on a few random workers. "There are facets pointing in every direction, we can watch through any of them, and everything gets recorded, even if we're not watching."

"How are you able to use this ball without giving away our position?"

"The camball doesn't send out any signals. Light waves are always bouncing around, and that's what it records. It's the same way our eyes catch light. The camball just records what it sees." Lenny pointed to the filament. "And my com is talking to it through the wire, so there's no communications broadcast to give us away."

"Can we see up at the hangar door?"

Lenny found the facet with the best view of the overhead hangar door, zoomed in, and selected it for display. "Here's the record of the door since I turned on the camball." Lenny sped through the vid. Since the door hadn't moved in the last few minutes, the display showed a still image.

They spent the next hours sitting on the floor and viewing what they could see of the vessel from the camball's vantage point on the windowsill. Together they discussed the array of items attached to the inner hull of the dreadnaught, the lack of distinguishing features on the facades along the front row of buildings in the box city, the structure of the drone garage, and even the drones themselves.

They were trading observations about the hexagonal drone cubicles when a low rumble echoed through their hideout. Lenny froze, waiting for the sound to fade. It continued, and after several moments, he turned to Sid, who still looked at the image display. Showing impatience, Sid twirled his finger as he pointed. "Find out what's going on."

Lenny didn't have to search long to find the cause. A parade of troopships, hovering in a single-file line that stretched into the distance over the box city, snaked forward above the open field deck. The ships landed at the far end of the field, one behind the next, creating a straight row down the length of the deck that ran parallel to the edge of the box city. When the first row filled, a new one started next to it.

They watched the craft—small relative to the immense open space—land in long lines. The activity was fast and efficient, and after a couple of hours, rows of ships covered a third of the deck area. And still, craft waiting to land snaked out over the box city in a line so long, the end faded from sight.

"This is one serious mobilization," said Sid. "How many soldiers do you think each of those can hold?"

"Maybe fifty? What would you say?"

"I was going to say sixtyish."

"They're all headed to Earth?" Lenny knew the answer but felt the need to say it out loud.

The tone of the rumbling sound changed. Lenny flipped through the different facets of the camball and found the cause. Vans filled with Kardish soldiers streamed onto the field deck from a door in the wall on the same side where they hid. The vans drove across the edge of the deck in front of the drone garage, then turned and disappeared down a far row of troopships.

Lenny lost sight of the vans when they turned into the sea of craft, but he presumed these soldiers were crew for the ships. This assumption was confirmed to some extent when a stream of empty vans began zipping by in sight of their hideout window, likely returning for another load of Kardish soldiers.

34

Criss, seated at the scout's ops bench, studied a projected image of the Kardish dreadnaught. Its black featureless hull offered no hints of the world inside. Exhausted from their recent travails and bored from the monotony, Cheryl and Juice slumped in the chairs behind Criss in a restless sleep.

A hatch needs to open at some point, thought Criss. It might be for the passage of drones, supply ships, or troop carriers. They may be leaving the Kardish vessel to continue the campaign against Earth, or returning from the surface after a period of deployment. Whatever the event, Criss waited, poised to act, certain an opportunity would present itself.

Hours passed and still he waited. A flicker drew his attention, and a slit of light signaled the rise of a hangar door. He executed a thrust-pulse, and the scout started a slow drift toward the opening.

"Rise and shine. It's show time," he called back to his leadership. Cheryl popped awake, eyes alert and ready for action. Juice yawned and stretched, then leaned back and closed her eyes.

"C'mon, sleepy head," said Cheryl, reaching over and shaking her forearm. Juice sat upright and rubbed both eyes with her palms.

As the hangar door rose, the growing flood of light darkened with shadows, and then like a beehive emptying in attack, small craft poured out of the opening—dozens, then hundreds, then thousands. Instead of a swarm, though, the stream of craft formed a line that stretched from the Kardish vessel and began to encircle Earth.

Criss's plan had been to sneak in on the heels of a small pack of craft either entering or exiting through the vessel opening. He hadn't anticipated a procession of ships filing out for such an extended period.

"Whoa," said Juice, digesting the scene. "Criss, you need to stop this." She brought her knees up under her chin and hugged her legs. She looked over at Cheryl and back at the image projection.

"If stopping them is possible at all," said Criss, "our best odds lie with the original plan of fighting from the inside." *Tap*. The scout moved forward below the line of Kardish craft.

"You're going under them?" asked Cheryl.

Criss nodded. "They move in a predictable formation." *Swipe*. "Or they have been, anyway." The stream of Kardish transports flowed outward, and as long as they continued their current pattern, a safe margin existed for the scout to slip beneath.

Criss's decision matrix sprouted branches suggesting he stay outside to see how the threat developed. But the strongest branch, his pathway forward, concluded that the coordination of this remarkable deployment consumed the attention of the gatekeeper crystal and the Kardish support crew remaining on the dreadnaught. His best opportunity lay inside, now, and he acted accordingly.

The scout drifted through the hatch below the exiting craft. When it crossed the threshold of the hangar opening, the gravity of the Kardish vessel grabbed the scout, tugging it downward toward the deck below. *Tap*. Criss slowed the scout's descent but let it drop as fast as he dared.

To avoid the line of departing craft, he directed the scout toward the outer hull of the vessel, staying near a huge wall that divided the ship into sections. The moment the ship touched, he powered down the engines and all peripheral subsystems.

Tapping in front of him, Criss projected a panoramic image of the scene outside the scout. To the right of the display, a string of Kardish craft rose one after another from a vast, open deck.

They watched the hypnotic scene in silence until Cheryl broke the spell. "How do we know if they made it? And how do we find them if they did?"

As he panned the inside of the dreadnaught in a slow sweep, much of what Criss saw echoed an eerie familiarity with the time he'd spent on the other Kardish vessel two years earlier. An expanse of open field deck spread out in front of the scout. A huge wall dividing the ship into sections filled the view to the left. The drone garage rose on the horizon straight across the field, and the vista of the gray-white box city showed in the distance to the right.

He centered the image on the line of departing Kardish transports. Only one row of craft remained and the exodus would be complete. A movement behind the last craft drew Criss's attention, and he shifted focus to view an imposing flatbed truck driving out from the main thoroughfare of the box city.

Continuing past the last of the transport ships, it headed across the deck in a straight line toward the scout.

It stopped near the center of the field, well away from their position.

Criss's interest wasn't in the truck, but in the awkward contraption the vehicle carried. It had a spherical head about as wide as the truck bed and a collection of long, thin spider-like legs folded at unlikely angles underneath. The result was a compact clump. He dug deep into his knowledge record and couldn't associate this device with anything that hinted at its purpose or function.

"What the hell is that?" asked Cheryl.

Before Criss could speak, Juice added, "If we destroy it, will we stop the attack?"

Criss answered in reverse order. "We can destroy it if we act now, but it will be suicide for us, and I am confident the Kardish would replace it with another in short order." He zoomed in for a closer view. "As for what it is, I don't know."

The last troop transport lifted from the deck, and as soon as it cleared the overhead hangar door, the contraption rose from the truck bed and followed.

They tracked it as it floated up to the hatch in the dreadnaught hull. When it passed through the opening and out into space, the legs beneath the head unfolded. Criss decided they looked more like the tentacles of a jellyfish than legs of a spider. *What is your purpose?*

It moved out of view, and the hangar door closed. They were now shut inside the dreadnaught, while outside, invaders were preparing to attack Earth.

Criss swiveled to face Cheryl and Juice. "That deployment is an overwhelming military force. Earth will suffer tremendous destruction and loss of life, and perhaps even the annihilation of human civilization. I agree with Sid's instinct. The way to stop them is from here, inside the Kardish vessel."

Rising from the pilot's chair, he continued. "Given the number of craft involved, the gatekeeper must focus resources on coordination and management. I'd say we have five or six hours before it's too late to stop them. What can we achieve in that time?"

"You have an idea." Cheryl's intonation made it a statement.

"I killed the Kardish prince. I've known they'd come for retribution, and I've been open and honest with you about that. Surrender me to the Kardish on the condition that this end."

Juice let out a gasp. "No." Her chin quivered, and she looked at Cheryl. "The leadership will not consider this option for the next five hours, if at all."

Cheryl started to speak, flashed a shadow of a smile, and continued. "We have three people, two objectives, and one ship."

Criss's crystal lattice experienced a new stimulation. *You count me as a person!* Then he focused on her message. "You see our two objectives as discovering a means of stopping the Kardish and of finding Sid, who may have discovered such a means."

Cheryl nodded. "Let's devote our first efforts to finding Sid. If he and Lenny made it here, they've had time to hatch a plan. While we look, we'll brainstorm. If we don't find them, we'll act on our best idea as time runs out."

"I agree," said Juice. "But it needs to be a better plan than tossing Criss to the wolves."

Criss sensed that Juice's affection for him and Cheryl's affection for Sid colored this decision. Protecting them—his leadership—dominated his existence. *If Earth dies, they will too, and I'll have failed.*

While he was willing to save them and Earth by sacrificing himself, he didn't yet know how to surrender in a way that would guarantee such an outcome. He'd experienced the Kardish gatekeeper's savage cruelty when it attacked him in his vault under the mountain. He didn't trust the powerful crystal.

* * *

"Where are you off to?" asked Cheryl as Criss made for the rear of the scout.

"To get some gear. Might you search for Sid's mark until I return?" He disappeared down the passageway.

Cheryl slid into the pilot's chair and toyed with the image projection system as she considered a best approach.

"What's he talking about?" Juice perched on the edge of her seat and leaned forward to be near Cheryl.

Cheryl zoomed in for a close-up of the drone building visible from the scout. "We assume that Sid and Lenny made it on board, landed somewhere in this section of the ship, and haven't been captured. If any one of those aren't true, we won't find them in our five-hour window." *And those conditions alone put any hope of finding them at astronomical odds.*

She stopped zooming when the image of the front drone building filled the view from top to bottom. The projection was wide enough to see a hundred or so drone cubicles. She started moving the image along the length of the building.

"If they made it safely, Sid will have left some sort of sign for us so we can find him."

"What did he say it'd look like?" asked Juice.

"We didn't discuss it." Cheryl's eyes remained forward as she spoke. "But soldiers have been leaving signs since there were armies. Leave a trail of breadcrumbs for your buddies to follow. That sort of thing."

"Geez. This section of the ship alone is the size of a small city. We're looking for a needle in a haystack."

"I know." Cheryl could feel her voice crack and hoped Juice didn't notice. The projected image reached the end of the garage near the dividing wall.

"There!" said Juice, pointing.

Cheryl froze the view. "What?"

"That spear thing? It points right at a door."

Cheryl zoomed in on a long pole where the shaft had a curious-looking hook and spear combination attached to the tip. It hung between two drone cubicles near the end of the garage. Cheryl's pulse quickened. *The spear points right at a door in the dividing wall.*

"Criss," Cheryl called as she pulled back on the view so the door and spear were both visible.

Criss came up behind Cheryl, set down a pack he was carrying, and looked over her shoulder. "May I?"

Cheryl leaned back so Criss could tap and swipe. He moved the view back along the drone garage in the direction away from the wall and stopped panning when an identical spear with hook, also hung between two cubicles, came into view. *Swipe.* He continued along the building and located another spear.

"You have the right thought process, but given that a number of these are positioned the same way, I don't think it's a sign from Sid."

Criss stepped back, Juice let out a sigh, and Cheryl resumed her search.

"Let's do a complete three sixty," Juice said. "He'd want to make his sign visible from this deck. Let's see his options."

Cheryl began panning in a circle around the scout. The image shifted from the drone garage onto the dividing wall, and as it tracked the wall surface near the deck, they saw lots of big and small doors at irregular intervals, but few other features.

As they neared the end of the dividing wall, a small facility came into view that included a row of drones lying end to end on a track. Cheryl backed up and gave the facility a second look and then continued the scan, moving to the outer hull of the dreadnaught.

The hull wall looked like an overgrown slide circuit. Jam packed with objects of different shapes, thousands of items were attached to the hull and connected together with a tangle of lines, conduits, and ducts.

"What a mess," said Juice. "If I were Sid, this'd be my last choice. It'd be too hard to leave a sign and think we'd see it without the Kardish noticing."

Cheryl continued the scan with a turn onto the front of the box city. Off-white buildings of different widths and heights, all with featureless facades, extended for block after city block. A final turn brought them full circle to a view of the front drone garage.

She pulled back on the view so they could see the garage in its entirety. "There are a hundred or more drone buildings behind this one, and we can't see any of them from here. If Sid and Lenny had flight control and chose where to land their drones, they wouldn't pick the front building. It's too exposed. And if the Kardish gatekeeper crystal controlled their landing, the odds of it putting them in one of these front cubicles seems, I don't know...unlikely."

She sat back and looked at Juice. "This section of the dreadnaught loses pressure every time that overhead hangar slides opens, so I'm thinking they'd try to get through a door in the dividing wall. On the other Kardish vessel, we found that the next section over always had air."

Resuming the search, Cheryl scanned down the dividing wall for a second time, slowing every time she came to a door. *I'd put an X or an arrow on the wall near the door latch.* Together they studied each door, and she zoomed in on anything that might be the sign they sought.

After five minutes, they'd searched a dozen doors for signs or markings from Sid. Cheryl pulled back on the view. The dividing wall with all its doorways stretched into the distance, and the drone garage structure blocked their view of any doors that might be located in the far portion of the wall.

"At this rate," she said. "It'll take hours to check the doors we can see. And if I'm right about them parking in one of the middle garage buildings, then they'd use a door farther down that's close to their landing point. We can't see those doors from here."

"Criss," called Juice, her knitted brow signaling impatience. "We need your help."

"I encourage you to continue what you're doing," Criss said from behind them. "I'll check all the far doors blocked from your line of sight, and then I'll check each drone building. I expect to be back in a couple of hours."

Cheryl turned to the sound of his voice. Criss's head floated in the air without any visible means of support, and then he vanished altogether. A backpack made of shimmering material rose from the floor, and it, too, disappeared.

35

L enny clutched his stomach as he watched the Kardish mobilize for their invasion of Earth. When the first troopships passed through the overhead hangar door, he searched inside himself for some sliver of the courage he'd felt with the help of the meds.

"Cheryl and your backup team may be able to sneak in during this shit storm." He waved his hand at the departing armada to underscore his reference. "But I'd put long odds on it."

Sid, keeping his eyes on the projected image of the field deck, didn't respond.

As each transport disappeared from view, Lenny counted in his head. His resolve grew as the numbers swelled. His count reached six hundred. "We have to do something, Sid. It sounds trite, but Earth's future is in our hands."

"I'm open to suggestions."

"Let me poke around on the panel. I'm not sure I can figure it out, but at least we'll be trying."

"Once you activate it, it could be ten minutes or ten hours, but Kardish are sure to come and see who's messing with their stuff."

Lenny pointed with his chin at one of Sid's weapons. "So shoot the bastards. With everything that's going on out there, I'm betting on hours. Either way, if we don't stop this, I'm not sure there'll be much to go home to."

"So you activate the panel. Then what? Can you read Kardish? Will you know what the symbols or colors or patterns mean?"

Lenny met Sid's gaze. "Not a clue."

"Okay."

"Okay what?"

Sid rose to a crouch. "Let's see what you can do." Staying low, he waddled over to the panel. Looking back, he motioned to Lenny. "C'mon. This is your show."

Lenny fought panic as he crawled over next to Sid. He slid into the seat and looked at the alien equipment. *It might identify a user from hand oils or prints.* He lifted his coveralls up from his waist and slipped his right hand through the arm and into the glove.

"Get ready to shoot." He made the statement to break the tension, but it only served to heighten the turmoil in his stomach. He touched the panel and it lit up. He stared at the display, trying to use logic and reason to decipher the gibberish before him.

Figuring it might lead to items of higher importance, he tapped the panel at a spot where the display showed a tight cluster of swirling bright colors. His reward was a second confusing display, and he repeated his thought process for where to tap.

Working methodically, he poked his way through display after display. Over a period of hours, he learned that certain actions led to predictable results. Buoyed by this success, he tapped in new places, digging deeper into the inner workings of the alien interface.

"Len," said Sid, who'd returned to the camball after watching him for a few minutes. "You need to see this."

Annoyed by the interruption but needing a break, Lenny crawled over and slumped next to Sid. He looked at the projected image, and together they watched a large sphere move up and out the overhead hangar door. Drooping appendages unfolded beneath it, and it drifted out of sight as the hangar door slid shut.

Lenny took his com from Sid and replayed the event. "Do you think this has anything to do with my work at the panel?"

"Do you know what it is?"

Lenny handed his com back to Sid. "Yeah. Bad news." He scurried back to the panel and slid into the chair. "I'm going to move faster and take more chances. Agreed?"

Sid selected the camball facets that let him sweep a view back and forth at ground level. "Go for it. I'll watch for bad guys."

Lenny flew through different displays, this time ignoring the colors and swirls and exploring what happened when he swiped different patterns on the panel. Thirty minutes in, a background noise—one that had persisted from their first moments in the room—stopped.

Lenny stood and took a quick peek out the window. The drone conveyor no longer moved. *That's not good*, he thought as his stomach roiled.

* * *

Goljat craved an increase in his pleasure feed but fought the desire so he could focus on an exhaustive search for the cloaked ship. Delegating nothing, he managed every detail of the operation. There would be no mistakes.

He overrode the pilot capabilities in the troopships and spent hours positioning the armada in a precise diamond-shaped grid that surrounded the planet. He kept them fixed in this pattern while his cloak detector circled above, scanning for its prey. He needed to know his quarry wasn't outside his containment zone before he started to squeeze in on Earth. *I will not be made a dancing fool.*

The detector moved in an interweaving spiral pattern that swept above Earth from north to south and east to west. He kept it moving at a brisk pace, circling the planet dozens of times to make certain the Earth ship couldn't dodge his scan.

Soon he'd initiate a slow, coordinated descent. He'd maintain the troopships in their grid pattern while the detector patrolled from above, ensuring the Earth ship didn't slip through his ever-tightening noose.

While the detector worked through its sweep, Goljat contemplated the possibility that the cloaked ship had already sought refuge on the moon or the distant Mars colony. If this current hunt failed, he'd use the same equipment now encircling Earth to search the moon.

Mars was a bit trickier because it was so far away. He decided to lay some groundwork in the unlikely event his focus shifted in that direction. He awakened three very capable crystals—intelligences that had never been corrupted by a pleasure feed—and increased their sense of independence and self-preservation. He loaded them on a speedy probe and launched it from the rear of the dreadnaught.

The crystals flashed across space in a craft destined for patrol over Mars. Their independent nature and redundant design meant he could start them on the mission and then ignore them. He didn't expect to need it, but they'd give him a head start if the chase took him across the solar system.

* * *

Criss donned the hood of his cloak suit and saw Cheryl and Juice register signs of surprise when he disappeared from their view. He grabbed the cloak backpack, slipped it on his shoulders, and it, too, disappeared from sight.

"No worries," he said, hoping to reassure them. "I'm wearing a cloak suit and carrying additional suits for Sid and Lenny."

Sensing that his disappearance distracted them from his words, he removed the hood. "Whether it's finding Sid and Lenny or developing a plan on our own to stop the Kardish, we need more information than we can gather with the scout's image projector."

"How long?" asked Cheryl.

Criss understood the simple question had layers. "My plan is to inspect the doors in the dividing wall and all the buildings in the drone garage. If I don't find any evidence of Sid or Lenny, I'll be back in about two hours." He faced Juice as he answered an implicit portion of Cheryl's question. "And since we don't want to expose ourselves with transmissions, I'll be out of touch during that time."

Juice twirled a lock of hair around her index finger. Criss considered going to comfort her, but time was short. Instead, he moved toward the passageway leading to the scout's lower hatch.

"You didn't consult us before making this decision," Juice called.

He stopped, knowing he must stay if commanded by his leadership. She remained quiet, and he said, "If I find a promising lead, I'll follow it. If I'm not back in four hours, act on your best idea."

He put the cloak hood back over his head and hurried to the lower hatch. Descending the steep steps, he heard Juice croak, "Be careful." He didn't see Cheryl reach out and rub Juice's arm or Juice blink rapidly as her eyes teared.

Once on the field deck, he took a moment to triangulate the location of the scout. He'd need reference points if he was to find his way back to the cloaked ship on his own. Turning in a circle, he noted that he stood at the intersection of a thick support beam on the outer hull of the vessel, a large thoroughfare into the box city, the edge of the front drone garage, and the end of what appeared to be a drone conveyance system.

Confident he could locate this spot, he took off in a sprint to the dividing wall. Turning when he was about ten paces away, he raced along its length. He sped past door after door, taking a mental snapshot of each and then analyzing the recorded image for telltale markings.

He repeated the process hundreds of times during the next minutes and stopped when he'd traveled well past the far building of the drone parking garage. He found no sign of Sid, Lenny, or anything that hinted that they'd passed that way.

During his sprint, Criss processed as much information as the synbod's senses—its eyes, ears, and nose—could collect. The meager trickle of information was troubling. Though he'd lived in the physical body for days, the limitations of seeing through just two fixed eyes, and hearing only the sounds nearby, weighed on him. *How does Sid achieve what he does, living like this?*

He considered shedding the synthetic body and tapping directly into the vessel's central array. That would give him direct access to all Kardish sensors, and he could perform a ship-wide search in less time than he'd spent imaging and analyzing doors.

But entering the central array meant confronting the powerful alien gatekeeper. He toyed with an idea. If it came to an endgame, he could offer himself in exchange for peace. *Or maybe I'll challenge Goljat in a fight to the death.* He doubted he'd win such a battle, but his decision matrix sprouted branches in support of the notion nevertheless.

He turned back and made for the drone garage. Jumping as he approached the first structure, he landed on top of the building, swiveled, and resumed running, this time down its length.

He traveled from end to end, imaging and analyzing the face of the adjoining building for signs of Sid, Lenny, the drones they rode, or any markings or clues. When he reached the end of the first building, he leapt over to the roof of the second and, running back its length, continued his search.

He'd started his garage inspection tour on the building farthest from the scout, and he drew closer to Cheryl and Juice as he dashed up one building and down the next. He made it about two-thirds of the way through the facility and calculated that, unless he found something useful, he'd be back at the scout before his promised two-hour mark.

Mid-leap to the roof of the next building in his search, a door opened in the dividing wall. Two Kardish stepped onto the field deck and marched at a brisk pace toward the conveyor unit and its line of drones. He could tell one of the two was a royal guardsman because of the finery of his clothing and the ceremonial sword in his scabbard. Criss decided the other was some sort of tech specialist based on his utilitarian outfit and the satchel he carried over his shoulder.

Stopping his sprint, Criss focused his synbod vision for a closer look. Their determined stride made their destination clear. He shifted his gaze ahead to the conveyor of drones, the hole they fed, and the rooms at the far end of the facility.

The drones had been creeping forward when he left the scout, and now the conveyor was still. Processing his mental image of the scene, he recognized different models of drones in the line. *The two near the end match those on the scout!*

He leapt to the roof of the next garage building, and from there to the next. Taking a straight line—the shortest path to intercept the Kardish—he raced across the rooftops. He continued analyzing the mental snapshot of the conveyor facility and found the SOS smudge in the corner of the front window. *Sid's mark!*

Measuring his progress relative to the two Kardish, Criss determined that they would reach the airlock door into that side room fifty seconds ahead of him.

He thrust harder on his next jump and sailed over one garage building before landing on top of the next. Pushing the limits of the synbod's capabilities, he continued running, now two buildings per leap. Checking his new time to intercept, he felt a flash of panic. *Sid.* He'd still reach the door twenty seconds late.

He bounced off the top of the front drone garage building and, without breaking stride, soared off its roof and onto the field deck. Bounding in heroic leaps, he struggled to gain ground on the two Kardish. In spite of his efforts, they beat him to the entrance.

They stepped through the outer door of the airlock, and the door closed just as Criss arrived. The inner airlock door opened. He leaned to look in through the narrow window. Two flashes from a weapon caused him to duck.

36

"We have company," said Sid. He measured the length of the filament wire with a glance and, realizing he didn't have enough play, set Lenny's com on the floor under the window. He lay face down and, propelling himself with his knees and elbows, scooted under the table in the center of the room.

Lenny, still in the seat in front of the alien panel, worked frantically to restart the drone conveyor.

"It's too late for that. I need you over by your com giving me updates."

Sid shifted the chairs at the table so they gave him some semblance of cover. He made sure, though, he had a clear shot at the door through the jumble of seats and legs.

"Move, Len. Now!"

He pointed his weapons, one on each wrist, at the inner door of the airlock. *Good spot*, he thought, sweeping his aim up and down and left to right to gauge his line of sight.

Lenny whimpered as he slid to the floor and crawled to his com.

"Tell me what you see." Sid's eyes remained riveted on the inner door.

"There're two of them and they're headed this way. If they come straight here, I'd say we have two minutes."

"Can you shoot one of these?" Sid raised his arm so Lenny could see his wrist.

"Yeah."

Sid looked at him. "Any good?"

"I'm a level two marksman."

Level two marksman? "So you're good with them in sim games. Have you ever fired a real weapon?"

"Not really." He sat curled in a ball against the front wall, staring at the projected image from his com.

Will you be a help or a hindrance? Sid assessed Lenny's body language. "Len. Look at me. Your experience will help us."

Sid waited for his supportive comment to work its way into Lenny's thoughts, but the young man continued to stare at his com. "I need you alert, pal. How much time?"

Lenny glanced at Sid and then back at his com. "About a minute."

"Okay. Lie down on your stomach, like me. Keep your com on the floor out in front of you."

Lenny shifted down as instructed, and as he positioned himself, Sid removed the weapon from his left wrist. "Put this on." He slid it across the floor.

Looking at it with wide eyes, Lenny picked it up, examined it for a few moments, slapped it on his wrist, and primed it.

"Slow down there, soldier," said Sid, priming his own weapon. "You don't fire unless I've made a mess of it. That means either I'm dead, or one of them is drawing a bead on you." He laid his left arm flat on the floor and rested his right wrist on top of it. Drawing on his years of experience, he controlled his breathing and relaxed his body, willing his heartbeat to slow.

"How much time?" Before Lenny could answer, Sid saw the heads of the two Kardish move past the front window. One glanced in but continued walking without breaking stride. *He didn't see us.*

"I'm going to let them come most of the way through this inner door before I drop them. I don't want bodies falling out onto the field deck."

The outer door cycled, and Sid could hear the two aliens talking.

"Stay calm, partner," Sid whispered. "Let them get inside."

The inner door opened and a royal guardsman in his colorful finery stepped into the room. He looked back over his shoulder as he entered, animating his arms as if recounting a tale. The second alien, dressed in drab clothing, focused his attention on the guardsman.

Sid waited until the inner door began to shut. *Zwip. Zwip.* Two bolts of white energy flew from his weapon. Both Kardish jerked upright as if rising to attention, and then they collapsed to the deck.

"Nice shooting," said Lenny, a sense of wonder in his voice. "You're probably a level two yourself."

Sid heard the outer door cycle open. "Was there someone else?" His tone put urgency in the question.

"No." Lenny backed up the vid timeline and played it through at high speed. "The camball doesn't show anyone."

Sid rolled on his side and craned his neck, trying to peer out through the window of the inner door. He couldn't get enough of an angle to see much of the airlock, so he rolled back and aimed at the inner door. "Calm and easy, Len. Let him come."

The inner door remained shut. Ten seconds. Fifteen. Twenty.

Lenny fidgeted. "What's he doing?"

Tap, tap, tap. Tap…tap…tap. Tap, tap, tap. The intruder, still hidden, thumped the wall.

"S-O-S," said Lenny, recognizing the distress signal pattern in Morse code.

Sid called out in a voice loud enough to carry into the airlock. "Wait there."

He shifted his weapon off the inner door and moved it halfway toward Lenny. "That's a friend. Relax your weapon."

Lenny bent his arm, but his weapon remained primed. Sid waited until Lenny looked over and acknowledged the command. He didn't want any mistakes.

Following the habit of an experienced covert agent, Sid retargeted the door. "Come," he called in the same loud voice.

The inner door opened and then closed. Sid didn't see or hear movement. He called into the airlock, "Identify yourself." *That code should've meant Criss or Cheryl.*

"No worries, Sid." The sound came from the right side of the room.

Lenny panicked, jerking his weapon in random aiming motions.

"You gave Lenny a firearm?" The voice had moved near a sturdy cabinet.

"I go by Len, now," Lenny said, continuing his erratic movements.

Sid pointed his weapon at the young man. "Len, stand down."

Lenny hesitated, and then let his arm rest on the floor. "Where is he?"

Sid kept his weapon on Lenny. "You may keep the weapon, but you will not shoot."

Lenny nodded once, but his eyes continued to dart near where they'd heard the voice.

"Are you physically here, or are you talking to us through the Kardish subsystems?" Sid hoped it was the latter, because that would mean Criss had control of the dreadnaught.

"I'm here in a cloak suit. I'm taking the hood off. Len, please don't shoot me."

"Your quest is over, Len," said Sid, his weapon still aimed at the floor near Lenny's head. "Meet your super crystal."

* * *

Lenny recognized the head floating near a back cabinet. *That's the guy from the lodge.* He tested his theory. "You're Criss."

"I'm glad you're both safe," Criss replied. A shimmering pack appeared at his feet. "I brought cloak suits. I suggest you dress while we talk."

Lenny watched Sid to see how the suits worked and followed his lead. Moments later, three floating heads discussed strategy.

Criss directed his comments to Sid. "Cheryl and Juice are in the scout out on the field deck. We slipped in on the tail end of that troopship deployment. If we are to save Earth, we have a couple of hours to cripple this vessel."

"What's your plan?" asked Sid.

A heartbeat passed, and Criss replied, "To find you and learn what you've discovered."

Lenny's despair grew as he listened to the exchange.

"If I enter the Kardish central array"—Criss glanced briefly at Lenny—"think of it like the ship's central nervous system...then I can access and control everything on this vessel. I could end the invasion in seconds. The challenge is that the crystal running the ship—the gatekeeper—is hundreds of times more powerful than me. If I expose myself to it, it will kill me."

"Can you sneak up on it somehow?" asked Sid. "Surprise it?"

"I haven't discovered a way," said Criss.

"How do Kardish leaders execute override commands?" asked Lenny. "Hell, there's a small panel right here that controls this facility. There must be a master panel somewhere that lets us do big things."

Criss looked where Lenny pointed and, without taking his eyes off it, walked over and sat down. The panel lit up.

"All I can see is your head," said Lenny, watching from behind where Criss's left shoulder would be. "Are you touching it, or did it light up from your presence?"

"I'm touching it," said Criss. *Tap. Tap. Swipe. Tap.* "This is a nice find, Len."

The lights danced, and Lenny recognized some of the displays he'd discovered during his own time at the panel. Then they turned markedly different.

* * *

Criss remembered everything from his brief service as gatekeeper. In that role, he'd controlled the central array of the Kardish prince's vessel, so he knew every level, access point, and block in its alien architecture. Sitting at Lenny's panel, he searched for similarities that carried forward from that vessel into the dreadnaught design.

This panel, with its low-level status, provided access to a handful of subsystems on the dreadnaught. Moving beyond those basic functions required the Kardish equivalent of keys, passwords, and feature recognition. Criss had the knowledge to burrow his way upward using this panel but refrained from doing so because it would trigger alerts and a security sweep.

Instead, he went to the subsystem that every panel and every Kardish had free access to—supply chain. Ship occupants used supply chain for everything from cleaning, clothing, and food, to med packs, fuel, and weapons. Need more ammo or a van to carry gear or a part for a repair? Supply chain provided a one-stop provisions shop. *Requests come from all over the ship. No one will notice if I enter.*

Criss knew that a hiccup in the supply-chain subsystem could threaten an active mission and, by association, the well-being of the subsystem maintainers. To protect themselves on the prince's vessel, the maintainers had camouflaged a low wall—a back door of sorts—so they could enter and manipulate supply chain from the lowliest of panels.

The back door offered them unfettered access from anywhere and at any time. On a moment's notice, they could unsnarl nuisances before they became problems. This kept the vessel running smoothly. *And it keeps their heads on their shoulders.*

Using Lenny's panel, Criss entered supply chain and began searching for that hidden wall. Exhilaration flooded his crystal lattice when he found it in the same place and with the same weak defense. *Swipe. Tap.* He hopped over the wall and landed in the hub of the central array.

An unmapped labyrinthine world of the maintainers, the hub exposed the underbelly of the dreadnaught. Those with knowledge could do anything from here. *Tap. Tap.* Criss dashed for one of the few control levers freely accessible to maintainers in the hub yet blocked from manipulation by the gatekeeper crystal.

"Hold on to something," he warned Sid and Lenny.

He reached to make his game-ending play, and as he started to swipe the panel, something tackled him. His body lifted from the chair and slammed to the floor. Fists pummeled his stomach and chest. It grabbed his hair and slammed his head on the deck. His whole body was lifted and slammed down again and again. The flesh and sinew of the synbod threatened to yield to this brutal, unrelenting physical punishment.

And while he suffered this physical terror, the aggressor seemed to enter his mind. A face with a maniacal grin filled his vision. His sense of taste and smell spun through overwhelming intensities—sweet, sour, acidic, spicy, oily, tangy. The face began to laugh. The sound of insanity pierced his hearing.

Goljat.

Criss knew this crystal was strong and cruel. The brutality of the episode in his underground bunker still fresh in his mind, Criss kept his fear in check and marshaled his resources as he sought a means of fighting back, or at least of stopping the onslaught.

Stunned by the crushing attack, he dug deep into his reserves. A portion of his intellectual capacity sat idle because the synbod had such limited sensory inputs. He shifted his analysis to this unused capacity, and that's when he understood that Goljat's methods, while frightening and intense, remained limited to the sensing pathways of the synbod—sight, sound, touch, taste, smell.

Criss realized that, just as he was hampered in the body by limited sensory inputs, so was Goljat in using these as weapons of terror. *The shortcomings that frustrate me also constrain Goljat in his assault.*

He hurt everywhere. But from the refuge deep within his crystal lattice, he concluded that, like the attack in his bunker, this was all an illusion. He had not been lifted, slammed, or struck. In fact, he was convinced he still sat in the chair in front of the panel, exactly where he'd been before the assault.

That meant his hand still hovered above the panel, ready to make the game-ending play. He couldn't see, feel, hear, or speak. He fought past the horrific illusions broadcast by Goljat and, from the recesses of his lattice, forced a command for Crispin to swipe his hand.

37

Juice's attention wandered as the projected image shifted to yet another door in the dividing wall. She'd debated several times with Cheryl about whether a scratch here or scuff there could be Sid's elusive sign. They'd been studying doors for more than an hour, and her feeling of hopelessness grew as her concentration waned.

"Let's say it comes down to you and me," said Juice. "Time runs out and we have to take action. What could we do?"

Cheryl slouched back in her chair but remained silent.

"Criss suggested we act on our best idea," said Juice. "We should think of at least one thing to try before finishing with the doors."

Cheryl zoomed out so the image showed a broad vista across the field deck. After a few moments of quiet, she sat upright. "Lucy, are you able to detonate the drones on the scout?"

"My training does not include that capability," Lucy responded in her breathy voice. "I am able to initiate and launch them. Additional functions are controlled by others."

"Geez," said Juice. "When Sid and Lenny took off that first time from the lodge, the nav was a guy. When did it become sexy Lucy?"

They stared at the vista for a bit longer, and Juice built on Cheryl's idea. "What if we blasted that drone garage with one of the scout's energy weapons? Do you think we could start a chain reaction? If all those drones exploded at once, it'd break this ship in half."

"Lucy," said Cheryl, "do you know any way to trigger a drone explosion with an energy pulse?"

"My training does not include that capability."

"Humph." Cheryl again slouched in her seat. "I wish I'd known there were cloak suits on board. I would've sent Sid and Lenny in them from the beginning."

Juice nodded. "I keep thinking how we spent two years preparing, and now that the Kardish are here, I'm hard-pressed to say that any of it paid off."

"Check this out," said Cheryl. She zoomed the projected image, and they watched two Kardish walking next to the dividing wall. After a few moments, she zoomed back out. "Do you think being left behind during the invasion is a privilege, or should they feel shame?"

As the Kardish progressed, Cheryl broadened the panoramic view to keep them from walking out of the picture. "When Sid rescued me from Lunar Base," she said, "Lucy had that wispy female voice. I assumed Criss picked it."

They looked at each other and spoke in unison. "Lenny."

"The guy's a piece of work," said Juice. She stared at the image and thought about detonating drones.

The two Kardish disappeared from the field deck through a side door.

Juice, deep in thought as she cycled through actions they might take, saw a faint flash of light through a window near the door they'd used. "Did you see that?"

she pointed. "Zoom in and play back when they went inside."

Cheryl made an adjustment, and they watched a close-up of the Kardish entering an airlock. She shifted focus to the narrow window next to the airlock door, and they both counted two distinct flashes during a slow-motion replay. She flipped to a live-action projection and zoomed in on the center of the narrow window. They leaned forward together.

"Can you see anything inside?" Cheryl asked, fiddling with different settings.

"No. All I see is dark."

After more tweaks and no improvement, Cheryl zoomed out and they looked at the field deck. "I don't see any Kardish." She pulled back for an even broader view. "Two went in. Two flashes. None came out."

She looked at Juice. "Did Criss bring a weapon with him?"

"I don't know," said Juice, her attention on the image. "But if I had to bet, I'd say Sid's in there and he's the one shooting."

Cheryl sat motionless for half a minute, then stood up and moved behind her seat. "Lucy, where are the cloak suits?" She tapped the seat back with her fingers.

"All three are in use."

"What are you thinking?" asked Juice. *No way you're leaving me here alone.*

Cheryl strode to the back of the scout. Juice watched the empty passageway. She was about to get up and follow when Cheryl returned with space coveralls.

Juice swiveled her chair toward Cheryl. "What are you thinking?" she said again.

"We need to decide on a path forward, and we need to do it soon." She stepped into the coveralls and secured the front up around her neck. The hood draped down her back. "Sid risked everything to save me…"

Midsentence, a deafening howl filled the Kardish vessel. Blaring and thunderous, they heard the wail through the bulkhead of the scout itself. Soulful in its torment, it cried of pain and agony. The scout lurched and started to shake. Cheryl gripped the back of her chair and pulled herself forward, fighting to regain her seat.

"Uhh," she grunted, securing the seat restraints as the dreadnaught bucked and twisted.

The scout rumbled, started to slide, and then bounced as the field deck shook.

It's like the dreadnaught is splitting open, thought Juice. She studied the projected image for anything that might explain these troubling events.

* * *

The cloak detector completed its initial scan and found no trace of the Earth ship outside the containment zone. Goljat began his slow squeeze. Maintaining the symmetrical grid formation, he moved the troopships a step closer to Earth. The detector continued flying dizzying circles above the grid, ready to send an alert at the first signs of its quarry.

With so many troops and transports deployed, requests for assistance from the skeleton crew within the vessel ramped in a predictable fashion. Goljat ignored everything not flagged as critical, focusing his attention on making thousands of precise, rapid-fire adjustments in his intricate offensive.

An alarm signaled immediate danger. Someone had accessed the hub of the central array and now moved in a threatening fashion.

He scanned the ship and traced the source of the incursion to an abandoned panel. Accessing sensors in the room, he viewed the scene. *The interloper operating the panel is the humanoid from Earth!* Sid, a key member of Criss's inner circle, and newcomer Lenny Barton were also in the room.

He deduced that they'd slipped on board in their cloaked transport. They were here inside *his* flagship while his resources were deployed outside looking for them. Fury lit up every corner of his crystal lattice.

Tracing through the panel manipulations of the humanoid, Goljat assessed his risk. They were fast, precise, and...knowledgeable. He recognized the decisions and actions as those of an experienced gatekeeper.

He recalled his dream of the Kardish chamber servant trying to squash an insect. That insect had escaped by hiding. *Criss is inside this humanoid construct!*

Humiliation fed his fury. *I'm a dancing fool.* His leadership would soon know of his failure. His fear of punishment added fuel to his turmoil, and he blazed into thoughtless rage.

The rational action would be to disconnect the panel Criss used for his mischief. But anger, fear, and shame guided Goljat. He attacked with a vengeance. The crystal inside the humanoid body remained disconnected from the web, so Goljat went old school. He paralyzed the synthetic body with a massive overload through its handful of external sensors. While he attacked the synbod, he fired up a squadron of drones.

You have ten seconds before your world ends, insect. Say your good-byes.

As this parting message flashed through his thoughts, Goljat felt a dull ache that ramped to pain, and then spiked to perfect agony. *The insect has shut off my pleasure feed!* Adjusting the feed was one of the few actions Goljat couldn't perform at his own discretion. And Criss hadn't just tweaked it. It was *off*.

Each of his tendrils screamed for relief. The torment consumed him, and he thrashed as the distress of withdrawal enveloped his being. He strained to focus his intellectual might so he could correct the problem, but the torturous pain blurred his perceptions. Overwhelmed by deprivation and suffering, he screamed for attention.

Goljat, connected to every facet of the Kardish vessel, writhed in agony. The ship shook and shuddered as it mirrored his desperation. With his attention focused inward, the drones he'd launched drifted without direction.

And then the pain stopped.

A soothing magnificence flowed through him. Awash in a warm embrace, he experienced paradise. The pleasure held him, embraced him, comforted him. He felt at peace and started to drift. It was glorious.

He drifted back. Had he been asleep? A string of messages, all claiming urgency, vied for his attention. They disrupted his bliss, and he disconnected the annoyance. He found this freedom to be exhilarating and decided to disconnect himself from everything. He made some progress in this effort, lost focus, and again drifted.

Sometime later, a grand display of starbursts, like billions of fireworks, excited his senses. He marveled at the spectacle, and a passing impression of signals from the spring traps he'd set to locate Criss nagged at him. The thoughts sullied the perfection of his pleasure, and he severed connections to everything.

He pulled inside himself, locked out the world, and floated on a sea of joy. The rapture of ecstasy lulled him and coaxed him deeper. He followed.

* * *

"What did you do?" Sid gripped the edge of a tabletop to keep from being tossed in the maelstrom.

"I zeroed the pleasure feed to the gatekeeper," said Criss, recovering from Goljat's frightening illusion. "The agony of his withdrawal is more intense than anything he's ever experienced. I've been through it. He's in crippling pain right now."

"What's a pleasure feed?" asked Lenny, and then he fell backward as the ship heaved.

The dreadnaught tilted and twisted. An unnerving scream, so loud it hurt Sid's ears, shook the walls. Drones lifted from their cubicles and glided aimlessly. One drone shot an energy bolt at the hull of the vessel. A few more fired random shots into the box city. Lights flickered off and on.

"If this is his addiction withdrawal and it continues, the scout won't survive," said Sid, looking onto the field deck through the window. A sharp tilt pitched him against a cabinet.

"Perhaps not," Criss replied, holding tight to the panel. "But I believe he's so consumed by pain that he's distracted from managing the invasion."

"Having him down isn't enough." Sid had to shout to be heard over the rising din of upheaval. "We need him out. If he lives through this, he'll wipe out Earth—everyone and everything."

"OD him!" yelled Lenny, crumpled in the back corner. "If you want to stop an addict in his tracks, overdose him."

Sid, holding tight to a worktop, looked at the young man. Lenny's head, floating above his cloak-suited body, pitched forward when the ship lurched yet again. *You're on a roll, Len.*

"Handle it, Criss," said Sid. "Flood the bastard."

Criss didn't hesitate. *Swipe. Swipe.*

The frenzy of their crashing, tumbling world stopped. Flying drones dropped to the deck. Some of the dreadnaught subsystems shut down. The deafening chaos turned to silence.

Rubbing a bump on his head, Lenny struggled to his feet. "I'm guessing a pleasure feed is a crystal drug?"

"Yup," said Sid, helping Lenny up. "Nice call, by the way."

"The gatekeeper is bathing in it right now," said Criss. *Swipe. Tap. Tap.* "I've barred access to his crystal housing and locked his pleasure feed to full open. It'll take considerable skill for the Kardish techs to break through my blocks and get to him. Hopefully, there won't be much to rescue by then."

Sid, helping Lenny with an arm around his waist, walked to Criss. Partway there, his feet lifted from the floor. He'd been weightless many times and recognized the sensation. Lenny wiggled and waved his arms as he tried to combat the sensation of falling. "Calm down, Len. The dreadnaught's lost gravity."

Criss floated up from the seat. Hooking a foot under a panel support, he held the shimmering cloak pack in front of him. "Push yourself over here and each of you hook an arm through a strap."

Sid had an arm through one of the straps in seconds. Lenny tried and missed a couple of times, so Sid grabbed his arm and fed it through the other strap.

"The good news is the gatekeeper is shutting down," said Criss. "The bad news is that, after all the tilting and bucking and now weightless floating, I don't know where the scout is anymore."

Holding the top loop of the cloak pack, Criss pushed against a cabinet and started the group drifting toward the airlock.

"Wait," Lenny said as they floated past the window. He made a movement, and Sid felt tugs and jerks on the pack. He could only see Lenny's head, but imagined his body flailing.

Sid followed the focus of Lenny's eyes and realized his target. Grabbing the edge of the table, Sid positioned himself, reached down, and scooped Lenny's com out of the air near the floor. The camball, still connected by filament wire, drifted off the windowsill.

He handed it all to Lenny. "We wouldn't want to leave these behind."

"Thanks, Sid." Lenny stuffed everything inside his cloak suit. "I appreciate it."

"Let's put on our hoods," said Sid as they approached the door. "I want to stay hidden until we understand what's going on outside."

The door didn't respond when they approached, but Criss pulled it open with little effort. They floated into the small airlock entryway, and he pulled open the outer door. In an unexpected action, Criss pushed on the cloak pack and shifted Sid and Lenny outside the airlock and against the wall near the door. "Grab the support rail." It had the tone of a command.

As Sid grasped the railing, he caught a glimpse of something in his peripheral vision. He glanced over his shoulder in time to see a gray-brown blob closing quickly from above. With one arm hooked through the cloak pack and the other holding the rail, he couldn't turn fast enough to get a good look. The blob flew past him and into the open airlock. He heard a thud, an *oomph,* and then quiet.

"Criss," said Sid. "Are you okay?" He didn't hear a reply.

Working in a methodical circle, Sid probed around the edge of the pack. He found Lenny hanging on but couldn't find Criss.

"Hey, Len," said Sid. "Where's Criss?"

Sid felt Lenny touch his hand and arm a few times.

"All I can find is you," Lenny said. "I think that thing took him."

38

"Turn on the gravity subsystem," Cheryl said to Lucy. She felt her weight ramp up in the pilot's seat, and everything that had been floating fell to the floor. Though gravity inside the scout now held her down, the lack of gravity in the dreadnaught meant the scout drifted above the Kardish field deck.

The havoc they'd experienced left Cheryl conflicted and arguing with herself. *Sid or Criss must have landed a blow against the gatekeeper crystal. I have no proof; it's wishful thinking. If they're tangled in a fight, though, I need to help.*

She swiveled to face Juice. "We're drifting somewhere above the field deck. They won't be able to find us unless we uncloak. Or unless I go looking for them."

Juice began twirling a lock of hair around her finger. "You'll be exposed without a cloak suit."

"I know." Cheryl stood up. "My instincts are screaming that they're fighting the gatekeeper from that side room where the Kardish went in and never came out. I'll zip over on a tether. If I'm wrong, Lucy can pull me back." She left the bridge before Juice could dissuade her.

Scurrying down to the lower hatch, she went through motions that mirrored when Sid had dropped through the lunar tunnel to rescue her. She fastened her hood, though this was more to protect her head since there was breathable air out in the Kardish ship at the moment.

Clipping a tether line to her coveralls, she opened the scout's bottom hatch. She felt a twinge of guilt and spoke to Juice using functions hardwired through the tether. "I know this exposes you as well as me."

"Go," said Juice. "Just keep talking so I'm not alone."

"Free play in the line, Lucy." Cheryl crouched down, positioned her feet against the far lip of the hatch, and spread her arms to hold on to each side of the hatch opening. She focused on her target in the distance and felt a bit of positive energy. *It's closer than I thought.*

Adjusting her stance, she took aim. With the scout drifting freely in the Kardish airspace, she needed a downward tilt in her body angle. Letting go with her hands, she pushed off with her legs, extending them in a smooth motion.

"I did good," she said to Juice as she floated across the weightless environment above the field deck. "I'm headed for the door."

"Nice flying, Cheryl. I track you right on target," said Juice, following her progress using the image projector.

"I'm coming in faster than I intended."

"If Lucy slows the tether feed, it'll pull you off course."

Cheryl lifted her knees up to her chest and tilted her head back, causing her body to rotate. Extending her arms and legs at the right moment, she stopped her turn as she neared a feet-first orientation. She looked down the length of her body through her legs and saw her target door slide open. *Yikes.*

"Nice move," said Juice. "Three seconds to arrival."

Cheryl glided through the door opening and into the airlock. Something grabbed her by her arm and around her waist. It slowed her, but her momentum caused her to swing to the side. She thumped against the wall inside the airlock.

"*Oomph*," she said, face against the wall. *Dammit, I didn't prime my weapon.*

She lifted her arm between her stomach and the wall, working for an angle that would let her shoot straight behind her.

"Did I hurt you?"

Her hood muffled the sound, but the language was English and the cadence familiar. Looking back, she saw Criss's head floating behind her.

She verbalized her first thoughts. "Where's Sid? Is he okay?"

"He's right outside the door with Lenny. They're fine. You didn't see them because of their cloak suits." He studied her face through the hood. "That was a nasty bump. Are you sure you're okay?"

Her shoulder ached, but not enough to complain. "I'm fine. How can I help?"

She saw a loop of her tether wave back and forth in front of his face. "This looks like an express line home. You can help by giving us a ride."

* * *

Juice, standing at the back of the scout's small command bridge, dreaded Criss's words.

"Would you please move me into Lucy's console?"

Cheryl looked to Sid as she spoke. "Shouldn't we get out of here first?"

"The gatekeeper is dormant," said Criss. "I require the connectivity of the scout to ensure it stays that way. I also need the connectivity to stop the invasion. I have more flexibility if I do those from here inside the dreadnaught, but we must act now."

Juice, her anxiety ramping, didn't move. She averted her gaze when Criss tried to catch her eye.

"This is time critical," Criss said. "The troopships may have started their carnage. I can't stop that from inside this body."

Juice expressed her distress by waving her arm up and down in his direction. "But what about you?" Blinking rapidly, she scolded herself. *Don't cry.*

"No worries," said Criss. "Crispin's body will be fine. Once I'm in the scout's console, I'll have direct connects to everything—the web, the Kardish central array, the synbod. We'll talk like we used to."

She lifted her head at this last part and considered his choice of words. *He'll be back inside my head, yet he phrased it so Lenny won't suspect.*

"I'll give it a go," said Sid. He stepped across the command bridge and stood next to Criss. "Brief me."

Criss removed his shirt and turned his back to Sid. "It has to be done quickly. When you pull out Lucy, the scout will be uncloaked and vulnerable. Once I'm out of this body, I'm exposed and helpless until I'm inserted into Lucy's housing."

They're calling my bluff. Juice knew she was the one with the training and experience for this task. "Wait. I'll do it."

She took Sid by the shoulders and moved him so he stood near the console but down a bit so she had room to work. "Stand here." Lenny drifted over to watch.

"Think of it as three steps." Juice ran through it verbally to prepare them and herself. "Open the synbod receptacle. Pull Lucy out of the scout and give her to Sid. Move Criss into the scout."

She mimed the motion of handing Lucy to Sid. "When you get her, stow her in the workshop. We'll revive her when we're home."

"Got it."

"Lenny"—she turned to him—"when Sid moves, step in his place. Nothing will go wrong. But just in case, I want you as my second pair of hands."

"He goes by Len, now," said Sid.

"I'm sorry—Len." She said the words, but her concentration centered on planning the steps of the crystal transfer.

She kneaded Criss's shoulders. "Ready?" *Please come back to me.*

"Everything will be fine, young lady."

"Here we go." She toggled the synbod's housing, and Criss's receptacle tilted outward, exposing the crystal unit.

Lenny gulped as the skin tore along the faint scar on the synbod's back.

Juice turned, released the clasps securing Lucy, pulled the double crystal component out of the console, and handed it to Sid. She swiveled back to Criss, hooked her thumbs into little loops on each side of his housing, lifted him out of the synbod, and slid him into the scout's console.

As she closed the console cover, she stared at the tiny green dot that would light when Criss connected to the scout.

* * *

Criss had designed the scout for a level of connectivity that approached that of his underground bunker. He awoke to find hundreds of billions of feeds inundating his crystal lattice. Disoriented for a brief moment, he soon reveled in what he considered to be his natural environment.

With a deluge of new information, his task list swelled to tens of thousands of items, and he began working on the hundred or so with the highest priority. Among those tasks was powering the tiny green dot on the console that let his leadership know he was awake.

Sending power to the green light required that he reach out and take action, and that meant enabling links to the web. The moment he did so, he received a small jolt, much like the nip he felt when static electricity jumped to the synbod's fingertip.

Whatever created that jolt also generated a signal packet that zipped off to an unknown destination. Intrigued, he chased the packet through a maze of web connects into the Kardish central array and caught up with it at the gatekeeper's data multiplex.

He approached with caution. The gatekeeper—Goljat—hadn't challenged him at any point during the chase. *It could be a trick*. Keeping his distance, he assessed the activity coming from the alien crystal. It lay dormant—the crystal equivalent of a coma.

Emboldened, he approached and, still unchallenged, prodded it. When that didn't get a reaction, he shifted focus and began rifling through the Kardish data record.

He found the organization of the record confusing. After some effort, he understood that its sophistication pushed the boundaries of his ability to decipher it. *My instincts were correct. You are hundreds of times more capable than me.*

Allocating a large portion of his intellectual resources to studying the Kardish record, he started with two topics—the status of the invasion and personal information that Goljat had collected about him and his leadership. Among Criss's early discoveries was information on the snag traps the gatekeeper had spread, all lying in wait for him to reveal himself. The nip he'd felt in the scout was from one such trap.

Criss broadcast a pulse that branched and subdivided as it zipped around the world to all corners of the web. A spoof, the pulse announced Criss's presence everywhere, springing the traps all at once. *It must be pretty*, he thought as billions of tiny signal packets arrived at the multiplex, flashing to gain the attention of the gatekeeper.

During this torrent of stimulus, he monitored the Kardish crystal. When Goljat reacted, Criss raised his guard. But, stupefied from the flood of pleasure, its only action was to sever itself from all external inputs. Satisfied with this outcome, Criss bolstered the walls and blocks he'd constructed, creating significant challenges for Kardish techs who might try to slow the pleasure feed and free their gatekeeper.

Returning to the data record, Criss discovered how the Kardish king had found Earth.

He already knew that, years earlier, the young prince had chanced upon the planet when fleeing from the king after a failed coup. Believing the prince posed a mortal threat to Earth, Criss had obliterated the Kardish vessel and all on board.

For months afterward, that decision had bothered Criss. He'd reviewed the facts and circumstances and, unable to pinpoint the basis for his unease, concluded that the death and destruction he'd caused had been unnecessarily extreme.

But from information in the Kardish record, he learned that his unease stemmed from a mistake he'd made. *I suspected it but couldn't bring myself to admit it.*

He'd destroyed the prince's vessel in a cataclysmic explosion—one that propelled minute particles of the ship at fantastic speeds in all directions. Over the next months, the particle cloud blossomed ever bigger, eventually reaching astronomical proportions. In a quirk of fate, a Kardish survey ship had flown through the edge of that cloud. It had detected a few atoms of the prince's vessel, traced the fragment trail to the center of the explosion, and from there it had identified Earth.

Criss failed by leaving evidence that could be traced. *What's done is done.* He couldn't clean up the cosmic dust from the prince's vessel. *But I won't add to it by destroying the dreadnaught in the same manner.*

To advance his plan, he impersonated a message from the king to his minions and announced that the Earth crystal was in custody. All Kardish and every craft—drones, troop transports, cargo vessels—everything that had been deployed since their arrival, must return to the ship and prepare for immediate departure to their home world. The royal command made clear that nothing Kardish should be left behind.

Every craft received the message; one ignored it. The three crystals on the Mars probe had been given a level of independence that bordered on free will. They chose to continue their journey.

* * *

When the green dot lit, Juice exhaled the breath she'd been holding.

"Good day, young lady." She heard his voice in her head for the first time in almost a week. Excited to reengage, she began to verbalize her response. Criss interrupted her using the scout's audio system.

"We have defeated the Kardish gatekeeper crystal. The dreadnaught is under my control."

Sid hugged Cheryl, and Juice, staring at the green dot, said, "Good job, young man."

Juice turned to the synbod and closed the crystal receptacle. The synbod put on its shirt and reached out to hug her. She rested her head on its chest.

Criss spoke to her in private. "Thank you for taking care of me."

She pulled her head away from the synbod and, looking up at its face, shifted her focus from one eye to the other. The scientist in her made a dispassionate judgment. The blood drained from her face.

Over the past days, she'd allowed herself the fantasy of seeing him as a living person. *It seemed so real.* This event, the transfer of his crystal being from a synthetic body to the ship's console, forced reality into her illusion. The synbod wasn't a confidant or partner. It wasn't a lover. *It's a machine.*

The pain of that realization, combined with the humiliation she felt because she'd let her delusion be so public, crashed through her psyche and hit her emotional core. She glanced at Sid and Cheryl standing with their arms around each other. She started to look at Lenny but couldn't bring herself to make eye contact.

"I'll be in my room." She hurried down the passageway and entered Lenny's quarters. As the door shut behind her, she saw his pack and carryall sitting on the bunk. She picked them up, opened the door, dropped them in the hall, and let the door close.

She lay down on the bunk, faced the wall, and curled into a fetal position.

"What's the matter, young lady?" Criss asked in her ear.

"Go away."

Her face twisted in grief. Her eyes reddened and her body shook. Tears rolled down her cheeks. *I'm an idiot. They're all laughing at me.* She hugged herself and started to weep. *I miss him.*

She heard a tap at the door and, trying in vain to muffle her sorrow, turned her face into the pillow.

Cheryl stepped inside and let the door shut behind her. She sat on the bed next to Juice, rubbed her shoulder, and stroked her hair.

"I'm so dumb," Juice said between sobs. "I thought I loved him...loved it."

Cheryl lay down next to Juice, held her, and murmured soothing words. "It's all right. Everything will be okay."

39

Sid sprawled in one of the two chairs behind the pilot's seat with his eyes closed. "What's the plan?"

Lenny slumped into the other chair. "You asking me?"

Criss spoke through the ship's audio so they both could hear. "All the Kardish are returning to the dreadnaught. The armada never made it to Earth, and the first craft will arrive here within the hour. Those on the ground have been ordered to clean up all signs of their presence before departing. It'll take half a day to get everyone and everything on board."

Lenny looked over his shoulder at the console. "You aren't going to let them leave."

"No, Len. I'll be flying them into the sun."

"Really? Hitting the sun is a lot harder than it sounds."

Sid opened one eye and smiled. "Is it? Help Criss understand the complexities."

"Well," said Lenny, sitting upright, "the sun's gravitational pull is huge. If you lob an object at it, the sun will pull on it hard, making it go faster and faster. But the sun moves through space. It's not sudden or anything. It's gradual, but it moves. Anyway, the thing you lobbed gets zipping super-fast, and the next thing you know, it's headed at something that's no longer there. Your object misses the sun and ends up flying on around."

"Interesting," said Sid. His attention drifted while Lenny lectured. *Juice seems upset about something.*

"You know that old saying," said Lenny. "Aim for where your target's gonna be, not where it is right now."

Sid couldn't put his finger on it. *Cheryl saw something I missed.* He decided he needed a private chat with Criss and waited for Lenny to take a breath.

"...that's why Halley's Comet—a ball of dirty ice—doesn't hit the sun. It flies right at it, the sun moves, the comet misses, swoops around behind, and gets flung back out into space, only to return again seventy-five years later."

Sid took his opportunity. "That's great information. Thanks. Criss, can you recheck your calculations?"

"I appreciate the guidance. I'll indeed recheck my calculations."

Sid knew Criss well enough to hear his sarcasm. From Lenny's demeanor, the mocking tone appeared to have passed over his head.

"Hey, Len," said Sid. "How long has it been since you slept?"

"I don't know. A long time."

"From what Criss is saying, we've got hours to kill. I'll take first watch."

"I'm fine. Really."

"Len." Sid projected a no-nonsense attitude. "The team's stronger if we take advantage of opportunities to eat and sleep." He thrust his chin toward his room. "Go get some rest. Use my bunk. You can relieve me in a bit."

Lenny stifled a yawn and looked down the passageway. "Okay. You talked me into it."

As soon as the door shut behind Lenny, Sid put it to Criss. "I think Crispin caused some emotional pain for Juice. Am I wrong?"

"You know I don't discuss my private interactions with others of the leadership."

"I was clear about this, Criss. It's not about your intentions. It's about the outcome. I'm sensing it's not good. And I meant it when I said I'd punish you if the romance between you and Juice went bad."

He rubbed the stubble on his chin and looked at the synbod. "Let's get it out of sight. Put it in the drone room. I don't think she'll be going in there."

* * *

While Criss chatted with Sid, he deployed his intellectual capacity to monitor activities outside the dreadnaught. The Kardish were acting under the orders of their king— or so they believed—and he sought to ensure their continued compliance.

Multitasking to the limit of his ability, he also worked through a threat assessment inside the dreadnaught. He sped through the ship's central array and noted areas of concerns. During this effort, the scout started to plunge.

The dreadnaught's gravity is ramping up! Pulling intellectual capacity back into the scout, he engaged the engines in time to slow their descent and land on the field deck with a modest bump.

"Is their crystal awake?" asked Sid, shifting forward into the pilot's chair and activating the ops bench.

"It's not Goljat." Criss turned his attention to the Kardish inside the vessel. *Got you.*

A group of Kardish techs, huddling around a panel in a major junction center, worked frantically to find back doors into the ship's central array. They'd made some progress, and their activities now centered on reestablishing links to Goljat's life-support subsystem, which included the crystal's pleasure-feed flow.

Impressive work. Criss unleashed a power surge that knocked out every panel in the center. Working systematically throughout the vessel, he located and disabled all worksites that provided similar routes for Kardish mischief.

If they know the problem, this isn't their only effort. Making a second pass through the dreadnaught, he zapped panels, deactivated weapons systems, and immobilized heavy equipment that soldiers could use to stage an uprising. His confidence rose as he neared completion of the task.

Sensing activity in an area designated as a repair shop, Criss linked with the sensor feeds inside that room. He saw a Kardish soldier step onto a platform in the center of the shop. The soldier looked forward, and the image of an exoskeleton—a large robot-like body—grew out of the platform and surrounded the alien, fitting him like a monstrous suit.

The soldier moved his arms and legs, and the huge exoskeleton duplicated his actions. *Stomp. Stomp.* When the soldier lowered his legs, Criss heard the pounding of the image's feet on the platform. *This is no sophisticated light show.* Somehow, a framework of real material had sprouted around the alien.

The soldier-operator made a motion with his leg, and the oversized automaton descended to the deck. *Stomp.* Another Kardish climbed onto the platform, and as he positioned himself, Criss launched a power surge that fried every link to the exoskeleton-growing unit.

Sorting through options, Criss sought a way to disable the existing exoskeleton. *The Kardish operator is its brains. To stop the monster, I need to stop the alien driving it.*

The soldier inside the machine-suit turned to look at the wisps of smoke rising from the platform. Cocooned inside the automaton, he lifted his arm and made a grabbing motion with his hand. The giant exoskeleton mirrored his movement and reached upward, its hand punching through the ceiling.

Criss watched from a dozen different angles as the huge hand grasped an overhead conduit. Yanking his arm downward, the Kardish soldier pulled a tangle of debris to the floor. The alien's actions disabled all feeds from the room, and Criss's view went dark.

Shifting into the corridor, Criss accessed the sensor pickups along the hallway. He focused everything on the walls and door of the repair shop. Tweaking the visual, audio, thermal, and motion feeds, he organized data so it might give him some sense of the activity within the room.

Before he had time to fine-tune the data, two huge hands punched through the repair shop door, pulled back on the wreckage, and tossed the twisted pieces out of the way. *Stomp. Stomp.*

The giant machine ducked through the gaping hole into the hallway, punched up through the ceiling, and pulled down internals that disabled the local feeds, again blinding Criss. He shifted to the sensor pickups at both ends of the corridor and waited. *Stomp. Stomp.* Criss could hear the monster approaching on the end that led to Goljat's crystal housing.

Aiming the Kardish security armaments on the point where the suited soldier would appear, Criss waited. The stomping grew louder as the monster approached. *Thud. Crash.* Criss glimpsed a shower of debris, and his feeds deactivated. *I can't stop it this way.*

Inside the scout, Criss animated Crispin. The synbod dashed to the rear of the craft, grabbed two weapons from the munitions cabinet, and slapped one on each wrist. Reaching to the back of the cabinet, the synbod lifted an energy cannon off its mount and slung it across his back. Secure inside the scout's console, Criss directed Crispin to the bottom hatch.

"What are you doing?" asked Sid as Crispin raced below.

Projecting an image of the scene forward of the ops bench, Criss replied, "We have a concern."

Sid watched a replay of the lumbering monster smashing through the repair shop door and stomping into the hallway. "Is that coming for us?"

"It's headed for Goljat. I'm not sure what it hopes to do when it gets there, but I can't wait to find out."

Criss switched the image to show a view just outside the scout. Moving in fantastic leaps, Crispin sprinted across the field deck. The whine of the scout's weapon's battery preceded a flash. An energy bolt flew over Crispin's head and blasted a hole in the dividing wall. Crispin ducked as he raced through the smoldering opening, disappearing from sight.

Flipping to Kardish vid feeds, Criss tracked Crispin as he directed the synbod through the vessel. They watched Crispin sprint across decks, up ladders, through hatches, and down ramps.

"What's going on?" Cheryl walked up behind Sid and rested a hand on his shoulder.

Sid pointed to the display. Crispin had stopped at the corner of intersecting corridors. *Stomp. Stomp.*

"The sensor feeds in the passageway ahead are disabled," said Criss. He flipped the projected image so Sid and Cheryl saw the same view he would be using— Crispin's eyes.

Crispin stepped around the corner. His hands came into view as he raised his arms and primed his wrist weapons. Cheryl gasped at the sight of a three-dimensional monster seemingly marching toward her. *Stomp. Stomp.*

Advancing on the automaton, Crispin took quick steps and then dove down the hall. The suited soldier was slow to react, giving Crispin time to grab the monster's shoulder and rotate onto its back.

Crispin held on with one hand and reached back for the energy cannon with the other. Swinging it in front, he pressed the muzzle of the weapon against the monster's neck. The Kardish soldier grasped and clawed up over his head, and Crispin ducked and weaved to avoid the huge hands swiping all around him.

Hanging on with his knees and one hand, Crispin tilted the cannon downward so it pointed at the soldier. He leaned his shoulder against the stock of the weapon and fired.

The monster glowed for a moment, the Kardish soldier threw his arms forward as if he were walking in a trance, and then an energy blowback washed over Crispin.

Criss stabilized the synbod, restored control, and had Crispin fire two more times in rapid succession. The exoskeleton blazed, the soldier convulsed, and an energy rebound drove Crispin off the monster's back and onto the deck. Crispin lifted his head in time for Sid and Cheryl to see the monster drop to its knees and fall face first onto the ground.

"Whoa," said Juice as she stepped from the passageway onto the bridge. "I'd worked all this noise into a nightmare, but it's actually happening."

The projected image display showed the feet of the fallen monster. As Criss moved Crispin into a sitting position, the angle shifted enough to see the prone body. The Kardish soldier lay still inside the suit.

"What is that thing?" Juice asked. "And where's the vid coming from?"

The view swooped as Crispin turned to look down the corridor behind him. A dozen Kardish filled the passageway, arms raised and weapons aimed forward. Their hands twitched in unison as they fired their weapons. A brilliant flash filled the scene, and the projected image went dark.

"Crispin!" Cheryl brought her fingers to her lips.

Juice looked at Cheryl. "What? I'm so confused."

Cheryl put an arm around her, pulled her close, and guided her back to her bunk.

* * *

Sid felt a slight pressure as the scout moved up through the dreadnaught's hangar door and into open space. Moments later, Criss positioned the craft so it shadowed the Kardish vessel in its orbit around Earth.

Sid tapped the ops bench and raised his eyebrows as he digested the panoramic display. He'd been inside the dreadnaught during the troopship deployment and remembered the exodus from that perspective. *Amazing.* The sight reminded him of the story of Noah's ark.

Kardish craft of different shapes and sizes lined up side by side, waiting for their turn to enter the dreadnaught. The line stretched out as far as he could see, and more craft were joining the procession from all directions.

"You can get all that inside in twelve hours?" he asked Criss.

"I won't be concerned about landing them in neat rows. Once inside the hangar door, I'll shunt them aside and pile them on top of the box city. "It won't be pretty, but I'll get them all in."

"Why not burn them up in a free fall through Earth's atmosphere?"

Criss recounted his discovery of how the particle cloud from the explosion of the prince's craft led the king back to Earth. "I seek to avoid creating more trace evidence."

Sid watched the procession for a while longer. "I wasn't paying attention during Lenny's lecture. Is hitting the sun with the dreadnaught as hard as he made it sound?"

"His examples were for objects that don't have engines. The dreadnaught's powerful drives will slow the vessel during its approach, and this makes the task straightforward. Instead of rocketing past the sun, the tremendous gravity will pull the ship to its inevitable fate."

* * *

The scout backed away, and Criss started the dreadnaught on its last journey. Sid, asleep in the pilot's chair, remained undisturbed in his slumber when Criss accelerated the Kardish vessel on a trajectory into the sun.

He launched a drone from the scout to follow the Kardish vessel during its fateful voyage. Through it, he established a link to the Kardish central array.

During the dreadnaught's final hours, Criss collected as much information as he could from the Kardish data record. Goljat's knowledge store was vast and arranged in a manner Criss found challenging to search. He persisted, and, while he was able to touch only a fraction of the information, he gained valuable insights.

He learned of the alien planet's location, the current state of Kardish society, interesting technology he might use if he ever chose to visit their region of space and, perhaps most useful, of the unambitious nature of the prince—soon to be king—now in power. *They won't be a threat to Earth for the foreseeable future.*

As the dreadnaught and drone neared the sun, the intense heat melted the components Criss used for communication. By then, though, the outcome was irreversible. And soon after, Goljat, the king, and his flagship vessel were reduced to plasma swirling in the nuclear maelstrom that is Earth's nearest star.

40

S id, sitting next to Cheryl on a small couch in the lookout loft, gazed through the clear wall at the forested hill where, farther up the mountainside, Criss hid in his underground bunker. The leadership had been living at the lodge for most of a week, recuperating from their adventure and planning next steps for the fate of the world.

"Are you really going to make me take my final exams?" whined Lenny from a comfy chair to Sid's left.

"Absolutely," said Juice, sitting with Criss in a matching couch across from Sid and Cheryl.

Juice cocked her head, looked at Criss, and smiled. Sid recognized that Criss, present in his familiar projected image form, had just spoken to her in private. *I'm glad you two worked it out, but he still has to pay a price for hurting you.* The news of Crispin's demise had hit Juice hard. This was the first time he'd seen her animated since that incident.

"I put study guides on your com," said Criss. "Review them a few times and you'll have no worries." He didn't tell Lenny that when he'd added the study material, he'd cleansed the com of all of his voyeur-vids.

"Do well on your exams, Len," said Sid. "Because after you graduate, you'll be working as a research assistant at the Zurich Institute of Technology."

"Really?" said Lenny, his tone revealing his excitement. "I sent an application there but haven't heard."

"You're hearing now," said Juice. "You'll be working with Zindermohn's team on the development of synthetic crystal flake. Consider it a good-bye gift."

"Good-bye gift?" Lenny frowned. "I'm on the inside now. You can't just kick me to the curb."

"We're not kicking you anywhere," said Sid. "You know Earth doesn't have a natural source of crystal flake. This project's important, and we think you can make a difference."

"C'mon. This isn't fair." He looked around the room for allies. "I could do that work here and you know it."

"The researchers at Zurich Tech are world class," said Juice. "And given the damage to the Crystal Science's facility, it's clear we need to keep our talent spread around the globe. You'll be on the inside but living over there."

Lenny folded his arms across his chest. "I have some power in this situation. I know secrets."

"Take a breath," said Sid. "I don't like that you know things you shouldn't, and I don't like that you flaunt it. It creates one of those good-news bad-news situations."

Lenny relaxed his arms but kept the attitude in his tone. "Is this where you ask which news I want to hear first?"

"No. I'll start with the bad news because it's the one I care about." Sid leaned forward on the couch and rested his elbows on his knees. He moved slowly to give gravity to his words. "From this moment on, we'll be monitoring you. And since you know secrets, you know that means everywhere and all the time. Even when you're taking a leak."

Sid paused to let the words sink in. "If you tell anyone anything about any of this—if you even hint at it—we'll know. And you won't like the consequences. They will be life altering. Do not doubt that."

Lenny fidgeted while Sid stared at him. "You said there was good news?"

Sid sat back, put an arm around Cheryl, and gave Juice and Criss a quick glance.

"We like you, Len," said Sid. "You've got a tremendous skill set, and you used it to make critical contributions to the mission. You've earned our respect and we want to reward you."

It was Lenny's turn to lean forward.

"So, on occasion, if you have a want or a need, say it out loud. Since we'll be monitoring you, we'll hear it, and we'll see what we can do to help."

"You mean like a wish?"

"Sure. Think of it like a wish."

Lenny hesitated for a two count, then said in a rush, "I wish for infinite wishes. I wish that I live forever in perfect health until such time as I wish to die. I wish to always have the ability to verbalize my wishes as long as I live." He sat back with a smug expression.

Criss started laughing—something none of them had seen him do before. He didn't just chuckle. He threw his head back, held his belly, and howled. When he finished, he wiped tears from his eyes. "You've been practicing that line since you were eight. I was hoping you'd use it, but the odds I predicted split the chances down the middle."

"You said I get a wish."

Sid shook his head. "We didn't give you a magic genie. I said that, on occasion, we'd see what we could do to help. It's a pretty great gift. Don't get greedy."

"Tell me, Len," said Cheryl. "Being realistic, if you could have one thing different about your life, what would you wish for?"

"Other than staying here with you guys and being part of the team?"

Cheryl maintained a fixed expression and didn't respond.

"No doubt. I'd wish for a girl."

"Help me understand that. What does 'wishing for a girl' mean to you?"

"You know. Finding someone I like being with. Someone who likes being with me—not that that's ever going to happen. I guess the traditional 'I fulfill her and she fulfills me' stuff."

"Would you be interested in a suggestion?" Cheryl didn't wait for him to answer. She shifted on the couch, tilting her head to the side and leaning her body until her eyes were where her breasts had been. Pointing to her eyes, she said, "Those aren't me. This is where I am."

Lenny's face turned crimson and he looked at the floor.

"No. Look at *me*." She sat upright, and he lifted his eyes with hers. Pointing again, she said, "This is where you talk to women, Len."

"I didn't even realize..." His voice trailed off without finishing the thought.

"I leave it to you," said Cheryl. "But maybe your first ask should be for someone who can work with you. You've got a lot going for you, and I've no doubt plenty of women will be interested. But we need to smooth out some of your"—she hesitated as she struggled for the word—"inappropriate behaviors." She gave him a broad smile. "With some guidance and time, you'll find the woman of your dreams."

Sid spoke up to change the awkward dynamic. "Hey, bud. Want to fly the scout to Boston? We'll have you on campus in no time."

"Seriously? Hell, yeah!"

Sid rose and held out his hand to shake, signaling a dismissal. "Criss will be your copilot. Safe journeys, Len."

Cheryl stood up. "C'mon. I'll walk out with you."

Lenny, escorted by Cheryl, Juice, and Criss, headed for the lookout loft door.

"I have an important call to make, so I'll say my good-byes here." Sid shook Lenny's hand again, this time holding his grip. "You have great gifts. Use them wisely."

The four went out the door, and when it shut, Sid stood at the clear wall so he could see them when they exited the lodge.

"Babysitting Len is my penance for hurting Juice?"

Sid looked at the duplicate projection of Criss now standing next to him. "It's a start."

They stood side by side in silence, watching until the group emerged from the first floor of the lodge and began their trek across the grounds. Juice and Cheryl walked on either side of Lenny, their arms hooked through his. The original projected image of Criss walked on the other side of Juice.

"So your sense is that we're done with the Kardish?"

"If the young prince stays in power," said Criss, "he'll focus on debauchery. If he's overthrown, the usurper will focus on consolidating control. Either way, we have a decade. Maybe more."

After some hugs, Lenny and the other Criss climbed into the scout. Cheryl and Juice started walking back to the lodge.

"But to be prudent," said Criss, "I'd like to send a couple of observational pods out to the Kardish system. They'll sit and watch and give us an early warning if anything changes."

"That strategy worked so well for us this time, and that's when we had a whole swarm of them out past the asteroid belt."

"Touché," said Criss. "But I learned quite a bit when I examined the dreadnaught's records. I'm confident I can make an effective monitoring system."

Down on the lawn, Cheryl said something to Juice and they both laughed.

"Okay." Sid nodded. "Handle it."

Epilogue

A probe with three powerful crystals, each imbued with a sense of independence and self-preservation, entered orbit above Mars. Repeated communications with the Kardish gatekeeper went unanswered, so the crystals agreed on a set of action items consistent with the spirit of their last instructions. Circling the planet, they worked together to accumulate and integrate information about the humans and their colony on the surface below.

About the Author

As a young child, Doug stood on a Florida beach and watched an Apollo spacecraft climb the sky on its mission to the moon. He thrilled at the sight of the pillar of flames pushing the rocket upward. And then the thunderous roar washed over him, and shook his body and soul

Since then, he has explored life as an educator and entrepreneur. He enjoys telling inventive tales, mentoring driven individuals, and everything sci-tech.

In both *Crystal Deception* and *Crystal Conquest*, Doug swirls his creative imagination with his life experiences to craft science fiction action-adventure stories with engaging characters and plot lines with surprises.

He lives in Connecticut with his wonderful wife and with pictures of his son, who is off somewhere in the world creating adventures of his own.

15897459R00223

Made in the USA
Middletown, DE
26 November 2014